The Wanderer
By Crystal Jordan

Love is the most dangerous experiment of all.

There is only one rule in the Wasteland: survive.

The few remaining women are as reviled as they are worshipped, a commodity any man must pay to touch. And to touch a Wanderer, he may pay with his life.

For Ezra, the risk is worth the reward. People speak his name with the same reverent terror reserved for ancient wrathful gods, but he must always be ready to fend off those who would take what's his. And what he wants to be his is Kadira.

Kadira, adopted after she witnessed the slaughter of her devoted parents, has vowed never to love or need anyone. It seems only fitting that she, an outsider, accept Ezra's demand in trade for the fuel technology her clan needs—but her deep, unexpected need for him is the torture she's fought all her life to avoid. Worse, the greater her wrath, the more he seems to like it.

Ezra's mercenary half delights at having the warrior woman in his arms. His scientist half can't resist the urge to see what makes her react—and what makes her explode.

The real experiment: if the bond they forge is strong enough to make her want to stay.

Warning: Threesomes, foursomes, boy on boy, girl on girl, boy on boy on girl, voyeurism, exhibitionism, sex at knifepoint, anal sex, ritual orgies, and, well...it's just a really dirty book.

The Whore
By Lilli Feisty

Her quest for freedom plunges her into dangerous waters...of desire.

Bryn is a "Rose", but her life is no garden. A stolen child, prostitution is the only life she's ever known—except on the nights she sneaks out in stolen men's clothing to explore the city. A tiny taste of freedom that makes her long for a life outside sexual servitude, at the mercy of any man who can pay.

Xander remembers no other home except his pirate ship, smuggling weapons or anything else for a fee. He's been happy with his life and his lover, Hawke...until he rescues who he thinks is a young man from robbers.

Figuring she can blend in with the crew, Bryn jumps at the chance to escape the Brothel. Then she discovers Xander and Hawke have a taste for pretty boys—and that she has a taste for them. In their arms, she embraces their incredible gift: control of her own sexuality.

Though women are considered bad luck at sea, Xander isn't of a mind to give her up. Yet the time is drawing near when the ship must return to Wasteland to resupply. And what awaits them there is a danger that could tear them apart.

Warning: Contains hot pirates, bad boys, pretty boys, lots of three-way pirate sex, a woman spanking a pirate with a rare-wood paddle, a glass dildo used on a pirate—have we mentioned the pirates?

The Breeder
By Eden Bradley

Destined to serve the desires of an entire city, all she wants is one man. Or maybe two...

Born to the Temple, Nitara knows the Great Goddess's plan for her: to bring life into what is left of an arid and wasted Earth. Since puberty she has been trained to arouse and titillate, to ensure the continuation of the human race.

As is the custom, the man captured for her is strong of blood, though considered little more than a wild animal. Yet when she looks into his eyes, she sees no primitive creature, but the man whose face and hands haunt her sensual dreams.

For Akaash, a hunter and warrior, it's his shame that he will be sacrificed to a goddess he doesn't believe in, for a people who are not his own, leaving behind his Wanderer clan—and his bonded lover, Dhatri. Locked in the bowels of the Temple, he has a month to ponder his fate, all while falling helplessly under the spell of the virgin temptress who will soon take his life.

With each torturously erotic encounter, however, Akaash realizes that Nitara is as much a prisoner as he. If he can just get a message out to Dhatri, there may be a slim chance both of them can escape...

Warning: Sexual acts in a prison cell, by the sea, in the desert, on an altar, with every possible combination of dirty deeds between two men and one very lucky woman, and all of it hot enough to melt sand! And her panties. If she were wearing any.

The Priestess
By R.G. Alexander

Damn the rules, damn the gods...even if he has to share her, she belongs to him.

High Priestess Xian has followed the Path of the Peaceful Sun since she was chosen at birth. Yet the joy she receives from helping others is overshadowed by her growing belief that the world they live in is...wrong.

At a crossroads, unsure of her ability to do her job—unsure of anything—she journeys to the ruins of the old city, hoping to uncover secrets that will give her clarity. Instead she finds the path to her goal clouded by an unexpected desire for her handsome guard, Hel, and for the battered stranger they find along the way.

Hel can't prevent Xian from reaching out to the mysterious Siraj, but there is danger in allowing him to stay. Siraj belongs to no caste, follows no rules but his own. And Xian's fascination with him makes Hel's blood boil. No one can know that Hel has always loved her, or the secret he's kept hidden for years. But Siraj's advances and Xian's curiosity force Hel to cross lines he never before dared...

Warning: The word of the day is Voyeurism. Oh, and explicit sex with two men and one previously repressed High Priestess. Bi ménage, anal sex, oral sex, kissing, licking, rimming, author blushing ...so you know it must be good.

Wasteland

SAMHAIN
PUBLISHING

Samhain Publishing, Ltd.
577 Mulberry Street, Suite 1520
Macon, GA 31201
www.samhainpublishing.com

Wasteland
Print ISBN: 978-1-60928-085-7
The Wanderer Copyright © 2011 by Crystal Jordan
The Whore Copyright © 2011 by Lilli Feisty
The Breeder Copyright © 2011 by Eden Bradley
The Priestess Copyright © 2011 by R.G. Alexander

Editing by Bethany Morgan
Cover by Kanaxa

The Wanderer, ISBN 978-1-60928-031-4
First Samhain Publishing, Ltd. electronic publication: May 2010
The Whore, ISBN 978-1-60928-039-0
First Samhain Publishing, Ltd. electronic publication: May 2010
The Breeder, ISBN 978-1-60928-034-5
First Samhain Publishing, Ltd. electronic publication: May 2010
The Priestess, ISBN 978-1-60928-045-1
First Samhain Publishing, Ltd. electronic publication: May 2010
First Samhain Publishing, Ltd. print publication: April 2011

Contents

The Wanderer

Crystal Jordan

Dedication

For Frank, the semi-dastardly Professor Moriarty. *Ich liebe dich, mein Liebling.* For my best friend, Michal, because we're at a decade and counting. For my sometimes critique partners and sometimes writer OCD support group, Rowan Larke, Loribelle Hunt, Kate Pearce, Elaina Huntley, Rhiannon Leith, and Patti O'Shea. For Rolf Potts, who was kind enough not to be offended that I borrowed his face for one of my characters. Anything beyond looks is pure fiction, I promise. For my awesome editor, Bethany Morgan, who agreed to our crazy scheme to write this series. And, of course, for my Smutketeers, Eden Bradley, R.G. Alexander, and Lilli Feisty. All for Smut, and Smut for All!

Prologue

In 2012, the world came to a grinding halt as radiation hit from a massive solar storm. Crops died, animals perished, cities fell and humans became little more than beasts themselves. Under the threat of starvation, civility was reduced to mere memory. Only the strongest men survived, and physically weaker women and children wasted to nothingness.

More than a century later, humanity struggles in the desert Wasteland. The solar radiation rendered most women infertile, and the population dwindles more with each year that passes. Scattered up and down coasts, isolated cities eke out an existence from fishing, foraging and hunting for what little game is left. Outside the city walls, men face the threat of pirates and raiders.

Few women remain, divided into four classes—Whores, Breeders, Priestesses and Wanderers. They are as reviled as they are worshipped, a commodity any man must pay to touch. To touch a Whore, a man must sacrifice his riches. To touch a Breeder, a man must sacrifice his freedom. To touch a Priestess, a man must be chosen by the gods. And to touch a Wanderer may end up costing him his life.

There is only one rule in the Wasteland—survive.

Chapter One

The drums pounded through her like a second heartbeat.

Kadira sat cross-legged before the great bonfire, her palm slapping against the tight skin of the drum cradled between her thighs as others beside her did the same. The Rites of Spring unfolded before her, the month of celebration where the goddess Ela ascended and took control of the seasons from her consort, the god El.

The days would be filled with peace and prosperity, where Clan Mutairi traded with Clan Duaij, Clan Tayi drank with Clan Jassim, and the nights would be filled with feasting and carnal worship, where fertility was rejoiced and all Wanderer clans set aside the pleasures of their feuds for a deeper ecstasy.

Naked bodies danced before the huge blaze, others twined together in the sand, the heat they created more than enough to stave off the cold desert night. A rough shout captured Kadira's attention.

Two men and a woman writhed together not far from where she drummed, caught in the flickering amber light. The woman lay on her back, her legs braced against a man's heavy shoulders as he sank his cock deep inside her pussy. Kadira recognized the other woman. Fatin, whom Kadira had faced over crossed blades before. A fierce warrior, and even fiercer in her passions now. Fatin caressed her breasts, plucked at the stiff nipples, a smile playing over her lips. The man impaling her groaned as the second man pounded hard into his ass, their flesh slapping together in counterpoint to the drums. The family tattoo on the back of the second man's neck declared him a Jassim, son of the clan chieftain. Bachir was his name, though Kadira knew him only by his reputation in battle.

Bachir's long cock slid out, the shaft glistening in the firelight, and his teeth bared as he shoved back into his lover's anus. The muscular buttocks of both men flexed as they moved, like a horse and rider in fluid gallop.

It was erotic to watch, mesmerizing, and heat suffused Kadira's body, her pussy flooding with juices. Her thighs unconsciously clenched on the drum between them.

"Ezra, yes!" Fatin moaned, lifting her hips into every thrust.

Kadira shuddered at the sound of his name. The man in the middle, the eye of the storm. Ezra. Inventor, mercenary, warrior. Chieftain of Clan Haroun. People spoke of him with the kind of reverence reserved for ancient, wrathful gods. The woman beneath him screamed, clawed at his chest, arching as she came. He rode her through her orgasm, jutting into her with harsh precision until she was twisting against him, demanding he fuck her harder, make her come again. All the while Bachir rode him with just as much violent ardor. Kadira felt her nipples harden to tight buds, and it was all she could do not to stimulate her clit against the base of the drum. She wanted to come so badly she ached. Her skin was aflame with her longing, her heart thundering in her chest, her breath speeding to a quick pant.

Just then, Ezra turned his head and met her gaze, smiling as if he'd known she'd been watching and was pleased. She shivered, her nipples beading tighter. The way he stared at her made her uncomfortable, with an intensity in his golden eyes that caused her insides to clench in utter want. Always it had been so, since her first Rite when she had reached maturity, years ago. His grin turned wicked and he held a hand out, flicked his fingers in invitation.

Her body urged her to accept, to ease the need that built higher and hotter than the great bonfire itself. Her muscles shook with the effort it took to keep her seat, to keep her hands moving in smooth rhythm on the drum. Even if she had wanted to fuck him, she could not. As a kabu shaman, she had to remain purified until the end of the first week of Spring Rites, a time when it was her duty to mark those who had come to sexual maturity since the previous Rites, last fall.

But she was tempted beyond anything she had ever known.

Why Ezra should fascinate her, she didn't know. She deliberately looked away, as though he were no more interesting than any of the other people coupling wildly in the night. She caught his frown out of the corner of her eye, but she refused to give in to the temptation he presented. He knew she was a shaman, knew she could not indulge in her desires yet. Did he think because she was not born a Wanderer, because she had trader blood in her veins, that she was not dedicated to her shamanic training? Anger sliced through her. How long would she fight the stigma of her birth? How many would she have to kill in battle, how many times must she prove her skill as a kabu practitioner before she was accepted? It was a blow to the soul to recognize that the answer was *forever*. The mark on the nape of *her* neck would always show she was born an outsider, that she had only been adopted into the Badawi clan.

She would never fully belong, and at the moment, she hated Ezra for pointing it out to her, for questioning her honor, for assuming she would break her vows for an orgiastic fuck with him.

"Bastard," she hissed, and the drummer beside her startled and cast her a wary glance. There was no greater insult among the Wanderers. To be a bastard was to have no family, no clan, no honor. To be a bastard was to be nothing.

Rage made her jaw tighten, and she looked back at Ezra, more than ready to take her blade to his flesh and peel it away a strip at a time. She allowed herself the satisfaction of that fantasy for a few moments, knowing it would not happen. At least, not at a Rites gathering, and not while Clan Badawi was on good terms with Clan Haroun. But loyalties among the constantly warring Wanderers could change from one day to the next. She could only hope to let her dagger kiss his skin...soon.

Blinking, she was once again enraptured by the scene unfolding. She cursed herself under her breath, slamming her fist down on the drum, taking her frustration—sexual and otherwise—out on the defenseless instrument. Still, she was unable to turn away, was only thankful Ezra's attention was focused on his lovers.

Bachir's hips hunched forward, powering his thrusts. His groan was long and loud, his face flushing in the firelight, his eyes closing as an agonized ecstasy reflected on his features. He shuddered, arching once more, digging his cock even deeper into Ezra's backside. Ezra reached over his shoulder, grabbing a fistful of the other man's hair and held on while Bachir came. It was rough and wild, two ferocious animals mating.

Wrapping an arm around Bachir's waist, Ezra flipped him neatly over his shoulder and tossed him onto his back beside Fatin. Quick as a striking snake, Ezra snapped his hands around Fatin's slim waist and set her atop Bachir's face. The woman arched, crying out as Bachir's mouth opened on her sex. She ground her pelvis downward, pumping her hips in hurried desperation.

Ezra laughed, the rich sound floating through the air. Shoving Bachir's thighs open, Ezra pierced the other man's ass in a swift thrust. The thick muscles of Bachir's body tightened, and he bowed in a hard arc at the forceful penetration. Ezra's haunches flexed with every movement, battle scars and kabu markings carved into his flesh, his auburn hair burnished to dark flames by the dancing light. He withdrew from Bachir's anus with slow relish, his features taut with unspent lust. Then he drove forward, between Bachir's buttocks, and both men groaned. Fatin cried out, falling forward, but Ezra caught the back of her neck and pulled her toward him roughly, claiming her mouth as he fucked the other man into the sand.

They twined together, their bodies twisting, harsh groans echoed by the other people copulating around them. Ezra thrust deeper and deeper into Bachir's ass until he froze, his big form heaving as he reached orgasm. Fatin broke her mouth from his, throwing her head back to scream her release to the night sky.

A shudder passed through Kadira. She swallowed, her sex so alive with cravings she knew a single touch, the brush of a finger over her clit, would make her come. Biting back a helpless whimper of frustration, she jerked her chin at a nearby Badawi clanswoman, Akilah, who rose with the contained grace of a warrior and strode over to take her place at the drum. Kadira brushed the sand from her legs with an impatient hand.

"Thank you." If her voice came out too gruff, she hoped her clanswoman wouldn't take offense. If she did, they could work it out on the practice field. A feral smile curved Kadira's lips. She would welcome the challenge, the chance to burn away some of this unsettling, unwelcomed longing. It would be days longer before she could throw herself into the nightly festivities.

Akilah caught her arm, her grip almost painful. "Soon, my friend. I am relieved I don't have to share in the sacrifice you make as a kabu shaman, that El and Ela do not require it of me." Her grasp gentled into a caress. "When you can partake of the Rites, I would be more than pleased to ease your suffering."

When she stroked her thumb over the pounding pulse at Kadira's wrist, Kadira almost broke. Many a night had been kept warm by this woman, and the hot throbbing of her pussy urged her to take advantage of so talented a lover.

No.

Trader born or not, Kadira had been a Wanderer since she was eight summers old. She would not break her vows. She didn't even want to imagine how the Badawi chieftain would react if she did. The Badawi had taken her in, but they didn't have to keep her. She wasn't born to their clan, and a part of her that she knew was foolish always doubted her right to stay, always gnawed at her with worry that if she wasn't useful enough to them, then she was one wrong step away from losing everything she'd ever worked for. Being a woman—one who *might* produce more members for their clan one day—made it unlikely she'd be disavowed. But unlikely didn't mean impossible, and she wondered if she'd ever feel secure enough to relax her guard around anyone. Even more unlikely. She clenched her jaw. It didn't matter what her chieftain would do, because Kadira would never break her word or sacrifice her honor. When she made a vow, she kept it. She would prove as many times as she had to that she was as expert a warrior, as devoted a shaman, as any who had Wanderer blood coursing through their veins. With that thought, she sheathed her broadsword, adjusted her belt and spun away. She disappeared into the darkness and refused to look back to see if Ezra noticed her departure.

He loved watching her work.

On the battlefield, with a sword in her hand, she was intense, fierce. A dangerous adversary that kept her skills sharpened to a fine edge. Many liked to test their strength against hers, and more often than not, they fell before her. At the Rites, it was for practice, as the feuds would resume once the month had passed. No one wanted to let his or her swordsmanship slip. To do so could mean disaster for a clan. Kadira pushed herself harder than most, and Ezra loved the way her slender body moved, as graceful as any dance, and twice as deadly.

But now, when she set aside her blade and plied her other trade, he could gaze on her with the unguarded zeal of everyone else who gathered about the large woven mat upon which a young woman lay, receiving her mark of adulthood that would allow her to participate in the Rites.

It wasn't the girl that interested him. It was Kadira. Always Kadira.

The crescent moon engraved between the dark wings of her eyebrows marked her as a kabu shaman, a master in the sacred art of tattooing. Unusual for a woman to choose to train as a shaman—but, then, women were unusual, outnumbered five to one, even among the Wanderers, and it was worse in the cities. Kadira leaned closer to the girl's arm. Ezra had never seen her face so unguarded, so serene. She'd lost herself in the kabu ritual, the god and goddess moving through her and her tools to shape the designs she carved into the flesh. It was beautiful to watch. *She* was beautiful to watch.

Her waist-length ebony hair was separated into dozens of slender braids, the top half pulled away from her face so she could work for hours without the desert wind blowing the plaits in her eyes. Amulets and beads hung from her neck, etched with blessed symbols. A black leather band covered her breasts and a loincloth stretched around her narrow hips. Rich white pelts dangled from her belt, concealing pouches that held her shamanic tools. Her legs were bare to the knee, where boots encased them like a second skin.

He'd wanted those long legs wrapped around his waist for years.

An apprentice held the skin taut while Kadira dipped a serrated chisel attached to the end of a stick into a jar of black ink. She pressed the blade to the girl's skin and used another stick to tap the chisel and ink into the flesh. The rapid sound of wood smacking against wood was hypnotic, and more Wanderers gathered, entranced, to observe the kabu ritual performed.

Kadira pulled in a deep breath, her breasts threatening to spill from the leather containing them. Biting back a groan, Ezra was unsurprised by his body's reaction, his cock hardening to a painful degree. Always it was so with her, but she had never allowed him to touch her, even in the orgiastic indulgence of Spring and Fall Rites. Not once. It made him burn with frustration. He knew she was aware of him, had seen the keenness of her interest the night before. The lust shimmering in those midnight eyes had nearly driven him past his endurance. He'd beckoned to her before he'd recalled her vows required a time of sexual purification. Only that recollection had kept him away from her. He wanted to take, to claim.

This Rite, he would have her. In any way he could. She would be his and his alone. A shudder rippled through him as the thought made his cock throb. Yes. He refused to hold back any longer, refused to wait. Why he'd delayed this long, he didn't know, but the time had come for action.

Soon he would have that graceful body beneath him. Soon he'd sheathe his cock in her tight, wet pussy. Soon he'd taste the sweetness of her juices, hear her scream his name as he made her come for him. Soon he'd have all that wildness in his arms.

Soon.

Chapter Two

Kadira stretched, feeling the kinks work themselves out. Satisfaction rolled through her as she watched the boy admire the kabu mark on his arm. He tested the muscles and flinched, but nodded solemnly. "Your work is the finest there is, Kadira. The god and goddess blessed me when I was able to place myself in your schedule."

Pride suffused her heart, and she allowed a rare smile to curve her lips. It was the last day of her purification time, and this young man had elected to wait until she was available, delaying his entry into the Rites so that he could be marked by her. She bowed her head, one warrior to another. "I am pleased you think so."

He returned the gesture. "My thanks, shaman."

While he heaved to his feet, she stayed within arm's reach in case he stumbled. It would wound his dignity, but she'd rather that than he injure himself in a fall. Each excruciatingly painful kabu ritual took hours, and enduring one was a rite of passage in and of itself. Depending on the kind of marking, some took multiple rituals to complete. The young man remained steady on his feet, brushed a hand over his short hair. He collected his weapons from beside the mat and moved to join a group of boys near his own age. Several wore fresh tattoos, and Kadira eyed them critically. Hers were just as good, she thought. The young Jassim she'd just marked seemed to think her work fine, and she'd been busy with requests this past week from Wanderers from every clan present. Most had been younglings, but there'd been a few warriors wanting proof of their battles, their kills engraved upon them. Couples and triads had asked for permanent bond marks to be set into their right wrists, signs of their lifelong commitment.

Here, people from any clan might ask her to perform the kabu ritual upon them. Feuds didn't matter at Rites, so she'd even marked a few who openly warred with the Badawi. She shook her head. It was a time away from time, the Rites.

Cleansing her tools, she placed them into her belt pouch. A few quick snaps and her mat was folded and tucked under her arm. She kept her sword hand free. Though it was Spring Rites, some habits never died. Caution was second nature to her, to anyone who wished to survive in the Wasteland.

The harsh sun reflected off of her clan's auto. Flaking rust made holes in the metal, but having a running motor was a sign of prosperity few clans could manage. She laid the mat in her satchel and slipped it behind one of the hammered metal wheels. They'd need to trade with Ezra's clan to get a few spares. These were corroding in the desert sand. More important than new wheels, they'd need fuel to power it. The noxious concoctions Ezra created could keep it going for much longer than what had been available to her father's trader caravan. If their fuel ran dry, they had to use their few precious horses to draw the auto. Kadira sent a swift prayer to the goddess that negotiations went well with the Haroun chieftain.

Akilah approached, and Kadira's pulse quickened. Her clanswoman's promise of fulfillment echoed in her mind. At nightfall, Kadira's purification time would end. Only a handful of hours remained.

The other woman dipped her chin in a swift nod, her face set in stern lines. "You need to come now."

"Trouble?" Kadira's hand flew to the hilt of her sword.

"Yes, but not the kind that requires a blade." A smile slashed across her friend's face. "The bartering with Haroun has taken a disturbing turn, one that will interest you."

"Disturbing? How?" She shook her head, unable to fathom what could interest her specifically. She was a warrior and a shaman, not a chieftain or even an advisor to one. "What does Haroun want?"

"You."

She blinked. Blinked again. Then she pivoted on a heel and marched across their camp to the large tent where the chieftains and advisors of both clans sat cross-legged in a loose circle, all men except the Badawi chieftain.

But her chieftain's words made Kadira's heart skip two full beats.

"Are you offering a bond to Kadira?"

Ezra stiffened, utter horror widening his eyes. Because of her approach or because of the question put to him? "No. I have no wish to offer a bond to any partner." He inclined his head to Kadira, who kept her face impassive. "Though it would be an honor to any man or woman to bond with your clanswoman."

"What exactly are you offering?" She knew she spoke out of turn, but Chieftain Safia gave a small nod. She tried to read the older woman's expression, to see what her leader wanted, but could decipher nothing.

Unfolding his long length from the floor, Ezra turned to Kadira. He wore only a loincloth, and she had to fight to keep her gaze on his face. His golden eyes met hers, the dappled light of the tent playing over the curving kabu marks on the left side of his face. The marks of a chieftain. "I am offering to provide fuel to last your clan until the Rites of Fall."

So much. Shock rocked through her, but she compressed her lips and refused to let her surprise show. "What are you asking in exchange?"

His gaze flickered for the briefest of moments, and she noted a fine tension running through his muscles. Like her, he was not as casual as he seemed. "You. In my bed, exclusively, for the three remaining weeks of this Rite. I understand that you cannot engage in sexual activities until sundown this day, and the term of my agreement begins then."

This time, she knew her shock reflected on her face. Anger hit her with all the force of a broadsword. She stepped forward until only a handspan remained between them, narrowed her eyes to slits. "I think trading your wares in the city has tarnished your view of women, Chieftain Haroun. I am no Rose. I do not sell my body as Whores do. I am a *Wanderer*, a warrior. *No one* takes of me what I am not willing to give."

Ela curse him for treating her as he would no woman born a Wanderer, for singling her out and degrading her.

He drew in a breath, his broad chest expanding to the point he nearly brushed her breasts. Unwanted, unwarranted longing suffused her, and she curled her fingers into fists. His voice was quiet when he spoke, intimate and just for her. "I have never had an unwilling woman in my arms, and I do not wish for one now. My offer was to acknowledge the sacrifice you would make in not participating in the full extent of the Rite. If the thought of my touch sickens you, then I withdraw my offer and extend an apology to you and to your clan."

"And does this *offer* require your fidelity to me as well?" She kept the sneer out of her tone. Barely.

"It does, yes." The heat of his body enfolded her, sent prickles down her skin. "I have always desired you, this you know."

Yes, she knew. Just as she had always desired him, but had been reluctant to give in to the temptation of a man who drew her in like a moth to flames. In the end, the moth was burned, and she'd suspected she would fare no better. She cast a glance toward Akilah and saw a moment's anxiety flitter across her friend's features. His offer was generous, would do much to help her clan. Would he decline to bargain further if she refused him? She'd never heard that he was a petty man, but he was a man and had a man's pride.

"A year." The words fell, unbidden, from her lips.

"Pardon?"

Her gaze went back to him, and she arched an eyebrow. "I will agree to your arrangement if you provide a *year* of fuel to Clan Badawi, from this Spring Rite to the next Spring Rite. For my...sacrifice."

This time, when he drew in air, he did rub against her breasts. She refused to back away, and she knew he would not. Even her outrageous counteroffer wouldn't dissuade him from the course he'd set. Excitement sizzled through her veins, speeding her pulse. His mouth worked for a moment before he bit out, "Done. Be in my tent at sunset."

He dipped his chin in a sharp nod to Chieftain Safia before he strode out of the tent, his advisors hastily standing to follow.

A great sigh bellowed out of Akilah, and the tense silence Kadira had barely noticed when she had confronted Ezra dissipated. Chieftain Safia stretched her legs out before her, and her consort stroked a hand down the kabu markings on the right side of his face, those that designated him a consort rather than a chieftain in his own right. He sighed. "Mighty El."

Safia grinned. "I thought you would gut him."

"I considered it, but decided there were better ways to bleed him dry." Kadira shrugged, caressing her dagger.

"My thanks for your restraint. A feud with the Haroun would be unwise." The chieftain flicked her fingers. "I cannot believe he consented to such steep terms." Her grin widened. "Your reputation in battle is excellent, but I've not heard of your great prowess as a lover."

Akilah chuckled, the sound mellow. "She *is* that good. Perhaps you should try her, Chieftain."

Rolling her eyes at both women, Kadira shook her head. That both the chieftain and her consort had looked her over with sudden interest was unnerving. She held up her hands. "I can only satisfy one chieftain at a time, especially with the conditions of Haroun's offer."

She bowed to Safia and her advisors, wishing to extricate herself as quickly as possible. Akilah followed behind, exiting the large tent with almost as much haste. She swung an arm around Kadira's shoulders. "We will have to delay our pleasures until after the Rite ends. Pity, but I'm most certain Ezra will keep you entertained." Her tone lightened with teasing. "Just not *quite* as entertained as I could."

"You've lain with him before?" The question was sharper than Kadira liked, and she knew Akilah noticed.

"No." Akilah's pale eyes squinted. "He has many lovers at Rites, but never me. His demand of exclusivity is odd. Even most bonded mates do not require it."

"Some do. Such things are negotiated between the mates." Kadira shrugged. "What do I know of such things? I have never been bonded, not even temporarily."

A tiny sliver of her wondered if she had never been offered any kind of bond because of her trader blood. Ezra's obvious disgust at the suggestion made renewed rage bolt through her. He thought her good enough to bed, to *buy*, but not good enough to bond with. Her hand locked tight around her dagger. He wanted a willing woman, did he? A thin smile flicked on and off her face. She'd show him just how willing a warrior could be, and how much it cost to tangle with one.

Ezra swiped the rough cloth over his skin, removing the excess moisture from his ablutions. The deep caves where his people encamped during the winter months, where he kept many of his supplies for his inventions, had an underground spring used for bathing. Water was too precious to spare in the open Wasteland, but he missed submerging himself in the warm liquid and was eager to return home after the Rite. Despite the cold, he and a contingent of his warriors had been away trading for many months, as did most Wanderer clans. Unlike most Wanderers, he could trade in the cities, where most of his kind were targeted by the Sun Guards who captured Wanderer males to strengthen their own bloodlines. None who were captured ever escaped. Or survived.

If they had, none had returned to their clan. Then again, the shame of being captured would discourage returning. Loss in battle was humiliation enough, but death in battle was preferable to capture by the city's guards and an end as a stud horse in chains, given over to the Breeder women as a sacrifice to their spiteful god.

Ezra shook his head. Doubtful any man could hope to regain his honor after such disgrace. A slight smile curved Ezra's lips. The Haroun clan didn't have to worry about such attacks. Even the Sun Guards didn't wish to anger a man who held the key to restoring some of their meager technology. Unlike the trader families and Wanderer clans—and even the pirate raiders—the cities hadn't managed to maintain their advances after the Mighty El scorched the earth, and Ela had retaliated by refusing to allow anything to grow on her plains, making the planet the Wasteland it was now. Always they fought, battling for supremacy with driving sandstorms and sucking funnel clouds, as contentious as the clans themselves. The cities had huddled together, herded there like animals by their foreign goddess, while necessity made those outside snatch up any machinery they could lay their hands on. Whatever it took to survive the sea pirates, the road pirates, the feuding clans, the city guards.

Legend said the world was once an ocean of lights and autos and buildings that reached to the sky. All that remained were rusted scraps of metal that Ezra repurposed into useful objects. Objects people paid him dearly for. He did not look to the past, as those in the city did. He looked to the future. Security for his clan, honor for his people. And a blade through the heart for anyone who got in his way.

He scrubbed the cloth over his hair and face, setting aside his musings as anticipation thrummed through him. The sun had set, and Kadira would come to him soon. Her honor would demand it, even if her pride balked. He'd assumed his offer would either get her to agree with him, or it would make her so angry she tried to kill him, and he could twist that into a different kind of passion. She need never know he would have paid a great deal more to have her, to push past her resistance and force her to acknowledge their attraction to each other.

The sound of drums broke the silence of the gathering night. The beginning of the evening's festivities. He had more private festivities in mind. There was no scrape of boots on the ground, no rush of wind as the tent flap was pushed aside, but he became aware of Kadira in the tent with him. He tossed the rag to a low table, turned to face her, and felt his cock rise at the sight of her. Gone were the amulets and the pelts that held her kabu chiseling tools, though she still wore the brief leather outfit. Her hair had been freed of the ceremonial braids, rippling in dark waves to her hips.

Not speaking, she approached with the predatory stride of a hunter. His eyes narrowed, but he didn't back away. He'd waited too long for this moment, and had paid dearly to get it. Her head tilted back, and her gaze met his. He drew in a deep breath at the naked heat reflected there, and he leaned forward, wanting to taste her luscious mouth.

He froze when he felt the prick of a blade along the underside of his jaw. A smug grin flickered over her face, and he shifted away from her, but her dagger stayed at his jugular. His heart thundered in his chest, and his cock grew even harder.

"On the pallet." She pressed the knife deeper into his flesh.

Taking a step back, two, he eased down to the thick bed of layered rabbit pelts. She came down on top of him, straddling his waist. The feel of her naked sex against his almost made him groan. She rocked on him, and he realized she was as primed as he was, her folds plump and slick. He swallowed, and the blade nicked his skin. A bead of blood trickled down his neck.

Her gaze followed the path of the blood before she met his eyes again. Only a fool would call the baring of her teeth a smile. She reached her free hand between them to grasp his cock, then she lifted herself to take him inside her hot pussy.

The dagger bit into his skin as she impaled herself on his cock. He understood the unspoken message. If he failed to make her come, she would slit his throat.

He would not fail.

The rhythm she set was fast, punishing. Their skin slapped together, a carnal contrast to the drums pounding outside. His fingers fisted in the furs beneath him, fighting the need to touch her, to come deep inside her. She was tight and wet around him, the feel of her better than he had dared dream. The leather of her loincloth stroked him as he rolled his hips, grinding his pelvis into her clit. Air hissed between her teeth, and moisture gushed from her core, but he didn't allow himself to smile. The dangerous woman had a knife to his neck, after all.

Their breathing sped, lungs bellowing as sweat slid down their skin. Her lush scent, aroused woman and something uniquely Kadira, teased his nose. He groaned, the sound low and tortured even to his own ears, but still he never looked away from her. Their gazes locked, and he imagined his expression was as taut with lust as hers was. Her eyes gleamed with dark fire, and she rode him harder, faster. Her pussy flexed around him each time he pierced her, and it was almost enough to drive him to lunacy.

Moving to change the angle of his thrusts, he dug his cock deep, shoving upward every time she pushed down. She froze over him, her gaze going glassy and blank, and then her sex pulsed hard around his shaft, squeezing him so tight he could barely breathe. He clung to his control by the very tips of his fingers, determined not to end this little game just yet.

"Oooh." The softest of shuddery moans slipped past her lips, and her eyes closed for just a moment.

The tiny opening was all he required. His hand snapped around her wrist, a quick press of his thumb, and her fingers went slack on the blade. It fell away, and in a swift roll, he reversed their positions until he laid atop her, his cock still hard and buried within her pussy.

Her free hand shot out to jab into his ribs, but he caught it, imprisoning both her wrists in one of his hands and pulling her arms over her head until she was forced to arch into him. Rage tightened her features, and she growled at him. "I will kill—"

He covered her lips with his, and she bit him hard enough to draw blood. The iron taste coated his tongue, but he thrust it into her mouth and did the same with his cock in her wet sex. She bucked against him, her heels slamming into his legs. He winced at the pain, but her movements only drove his cock deeper inside her, and he groaned. She twisted her arms, and he tightened his grip. Using his other hand, he jerked at the leather ties on her breast band, loosening it until he could cup her and tease her bared nipple.

A shiver passed through her, and she pushed her breast deeper into his palm, her resistance abruptly leaching away. He broke his mouth from hers, and her eyes were wide and wary, her breathing uneven. Searching her face, he found none of the fury of moments before. He leaned in and brushed her mouth with his, tasting her the way he'd wanted to when she'd entered his tent. Sweet, tart, the flavor making his cock throb where it nestled within her. He licked her lips, suckling the bottom one.

She seemed startled by the gentle contact, but she sighed a little when he pulled away again. "Let my hands go."

Jolting, he obeyed. He'd forgotten he held her down, so lost was he in the feel of her, the taste of her. Bringing one wrist to his mouth, he kissed the tender flesh, and her pulse pounded under his lips. He smiled, flicking his tongue out to savor the salty essence. Rocking his hips in infinitesimal strokes, he stimulated them both.

"Kadira." He drew back, propping himself on his forearms. It shoved him deeper between her thighs, and they both groaned. Leaning to the side, he tugged at the ties on her clothes until he could peel them away and toss them over his shoulder. Soft, naked flesh sliding against his. Her hot, wet channel clamping down on his cock. "Mighty El, you are tight."

Her gaze fastened on his lips when he spoke, and she pressed her boot heels to the backs of his legs, pushing him closer. He leaned down to offer his mouth, and she met him halfway, her tongue eagerly meeting his. So, she enjoyed his kiss. Satisfaction pulsed through him at the realization. He matched the mating of their bodies to the mating of their mouths, plunging into her, soft, then harder, deeper. Her beaded nipples rubbed against his chest, and when she fisted her walls around his cock, every thought drained from his mind.

Tilting her head, she changed the angle of their kiss. Her tongue dueled with his, but her fingers were tentative when she slid them through his hair. He choked at her touch upon him, tore his mouth away. "Yes. I want your hands on me, Kadira."

The tips of her fingers trailed down his spine, and she curved her palms over the cheeks of his ass, digging her nails in. He grunted, grinding his pelvis against her clit in retaliation. She bit her lower lip, her lids dropping to veil her eyes. He did it again, angling his thrusts to bring her as much pleasure as he could. A stifled sound of need poured from her throat, but she pressed her lips together and arched under him, her hands demanding as they pulled him closer. Her sex cinched around his cock, and he felt her shiver. The slickness coating his shaft made each stroke a struggle not to come. Fire licked at his belly, fisting tight, and pinpricks of sensation rushed over his skin everywhere they touched. Sweat from the heat they produced welded them together, and the coolness of the night air moving over him made him shudder. He drove deep, a harsh cry ripping from him. He'd be unable to contain himself much longer.

El and Ela, she was divinity incarnate.

Her head fell back, and he took advantage of the exposed position to nip and suck at her throat. She gasped, writhing beneath him. He sank his teeth into the sensitive spot that connected shoulder to neck, and she arched so hard, she lifted him with her. Her channel contracted around his cock, gripping him tight enough to make his skull feel as if it would explode. He released his hold on his restraint, and spilled his seed inside of her. Her inner muscles milked spurts of fluid from him, and he couldn't stop the harsh sounds he made.

Spent, he collapsed on top of her, burying his face in the lush valley between her breasts. He turned his head and kissed one soft slope. She panted, her muscles trembling, her breath rushing in and out, and he could hear her heart thundering under his ear. A smile curled the corners of his lips.

Never had he known pleasure this deep. It had been better than he'd imagined, and he had imagined it for more years than he'd care to admit. Her hands stroked his buttocks for a moment before she let them fall to the furs. He shuddered at the sweetness of having her hands caress him. He wanted more of it, of her, and he would have it. Weeks more of it, where he could finally burn her from his mind and body, glut himself until he was satisfied.

He leveraged himself up on his forearms so he wasn't crushing her. She shifted beneath him, but he didn't wish to slide his softening cock out of her just yet, so he stayed where he was and gazed down at her face, brushed his lips over the crescent moon on her forehead. "You are quiet."

"Am I?" Her brows pinched together, and she pulled in a deep breath that pressed her firm breasts to his chest. "You wish me to have a conversation during sex?"

It did sound odd when she put it to him that way, and he *was* still inside her. He frowned. It wasn't that she hadn't conversed; it was that she'd made little noise at all. She'd clutched at him, kissed him hard, but he'd seen her grit her teeth to hold back a scream, to muffle a moan. Her actions had spoken more than she had, and he wondered at her reserve and how to break through it. He wanted her as uninhibited as she was on the battlefield, wild and fierce. Had he ever seen her cry out a lover's name during the Rites? She'd drawn his gaze often, and he realized he had not. Her control always held. Interesting. A puzzle to decipher. Something he excelled at. He would consider it. Later. Instead of answering her questions, he offered a query of his own. "I hope you weren't...upset that I did not offer a bond."

"Not at all." Her eyebrows arched, and a coolness filled her gaze. She pushed at his shoulders until he rolled off of her. She sat up, brushing her hair away from her face. "I would never bond with someone who wished to cage me the way this arrangement does. I prefer the bond matings that are more open to experimentation."

"Experimenting is my trade." The irony of that made him smile a little.

What was almost a grin fluttered the sides of her mouth. "Your trade, but not your bond."

"No. Opening up a bond in that manner causes more problems than it solves." Discomfiture made him sit up as well, and he propped an elbow on a raised knee. Ugly memories, old taunts and humiliations, sparked through his mind. Why had he brought up the subject of bonding? Perhaps because of the way her expression had closed when he'd told her chieftain he wouldn't offer her one. He wouldn't offer anyone a bond. Ever. His parents' example was seared into his mind, and he knew how badly such arrangements could go. Better to seek the fleeting pleasure of a lover than the perpetual agony of a bonded mate.

"I disagree." One of her shoulders twitched in a shrug, but she'd turned her face away from him so he couldn't read whatever emotions she might allow to show on her features. Her fingers clenched into the pelts beneath her. "If a bond is secure, nothing can break it, and sexual play doesn't change that."

"You've been bonded before?" Jealousy ripped through him at the thought of anyone else possessing her in such a way, receiving her devotion. He shoved that unwarranted feeling aside. He didn't wish to bond with her, so why should it bother him if some other man or woman did? He shouldn't. It didn't. Of course.

She shook her head, flicking a glance at him. "No, but I've seen such bonds...in others."

"Others who were in love?" He couldn't keep the scorn out of his voice, and he almost missed the haunted expression that flashed through her gaze.

"I suppose." She scooted to the edge of the pallet and jerked her clothes off the woven grass mat on the floor. "Love makes you weak, leaves you open to pain. It'll put you on your knees if you let it. I can do without."

"I could not agree more, and I never intend to bond, which is the only reason I mention it. I meant what I said, that anyone should be honored to mate with you, if they were seeking a mate. I am not, so my refusal was not personal, and I wished to make certain you understood no offense was intended." Reaching over, he pulled her clothes away from her and threw them back to the mat. He scooped her into his arms and began working her boots off so she was as naked as he. He scowled down at her. "We're not done yet, Kadira."

"I took no offense." But her eyes told the truth. His denial had upset her. The knowledge twisted something deep inside him. Had she *hoped* he would bond with her? Impossible. He would never allow anyone that close. He had always imagined a woman as contained as she would agree, but he sensed there was more to her story than what she had said. Some wound that was still tender. Another puzzle. No wonder she fascinated him. And he had days upon days to unravel the mystery of her. Excellent.

She folded her arms over her naked breasts, shifted uncomfortably in his lap and cleared her throat, obviously groping for another topic. He would welcome one as well, so he waited for her to speak. "What is that?"

He followed her gaze to the small table beside the piled furs. "I call it a pharos."

Leaning away from him, she examined it more closely. "It is...not fire that makes it burn."

"No, you leave it out to catch the sun during the day and it'll burn all night, if needed. It works better than those powered by our regular fuel, and requires no horse chips or precious wood to sustain. Difficult to find the materials to create, so I don't trade them. Yet." He stroked his fingers in circles on her skin, thinking. "I need to consider ways to simplify the design."

"They say your mind does not work the way a normal person's would. That El and Ela made you...different." Her dark eyes studied him, and he couldn't prevent himself from stiffening. How often had he defended his own thoughts? He could not explain the unexplainable. He'd thought such sensitivity buried under heavy calluses, but it stung to have her point out his freakish nature as so many had done before her. In his youth, anyone who'd mocked him had been battered into unconsciousness on the practice field. His clan had quickly learned that even if his mind was different, his fists and sword hurt as much as anyone else's when they struck.

"Are not we all unique? Different?" Though he managed the light voice he usually used when people asked such things now, his shoulder jerked in a shrug. He snapped off the pharos, throwing them into darkness. He rolled them so she was on the side of the pallet farthest from the door, to protect her or to keep her from escaping, he was uncertain, but he knew neither would be a gesture she appreciated. "Sleep, Kadira."

"You...want me to *sleep* in your tent too?" The incredulousness in her voice irritated him, made him want to growl at her. Why she should be able to set him so on edge, send arrows to all the chinks in his armor, he didn't know.

"Only a Rose slinks out of a man's bed when he is done fucking her. You are not a Rose."

She went rigid beside him. "No. I am not. Say so again, and I'll put a blade in you."

"Good. You do that." He hooked his arm around her waist and pulled her back against him. "Now stop talking and allow me some rest. I have to keep up my strength if I'm going to help you work off the cost of a year's supply of fuel."

Snorting, she drove an elbow into his belly, and all the air rushed out of his lungs. He choked and laughed at the same time. She groped around in the dark for a moment, pinched his ass and then pulled a blanket up and over them. "Go to sleep, Chieftain."

A sigh eased out of him, and instead of keeping him awake, the sound of the Rite drums lulled him to unconsciousness, his face buried in the nape of her neck.

The sweet scent of her teased his dreams.

Chapter Three

His hair looked like fire in the morning light, turning it a brighter shade of red than it actually was. Leaning away from him, Kadira allowed herself a thorough look while he still slept. It was odd, waking beside someone. She usually found her own pallet after a bout of sex.

The lightest brush of freckles shown under his browned skin, and on anyone else it would have been endearing, but his body bore too many scars for him to be seen as anything other than what he was—a ruthless, dangerous man. Black whorls of tattooing curled from his brow to his chin on one side of his face, the high cheekbone making the ink stand out. His skin was paler than hers, making the dark marks all the more apparent. His warrior kabu sliced and swirled from his wrist to his shoulder and around to the upper portion of his pectoral muscles. Chronicles of his many kills, battles he had won. The victories hadn't been easy, and his body showed those marks too, white scars lanced down the biceps on his right arm, opposite his warrior kabu. A puckered puncture wound in his side where a spear tip had struck. A broadsword had carved a path down his left thigh, and a tattooed thigh band asking for protection and good fortune from El and Ela circled his right leg.

Her fingers itched to touch, and she told herself it was because she felt the call to chisel kabu marks into his flesh, and she did, but she knew that was not the whole of the truth. His muscled chest drew her gaze, too, the flat brown nipples, the dusting of dark red curls that led to the ridges of his abdomen. The indentation of his navel made her wish to nip with her teeth, and she wanted to pet the rougher hair at his groin that surrounded his cock.

His erect cock.

Her gaze flew to his face, found his eyes had cracked open and glittered like gold as he looked her over as thoroughly as she had examined him. "Bright morning to you."

"And you." She watched his lips form the words and hoped he kissed her again. She'd never had a lover kiss her so well, so thoroughly before. The intimacy of it had been...surprising, startling, but she wanted more. The man had a gift, and if she must confine herself to him for the next several weeks, then she should reap the benefits of his many talents.

"How are you?"

The way he stared at her still had the power to make her uncomfortable, and she didn't like it. She didn't like how he constantly threw her off balance. During Rites, she'd seen him rough and wild with his lovers, and she'd expected that the night before, but when he'd put her on her back he'd been gentle...almost tender. She'd braced herself for retribution and pain for holding a knife to his throat, but her point had needed to be made—all the power was not his, and their arrangement did not make her his plaything.

He'd understood. She'd seen it in those golden eyes, watched his thoughts process. His mind was odd. Perhaps he saw more than other people could, and the thought made her wary. She'd hit a sore spot when she'd mentioned his genius to him. She could understand how isolating it was to be different, and unexpected sympathy wound through her. Such sentiments were foolish and would likely insult him if he knew of them. He was not a man to be pitied, any more than she was a woman who would accept commiseration on her position in life.

"Kadira?"

She started, and it took her a moment to remember his question, she was so lost in thought. "Fine, though I need to rise and get to the practice field before everyone's too tired to be a worthy challenge." She stretched and prepared to sit up. "You'll want me back here at sundown, yes?"

"Yes, but don't leave just yet." Something wicked flared to life in his eyes, and he rolled smoothly on top of her. A hot thrill bolted through her at the feel of his hard body, his coarser flesh. Her nipples contracted to points, stimulated by the crisp hair on his chest, her sex clenched, flooding with juices. She'd never reacted this quickly to anyone, man or woman. She grabbed for his shoulders, tried to hold him in place, tried to contain the anticipation his mere touch sent buzzing along her nerves. Her attempt failed miserably when he swept his lips over hers in a featherlight kiss. "I think we did not properly display our spiritual devotion in the Rite last eve. We are here to celebrate the ascendance of the goddess, are we not?"

"Yes," she gasped. Every inch of her body throbbed in awareness of him. El and Ela, but she wanted his hands on her, his mouth, his long cock pushing into her wet sex. Making the agreement she'd made, she no longer had to pretend this wasn't what she craved, and when it was over, they would part ways. Nothing permanent would ever come of this, and they both knew it. He wanted no bonds on him. She could never bond with a man who'd force her to deny her sexual needs. It was freeing. She could savor every moment and never have to fear that either of them would expect anything more than a simple transaction. A trade agreement. He'd made an exchange for her time at Rite. Her clan got what it needed, and they could scratch an itch they'd been avoiding for years. *She'd* been avoiding for years. If the simplicity of her justification rang hollowly, she ignored it.

His auburn head dipped and he kissed the upper slopes of her breasts, sucking each tip in turn, hard enough to make her breath catch. Sliding his tongue down the centerline of her torso, he nibbled at the sunburst kabu that ringed her navel. She arched beneath him, her hands sliding into his hair to urge him lower.

"Now is the time for worship of the female form, yes?" She felt him smile against her skin while he slipped down until his breath rushed over her slick folds.

The very breath stopped in her lungs, her heart stumbled as she waited, the tension building higher and higher until she had to clench her jaw on a scream. Shudders ran through her, flames bursting to life within her. Dipping forward, he shaped his mouth around her clit, sucking hard. She gasped, heaving under him, and she couldn't stop the soft words from spilling forth. "*Yes.* Yes, Ezra. Yes, yes, *yes.*"

He chuckled, released her sensitive flesh and moved to kiss his way down the geometric pattern tattooed on the outside of her right thigh. Her muscles flexed, and she moaned a low protest at his abandonment of her pussy. She craved his touch there, her channel clenching on emptiness. His thick cock needed to be inside her, shoving her toward that earth-shattering pinnacle. Her skin felt aflame, but she stopped herself from demanding he take her. She didn't want this to end. The slow, insidious heat rising in her core was too good, so she let him pleasure her.

And he did.

He stroked her, kissed every mark, every tattoo, every scar, worshipped her body, but didn't touch her where she needed it the most. Her fingers bunched in the furs, and she writhed, her breath strangling in her throat when he returned to suckle her breasts. He batted his tongue over the stiff crests, teasing her nipples to points so tight they ached. Then he drew them into his mouth again. She choked, dragged in a ragged lungful of air, but it did nothing to calm her raging excitement. His scent teased her nose, rich and masculine and Ezra. She reached out, her hands twisting in his hair so hard she felt him wince, but her body hungered for him. She could feel each pulse of her blood moving beneath her skin.

"Ezra," she moaned.

He released her breast with a pop of suction that made her squirm. "Yes?"

"Touch me."

"I am touching you." Rubbing against her, he demonstrated how every inch of him pressed to her, stimulated her. She could feel his cock, hard and heavy against her belly. Close, but not close enough.

She licked her lips, groped for some coherency. "Between—between my legs."

"Here?" He moved to kneel in the spread vee of her legs, and the very tips of his fingers feathered over the insides of her thighs.

Amusement, annoyance and streaking lust warred for dominance inside her at his perversity. She was dying, and he was *teasing* her. "A little higher, and if you require me to be more specific, I'm going to go find someone else who actually knows what they're doing."

He growled, some of the irritation she felt showing in his expression. "That would violate our agreement."

"Then perhaps I should go find someone who can instruct you on—"

Shoving her legs flat to the pelts, he buried his face between her thighs and feasted on her damp, needy flesh. Finally, *finally*. A smile stretched her lips wide, though she knew he couldn't see it. She wanted to laugh, but his tongue thrust into her channel, lapping at the thick cream. Ela, but she'd never been so wet.

Sweat sheened her body, and the tent grew brighter with every moment as the sun rose, the day heating to match the way her blood boiled in her veins. Her muscles strained as she lifted herself into him, pressing as close to his mouth as she could. He licked her slit, suckling her clitoris while his fingers delved into her channel. He teased more moisture from her, hooking his digits so that he rubbed her in just the right place. Twisting in shameless ecstasy, she reached out to sink her nails into his shoulders. He jerked his fingers out of her, and she raked her nails over his skin for denying her what she wanted. He rumbled a laugh, and the vibrations had her writhing, the soft pelts she lay on stimulating her skin as she moved. Slipping his fingers downward, he stroked her anus. She froze, then opened her legs wide to give him access. He pushed in, his digits slick with her juices. Her muscles gripped him tight, and she had to concentrate to relax for his penetration. He added a second finger, working her open so he could thrust into her. She bit her lip on a whimper, shivers starting deep within her and spreading outward. Her sex flexed once, hard, and she knew she'd come soon. Another few plunges of his fingers, flicks of his tongue, and she'd shatter.

"Scream for me, Kadira. I want to hear how much I please you."

He did please her. El and Ela, how he did. Panting for breath, she couldn't drag in enough air to tell him. Her head tossed on the thick furs, and her sex spasmed every time he stroked her with his hand and tongue. The way he made her feel was so very fine. Nothing had ever been this sweet before, made her experience such a rush of elation. It was terrifying. It was perfection.

Thrusting his fingers deep into her ass, he blew a cool breath over her slick, swollen pussy. "Scream, Kadira. Now is the time for worship, not restraint. Scream to the heavens."

She wanted to. She tried. Her mouth opened in a silent shriek, and when he withdrew his hand and pounded in again, every muscle inside her locked tight. His mouth closed over her clit, and she went off like one of his volatile concoctions. Her heels pressed to the pelts, and she arched high while he worked her faster and faster, dragging her into oblivion. When she could breath again, she collapsed back to the pallet, her entire body quaking.

Lunging upward, he shoved his cock deep inside her, and a broken cry bubbled from her throat.

"Good enough," he rasped. One, two, three strokes, and he shook as he joined her in ecstasy. He slammed deep, grinding hard against her clit and she imploded. Orgasm crashed over her again like a raging sandstorm, sucking and swirling around her, battering at her defenses. She clung to him, an anchor in the storm, the only link to sanity she could find.

She held him close when it was done. Held him while the sweat dried on their skin, held him while their breathing slowed and their heart rates returned to normal. Even then, nothing felt normal. Her response to this man had never been normal, and a tiny part of her was grateful her days with him were numbered. He unsettled her, and while she liked everything they'd done together, wanted more of it, there was comfort in knowing his unsettling effect wouldn't last past the end of the Rites of Spring, when their clans parted ways for half the annum. A relieved sigh heaved from her lungs, but she froze when she realized she was stroking his skin, petting him, curling and cuddling into him like a kitten. If she'd been one of the hunting cats the clans kept, she'd be purring.

When he hummed and nuzzled into the crook of her neck, she decided it was time to rise for the day. Sex was one thing, especially during the Rites, but these affectionate, caring gestures and letting herself go soft over a lover led to dangerous things—the kinds of dangerous ends her parents had met. No. Never. That path was not for her. She bucked hard, using his own weight against him in a move she'd executed in countless battles, and he landed on his back beside her with a grunt.

Rolling to her feet, she picked up her clothes to pull them over her head, twisting the leather pieces into place over her breasts and loins. Ezra's hand came up from behind her and tightened the laces on the bottom half while she did the same for the top. One teasing finger slipped under the garment and flicked over her clit, which raised her on tiptoe. "*Ezra.*"

He chuckled, and the sound was low and warm. Brushing her hair over her shoulder to trail over her breasts, he pressed his lips to the back of her neck. "This is a very interesting mark you have here."

A flinch she couldn't halt jolted her forward, and she twisted to get out of his arms. "The kabu says I'm not really a Wanderer. That's hardly interesting."

"If you were adopted into a clan, then you're as much a Wanderer as any other. That's our way." His voice was colored with confusion, as though he knew he treaded on treacherous ground, but wasn't certain how he'd stumbled upon it. "I'm afraid I hadn't known you were adopted into the Badawi clan."

"If you had, would you have chosen someone else for your arrangement?" She wanted to cut her own tongue out for daring to voice such a question.

He caught her shoulder, and she pivoted to face him rather than engage in a wrestling match over whether he could move her where he wanted. His expression was wary, but a tinge of annoyance shaded his gaze. "Do you really think your bloodlines have anything to do with why I want you?" He shook his head. "Is that why you train harder than anyone, became a kabu shaman, participate in the ritual drumming instead of just relaxing? Because of your bloodlines?"

"My parents were traders. That's my bloodline." It wasn't an answer to his questions, but she didn't want to think about the way he wanted her, about the way he made her feel, about why she lived her life the way she did. She owed him no explanations or justifications. Her jaw jutted. "They say the traders were once Wanderers."

He pulled a pair of supple buckskin breeches off a neatly folded pile of clothing. The table they sat on was...odd. Some invention of his, no doubt. She looked anywhere but at him, wishing she never had to speak of her bloodlines again, or the kabu that would always mark her an interloper.

Ezra's long fingers laced the front of his pants, and she couldn't glance away. "I wouldn't doubt that, since traders travel as we do, but they are not like us any longer. They are their own people, like the fisher folk and the city dwellers. Not bad, just...different. More peaceful, less prepared to defend themselves against threats." His gaze narrowed on her face, the intensity of his focus sending a shiver over her skin. "There are no female traders. Who was your mother? Or, rather, *what* was she, and how did you come to be raised by traders?"

"My mother traveled with my father, with our trader caravan." The mere mention of her long-dead parents sent a shaft of pain through her heart. She made her face go blank. She would not speak of them. Not ever. Not of how they lived, and especially not of how they died. Her gorge rose, and she fought to swallow before it choked her. Her words were clipped, making it clear this was not a discussion she wished to continue. "I was born and raised among them—my mother, my father and my many *uncles*, though I doubt any of them were related by blood."

"How did she—"

"I don't know." She lifted her hands and let them flop down. "I don't know how she came to be with a caravan of traders. I don't know how she met my father. I don't know if she was born a Priestess, a Breeder, a Whore or a Wanderer. Did she run away? Was she stolen? I was too young when they died to have ever asked. I just thought it was a special adventure for me when my father took me into the cities dressed as a boy to trade while my mother stayed behind with some of the other men in our caravan."

If anything, his scrutiny heightened, and she felt pierced by his amber gaze—those eyes that always saw more than she was comfortable with. He propped his hands on his hips. "Huh. That is an unusual upbringing, to say the least."

She merely shrugged, flashed a tight smile. "Are not we all unique? Different?"

"Ha." He slapped a palm against his thigh, his eyes twinkling. "My words used against me, clever woman."

The heavy moment passed, and she got the feeling he'd allowed it because he'd seen how desperately she needed to *not* talk about her strange upbringing, her time before the Wanderers, her family and what had become of them. He could push, but it would make her angry, so he didn't push. His courtesy irritated her, and she disliked how irrational that was. She hated how he threw her, how he peeled away her shields with just a glance. She knew her place, knew who she was, where she'd come from and where she was going. This time with him was simply a passing moment of sexual pleasure in her life. It should affect her no more than any other carnal encounter, no matter how much she enjoyed the encounter. Her body responded to the reminder of all they had done together, and how good it had felt to assuage her curiosity about him, to have his hands on her, his cock inside her, his mouth pressed to hers. El and Ela, but his mouth was divine.

As if he sensed her thoughts had turned to sex, he snaked an arm around her waist with that lightning speed of his and hauled her up against him. Her breasts flattened on the hard wall of his chest, and his hands curled over her ass to bring her up on tiptoe, mating their sexes. Goddess and god, they'd just fucked and her body was ready for more. A week with no sex had primed her like a powder keg for him. This couldn't last for the whole of their time together, but lying with him should have eased her sexual frustration, not sharpened it. His mouth slanted over hers, and he kissed her until she shoved her hands in his soft hair to hold him closer. His tongue mated with hers, and she ran her hands over the muscled planes of his back, her fingertips tracing a few scars, the raised skin of a kabu mark between his shoulder blades, the long line of his spine.

He lifted his mouth from hers, his lips as swollen and red as hers felt. His pupils were so huge they nearly eclipsed the gold of his irises. "Come to me tonight." He snorted and shook his head, self-derision flashing in his gaze. "I don't know if I can wait that long to have you again, Kadira."

"You have trading to do, and my clan will need me." She tried to be reasonable, but couldn't force herself to step away from him. "I also have a few requests to do additional kabu rituals for those wanting bond or battle marks."

Claiming her lips again, he explored her with a leisure that made her insides melt. He was panting when he released her, his hard cock branding her belly through his breeches. "Thanks to El and Ela that the maturity marking is done and you no longer need to remain pure."

"Yes." She pulled him down to her again, craving his taste. She could kiss this man forever and never tire of his distinctive flavor, but she pushed the notion away before it could drift into strange territory. Better to enjoy the moment than worry about the future.

Even if he was the best sex she'd ever had, it didn't change their arrangement, or the fact that neither of them was compatible with the other for a longer-term relationship. Three weeks of exclusivity was about as much as she could take, but she wondered at his demand for it if he wanted no part of an exclusive, permanent bond, ever. Another odd quirk to the man who was already so different than any other she'd ever known. She just wished that didn't fascinate her so much. Thank the god and goddess that the Rites of Spring would be over soon, and she could return to a life where she understood everything and everyone in it.

Including herself.

It had been a struggle to stay away from her all day, to keep his mind focused on business. Rites were some of the most important times for the clans, and he could not afford to misstep, yet he'd been unable to stop thinking about her and what they'd done, anticipating all he would do to her during their three weeks together, imagining what she might do to him. His cock had been semi-erect for hours, and it was a damned uncomfortable experience. He hadn't been this randy since he'd been a mere youth, fresh from his first Rite.

Even the desert night's frigid air couldn't quell the surging pressure in his loins. On the way out of his tent, he scooped up a new invention he thought might please Kadira and slipped it into his pocket. He wrapped a soft goat-wool blanket around his shoulders, accepted a peeled prickly pear from a passing clansman, and crunched on it as he went to find a large rock to sit on a short distance from the bonfire. He stretched his legs out and crossed them at the ankles as he watched the revelry begin. The drums thumped in time with pipes and mizmars, the music picking up beat, and many Wanderers leaped into dances of smooth twists and sensual undulations. Soon, they would move on to different, more sexual, kinds of dancing.

"Bla grog, Chieftain?" A handsome youth proffered a mug and meaningful grin. The alcohol made of blue potatoes was an offering to the goddess for Her Rites by the Haroun clan. Ezra had invented a new kind of distiller that enhanced the taste, and he was doing good business with people wanting to buy one for their clans. An unexpected boon for the Haroun.

Ezra accepted the mug with a grateful nod, and they sipped in silence as the bonfire carousing continued. The lad cast him a sideways glance that was almost hopeful, and Ezra shook his head with a small smile. Even if he weren't to be occupied with Kadira, he preferred his lovers a bit more seasoned. This youngling couldn't have more than a handful of Rites under his belt. "Enjoy your Rite. And the Haroun bla grog."

"I will. Thank you, Chieftain." Disappointment flashed in the boy's eyes, but he disappeared into the crowd of dancers without another word.

Ezra dismissed all thought of the lad the second he saw Kadira's form reflected in the firelight. Mighty El, but she was beautiful. The roll of her hips with each stride was unconsciously feminine, and her eyes focused on him, but she didn't so much as smile a greeting as she approached and stationed herself beside him. Though she wore a simple blue shift that ended at her knees, she must have recently performed a kabu ritual because her hair crinkled in such a way that said it had just been released from braids. An icy blast of wind swept through the camp, blowing her long tresses sideways.

"This night is cold." He uncrossed his ankles, set his drink on the ground beside him and sat up straighter on the rock, slanting an easy smile in her direction. She was far too contained and serious. He had far too many ideas about how to loosen her restraint. "Come share my blanket, and I'll warm you."

She tipped her head in a courteous nod. "I have no need of such comfort. I am fine."

The few comments she had made about her bloodline told him much about why she pushed herself so hard to be a better and stronger Wanderer than any other. The way she doubted herself and her place astounded him. It may not always have been thus, but she had more than proven herself a Wanderer. So little was thought of her adopted status that it had never even been mentioned in his presence. He would have noted any comments made of her—she had always roused his interest. She was like this night, fire and ice existing in the same environment, uninhibited and yet always in control. A contradiction that fascinated him, and that fascination had only increased in the last day. If it were merely the sex, he could explain it, but he found he wanted to know more than just what pleasured her most in bed. He wanted to uncover all her secrets. Only then could he move past his distracting fixation.

He shifted to look at her more fully. "You don't need to prove anything to *me*, Kadira. Your prowess as a warrior is not in question."

Folding her hands behind her in soldierly fashion, she lifted her chin. "Says the man whose rank in his clan was always assured."

He arched an incredulous brow. "Surely you don't believe that. My mind doesn't work the same way others do. As a child, they thought I might have been cursed by El and Ela. It wasn't until my skills proved useful to the clan that my place was assured." And it was only then that he'd been able to overcome the stigma of his parents' dishonor. His jaw flexed, and he had to force himself to relax. All of that was long ago and far behind him. "I fought for what is mine, just as you no doubt did, but there is no fight between us."

Unless they counted the rough sex while she held a blade to his throat. The thin cut was a small price for the pleasure of sliding his cock inside her slick pussy. Her hand moved to her hip, where she normally kept her dagger sheathed, so he knew her thoughts had followed the same lines as his. The slightest curve of her lips gave her away.

"Perhaps it is I who need your...*warmth* tonight." His voice dropped to a soft, coaxing purr.

Her breathing hitched, and his gaze fell to her breasts, outlined to perfection by the firelight filtering through her thin shift. He could see how her nipples beaded, jutting against the pale fabric. From the chill or something more? Her gaze sparked with heat when she looked at him, and his cock rose to full, throbbing attention. She swayed toward him, and he opened the blanket for her. Easing her weight onto his lap, she perched sideways in stiff silence.

Wrapping the blanket and his arms around her, he pulled her into his embrace. He rubbed a hand up and down her back, hoping to soothe her. The boisterous noise of the clans celebrating Rites roared before them, two men falling to the ground near them to couple in feral abandon. She stared at them, but her body only grew tenser. Ezra kissed the side of her neck. "Be easy, Kadira."

"I don't normally..."

"Relax? I know."

She nudged him with her shoulder, the barest hint of

tension leaching from her. "I don't normally sit on men's laps. I like to be more active than that." She slanted a glance over her shoulder. "Perhaps *that's* why I choose drumming when I cannot have fucking at Rites."

"We both know that's not true." This time he bit her neck, hard enough to make her squirm. He groaned when her movements rubbed her against his cock. "We both have our ways of proving ourselves useful because we are different. I, with my inventing of profitable things, and you, with your enjoyment of being *active*." He licked the spot he'd bitten, the sweetness of her skin bursting over his tongue. "We are so alike, you and I."

Her head fell against his shoulder, and her heavy-lidded dark eyes met his. She reached up and traced the kabu on his face. "You're a genius and the chieftain of a wealthy clan, and only growing wealthier with every invention. I'm a stray they picked up along the way."

"You are unique." He brushed his lips over hers, and the clamor of drums and laughter and dancing and fucking all faded as his senses centered on the woman in his arms. One side of the blanket fell open as he released it to fondle her breast. She arched into the touch, her body bowing in a tight line. He lifted his mouth to look into her eyes while he teased her nipple. "Are you wet for me, Kadira?"

"Yes." But she went rigid as an older man reached out to slide his hand down her arm. She caught his wrist in a tight grip, her nails digging into the tendons until his hand spasmed. The hot passion had fled her face, leaving only cold fury. "No one touches me without asking first."

She tossed the man's hand aside. Masud Tayi, advisor to the Tayi chieftain. Ezra fought the urge to set Kadira aside and break the man's nose. Only the fact that Rite was a ceremony of concordance kept him in his seat. He would never do anything to disgrace his clan. He had spent too many years trying to erase his parents' disgrace to bring more on his people, but possessiveness ripped through him and he resituated the blanket to cover Kadira from the man's lustful eyes.

Masud grinned slyly and wavered on his feet a bit, his mug of bla grog sloshing over the rim. "Careful, Haroun. I saw that look on your father's face once."

Ezra went as stiff as Kadira, and she shifted as if to rise, or to ready herself to spring free of combatants. He locked his fingers around her waist to hold her in place, knowing his grip would be painful, but also knowing she might be the only thing holding him back from the kind of youthful rage that used to flash out when such cutting comments had had him reaching for his blade. "I am not my father."

"Chieftain Haroun. Like your father before you." The older man gave an unsteady salute, all the more disrespectful for its drunken delivery. "He looked at your mother the way you look at her. Would a shaman have you for anything other than fucking after what he did? Ah, yes. You had to pay her even to do that, and she hides in your tent to do it with you."

Her fingers folded over his, tugging until she could lean back against him and pull his arms around her in an embrace. "I suggest you walk away now before he *accidentally* kills you on the practice field since the Rites is a time of peace. You are disturbing ours."

"My apologies." Masud nodded, his eyes suddenly clearer, and tinged with fear as he took in the icy anger emanating from the people before him. "Shaman. Chieftain. Enjoy your Rites."

Ezra managed to unlock his jaw long enough to grit out, "You do the same. Somewhere else."

"The edge of your sword—and hers—can't cut through the truth, Haroun." Masud's narrowed eyes reflected fury along with his apprehension.

Arching a brow, Ezra stared the older man down. "You forget, I never intend to walk down the same path as my father did with my mother. If you don't let yourself be marked, you can never wear the scars. Can you?"

"Never is a very long time, Chieftain. But tonight is short, so I'll take myself off to warmer company by the fire." Offering a final toast with his mug of bla grog, Masud made his way toward the bonfire, forced to step over the men fucking in front of them.

Kadira stirred in Ezra's lap, turning her head to look at him. She'd watched the exchange with interest, but didn't speak until their visitor had moved out of earshot. "You said you would never bond, but you never said why."

"My parents, of course." He snorted, and she twisted at the waist to face him, but it was he who stiffened while she leaned deeper into him. "You must have heard the story. Every

Wanderer has heard of my father's shame."

"I was not born a Wanderer." Her arms went around him, her hands on his bare back under the blanket. Her gaze searched his face, which he wiped clear of expression. "All I have ever heard of Ezra Haroun was of his mind and his inventions and the ferocity of his fury when it is invoked. They speak of you with the same fear the cities use for the angry Sun god they wish to soothe."

"And you want to soothe me?"

"No," she said softly. "I want to know you. Tell me what happened."

He closed his eyes to keep from drowning in the dark pools of hers. He'd never seen the female warrior so sympathetic. He liked that she offered it to him, and hated that it had anything to do with something he'd fight his whole life and never be able to overcome. "My parents were bonded, a permanent bond, the kabu marks carved into their wrists." He swallowed, his voice harsh. "When I was twelve summers old, my mother decided to take another lover. She wanted to...experiment...as she had in her youth. My father agreed, at first, but soon it became more than experimenting. She grew weary of my father's possession and wanted out of their bond."

"That can't be done, not with a permanent bond."

He choked on a bitter laugh. "Yes, but that didn't stop her and her lover from deserting their clans and running away together."

"El and Ela..." A shudder went through her—through him—and she held him tighter. He could feel her shock. The permanent bond was a sacred oath, inscribed in blood and flesh, consecrated by the god and goddess. To break it was to incur their wrath, to bring a curse down on a clan.

Wishing that were the worst of it, he swallowed the acrid anger that burned up from his belly. For so many years, they'd thought *he* was the curse upon his clan. He, with his freakish mind and freakish thoughts he couldn't explain to anyone. His freakish gadgets that did freakish things no one had ever seen before, but had heard about in ancient legend. Ezra, chieftain's child and Haroun clan curse, a punishment sent down to repay the shameful debt of his parents' perfidy. So many battles he'd had to fight, just to prove he had the right to live. He sucked in a deep breath. "That's not all."

"Tell me." She stroked her palms up and down his back.

He buried his hand in her hair, resting his forehead against hers, and shut his eyes so he couldn't see her reaction to the final, ugly revelation. "My father...my father peeled the skin from his wrist rather than wear the bond mark after she left him."

"Blasphemy," she breathed in horror, and it felt like ice ran down his spine. He'd thought she'd heard the tale before, that *everyone* had heard the tale before. Now he realized that Masud could be right. If she *had* heard, the shaman might never have lain with him.

"Yes." He wanted to beat himself into oblivion for voicing the question, but he couldn't stop himself. He had to ask. "If you had known, would you still have agreed to my arrangement, kabu shaman?"

She leaned back and stared up at him. A chortle sputtered out of her, and she repeated his own words to him, a habit he had a feeling he was going to regret laughing about. "Do you really think your parents have anything to do with why I want you? You are not to blame for what they did. It is the one thing I have never understood about the Wanderer ways. No person should be held responsible for another's actions. A whole clan should not suffer for one member's crimes."

Relief so great it would have driven him to his knees if he'd not been seated washed over him like an ocean wave. The power of the emotion jolted him, and he shoved it away, refusing to acknowledge what it might mean. "Thank you."

"For what?"

"For your absolution, shaman."

"You've spent too much time in the cities, with their wrathful, greedy deities. I cannot grant absolution to anyone. Such is not part of the Wanderer religion." She sat in silence for a long moment, and he wasn't certain he wanted to know what occupied her thoughts. "You said they thought you were a curse as a child, before your genius proved useful. They thought you were the punishment for your parents' sacrilege, didn't they?"

"Yes." He sighed. "I had to survive many *unfortunate accidents* after they sinned against El and Ela. Before then, I had just been an oddity, but...my freakish nature took on a darker meaning for everyone."

"People fear what they do not understand, Ezra. That is not

your fault." She rested her cheek against his chest, and the feel of her, soft and pliant against him, was sweet enough to stop his heart. "I'm glad you fought well and survived to be who you are now. I'm sorry for what your parents and clan did to harm you. Even if they are not."

Something deep inside him cracked and crumbled. A weight he'd born so long he'd forgotten how heavy it rested on his shoulders. Perhaps the wounds would never truly heal, but some of the childhood rage he'd locked away dissipated at her words. Someone looked beyond his genius and soothed the helpless boy he had been. Someone tried to understand. Kadira—a woman who was half-outside and half-in, just as he was. He swallowed and pulled a breath deep into his lungs, cupping the back of her head and stroking her silken hair. "You are a remarkable woman, Kadira."

"People are watching us." She shifted on his lap, and he became aware of just how much interest they were garnering from a crowd that should be immersed in carnal delights. "Is it because of what Masud said? That I'm a shaman, so I'll hide that I'm willing to fuck you because of your parents' shame?"

"More than likely, yes. Though Masud is still a horse's ass."

"Horses are rare and sacred animals." She sniffed. "They do not deserve such an insulting comparison."

He chuckled, then groaned when she tugged the blanket away from him and tossed it to the ground. She busied her hands unlacing his breeches. "Should I ask what you are doing?"

"If people intend on watching us, then we should give them something entertaining to look at." Her eyes flashed defiance, and she slipped his cock free of his pants. She pumped him between her fingers until he was harder than sun-glass. "And I wish to make it clear that I am not ashamed to sleep with you."

"Kadira..." He didn't bother finishing the thought. Voicing a halfhearted protest wasn't worth the effort it would take to form the words, and his wits seemed to have gone begging. Her thumb rolled over the head of his cock, smearing the moisture that seeped from the tip.

She let his shaft go long enough to tug her thin garment over her head and drop it on top of his discarded blanket. Having her slim body bared for him made him shudder. He arched her back over his arm and sucked her nipples into his mouth one at a time. Grabbing his free hand, she shoved it between her legs. "I want you, Ezra. Inside me. *Now.*"

He worked his fingers deep within her, until she writhed on his lap. Slipping his soaking fingers out of her hot pussy, he moved them to slide into her backside, stretching the tight ring of her anus. They both groaned, but she spread her legs for him. He pierced her with two and then three fingers, twisting them inside her until she was wide enough to take his cock.

Snapping her fingers around his wrist, she shoved his hand away. Her breasts heaved with each breath, her nipples tight points still damp from his mouth. She shifted around on his lap until she faced away from him, and then straddled his thighs. "I can't wait."

"Neither can I." He held her so she wouldn't fall off the rock they shared, guiding her backward until he could work his cock into her ass. She made a harsh noise that was almost drowned out by the cacophony of Rite, but he heard it and paused, waiting for her muscles to relax around his shaft so he could push his way deep inside her. She was so tight, it was almost painful, but it also made his blood roar in his veins.

A whimper broke from her. "They're still watching."

He glanced around, saw how many people stared as he penetrated Kadira's anus. Their eyes were envious, burning with lust as she began to move on him. She shimmied upward, then eased back down, letting her weight sink her onto his cock. He slid his hands up to palm her breasts, tweaking the hard little nipples. More than one warrior twitched in their direction, a few men and women beginning to move in time with them as they fucked. It was arousing, but not nearly as much as having Kadira watch him had been.

Now he had her in his arms—just where he wanted her.

Sucking her earlobe between his teeth, he bit down on the soft flesh. She choked, but didn't cry out for him. He breathed into her ear. "Do you enjoy having their eyes on you?"

"I would rather have a few of them join us."

Jealousy sank sharp claws into his belly, and he froze, his arms locking her in place so she couldn't move. She twisted in his embrace, sank her nails into his arm, and moaned an objection. "You would prefer their touch upon you?"

In that moment, he had a deeper sympathy for his father than he ever had before. To have a woman you craved more than your next breath want someone else instead could bring any man to his knees. Agony gutted him, and a hoarse sound ripped from his innards.

"It's not about preferring them," she gasped. "I want *you*, but I so enjoyed seeing you fuck Bachir's ass the way you're fucking mine now. It made me hot and wet for you. I almost came just from watching." Her words made his cock flex inside her, and he almost came just from listening to her speak of it. God and goddess, the things she did to him. She jerked against his hold on her. "Move, Ezra. I'm dying, burning up. Move, move, *move*."

Relaxing his grip, he let her ride his cock. He bracketed her hips with his hands, pulling her tight to the root of his shaft. She lifted and lowered herself, rocking faster and faster. Her ass closed around his cock, and the sensation was beyond amazing. The skin of her soft back rubbed along his chest. Her sweet scent filled his lungs, her long hair tickled his flesh as the wind made the strands flutter around them. And ever he was aware of the heated gazes that watched them, wanted them. It was erotic, and experiencing it with Kadira made it more so. He'd never been this conscious of how open the orgies of Rites were. Usually he was focused on his lovers alone, but now he absorbed all of it, every detail soaking in.

Her knees tightened on the sides of his legs, which dug the invention in his pocket into his flank. He grinned and wrapped his arm around her waist while he fished out the gadget with his other hand. Not only would he have her unashamed tonight, he'd have her unrestrained. He'd make her scream for him. "Well, I wouldn't want to bore you with my touch alone, my warrior shaman. Let me see what I can do to make this more interesting."

He held the cylindrical metal tube in front of her so she could get a good look at it. She ground her ass against him, and they both gave a low cry. She panted, reaching over her shoulder to grab a handful of his hair. "More interesting?"

"Yes. It's a gift. For your pleasure."

She chuckled. "I know what it's for. My father used to trade such items. Some were made out of metal, like that one, others were carved of stone or wood or sun-glass."

Rubbing it against her clit, he enjoyed her soft moans as he pressed the phallus into her pussy. She shuddered against him, her hand fisting in his hair as he stretched both her channels. Her muscles pulsed around his cock, and her moisture coated his hand as she gushed.

"Tell me, Kadira, did those pieces you traded do this?" He flicked his nail over a small knob near the base and the phallus began to quake within her, vibrating down the length of his cock as the movement pierced the thin wall that separated the two.

She threw her head back against his shoulder and screamed as she came. "Ezra! *Ezra!*"

The sound of his name on her lips was enough to shove him over the edge, and he released deep into her ass, his control shattering. He pumped his cock and the phallus into her until her muscles locked around him again, and orgasm shook her once more. Come spurted from him to fill her, his body jerking with each wave of ecstasy. Their shouts mingled with those of others celebrating the Rite, and for once both of them were a part of the Wanderers. No different than any other, integrated in a ritual that commemorated the purest aspects of their religion. Fertility, renewal, a strengthening of old bonds and forging of new ones. Peace, the meaning of El and Ela's Rites, flowed over Ezra as his heart rate settled and he held his woman in his arms.

Nothing had ever felt so good or so right.

Chapter Four

The clash of blades meeting rang clearly over the practice field. Akilah and Kadira circled each other, looking for openings in the other's defenses. They'd trained together so often, they knew every strength and weakness of their opponent, but that knowledge also made them evenly matched. Akilah's lower lip was split, and Kadira's left hand bore a weeping cut. They both sported an assortment of bruises. Akilah swung her curved scimitar, and Kadira met it with her broadsword, the long blades sparking as they connected. The hit vibrated up Kadira's arms, and she recoiled smoothly to absorb the impact. Sweat slid down her face to sting her eyes, but she didn't bother to try to wipe it away. It was all familiar. Thrust, parry, step. A deadly dance she knew every move to.

A feral smile curled Akilah's lips, and she taunted softly, "I hear the Haroun chieftain is doing excellent business on that little *toy* he used on you."

"You just wish he'd used it on you." Kadira blocked a swing and dropped to sweep Akilah's legs out from under her. The other woman went down in the sand, but arched and leaped to her feet, already slashing through the air to meet Kadira's next blow. "Two weeks, and he tells me the demands keep coming in for more. He's going to have to bring an auto full of them to the Rites of Fall." She sucked in a breath, and noticed Akilah was beginning to grow winded as well. They'd been practicing for several hours, and the sun was near to setting. Kadira usually trained in the mornings, but Ezra had pulled her under him at dawn and hadn't let her up until midday. Not that she'd tried to escape—no sane woman would. A fortnight in his bed and every time just got better as they learned what drove the other mad with lust. "I told him to take some with him the next time he goes to the city. Men and women can use them on themselves or a lover, and Whores would probably be wild for them. Might give them a chance to come."

A chuckle rippled out of Akilah, and she slapped her sword against Kadira's without much power. "Your trader blood is talking, there, my friend."

It smarted, yet another reminder that she would never be a true Wanderer, and from her friend, it was all the more painful. Anger pumped through her, her heart pounding and her fingers clenching on her sword, slicing her weariness away. She gritted her teeth, and with a thrust and twist of her blade, she sent Akilah's scimitar flying from her hand. The other woman's eyes widened, then narrowed, and she waited for a beat, then charged in low, catching Kadira around the waist and carrying her to the ground. Jerking her head to the side to miss Akilah's fist, Kadira dropped her own sword, and jabbed the tips of her fingers into her friend's ribs. A satisfying whoosh of air escaped, and she kicked out to send Akilah sprawling. Rising to her haunches, Akilah powered forward, sand spraying out behind her, but Kadira feinted to let her fly by, caught the other woman's arm as she passed, twisted it behind her back and slammed her face-first to the floor.

Quickly, Kadira straddled her friend's back, pulled her captured arm up between her shoulder blades, and pinned her down. Leaning close to Akilah's ear, Kadira all but purred, "I am what I am. Trader blood or not, I can still best the best of the Wanderers."

"I know what you are." Akilah grunted, tugging at the arm until Kadira let it go, and gingerly rolled to her back, still trapped under Kadira. Licking at the cut on her lip, Akilah made the action a sensual gesture. "And I know what you like. Perhaps you want me to use one of Ezra's gadgets on you?"

Kadira's body reacted to the thought, but reacted even more strongly when she thought of Ezra *watching* Akilah pleasure her that way. Her sex grew uncomfortably hot and wet in her leather breeches. She wished he weren't so set on an exclusive arrangement, but after hearing of how badly openness had gone for his parents, and understanding all the things he *hadn't* said about how he had suffered for their bond degrading, she could hardly blame him for his wariness of bonding and open sexual relationships, especially when the two were combined.

"You're ignoring me." Akilah's fingernail ran up the inside seam of Kadira's pants, and she shuddered, heaving herself away from her friend and rolling to her feet.

Offering her hand to Akilah, Kadira hauled the other woman up off the ground. "I'd never ignore you, but you know Ezra bartered for—"

"I was there. I remember." Akilah twitched her shoulders, strode to her fallen sword, and sheathed the blade at her hip. "He's an unusual man, Ezra. He must be good, or else you'd be discontent with his arrangement already. It's not like you to enjoy just one partner." She met Kadira's gaze briefly, then glanced away. "I'm...surprised."

Not just surprised. Her friend looked worried. Kadira couldn't fault her—she was worried herself. The longer she was with Ezra, the more she wished it could last, but that couldn't be. What they needed was fundamentally different, and she knew herself well enough to know she couldn't change her needs for him. She was what she was.

It made her inexplicably sad. She *liked* him. More than the sex, she liked talking to him, liked hearing his thoughts on his new inventions, liked the way he listened to her when she offered an opinion about his treaties and bargaining. He respected her, and showed it in a hundred small ways. Never once had he acted as though her trader blood mattered to him, made her less than a Wanderer in his eyes.

She would miss that. Miss *him.*

The few days they had left were slipping through her fingers like loose sand. She shook her head, retrieved her broadsword, and slid it home in the sheath on her belt. "He's unusual, as you said. Complicated. But the Spring Rites are over soon, and so is our arrangement."

"People used to say he was cursed."

"Now they beg him for his inventions." Kadira arched an eyebrow, containing the spurt of renewed anger on Ezra's behalf. What was wrong with her? Her temper never flashed hot this way, not so much that she lost her grip on it. "If only El and Ela would curse us all that way."

Akilah laughed, slapping Kadira on the back. "The drumming will begin soon, and I have plans for a pretty young

Tayi warrior. He needs some training."

"Be gentle with him." Kadira grinned and shook her head. She'd smiled more in the last two weeks than she had in years. It felt good.

"Never!" Tossing a quick wave over her shoulder, Akilah trotted toward the Badawi encampment. "He'll thank me before I'm through, and come back at Fall Rites begging for more."

Turning to the Haroun tents, Kadira left the field for her own evening plans. For the first time in the two weeks they'd been together, she finished her work before Ezra did. She strode into an empty tent, stretched her arms over her head and sighed. Setting aside her broadsword, she plopped onto the plush pallet and tugged off her boots. Her body ached from the hard work, but her muscles buzzed with energy the moment she entered the place where she and Ezra had had sex so many times. Tonight would be more of the same, and with any other man, that thought would have bored her days ago, but Ezra was nothing if not inventive.

His familiar tread came to her ears, and she couldn't help the smile that sprang to her lips. It died when another man followed him in. She rose to her feet, the palm of her hand resting on the hilt of her dagger.

The man was tall, a warrior, kabu markings down his left arm proclaiming his many kills. Not as tall or broad or well marked as her Ezra, she noted. Squelching the foolish thought—he was not *her* Ezra, and he never would be—she nodded in respect to this new male, and he responded in kind. A slight rustle sounded behind the men and a small, curvaceous woman with hair and skin the color of desert sand sidled in to stand beside the warrior.

Ezra stepped forward, moving to Kadira's side to face the couple. "Shaman, this is Gamal and Sahar of Clan Duaij."

The woman flashed a dimpled grin. "We are so pleased to meet you, aren't we, Gamal?"

"Yes." He gave Sahar an indulgent smile, the expression softening his face. Kadira noticed the hammered metal cuffs around their right wrists. A bonded pair.

Catching the direction of her gaze, Ezra chuckled. "They wished to ask you to perform the kabu ritual for their permanent bond marks."

"We were late to the Rites or we would have asked during

the first week." Sahar tucked a lock of her sandy hair behind her ear. "Our chieftain hired Gamal out to guard a trader caravan that was plagued by road pirates, and I didn't wish to come without him."

Traders. Road pirates. Kadira felt as if she'd been punched in the stomach, and it was all she could do not to double over with the pain. She stomped down on memories too crippling to withstand, locking them where they belonged—in the deepest, darkest corner of her soul. Struggling for normalcy, for control, she willed herself to think about something else, *anything* else. She unclenched fingers she hadn't realized she'd balled into fists and shook them out.

"Clan Duaij has a fine kabu shaman." She frowned, replaying the smaller woman's first sentence in her mind. "Why wait for Rites? Why me?"

"You marked my kinswoman, Ulima Tayi, last Fall Rites and I thought it was the most beautiful design I had ever seen. The goddess must truly move you." Sahar's green eyes went wide, her winsome smile managing to be both sincere and ingratiating. "Gamal consented to let me ask you instead of the Duaij shaman."

A short, breathy laugh escaped Kadira, and she ran a hand down her hair. "I would be honored to perform the ritual. How could I refuse?"

"Indeed. Sahar is a difficult woman to refuse." A little twinkle flashed in Gamal's midnight eyes, but he gave Kadira a formal nod. "It is we who are honored, shaman."

Ezra slipped behind her, looping an arm around her waist. He spoke softly in her ear. "Sahar does look like a difficult woman to refuse, though much...softer than you. Not a warrior." His fingers splayed across her belly, sliding down until he reached the edge of her pants. "Would you care to see how *soft* she is, Kadira?"

Both Sahar's and Gamal's gazes were fixed on the glide of Ezra's fingers, and Kadira saw the naked heat reflected in their expressions. A matching warmth built within her, melting her core. She embraced the feeling, using it to hold old memories at bay. Yes, this was just what she needed. She licked her lips and forced herself to maintain a grip on sanity for a few moments longer. "I thought the agreement was for exclusivity. Would this not violate our arrangement?"

"Ah, but I realized how selfish I was being. I do not wish to cage you." His hand moved lower until he cupped her through the leather. "If I participated in *all* your love play, I would be willing to share you." He kissed the side of her neck. "If you wanted to share our bed."

Gamal already palmed his mate's generous breasts, and she leaned back against his chest, their pose mirroring Kadira and Ezra's. Sahar whimpered, arching as she stared at them. "Please."

Kadira shivered, moisture flooding her sex at the other woman's pleading. How she would enjoy making the little blond beg. Ezra's chuckle was pure sin. "A difficult woman to refuse."

"Yes." She rocked her hips back into him, felt the hard length of his cock branding her backside. "I want to strip her and make her scream. I want to make her watch while you fuck her man."

Gamal groaned, a flush of lust running under his tanned skin. "I like that."

His hands slid up to the straps that held Sahar's doeskin dress on her shoulders, and he pushed them down one at a time, baring her breasts and her tight pink nipples. The dress pooled around her waist, and she pushed it down to the floor, slipping her fingers between her thighs to stroke herself while she gazed across the expanse of the tent.

"Ah, ah, ah." Kadira's body was engulfed in flames of longing. Ezra at her back, and two pretty new lovers to toy with. Her sex felt heavy with juices, and she couldn't imagine anything more erotic than this. With Ezra. Always with Ezra. She crooked her finger at Sahar. "No starting without us."

The curvaceous woman obediently removed her hand from her pussy, her green gaze moving over Kadira. "May I taste you?"

"Yes. Come here." The words were guttural, and she didn't care.

"A moment." Ezra froze all of them as he moved away from Kadira. If he changed his mind now, she might die of frustration. He dug around in one of his many odd-looking containers and came up with several small bottles of oil. "We're going to need these, I think."

He tossed one to Gamal, who's hand shot out and caught it with swift accuracy. A small smile quirked his lips, and he slid his thumbnail along the wax seal before he motioned to his mate. Pouring a small amount of the liquid in his palm, he set the bottle on the ground and knelt before her to work oil into her skin, from her ankles to her thighs, between her buttocks and into her anus, up to her high, round breasts.

Kadira was so immersed in watching them that she jolted when Ezra began tugging at her clothes. He was already naked, his cock a hard arc that danced just below his navel. She reached for the bottle in his hand, opened it and dumped oil into her palm. Then she stroked him while he stripped her, groaning each time she slid his shaft between her fingers. When she smoothed the liquid onto his soft sacs, he shuddered, and when she eased her slippery fingers into his ass, he cried out. "Mighty El, *Kadira*."

The ring of muscle was tight on her fingers, but she pressed closer to his big body, biting his nipple as she added another oiled digit to stretch his anus. His hands were frantic as they tore the rest of her garments away, grabbed the oil from her and used it to pierce her the same way she pierced him. She dropped her forehead to his chest, rocking her hips to take his fingers deeper into her ass. It stung, she was so full, but it was too good to stop now. Her sex clenched tight, and his cock prodded her belly.

A little whimper drew her attention, and she turned her head to see Gamal as slick with oil as the rest of them while he suckled his mate's breasts. Kadira wanted to do that. "Both of you, come here."

Sahar's nipple popped free of Gamal's mouth, and they moved forward as Kadira and Ezra slipped from each other's arms. She looked up at him, just to be certain that he was still willing to do this. His gaze flashed amber fire as he looked from her to the other couple and back again. She grinned and held her hand out for Sahar, who eagerly reached for her. The only kabu visible on her unblemished form was the one that symbolized sexual maturity. Her pale hair covered the one for her clan mark. "Let me taste you *now*. Please."

Wickedness wound through Kadira, and she shook her head, drawing the other woman over to the pallet and pushing her onto her knees. "Not just yet. I believe I said I'd make you scream while Ezra takes your mate's ass."

"Yes." Gamal stepped forward and sank down to kneel on

the piled furs.

"This might help with the screaming. It's always been effective for me." Ezra flashed a grin and held out something to Kadira. The toy he'd made her. They'd used it many times over the last few weeks, sometimes on her and sometimes on him, but it never failed to please, and never failed to make Kadira screech like a wild animal for him.

A laugh flowed out of her, and she felt a flush rise to her cheeks as she snatched the metal tube from his hand. "My thanks, Chieftain."

He winked at her and strolled over to settle himself behind Gamal while Kadira did the same with Sahar. The smaller woman's pert ass pressed to Kadira's stomach, and she twisted at the waist to offer her mouth for a kiss. Her lips were soft, and she stroked her fingertips down Kadira's shoulder as their tongues twined together. Fire burned through Kadira's veins, her heart thumping so hard and fast, the rush of blood was all she could hear. She cupped Sahar's full breast in her free hand, circling the nipple until the woman bucked and sobbed, her hips already moving in carnal rhythm. Kadira hummed in pleasure at her responsiveness.

Gliding the cool metal of the toy down the curve of Sahar's stomach, she teased her clit with it, letting it buzz for a single moment, rubbing the creamy folds of her sex, then flicking it on again. Sahar ripped her mouth away, gasping for air. "Please, please, Kadira. *Please.*"

A groan sounded from the men, and she looked, hypnotized, while Ezra gripped Gamal's shoulders tight, using them as an anchor while he thrust his long cock into the younger man's ass. Sahar's hand wrapped around Kadira's wrist, working them to the same cadence as Ezra fucked Gamal. Sliding the phallus deep into Sahar's wet pussy, Kadira set it to vibrating and used the heel of her palm to grind against Sahar's hard little clit.

Sahar screamed, arching helplessly. "Oh, god. Oh, goddess. Kadira. Gamal. Yes, yes. Oh, oh, *oh!*"

Biting the side of Sahar's neck, Kadira met Ezra's gaze. He groped blindly for Gamal's cock, pumping it hard as he watched Kadira slam the phallus into Sahar's pussy. His face was flushed, and it made his black kabu marks stand out in vivid contrast. Kadira's sex fisted on nothingness, aroused beyond measure at the scene before her, at the scent and feel of this soft female in her arms. Gamal's head fell back to rest on Ezra's shoulder, his muscles rippling as he pistoned his hips between Ezra's hand and Ezra's cock.

"Harder, Ezra. Harder, Kadira. Fuck us harder." Sahar's fingers gripped Kadira's thigh, shoving her hips forward to take as much of the phallus as she could. Ezra just laughed, his stomach slapping against the other man's ass as he obeyed the plea.

Licking Sahar's neck in the same place she'd bitten, Kadira rotated the vibrating toy inside her pussy. The blond woman squealed as she came, and Kadira felt the contractions against her hand. Gamal choked, a gurgle bubbling up from his throat as his come shot forward, spilling over Ezra's fingers. A moment later, Ezra groaned, freezing behind the other man as a look of ecstatic anguish crossed his sharp features.

Gamal fell to his hands and knees on the pallet, and a panting Ezra staggered to his feet to wash himself in the water he kept for just that purpose. Sahar sighed when the toy slid out of her, but Kadira's body still burned with unrequited need. She gritted her teeth when Sahar's soft form moved against her, stimulating her tight nipples.

"I don't think we took care of Kadira." Gamal's voice was rough, his dark eyes sliding over both women. "Let Sahar use her mouth on you. She has a gift for it."

"Gamal!" Sahar's hands fluttered in embarrassment, and her mate gave a rusty chuckle.

His hand shot out and wrapped around Kadira's arm, tugging her around until she faced Sahar. Excitement flooded Kadira, drenched her sex, and set her flesh on fire. The other woman's green eyes gleamed, and a smile unfurled on her lips. Gamal covered Kadira's breasts with his hands, his palms rough with calluses. He lifted her small mounds for his mate's mouth, and Kadira's breath stopped when those lush lips closed over her nipple. The warrior's fingers played with her other breast and she felt his thigh push between hers, widening her stance so he could enter her pussy from behind.

He filled her core, not quite as well as Ezra did, but that thought dissolved into nothing as Sahar abandoned her breast and licked a hot trail down her torso to her sex. Bracing herself on her hands, Sahar pressed her face deep into Kadira's pussy,

61

her tongue curling around the clit, sliding over the plumped lips and flicking against the cock that sank inside her. Kadira and Gamal groaned. His hands massaged her breasts, pinching the nipples hard. "Didn't I tell you she was talented?"

"Yes," Kadira gasped. Dark ecstasy shimmered through her when she felt Ezra's gaze on her. She turned her head to see him stroking his cock while his gaze remained fixed on them. Biting her lips on a groan as Sahar suckled her with delicate skill, Kadira beckoned the redhead forward. "Sahar's not enjoying this as much as she could be."

Golden eyes met hers, a question there that she smiled in answer to. She held out her hand, and he took it, pressing his lips to her fingers. With his other hand, he rubbed his cock up and down Sahar's slit, and then stabbed his cock into the blond woman's pussy. She whimpered, the vibration moving against Kadira's clit, who gasped in response.

Ezra drove his hand into her hair, hauling her forward so he could kiss her over Sahar's arching back. The woman's tongue snaked out, flicking over Kadira's clit so swiftly it left her screaming in Ezra's mouth. He drove his hips forward to spank loudly against Sahar's soft ass, his talented lips molding to Kadira's. Her sex fisted tight around Gamal's cock, and with his next rough thrust, he sent her flying out of control. Sahar's tongue and Ezra's mouth and Gamal's cock, working her at different speeds that spun her into beautiful, heart-pounding chaos. She came hard, light bursting in front of her eyes, caught between three lovers that pleasured her and pleasured themselves. Sahar bit down on Kadira's clitoris as she reached orgasm, moaning with each jolting push of Ezra's thick cock inside her pussy. Before she'd even finished coming, Ezra jerked out of her body. "I want Kadira next."

Rolling the blond onto her back, he picked up the discarded phallus and slid it home into her wet, gaping pussy. He wrapped her hand around it, showing her the knob that controlled its vibrations. Her lips parted in a wanton smile. "Ezra, I want one of these to take with me after Rites."

"You'll have one." He laughed and leaned down to suckle her nipples until she shuddered and squirmed. When he left her to toy with herself while she watched them, she bit her lower lip and worked herself on the quaking phallus.

"This is going to be fun, fucking your ass, and feeling his

cock while he takes your tight pussy," Gamal's voice gritted in Kadira's ear, his breath an excited rush. "And my Sahar's eyes on me." He groaned, slipped out of her sex to press his cock into her anus, and her own moisture and the oil Ezra had put there made the glide an exquisite pain.

Red hair glinted in the light from his pharos while he moved toward her. Pulling her legs even farther apart, he nudged the head of his cock against her wet entrance. The press of his thick sex made her moan. Both men were large, and they stretched her past bearing. She arched between them, but it only worked her on their cocks as one filled her and the other retreated.

They set a swift rhythm for her, their movements in perfect tandem. Gamal's hands gripped her hips, and her head rested in the crook of his shoulder, which bowed her back just enough to let Ezra suck one of her nipples into his mouth. He worried the tight crest with his teeth. A sharp cry burst out of her as one too many sensations piled like an avalanche on top of her. She reared up, but the two men just pinned her between them with their heavier muscles. Clutching at Ezra, she held on for dear life while the hair on his chest rubbed against her over-stimulated nipples. She slid her hands down his flexing back, grabbing the hard globes of his ass to pull him closer.

"*Oooh*, yes. Touch him, Kadira. Fuck her, Gamal." Sahar writhed on the pelts, gasping for breath as her gaze burned into their flesh. "This is the sexiest thing I've ever..."

Grinning at the blonde's enthusiasm, Kadira parted Ezra's buttocks and thrust her fingers into his anus. She pressed inward until she found the spot that she knew drove him to madness. His hips rammed harder, deeper, and he rotated his pelvis against her swollen clit. Gamal moved with them, letting Ezra's thrusts shove her backward to impale her ass more fully on his cock. It was too much. Fulfillment exploded through her body, and every muscle locked tight around the men's cocks. A shriek wrenched up from inside her as she bowed in their arms. Orgasm dragged her under, pulsing hot pleasure through her as both men groaned and bucked against her. First Gamal, then Ezra. Their shudders shook through her, and she let her fingers slip from Ezra's anus while his seed flooded her clenching sex. Sahar sobbed and stuffed her pussy full of the vibrating toy, her heels bracing on the furs and her hips lifting high as she came with them.

Ezra caught Kadira close when she crumpled against him, his arms cradling her to his chest. He kissed her sweaty temple. "Are you all right?"

"Yes." More than all right. She was as close to perfection as she'd ever been. Ezra held her, and two other lovers beckoned to both of them. She wrapped her arms around him as emotions clogged her throat. Something bigger and more terrifying than happiness swamped her, and she didn't know what to say or how to say it, so she lifted her mouth for his sweet kisses, and he gave her everything she wanted.

And it was perfect.

Hours later, Kadira's muscles burned with exhaustion. Her body had been well used in every imaginable position and combination, Gamal proving nearly as creative as Ezra. The younger warrior scooped a sleeping Sahar into his arms and nodded a farewell to Ezra, then he smiled at Kadira. "Will we see you in the morning, shaman? For our bond marks?"

"Yes." She yawned as the two disappeared through the tent flap. Ezra collapsed onto the pallet, a tired groan escaping as he rolled onto his back. Kneeling beside him, she pressed her palms to his chest. "All right. We're alone, so now you can talk to me. Why did you do it?"

"Because you wanted it. Because I meant what I said—I can cope with your desire to experiment if I am involved, but *only* then." Her heart squeezed at the sincerity on his face. He stroked a single fingertip down her cheek. "It was a gift. For your pleasure."

She chuckled and flopped onto the furs, then winced and lifted herself as something dug into her ribs. His vibrating phallus. She held it up and grinned. "You do give the very best gifts, Ezra."

He chuckled, snagged the toy from her hand and tossed it on a nearby table.

"Thank you. That was just what I needed." She kissed his chest. "I don't want to *replace* you." The way his mother had sought to replace his father. No. Never that. There could be no replacing a man like Ezra. "But I don't mind...sharing you. Occasionally." Or she wouldn't mind if they had more than a week left to call their own, but suddenly she felt selfish. She didn't want to share him again during their arrangement. She wanted every night and all his attention for herself.

He raised her hand to his mouth, brushing his lips over the tips of her fingers. "I'm glad you enjoyed it." He grinned, his golden eyes sleepy. "I know I did."

"Good." She sighed, letting some relief trickle through her that *he* seemed at peace with everything they'd done. "No bad moments?"

"With you? Never." His gaze unfocused, and his lashes made crescents on his cheekbones as his eyes slid shut. After a few moments, his breathing leveled out into deep slumber. She shook her head. Let a breathy laugh escape.

Such a remarkable man. Even if they weren't bonded like his parents had been, he'd still confronted something that he feared, just for her. What she wanted was more important to him than what troubled him. It took strength of character to do something like that, especially when he didn't have to. No one expected it of him—it wasn't a public gesture as a chieftain, but a private one for *her*. Even Gamal and Sahar would never know what it meant to him to invite them into his bed, or what it meant to her that he had done so. Was it any wonder why she loved him?

The breath seized in her lungs, and dread froze her down to the very marrow of her bones. *No.* No, that couldn't be. She closed her eyes and willed it not to be. Caring, respect, amazing sex, even bonding was acceptable, but love? Not that. Love made you weak, ate you up inside and made you scream and scream like a trapped and dying animal. Her belly heaved as memories she'd buried so many times she'd lost count resurfaced to mock her sense of security and control. Curling away from Ezra, she wrapped her arms around herself, as if she could ward off all the feelings that lived inside of her.

She *loved* him.

It was her worst nightmare, and that was the last thought she had before sleep claimed her, dragging her into blood-soaked dreams.

Ezra jerked from a deep slumber at the sound of her ragged moan. Something was wrong. He had his dagger in his hand before he was fully alert. Chills broke down his spine as he searched the tent for a threat and found none. He looked down at Kadira and realized she still slept. Sweat coated her skin, and she thrashed on the furs. He tossed aside the blade and caught her swinging fist as she fought imaginary foes.

"No." A wretched sob erupted from her lips, and she twisted to escape his imprisoning grip. "*No!*"

Shaking her shoulders to wake her, he leaned close to her face. "Kadira. *Kadira*, wake up. It's just a dream, beloved. Wake up, now."

She bolted upright, scrambling backwards. Her chest heaving with every breath, she snatched a dagger from the piles of clothing strewn across the floor, and rounded on him with it.

"*Don't touch me*," she hissed, her voice dropping to a low, ominous snarl. "You do not have my permission to touch me."

"I'm not touching you." He held up his hands for her to see. Unarmed. In fact, it was *his* knife she wielded. He rose to his feet, his movements unhurried and unthreatening. "I would never touch you without your permission. You know this."

Horror tripped through him as her words, her actions, the terror lurking behind her dark eyes, seeped into his conscious.

"Someone...violated you." The thought of his proud, brave, beautiful Kadira being forced in such a way made his stomach revolt and bile burn the back of his throat. Murderous rage ripped through him, and his fists clenched at his sides. He would hunt the bastard down and kill him with his bare hands. "*Who?* Who hurt you? Give me his name."

Her throat worked, and she shook her head. Her ebony locks whipped around her pale face, her pupils pinpoints of shock as her grip whitened on the dagger's hilt. "It wasn't... It wasn't *me*."

A shiver went through her, goose bumps roughing her bare skin, and he took a step toward her, but she stumbled back. He swallowed, wanting to pull her into his arms and protect her, but he couldn't. "Who was it?"

She swayed where she stood, and a moment of agonizing clarity shone in her gaze as it met his. "My parents."

"Tell me." His voice emerged a harsh rasp, and he was uncertain he wanted her to tell him anything.

"I... We..." She swallowed, her eyes staring into the distance as she looked at something that wasn't in the tent with them. Memories. Her past. "It was a bad expedition across the Wasteland. We'd had sandstorms, broken wheels, lost one of the horses. A few of my uncles had been injured and couldn't help keep the caravan moving. I was eight and small for my age, but even I was out in the winds trying to get us going. We were running out of water. It was...bad." She blinked, another shiver quaking through her. "They hit us so fast, I still can't remember when they...they were just there."

"Who was?" He wanted to stop her, wanted to tell her it was over and it couldn't hurt her anymore, but it wouldn't be true. It had hurt her, it still hurt her, and she needed to excise the wound.

"The road pirates." A harsh sound poured between her clenched teeth. "They killed my uncles, and made my father and me watch while they raped my mother. All of them. Again and again while she cried and reached for him and told him she loved him." She gagged on a breath, her shoulders bowing. "Then they raped my father, held him down, forced him. He never made a sound until..."

"Until what?" Horror curdled in Ezra's gut.

"They tied him to a pole and...roasted him over a fire." The hand with the knife pressed flat to her belly, and he watched her stomach heave. It was all he could do not to vomit himself. "He screamed for hours. The sound wasn't even...human. I didn't know a person could make such a noise." Her knees buckled, and she collapsed to the woven rug. "Then they ate him, feasted on his flesh and laughed and danced around the fire and drank the moonshine we'd brought with us to trade in the city." A painful, rasping laugh escaped her. "They were still busy raping my mother when the Badawi warriors overtook our caravan, and slaughtered them all."

He knelt beside her, too many realizations swirling through his mind. "They saved you. You and your mother." If they hadn't, Ezra might never have known her, and the thought was so alien, it didn't even register in his mind. He couldn't even recognize a life without her.

Kadira shook her head, then nodded, then shook it again. "She killed herself three months later...walked off the side of a mountain rather than birth the evil they had planted in her womb."

"El and Ela," he breathed, sickened once more by what she'd endured.

"Yes." A long pause echoed in the silence, then she dipped her chin in a sharp nod. "She is with my father now. Where she belongs. Where she would wish to be."

"Did they touch you?" He had to ask, had to know, and braced himself for an answer he didn't want.

"No." She ran a weary hand down her face. "I was too small to be of interest to them, especially when they had my parents to...play with."

There it was. The final piece of the puzzle, the reason Kadira was Kadira. Mystery solved. A part of him wished he didn't know the truth, and another part was humbled that she had told him. He doubted she had ever spoken of it to anyone, and only those who had rescued her knew what had happened to her family, how she had come to be among the Wanderers.

"Your parents and uncles... What were their names?"

She shook her head, pushing slowly to her feet. "Traders do not speak the names of the dead. To do so is to call them back from their final rest. It is forbidden."

He narrowed his eyes, tilting his head as he considered her. "Kadira is a Wanderer name."

"Yes. I took the name when I was adopted by the Badawi." Her expression flattened, and she refused to meet his gaze. "The trader's daughter died that day."

"And you will not speak her name?"

"I do not wish to call her back." She lifted her chin in that stubborn way of hers. "I am a Wanderer now."

Ah, his poor Kadira. She'd put aside the helpless child, too weak to save her family, and taken on the mantle of her saviors, become a strong Wanderer. He ached for her loss, for her suffering, for the confused child she'd been. Because he understood the desire to cut away the ugliness of the past, he questioned her no further. She'd been through enough.

Rising to his feet, he approached her, his movements still slow and unthreatening. He wrapped his fingers around her wrist, and she didn't protest when he removed his dagger and dropped it to the floor. Then he drew her into his arms, folding her tight against his chest. Her body stiffened, her breathing uneven. A great shudder passed through her slender form before she relaxed against him. One rough, ragged sob escaped her, the only sound of her great grief, and it made his heart literally stop. Moisture stung his eyes, but he held her closer while she trembled.

"I'm all right." She tried to pull away, but he cradled her

closer.

"Of course you are." He stroked his fingers through her long hair, kissing her cheek, her temple, her forehead. Anywhere he could reach. He held her for a long, long time, until her breathing leveled out and she grew pliant in his embrace. Rocking her gently, he rested his chin on the top of her head. "I just enjoy having you in my arms. You must have realized this by now."

A soft laugh slid out of her. "I noticed."

"Ah, such an intelligent woman. I have a deep weakness for intelligent women."

She didn't respond to that, remained quiet. Then she whimpered, the sound quickly cut off, but she buried her face in his chest. "I can still hear the sounds of their screaming. It haunts my dreams. It always will."

"No. No, you must not remember them that way." How often did she have such nightmares? Who comforted her in the night? He almost snorted. No one. She wouldn't allow it. He closed his eyes, more grateful than he could say that he was here for her this time. He groped for words that might comfort her in the future, when he could not. Pain knifed through him at the thought, but he pushed it away. Kadira was more important. "Think of how they lived, not how they died. The horror is natural, such evil cannot help but scar us as would any great battle we survive, but it is only a moment in time. Think of the other moments."

"They were good people. Honorable." She quivered once. "They loved each other and they loved me and the road pirates used that love to torture them." Her voice rose higher toward the end, and he could hear the tears she wouldn't shed.

"Think of how they were honorable, not of how horribly things went." He squeezed her harder. "I have no doubt they were very good people. They made *you*, did they not?"

She huffed out a breath, her lips moving against his skin. "I am not that good."

"You are." He leaned back to meet her eyes, let all of his admiration for her show. She shook her head, doubt in her expression, and he ached for that too. "A brave warrior, a blessed shaman. You look at yourself and you see what you are not. Nothing you do, no matter how hard you try, will erase that you were not born of a Wanderer clan."

"I *know* that."

"Yes, but you do not *know* that you are wonderful *just as you are*. Stop battering yourself into the ground for what you can never be, and respect what you are. You are a strong and gifted woman who has earned the respect of every clansman I have ever heard speak of you. That is difficult to achieve for anyone, regardless of their bloodlines. *You* are the one who sees you as less than a Wanderer, not me, and not the rest of the clans. They would never have allowed you to train as a shaman otherwise." He cradled her face between his palms, compelling her to listen to him. "For once, see yourself as I do, someone who has nothing left to prove to anyone. Someone who is capable and whole just as she is. Someone who *deserves* every good thing, every blessing, everything she could ever want." He stroked a thumb over her cheekbone. "Because you do."

Tears welled in her eyes, and she choked, jerked back and stumbled a few steps away. Her tattered breathing was the only sound for endless moments while she struggled to regain her composure. He let her go, knowing a show of weakness would wound her more than anything else, and he respected her pride as he did everything else about her. In her place, he would want the same respect.

When the tension escaped her, and she sighed, he approached to set his hands on her shoulders, pulling her back into his arms. "Come to bed."

"I'll have nightmares." The bleakness in her voice sliced through him.

He kissed the back of her head, the nape of her neck. "No, you won't. I'll keep them away from you."

Turning in his arms, she looked up at him, something almost desperately hopeful in her eyes. "You'll help me forget tonight?"

As an answer, he settled his mouth over hers, putting as much tenderness as he could muster into the gesture. He was a warrior, an inventor—a man of mind and body, but for her, he would sacrifice his very soul if it were what she needed.

Anything for Kadira.

Chapter Five

The strange whirring and thumping noises coming from Ezra's tent might have worried Kadira a few weeks ago, but not now. She was unsurprised when she slipped inside to see him sitting cross-legged on the grass mat with a mechanical contraption on a low table in front of him. He made a frustrated noise in the back of his throat, muttered to himself and used a multipronged tool to adjust something on his invention. The thumping stopped, and the thing purred like the hunting cats her clan raised.

A satisfied grin flashed across his face, and he rotated the machine on the table to fiddle with something else. She bit her lip to hold in a laugh when she saw a smudge of grease marred his untattooed cheekbone. Her heart squeezed.

Goddess, but she loved him.

The thought came easier now that she'd had some time to accept it, and even easier than it ever could have before she'd told Ezra about her past. It eased some of the burden to have shared her pain with him. She hadn't wanted to, but he'd told her of *his* childhood, and she'd been unable to refuse to reciprocate. She'd never spoken a word of it before, not even to the warriors who had saved her, so she hadn't had an inkling as to how he'd react, but then, he was Ezra. He was unlike any other man, and nothing had ever felt as sweet as his arms around her. Tears pricked at the backs of her eyes, and she hurried to blink them away. He'd been right, her genius. She had tried to run from her past and be *only* a Wanderer, but that wasn't who she was, no matter how she fought against it or denied it or tried to overcome it. As if she could. She was a trader's daughter, a survivor who'd become a warrior, a shaman, a *Wanderer*, but that didn't erase where she'd come from. She didn't even want to erase it. To do so would negate people who had loved her.

"Are you just going to stand there, or are you going to come in and talk to me?" Ezra's welcoming smile took any sting out of the words.

She grinned back and left the doorway, unbuckled her belt, and propped her sword against a tent pole. Strolling over to him, she bent forward and kissed him with slow relish. "We don't have to talk. We can occupy ourselves in other ways."

It was their last night together, the last night of Spring Rites. Tomorrow, there would be nothing left to mark their passing but the remains of the great bonfire and the tracks of departing clans. A few days in the relentless desert wind, and even that evidence would disappear as though it had never been.

Ezra's mark on her would be longer lasting. Indelible, like one of the kabu marks she left on other people's bodies.

And it felt like a huge, gaping hole opened in her chest because she knew he'd never be hers again. Even if they slept together at other Rites, it wouldn't be the same. She didn't even know if he wanted that much from her, and she'd found herself unable to ask. They'd grown closer than just sex partners in the last weeks, but proximity would do that. He'd said nothing about remaining together, never indicated he wanted anything more than what their bargain had originally specified. She'd dared to hope after he'd allowed Gamal and Sahar to join them, that perhaps they could give each other what they needed, that they could bend enough to fit together. She had certainly bent all her rules, falling hard and deep into the kind of love she'd sworn she'd avoid. But his silence was damning. He cared for her, she had no doubts about that, but he didn't want her enough to confront his own fears about bonding. The beautiful, shining connection she had with him, all these wild and wonderful feelings, were one-sided.

El and Ela, but it hurt to lose this, to lose him. A mortal wound that bled slowly.

"There was something I wanted to speak to you about." He caught her shoulders and pulled her down into his lap, his lips still sipping at hers. She wrapped her arms around his neck and held him tight, frantic for the taste of him, needing to relish every second they had left.

He licked his way down to bite and suck the pounding pulse point at her throat. She let her head fall back and moaned. He smiled against her skin, and she felt her own lips curve. He loved it when she was loud during sex. Sliding his hand up her leather-clad leg, he traced the laces that held her pants closed, but didn't unfasten them. Disappointment raged through her, but if he wanted to extend their love play, she wouldn't protest. Anything to put off the morning as long as possible.

He lifted his head and met her gaze. He swallowed, looking almost nervous. "I've been thinking. About after Rites."

"Yes?" Her heart slammed into her rib cage, and dizziness swamped her. She grabbed tightly to her control, tried to master the sudden geyser of hope that burst within her.

He glanced away, focused on his hand toying with the laces on her breeches. "You know, the Haroun kabu shaman died this past winter."

She blinked, sat up straighter in his lap. "Yes, I know."

"Doesn't the Badawi shaman have a nephew he's training to take his place?" His words rushed out, tripping over each other. "You will never be—"

"I know." Pain shafted through her soul, and she realized his offer wasn't what she wanted, what she needed from him. "I'll never be the Badawi shaman. I'll always be second." A part of her suspected that was why they allowed her to train with him, but she set aside those doubts and fears. Perhaps it was true, but perhaps Ezra was right and no one cared about her differences except her. Either way, it didn't matter. She was proud of her accomplishments, and she was good at what she did, both with her sword and with her kabu tools. El and Ela had blessed her in many ways, both before and after she'd joined the Wanderers, and she was grateful.

"The Haroun would honor you the way you deserve." Some desperate emotion flickered to life in those amber eyes. "Many of my clan came to you during the Rite to ask you to mark them."

A sad smile curled her lips, and she slipped out of his arms to stand. "I know."

"And, yet, you will still refuse." Hurt shot through his expression as he climbed to his feet.

She spread her hands, trying to find a way to ease his pain without causing him more. "The Badawi saved me, took me in, adopted me, trained me and fed me."

"You have more than returned their generosity to them." He snatched up her hand, squeezed too tight, his intense gaze burning. "You've served them nobly in battle, performed many kabu rituals and just this month have ensured their fuel supply for a full annum. They could ask no more than what you have already given as repayment."

"I can't," she whispered.

"Of course." He barked out a hoarse laugh. "Why would I think you would choose to stay with me? The curse of the Haroun chieftain—to want a woman who walks away."

"That isn't it, and you know it." Her tone was just as harsh as his, anger bubbling up inside her, twining with the anguish. "You are not your father, and I am not your mother. When I make a vow, *I keep it.* You are not cursed. You're a good man, a good chieftain to people who should have cared for you more as a boy instead of thinking you freakish. Do not lump either of us together with those who threw away their honor."

"Then, why?" His voice cracked on the question. "Why won't you stay with me?"

She realized she owed him the truth, even if it hurt him, even if it pushed him forever beyond her reach. Her heart bled, and she had to press her shaking lips together for a moment before she could speak. "You aren't asking me to stay with you *for you*—you're not offering me a bond. You're offering a shaman position in your clan. You...you were the one who said I deserved anything I wanted. You were the one who said my trader blood didn't matter, and I believed you. You *changed* things, made them different, made *me* different, and I cannot be the woman I was when this Rite began. Not even for you." She swallowed, shook her head. "I cannot simply be a member of your clan, even if I were its religious leader. I want more. I *deserve* more. I-I want what my parents had together. No matter how they played with others, with my uncles, their bond was to each other, permanent and unbreakable. Even if their *death* was one of suffering, the *life* they had together was one of joy. You were the one who reminded me to think of them as they lived, and the parents I knew would have made the same choices, even knowing how it would end. To them it was worth it. To them, love was a strength, not a weakness." She met his gaze, open and honest, her soul stripped bare for him. "And I want such a love. I deserve it. I deserve everything. You told me so, and I believed you."

His mouth opened and closed, opened again, but no words came out. For a heart-stopping moment, he looked as if he were going to cry, but then he nodded, wheeled around and stumbled out of the tent and into the night.

She sagged to the ground, pressed her forehead to the woven mat and choked on a sob. For the first time in her adult life, she'd allowed herself to be vulnerable, and she'd been shattered by the blow she'd had no armor against. Pulling in a deep breath, she picked herself up off the ground. It was no more than what she'd expected, no matter how much it hurt. And, god and goddess, but it hurt. She loved him, and nothing would ever change that. There were no defenses to be had against him, and she didn't want defenses—she wanted *him*. She just couldn't have him. She hadn't even gotten to enjoy her last night in his arms.

Hours too soon, it was over.

Misery twisted like a blade in his heart. How could she do this to him? To them? What they had was *good*. Why wasn't what he could give her enough? The thought sickened him, made him want to pummel himself into the ground. If someone else had said anything of the kind about Kadira, offering her less than *everything* she wanted, he'd have flattened them.

A harsh, painful laugh ripped out of him.

Wasn't everything different with Kadira? Hadn't it always been so? As she'd told him, things weren't just different with them, they had the power to *change* a person. Pride filled him that she had come so far, been so strong, survived so much and yet had managed to accept her past and integrate it into what she wanted for her future.

She amazed him, humbled him.

He wasn't certain he could do the same. To his mind, he *had* accepted and overcome his past, fought through his father's shame, his own strange mental processes and people's reactions to them, everyone's doubts about his cursed nature, and taken his place as chieftain of his clan. He'd decided the most logical way to avoid his parents' fate was to never follow their path into bonding. If he never took a mate, he could never have a failed bond and would never have to live with more of that disgrace—this time disgrace he had earned himself. It was rational, reasonable. As easy as piecing together one of his many machines.

Until Kadira.

How was he to avoid his parents' fate if the one woman he wanted would accept nothing less than everything? How could he offer a woman who meant everything to him less than she deserved?

He couldn't. He shouldn't. He no longer knew what the right path was, which route to follow. Keep the woman and risk himself, or walk away and never be tempted to stray from his set course again. No one would ever be Kadira. There was no one who could make him wish he were a different man with different experiences. A man who didn't know what bonding could cost.

So, he walked, his thoughts spinning in circles, his gut churning with disquiet. He just put one foot in front of the other and made himself continue. He knew not how far or how long he traveled, just set his feet to moving, needing the physical activity as his thoughts roiled. Hours. Miles. Not far enough or long enough. When he approached the camp again, saw the bonfire, the wildness of Rites, he stopped, turned his back and sat in the sand. He wasn't ready to return. Not yet. He sighed and let his head drop back.

The wavering green and purple, red and blue of the gloaming lights shot above the mountains in the distance, danced across the night sky, fading into the brilliant sea of endless stars. The lights were always brighter during Spring and Fall Rites, a blessing from El and Ela.

Soon the sun would rise in the east, and the yellow sky would heat the ground around him to unbearable levels. Legends said the sky was once blue during the day, but legends were not always to be believed. They also said there had once been as many women as there were men, and that all of them had been fertile, and children had been so plentiful, some had even been discarded as unwanted. Such was beyond his comprehension. Women were few and children were rare, and it was good fortune for a clan to possess either. And Wanderer women were more hardy breeders than any in the city. Perhaps that was why the Sun Guards coveted them so much, tried to recreate them by capturing Wanderer men. Only a fool would steal a Wanderer woman...likely every clan would go to war with the city to retrieve her. And if she were a warrior woman, like his Kadira, and lost honor for having been captured, she might tear the city to shreds just for the pleasure of her vengeance.

Kadira.

Even distracting himself with other thoughts just lead him back to her. He felt her behind him, knew it was she who approached. She didn't announce herself, just lowered herself beside him and opened her soft woolen blanket to wrap around him. Her flesh was so hot it seared him, and until that moment, he hadn't realized he'd been freezing, so lost in his musings was he. Instead of flinching away, he jerked her closer, situated her between his legs, her back to his front, and pulled the blanket tight around both of them.

She gasped as their bodies touched. "Your skin is like ice."

"Yes." Some of the tightness in him eased at having her near again.

Rubbing her hands up and down his arms, then his legs, she made a disgusted noise. "I should have brought bla grog. It would have warmed us."

As though he cared about drinking or warmth. "How did you know I was here? Why would you come to me after I—"

She shot him a sulfuric glance over her shoulder that didn't quite disguise the hurt, and her fingers bit into his thighs. "This is our last night, and we will spend it *together.*"

"Even if it means we're fighting?" He set his hands over hers, squeezing them until she relaxed her grip.

Arching an eyebrow, she jutted her stubborn jaw. "We are warriors. It is what we do."

God and goddess, how could he let her go? How could he live without her, take a single step away from her?

He couldn't.

And just that quickly, everything stopped spinning and settled into place. He couldn't lose her, would do whatever it took to keep her, he wanted her that much. He wanted to bond with her, wanted her mark on his skin, a mark that meant no matter what happened, no matter how far they roamed or how many they shared each other with, she belonged to *him* and he to her. Couldn't they give each other everything they needed?

Hadn't he enjoyed their time with Gamal and Sahar? Didn't they both crave the pleasures of their own sex? She was right...why should they give any of that up when they could experience it *together?*

The future opened up into something brighter and more wonderful than he had ever imagined. A woman who understood him, who stood by him and believed in him, who had never doubted him or thought him cursed. A woman with a past that haunted her, that set her apart and made her as different as he was. They were stronger together, and as she had told him, when she took a vow, she was honorable enough to keep it. So was he, and he would regret it all the days of his life if he let her leave without knowing how much he loved her. He rested his chin on top of her head, breathed in her feminine Kadira scent, and felt more at peace than he ever had before. "We are not just warriors, neither of us."

"No. We're not." She sighed, and the sound was sad. He squeezed her fingers again, just for the pleasure of touching her. How to say all the things he had to say? He knew where he should start, but everything after that wasn't so clear.

"I'm sorry, Kadira."

She stiffened. "Don't be. I'm not. I have no regrets."

"I do." When she flinched, he was sorrier than he could say. He brushed his thumbs over the backs of her hands. "I never wanted to hurt you, and I did when I walked out without saying anything—" She made a noise as if to speak, but he had to finish this. "No, I know I did. I am sorry. I just needed to think and...sort things out in my head. I'm ready to talk now, if you're willing to listen."

"Is this the part where we fight?" The lightness in her voice was unlike her, false and brittle. "Because I'm still not going to be your shaman."

"No?" He dropped his chin to her shoulder. "You don't want to mark me? I would swear you've given my skin the kind of look that said the goddess was moving you to do so."

Her short laugh was disbelieving. "You're offering up your flesh for my kabu chisel? That's...not what I expected."

"You know I like to keep things interesting for you." He laced his fingers through hers, rotating their hands until his was on top. "I thought perhaps you would grace my wrist...with a bond mark."

A tremor ran through her body, and her voice emerged grating and strained. "You wish to bond with me? A permanent bond? But...your father...your mother..."

"Yes. They chose poorly in each other. Neither was suited to a full bond, to the compromise demanded in a permanent partnership." He turned his head until he could meet her eyes, and his heart contracted when he saw hers swam with tears. "But I am not them. I do not have to make the choices they made. Or the mistakes."

"I love you, Ezra."

He closed his eyes for a brief moment, and let that wash over him. "And I love you, my Kadira."

Meeting her gaze, he saw a single tear had fallen. He released one of her hands so he could brush the moisture away. She sniffled and turned her head aside, coughing. He placed soft kisses along the column of her neck and down her shoulder. "You do not have to be the fiercest warrior. You do not have to be the greatest kabu shaman. You do not have to be a shining example of a Wanderer." He brushed his lips over the Badawi clan marks at her nape. "And if you are all those things, I will still want you. Just as you are. My Kadira."

"Nuri." Her voice was so soft, he almost didn't hear her speak.

"What?"

She pulled in a slow, quiet breath. "The name I was born with. Nuri."

Mighty El, but he loved this woman. Everything about her—her bravery, her vulnerability. She was everything, and he would worship her for the rest of his days, bond with her, stand beside her, give his life to defend her. Yes. He crooked a finger under her chin and swept his mouth over hers once, twice. "A lovely name. So we will call our first daughter, and give Nuri a chance to live again."

Her dark eyes were so wide, he could see the gloaming lights reflected in them. "You think we will be blessed with children? Not all women can have them."

"Why not?" He pressed his palms to her flat stomach. "I have so many other blessings, why not hope for one more?"

"Then I hope too." She laid her hands over his, and they sat there for a long while, resting against each other, watching the myriad of lights swirl overhead. Her fingers stroked up his arms and back down to his hands, and her touch had an inevitable effect on his body. He knew she noticed, because she wriggled her ass against his groin until he bit back a curse. She snickered, grabbed his wrists and slid his hands down from her stomach to the placket of her breeches. "I was thinking...maybe we should start trying for that blessing. The god and goddess help those who help themselves."

He had her pants unlaced in seconds, already delving into her damp folds. His cock throbbed, an incessant ache that only she could soothe. "Then I intend to help myself to you. Often."

The incoherent sound she made as she raised her hips into his touch only sent the blood rushing to his loins. He used her movements to his advantage, shoving her breeches down to her knees. She moaned when his fingers slid free of her sex, but made quick work of her boots, and then turned to help him strip. When they were both naked and he was seated on the blanket, she straddled his lap, stimulating her beaded nipples against his chest, her arms wrapping around his neck, and her gaze locking with his so he could see every emotion flashing in her eyes.

Her hand reached between them to grasp his swollen sex, and she rubbed it against hers. The wetness of her slicked the head of his cock, and he claimed her mouth while she pressed him into her pussy. Her tongue tangled with his, her addicting flavor filling his mouth. Thrusting into her was pure pleasure, one he would never get his fill of. He ran his hands over her resilient flesh, stroking every inch of her until he slipped his fingers between them to thumb her clit. She threw back her head and screamed for him, her sex fisting on his cock as she slammed over into sudden orgasm. He held her, continued to rock into her and soon she caught his rhythm, rode his cock with renewed fervor.

Her hands cupped his jaw, and she sucked in rough breaths. She looked into his eyes and his chest squeezed at the depths of emotion he saw there. "I love you, Ezra."

"Kadira. My Kadira." He groaned, thrusting harder and faster inside her, showing her all that he felt. No defenses, no running, no control. Just the truth. "I love you, love you, *love you.*"

The words jerked out every time he plunged inside her, and her walls clenched so tight around him, he thought he'd die.

Latching on to her hips, he slammed her down to the base of his cock, and ground himself against her clitoris.

"*Ezra!*" Her cries echoed across the open desert, as wild in his arms as he'd ever fantasized. Her pelvis thrust forward in convulsive snaps that took him hard and deep. Her slickness coated his cock, and the way her sex milked his shaft made him explode. He came inside her, groaning with each jetting of seed that jerked from his body. She held him and he held her, tight. Tighter.

Their muscles shook, sweat sealing their skin together and cooling in the morning air. They stroked each other, lips clinging even as they panted for breath. He collapsed back on the blanket and took her with him. Closing his eyes, he let himself savor the sweet blessing that was *her*. They lay quietly, and his heart slowed from its gallop. Her hair tickled his skin as she slipped to the side and propped her head on her hand, leaning over him.

"What are you thinking about?"

He opened his eyes and furrowed his brow as if in deep thought. "I wonder if Gamal and Sahar would be amenable to playing again at the Rites of Fall. When the god ascends, so you can spend the month worshipping me."

"You!" She smacked his stomach and pulled his chest hair, and he doubled up with laughter while trying to fend her off. "That's it. I've changed my mind."

His heart seized, his mirth dying as if it had never been. "No."

"Yes." She kissed him, and his pulse tripped for another reason. "I think I will be the Haroun shaman. It's an offer I can't refuse." She kissed him again, and his cock jerked to rigid attention. "But we don't have to do a permanent bond if you don't want to. I would be willing to wait until you've had some time to get used to it."

"Do you want to wait?"

She searched his face for an eternity, and his gut knotted. Loving him was one thing, but was she uncertain about *bonding* with him? Did she not want to take a vow her honor would force her to keep? "No, I don't want to wait. If I had my way, we'd ask the Badawi shaman to mark us before the Rites break up."

His breath whooshed out, and he grabbed her and rolled her under him. They both cried out when he surged deep inside her. "Then we'll ask. After I convince your chieftain to let you go."

"They will make it very costly for you, to take a woman from their clan." Her legs wrapped tight around his flanks, and their hips pumped together as they raced each other to orgasm, her pussy clamping around his cock with each stabbing thrust.

"You are the most precious thing in my world. Just as you are." Words poured from his soul with every ragged breath, and he knew they were the ones she needed to hear because she gave him a smile full of enough love to last a lifetime, through every trial and triumph. "There's nothing I wouldn't give to keep you. Always, *always*, my beloved Kadira."

About the Author

Crystal Jordan began writing romance after she finished graduate school and needed something to fill the hours that used to be eaten away by homework. Currently, she serves as a librarian at a university in California, but has lived and worked all over the United States. She writes paranormal, futuristic and erotic romance.

To learn more about Crystal please visit www.crystaljordan.com. Send an email to Crystal at crystal@crystaljordan.com or join her Yahoo! group to join in the fun with other readers as well as Crystal! http://groups.yahoo.com/group/crystal-jordan

Look for these titles by
Crystal Jordan

Now Available:

Treasured

In the Heat of the Night
Total Eclipse of the Heart
Big Girls Don't Die
It's Raining Men
Crazy Little Thing Called Love

Unbelieveable
If You Believe
Believe in Me

Forbidden Passions
Stolen Passions
Fleeting Passions

The Whore

Lilli Feisty

Dedication

My arre'te maker.

Prologue

In 2012, the world came to a grinding halt as radiation hit from a massive solar storm. Crops died, animals perished, cities fell and humans became little more than beasts themselves. Under the threat of starvation, civility was reduced to mere memory. Only the strongest men survived, and physically weaker women and children wasted to nothingness.

More than a century later, humanity struggles in the desert Wasteland. The solar radiation rendered most women infertile, and the population dwindles more with each year that passes. Scattered up and down coasts, isolated cities eke out an existence from fishing, foraging and hunting for what little game is left. Outside the city walls, men face the threat of pirates and raiders.

Few women remain, divided into four classes—Whores, Breeders, Priestesses and Wanderers. They are as reviled as they are worshipped, a commodity any man must pay to touch. To touch a Whore, a man must sacrifice his riches. To touch a Breeder, a man must sacrifice his freedom. To touch a Priestess, a man must be chosen by the gods. And to touch a Wanderer may end up costing him his life.

There is only one rule in the Wasteland—survive.

Chapter One

Aside from the worry of conceiving a child, Bryn considered sucking cock the worst part of her role as a prostitute. Leaning against the rails of the carved-earth tower above the brothel, she took a deep drag from the cinnamon-clove arre'te she held between her thumb and forefinger. By some twist of luck, she'd discovered she possessed an allergy to cinnamon when a trader had brought her chamber mate, Ayla, a tin of treats five years previously. At first Bryn had panicked when her mouth had gone numb after sucking the spicy delicacy, but Bryn wasn't the type of woman who panicked for long. She'd quickly realized a numb mouth made sucking a Jahns willy a lot less foul.

Another deep drag. The arre'te burned dangerously close to her fingertips, and a spark flew into the night air, disappearing into the sounds of a city bustling beneath her. As she watched the glow vanish, she felt an envy for that ember. Her heart lurched with a pain of longing as she listened to the noise reverberating against the exterior of the hills around her. Mostly she heard the clatter of men—fishermen announcing what they'd caught that day, traders hawking cigarettes and fresh water. All free men, roaming the dirty streets on their way to their next destination.

Men. Because they had a cock, they were free.

Bryn hated cocks as much as she wished to own one.

"Bryn. Your Jahn is preparing for you. He should be ringing the bell shortly."

Her stomach lurched as she listened to the servant's voice. "I'll be inside momentarily," she called over her shoulder. She'd already been prepared for the evening. Three servants had shaved her skin. One had cleaned her legs, one her underarms and one servant had gently run the edge of a deadly sharp knife over every crevice of her sex, leaving her pussy as smooth as silk. Another servant had massaged her body in agave milk, and her skin was as soft and pale as the plant's liquid.

Her arre'te was dark, dead. She flicked it into the night and watched it fall into the crowd. And there was a crowd. Tonight the city was bustling. The storm that had recently passed had left people relieved, and an air of excitement seemed to permeate the air. Storms were rare and fierce, and each time a tempest passed, the denizens of the sea came ashore. The fish were plenty, the air was clear and the men were horny. For that last part, if it happened to be a female a man wanted, there was only one place within a hundred miles to find such a commodity.

And, being such a commodity herself, Bryn was standing on the balcony of said establishment. The Dusty Rose. She rolled her eyes. It was a stupid name. After all, no living being had actually seen anything other than the desert rose, a mutation of the plant that survived. Now, they only saw illustrations that had been protected by the underground Librarians. Illustrations dated hundreds of years ago were the closest thing any being on the planet had come to seeing an actual rose. A sealed parchment with a photo of a rose hung in the entry of the brothel, given to the house by the High Priestess. The plant had been entirely destroyed during The Burning Time. So Bryn thought the name was hokey, some kind of cheesy suggestion of what was located inside the thick walls. Petal Pussies, Leaves of Flesh, Flowers for Hire—if they were going to pick a hokey name, any of those would be better and more accurate titles of what resided in the Dusty Rose.

She touched her right ear, where a red rose was tattooed on her lobe. Her fellow prostitutes were each marked similarly. A small symbol, but it said so much. The mark claimed her. Owned her. Kept her in her place. She was a Rose. A pretty word for whore. And that place was a fortress, an environment protected as tightly as any temple. A brothel.

Located in the center of Kroy Wren, the Dusty Rose was carved into the rocky walls of earth, the thick soil etched by the knives of highly skilled artisans. The balcony on which she stood was several hundred feet above ground and ornately chiseled with designs ordered by the High Priestesses. She shuddered at the memory. When the brothel had grown to the point where they required more room, the Roses had been the ones who'd traded for the artisans' services. Excited by the availability of sex each evening, the women had been kept busy. Bryn had taken so many cocks into her mouth during that six-month period, she'd thought her jaw would break.

The bell rang, a tinkling sound of burnt glass pebbles, summoning her. The elegant noise belied the sourness churning in her stomach.

With a deep breath, she tightened the scarves strategically wrapped around her body. Soft black fabric tied in a sash around her hips, and another piece of fabric draped across her breasts and tied over one shoulder. Men liked to see female skin, but they also loved the anticipation of finding out what was beneath the flimsy articles of clothing.

Like any prostitute, she was held in high regard. As she entered her chamber, crossed the room and stepped into the hallway, she reminded herself that despite her duty, she was in a caste higher than any man. She placed her hand on the doorknob and inhaled. Beyond, her Jahn waited. She lifted her chin and prepared to look down upon whomever waited inside.

She opened the door.

His chest was covered in a thick mat of dark hair, and large glass ear bobbles were affixed to his earlobes. Of course he'd leave those on. They were a sign of wealth and stature. He was probably an affluent trader. Now he reclined on the bed, a light sheet covering his sex. His erection was visible beneath the linen. Despite his freshly washed hair and body, there was an air of something dirty about him. Something in his eyes, the way he looked at her. Bryn's sex clenched unpleasantly but she pasted on what she knew was the perfect smile. Coy yet knowing. Innocent yet sexy. Ingenuous yet wanting. *Fake fake fake.* But it worked.

The man placed his hand on the sheet and grinned at her. He whipped the sheet off his body, exposing his cock. It wasn't very big, and the tip was already glistening.

This shouldn't take long.

"Evenin', Rose. I have a present for you," he said.

She dipped her head and looked up through her lashes. *Your cock. Goody. Just what I've always wanted.* Ignoring the nausea churning deep in her belly, she stepped inside. "Oh, sir.

How I do like gifts. And yours is just what I was hoping for this fine evening."

Licking her numbed lips, she closed the door behind her.

Captain Xander yanked at the hemp ropes binding his wrists behind his back. Fucking Viven's minions had tied them well. There was no way he was squirming his hands free. He looked up through a lock of brown hair that had fallen perfectly into his face to poke him in the eye. Puffing a burst of air out of his lungs, he attempted to blow the hair away. He succeeded. And then it fell back into place, more annoying then before.

But his unruly hair was really the least of his problems. The moment he'd stepped onto land he'd been abducted by his Payer's bodyguards. Now he stood in the fuckwad's office, and Viven looked none to happy to see him.

The tall, bald man leaned across his oversized marble desk, steepling his hands beneath his chin. He wore round dark goggles that hid what were rumored to be hollow eye sockets. He said, "Captain. You again fail me."

Xander took a deep breath and glanced to the huge guards flanking him. He had to keep his cool. He didn't have a choice. He faced Viven. "With all due respect, sir, I believe we were very close to finding what you desire this time out. But there was a storm, and we were forced ashore for supplies and to repair the boat."

Viven flicked a finger and a guard promptly shot a huge fist into Xander's gut. He doubled over as pain lurched through him, making his mouth water as a wave of nausea washed through his body. Still bent, he looked up through his hair. "Sir, I truly think we are on the verge of discovering what you seek. Just one more venture—uh."

Another punch assaulted his abdomen. One more hit like that and the remains of Xander's salt-cod breakfast would be spewed over Viven's expensive exotic rug.

Viven glanced to the small bowl of burning sage on his desk. "I am a forgiving man. I am a patient man. I paid you to do a job, and you have failed. Twice." He waved his hand at a guard, and Xander was thrust forward until he was bent over Viven's desk. Then there was a yank as his wrists were untied. The next thing he knew, Xander's hands were pushed flat on the marble surface, held firmly by Viven's minions. Xander struggled, but they easily overpowered him. And even if he could mange to free himself, the oafs had already disarmed him of the knives he kept strapped to his thighs at all times.

Hadn't you meant to brush up on your hand-to-hand fighting skills? He grunted. His knives were his weapon of choice. Fists were so...messy.

But, as Viven picked up a lighting stick, Xander had a feeling things were about to get a lot messier.

Fuck.

Every muscle in Xander's body tensed. "Sir, I assure you I'll attain what you desire. I just need a bit more time."

Viven placed the end of the burning stick into the glowing sage. "More time. We all need more time, don't we?" When the tip of the stick was burning with a small orange flame, he looked up. "I will give you more time."

"Great. Now I'll just be on my way—"

Xander tried to stand, but the guards tightened their grip, totally immobilizing him. "Not yet." Viven held the burning stick so it hovered just above Xander's right hand. "I want more."

"I understand."

"No. I don't think you do." Viven stabbed the fiery tip into Xander's skin. He screamed. The burn pierced his hand, pain shooting out of each nerve and up his arm. He sucked in a breath as the stick's ember died, buried in a small hole in his skin.

Finally, panting, he regained his breath. His mouth still watered, and he experienced a nearly overwhelming urge to spit into Viven's face.

You've just been beaten in the gut, and had a burning stick put out in your hand. You're restrained, and you have no weapons. Spitting in your Payer's face probably isn't a good idea at this juncture.

Viven lifted the smoking stick out of his skin. "The way I see it, you owe me, Captain."

"Fine," he bit out. "What do you want?"

"What I originally hired you to acquire." His pointy tongue darted out, and he licked his lips. "And more."

Xander stared into the black glasses perched on the Payer's face. "What more?"

"Your ship."

"No fucking way."

His outburst was rewarded with a kick to the back of his knee. His leg jerked forward, banging his kneecap on the marble of the front of the desk. Shit. Just because he was a pirate did not mean he wanted a metal leg. Still, he said, "With all due respect, sir, I can't give up my boat."

Viven leaned back in his chair and nibbled on the clean edge of the burning stick. "You misunderstand me, Captain. It's not just your ship I'm going to own. It's your ship, your crew and you. The way I see it, you owe me. Big time. And seeing as you can't possibly repay me, I'll take my payment how I see fit. And how I see fit is to own you—and what's yours."

"I hate it when you do this."

Brynn looked up from the men's shirt she was currently buttoning. "I know you do, Ayla. But I'm nearly out of arre'tes, and with the docks as busy as they are tonight, I need to seize the moment."

It wasn't a lie. Bryn's tin of the cinnamon mixture she used for rolling blunts was running low. That and she needed to obtain the rare sea sponge she used for contraception. Contraception wasn't allowed. Babies were immediately taken to the High Priestess and sent on a path chosen by a goddess. Bryn refused to produce another being who held no control over her destiny.

However, those were not the only reasons she was wearing men's trousers and affixing a large jewel to her ear, covering the rose tattoo. Her Jahn had given it to her as a gratuity, and she fully planned on using it tonight.

Restlessness seemed to be crawling over her skin. Listening to the hustle of the city caused her very insides to swirl with a need to leave the confines of the brothel. She got like this sometimes. Sometimes the desire to be free was so intense she thought her chest might simply explode.

Tonight was one of those nights.

"It's dangerous." Legs crossed, Ayla sat on her bed. Like Bryn's, it was high off the ground and adorned with luxurious and rare silken bedcoverings. Now Ayla leaned against a crimson pillow and began braiding her thick, bright red hair. "Think about what could happen if anyone discovered you're a woman wandering the streets alone."

"It hasn't happened thus far. And it's even less likely now that I've cut my hair."

It was true. One day Bryn had taken a large pair of shears and hacked off the long mahogany locks into choppy, uneven cuts. She wasn't sure why. She'd been staring into the mirror and had experienced the strong and sudden urge to free herself from the weight of femininity. So, she had done so. Then she'd taken a horsehair brush, dipped it in henna dye and brushed the color over the top layer of her hair. The result was jagged, sharp edges of hair with random, mahogany streaks. It wasn't much, but the result had given her a sense of control over something, even if it was something as simple as her hair.

The Madam had been none too pleased. After all, Roses were meant to possess the very essence of womanhood and femininity. With her short haircut and slight frame, the Madam said Bryn looked like a teenage boy.

Aw, but they swiftly discovered there was a market for such a thing. Soon Bryn had Jahns going as far as to request she wear men's clothing before she came to them, which came in quite handy. Now Bryn possessed several items in her wardrobe that she used during her ventures into the city.

She faced her friend. "Please don't worry, Ayla. I promise I'll be fine."

Ayla's brow was creased. "Can't you send a servant to the docks?"

Bryn sat on a stool and started lacing up her boots. "You know I'd never ask that of a servant. It's too dangerous."

"You do hear yourself, right? Too dangerous for a servant but not for *you*?"

"Do you think I'll be abducted by pirates?"

Ayla scowled. "You know that's not funny. My brother is a perfect example. He became a pirate, and now I never see him."

"That's because we can't see anyone. We're stuck behind these brothel walls." Bryn tied off the boot and started on the other one. Each second that ticked by the urge to flee grew, causing her heart to beat with anxiety. She *needed* to go. "I've done this a million times. Don't worry so." She stood, crossed the room and gave her Sister a kiss on the forehead.

Ayla took her hand and placed a soft kiss on the back of her wrist, followed by a gentle lick from her warm tongue. As usual, Bryn's sex swelled. She closed her eyes as Ayla moved

Bryn's hand to cup her breast. Bryn could feel Ayla's hard nipple through the soft fabric of her sleeping gown, and she took the beaded flesh in her fingers.

Ayla sighed. "Please. Stay."

For a moment she considered it. Ayla knew Bryn's body, knew her desires, more so than the other Roses. So many men... The only way Bryn enjoyed sex was to lay with her fellow prostitutes.

Sex was a job, a requirement. She didn't enjoy being forced to have sex with anyone who could afford it, but it hadn't ruined her own sexual appetite. Bryn refused to let her destiny ruin her body's desires.

Right now she desired Ayla. As her chamber-mate continued to rub her nipple with her fingers, Bryn's pussy dampened, started to throb.

Leaning down, she placed a soft kiss on Ayla's lips. "I'll be back," she whispered. "I promise."

Ayla leaned back onto the bed and lifted the fabric of her sleeping dress, pulling it to her waist. She opened her legs to reveal her smooth, glistening pussy. Reaching down, she dipped her index finger into the pink folds. "I'll be waiting."

It was difficult to pull herself away, but she did. Had to. Sex wasn't exactly difficult to come by—she lived in a brothel. It would be there when she returned. The desire to escape the walls of her fortress had been escalating with each passing second, leaving her with little choice but to fulfill that particular desire. Her escapes were the only thing that kept her from going mad.

She used the tunnels to reach the surface. Behind the walls of the brothel was a labyrinth of small passages. Hollow, narrow corridors that led to hundreds of exits. It was time for the servants evening meal, so Bryn expected barely any encounters as she made her way to the street.

Still, her heart raced. Although she tried to appear calm around Ayla, Bryn was well aware of how dangerous her actions were. If the Madam caught her sneaking outside the walls, she would be punished. Of course, a Rose couldn't have any visible marks of punishment. However, they had other methods. There were rooms located underground where Roses were punished for misdeeds. Like the sensory deprivation room. A woman was stripped nude, her wrists and ankles bound, and she was locked in a room of total darkness for forty-eight hours. All a person could hear in that room was the sound of her own breathing. Each time Bryn had seen a girl come out of such a punishment she'd had such an expression of insanity on her face—it made Bryn's blood run cold to think of it.

The punishment for leaving the brothel walls would be much worse than two days in the deprivation chamber. A year of penalty. Naked and chained. Spread-eagle on a table in the entry of the brothel. Each day, from sunrise to sunset. The small amount of freedom she knew would be taken away from her. She'd be nothing more than a receptacle. Anyone could touch her. Any servant could climb onto the table, kneel between her legs and fuck her. A group of men could surround her, stroke their cocks and shoot their come on to her naked flesh, where it would stay until she was released at night. Once the word spread that a Rose had fallen, there would be a line of men waiting their turn for a free fuck. She would have men sticking their cocks in her mouth and pussy and ass all day long—often simultaneously. No man would be turned away.

They said it was to ensure a Rose understood the dangers of being a woman alone in the Wasteland. Bryn thought it was a cruel joke. There was nothing in the barren lands that could be worse than what she found each day inside her prison walls.

Chapter Two

So, yeah. She had a lot to lose. Yet, here she was. Peeking through a tunnel door, her hands shook as she watched a group of men walking down the hallway in her direction, their voices and the sounds of their boot steps echoing through the corridor. When they had passed she quietly emerged, staying close enough so she seemed to be a part of their group as they strolled past the guards and into the street.

No one gave them a second look. It truly amazed her how much freedom a cock gave a person.

Dodging through the crowd, she went for a few blocks before dipping into an alley. She leaned her back against the side of a building. Her heart raced, beating so hard in her chest she could nearly feel it hammering against her breastbone. Taking deep breaths, she counted to twenty, then thirty. But she had to go up to fifty before her pulse began to slow. And then, her body lost some of its anxiety.

The energy of the city started to bleed into her, making her feel as if she'd taken a drag of a hemp arre'te. Tension drained from her body. The traders, the fishermen, the citizens—all exuded an unforeseen force that seeped into her, thrilling her. Freedom. For a few hours she had what they did. And it was exhilarating.

Pushing herself off the wall, she meandered toward the docks. She took her time. She paused to peruse a tray of sea stones a man had strapped to his chest. In awe, she watched a man wearing what could only be a coat made of leather, and straddling something even more rare—a horse—ride down the street. This was only the second time she'd seen such a creature in person, and the beautiful animal was so rare and expensive, four armed guards surrounded the rider and beast.

If she were free, maybe she could have worked hard enough to obtain something as magnificent as a horse.

If she were free.

You are, if only for a few hours.

With a sigh, she continued on her way. Closer to the water, the air became heavy and damp. Salty. She sucked in a deep breath and closed her eyes. Oh, how she longed to ride the sea. The sea was endless. No roads, no houses carved into the earth. She imagined herself on a boat, drifting day to day. Coming ashore only when a piece of land looked attractive.

A young man stopped directly in front of her. Two other boys flanked him. They looked dirty and poor and desperate. The hairs on the back of her neck prickled.

The one in the middle had shiny, sandy hair and a mean glint in his eye. He pointed to the jewel screwed to her earlobe. "Nice earbob."

A shiver of fear trickled up her spine, and she put her head down to step around them. But they intercepted her, moving to stand directly in her path.

"Where you off to in such a hurry?"

She met his gaze. One thing she'd learned was to show no fear. "To the docks. Now let me pass."

But his stare had gone once again to her ear, and she mentally kicked herself for being stupid. She should have worn a scarf, as she normally did. She reached inside her blazer to palm the dagger strapped to her side. She didn't think she could take the three of them. However, winning a fight wasn't her biggest concern. Any scene-making altercation, on the other hand, could be a problem. A big problem.

She fisted the knife's handle. "I don't want any trouble."

The sandy-haired boy reached out once again. "Then just give us your jewel, and you won't have any."

Fuck. She'd happily hand it over, but then her tattoo would be exposed. Again, she cursed her stupidity. Now, she had no choice but to fight. She drew the dagger out of her jacket and tried to look confident. "Fine. Don't say I didn't warn you."

The boys came at her, surrounding her. Her eyes darted between the three figures as she took a fighting stance. She'd watched the Sun Guards exercise, and had practiced their defenses. But that had been alone. Pretend. This was real.

She would lose.

Naked, chained to a table, a living fuck-toy.

No. You can not lose.

Backing up, she tried to lure them into an alley. The last thing she needed was to draw an audience. With her free hand, she beckoned them to her.

The leader came first. He swung a fist toward her head, but Bryn jerked backward, causing him to miss. She seized the opportunity. Gripping her knife, she stabbed him in the shoulder. He howled.

"Shut up," she hissed.

Then the two others came at her. Fuck, she couldn't take all three.

But she could try.

They swarmed. She backed up. One of the boys pulled his arm back and was about to swing at her. She thought she could duck again—

He was on the ground. She barely knew what happened. It couldn't have been more than five seconds before she realized her attackers were the ones under siege. Two men were making quick work of the boys. Breathing heavily, she watched as a man with white-blond hair in a long braid down his back punched the sandy-haired man in the jaw. Three punches and the boy was on the ground, unconscious.

The blond man appeared utterly unfazed as he quickly drew up a leg and spun around to plant the bottom of his leather boot in the second boy's chest. The boy flew backward, landing with a thud on the other side of the alley.

Her gaze landed on the blond man's companion. Tall and lean, he had brown hair and a handsome face. Like the blond man, he wore a brown tunic, tan breeches and leather boots. Each man had telltale shells woven into their hair. Pirates.

Pirates. They embodied everything she craved. Freedom. The sea. Power.

The brown-haired man held two daggers. Casually spinning the knives in his hands, he smiled at the third boy, who now had his back to the wall. Still focused on the boy, the man jerked a nod at Bryn. "You giving this chap a hard time?"

The fucker's eyes were wide, scared. "No—I just wanted

his—"

Bryn barely saw the knife fly out of the man's hand. She heard a whiz, and then the dagger was stuck in the side of the building, barely an inch from the boy's head.

His voice was high and full of fright. "Please...I didn't mean any harm."

"Get the fuck out of here."

The boy who'd wanted her jewel needed no further invitation. Seizing the moment, he fled, his footsteps falling hard and fast as he exited the alley.

Then, silence. The other two boys were unconscious lumps on the ground, leaving Bryn alone in the alley. With the two men. Facing them, she clutched her dagger to her chest. However, these were men—these were pirates. Fighters. She knew she wouldn't have a chance.

"Don't worry, boy," the blond man said. "We won't hurt you." In the dim light, she could see his wide blue eyes and thick black lashes. His face looked as chiseled as the exterior of the brothel walls, and a jolt of awareness shot through her.

Shaking it away, she looked to his friend. That was a mistake. A second jolt of awareness struck her, this time like lightning. In the moonlight, his shaggy brown hair flashed with sun-kissed tones. He possessed a tall, sturdy build and had an easy manner about him. But based on the way he'd overtaken the men who'd attacked her, she had a feeling his demeanor was deceiving.

He plucked the knife out of the side of the alley wall. "Fucking punks. I suppose they wanted your earbob."

Her fist clenched around the hilt of her knife. Eventually, she nodded.

"No worries, chap," the blond man said. His gaze raked over her and even though it was dark, she saw a glimmer in his eyes. "We won't hurt you."

She believed him. For some reason she believed him. But what did they want?

"Be safe," the brown-haired man said. Then, with one last glance he draped his arm over the shoulders of his companion, and they walked away.

Clutching her knife, she stared after them. If Bryn knew about one thing, it was sex. And, as she watched how they interacted—their constant physical contact, the way the blond man brushed a lock of hair out of his friend's face—she was quite certain they were more than friends. They were lovers.

That hot awareness from earlier? Yeah, it had just landed in her gut. Of course, all men lay together. She'd never been picked to participate in a ménage. However, on several occasions Bryn had spied on Roses who had participated in such scenarios. She'd found the scenes shockingly erotic, and had gone as far as to spy through a balcony window while she touched herself.

A hot flush crept up her neck at the memory. It was the one thing she'd actually wanted to do with a man. It was the one thing she'd seen men do that aroused her. She'd seen a Rose sandwiched between two men, both her holes filled at once. There'd been a tenderness in that encounter Bryn had never experienced. The ménages were always talked about with reverence, as the most desirable Jahns. They treated a Rose with respect and always gave her pleasure.

Watching the men kiss had been the most exciting thing. She wasn't sure why. Especially when they kissed each other while fucking the Rose...

It was a fantasy she'd held close to her heart, one she often played out in her mind while she touched herself...

The pirates were nearly out of her vision before she took off. She scrambled through the fishermen and traders, making her way across the dirty, twisting street until she was a few steps behind the pirates. Until she could overhear their words.

The blond man had long legs and an elegant gait. He said, "Half the crew has disappeared, Captain."

The man next to him—the Captain—was his opposite. His gait was more of a swagger. From behind, he seemed even taller than she'd originally thought. Her gaze roamed over his brown trousers, which hugged what even someone as jaded as Bryn would have to admit was a fabulous ass. Worn, knee-high boots hit the ground with sturdy steps.

She stepped up her own speed, listening to their conversation. She wasn't sure what drew her to them, but she was free, for the moment. So she didn't deny herself. And she wanted to know why half their crew had disappeared.

Curiosity killed the cat.

Good thing she wasn't a cat.

The skinny man said, "Word reached the ship about the

Payer, and five crew members were gone within the span of fifteen minutes."

"Fucking traitors."

"Mainly the new boys we picked up in G'huana. Probably would have jumped the second we reached Kroy Wren anyway."

The Captain ran his hand over his brown hair, which resulted in a bunch of chucks sticking up chaotically. "True. Still, I want to get the hell out of here tonight. Crew or no crew."

They dodged a group of traders carrying coils of hemp rope. "It's most likely going to be a skeleton crew, sir. Of course, we still have our core group. And a few citizens have inquired about passage."

"I suppose the deck swab is gone."

"Unfortunately, yes."

The Captain shook his head. "Damn. I hate a dirty ship."

"I'm aware of that, Captain."

"Fucker."

"I can clean."

As the men stopped and turned to face her, Bryn slapped a hand over her mouth. What the hell had she just said? Not only was the idea of working on a ship insane, but she'd never held a broom.

The Captain nailed her with his gaze, and her heart stopped. Brown eyes. Direct and intense and sparkling with intelligence.

She took a step back. "Or not..."

The skinny man gave her a slow once-over. Normally, such an obvious assessment would have disgusted her, but, oddly, it didn't. As his gaze roamed her body, a shiver of something went through her. Something she couldn't quite identify. Unfamiliar, but not unwelcome.

Strange, that.

"You looking for a job?" the thin man said.

She nodded her head. "Yes."

Their expressions were amused. The Captain stepped forward, and her heart skipped as he dipped his head to look her in the eye.

What were these men doing to her? Had she actually inhaled something intoxicating and was now suffering a contact high? That one trader's incense had smelled a bit funny...

The Captain put a hand on his hip. She noticed that hand was marked. A burn mark. And it appeared fresh.

Okaaay. That didn't look too good.

He said, "Yes or no, boy? We don't have all night."

Her hands clenched at her sides as her palms went damp. Her pulse hammered and her head spun. Was this really happening? Were they offering her a chance for escape?

She'd never cleaned a floor in her life.

She was posing as a man.

The ship was probably full of nefarious characters and big danger.

No one was more surprised than she was to hear herself say, "Yes. I am in need of a job, and I can clean. If you think you can take me on. On the ship, I mean."

The Captain's all-assessing gaze was much quicker than his friend's but it sent a shiver up her spine.

He gave her a quirked grin. "Oh, I think I can take you, boy. Now let's go."

What the hell was she doing?

As she walked up the pier and the gangplank to the ship, the men flanked her. Her blood rushed with nerves as doubt threatened to overwhelm her. Was she really doing this? Was she really going to just walk away from her life and pose as a man on a pirate ship?

She was. But there was something she needed to do before they set sail.

Set sail.

Never, not in a million years, did Bryn consider ever saying those words.

Her stomach lurched as they stepped aboard. Despite her nerves, a flash of excitement shot through her. She was, for the first time in her twenty-five years of life, standing on the water. The air seemed to leave salt on her skin, and she licked her lips. She glanced to the men beside her, and a shiver of responsiveness heightened her already-edgy nerves. She had spent much time with men, but it was never her choice. To be doing so now seemed odd...and oddly exciting. Something about the Captain and his friend was different than anyone she'd known thus far. She felt strangely safe with them, and she was well aware that fear should force her to run back home.

Except she'd never considered the Rose home. It had been a prison, a place where she was forced to spread her legs and open her mouth and service men. It wasn't a choice. Now, she was making a choice. It could very well turn out to be the most disastrous choice of her life, but at least she was able to make it for herself. For once.

"Captain—"

The words were spoken by a man with a voice so deep it sounded like thunder. He was taller than any man Bryn had ever seen. His hair was as ebony as his skin, and hung from his head in long, knotted ropes. He must have had five pounds of shells woven into the strands.

She felt the Captain tense beside her. "I know about the crew. But we need to get the fuck out of here. Now. And I already found one replacement." He gripped her arm and shoved her forward. "This is—what's your name, boy?"

"Bryn—Brian."

The thin man narrowed his gaze at her. "Bryn—Brian?" he asked.

"My friends call me Brian." She hoped that sounded believable. She really hadn't planned this whole pose-like-a-boy-and-sneak-away-on-a-pirate-ship idea, so if she was going to pull it off she was going to have to be able to think on her feet. "You can call me Brian. Too."

The Captain said, "*Bryn—Brian's* our new swab hand. I'm Captain Xander." He pointed to the man who'd been walking with them. "This is Hawke, my first mate." He pulled her deeper into the ship. "That man you just met is our purser, Adiv. You'll meet the rest of the crew later." He slanted her a grin. "Let's go have a drink to celebrate. And Bryn?"

"Yes?" she squeaked.

"Welcome to our ship. The Sugar Skull."

Chapter Three

They walked deeper into the ship. Bryn tried to school her expression, despite the fact that she was in total awe of being on a ship for the first time. It was much...shabbier than she'd imagined. It seemed like every inch of the boat was made of something recovered from the piles of scrap just outside the city. But she supposed, based on her sheltered existence, it wasn't surprising that the rest of society didn't live in the elegant environment she was used to.

She wondered if she'd miss it.

But the thought immediately reminded her of what she needed to do before it was too late. They pushed through a door to what appeared to be the Captain's chamber. A large bed hung from four lines of hemp rope that had been secured to the ceiling. The interior walls were made of various scraps of metal that had been pieced together and affixed to the surface. Captain Xander walked to a corner and lifted a bottle from a table. When he glanced up at her, through a lock of brown hair, something inside her chest did a little skip.

What was that about?

"You drinkin'?" he asked.

"Yes," she said. A bit too enthusiastically, perhaps, because he quirked a brow and grinned.

And that grin did that funny thing to her heart again.

What was wrong with her?

He poured the drink into a second mug, and a third. Then he carried the mugs over and handed one to her and one to Hawke. "Fuck," he said, lifting his glass.

Bryn took a small sip and tried not to spit it out. The stuff burned her mouth, and when she swallowed it trailed down her throat and pooled like a hot coal in her belly. "What is this?"

Xander drained his cup. "C'uerveh. It's made from leaves of cactus. Every time we have a job down south we pick up some bottles. Good, no?"

It wasn't exactly the desert berry wine she was used to, but she nodded anyway. "Captain Xander, I was wondering if I could ask a favor of you."

Turning, he headed back to the table of bottles and refilled his cup. "What's that?"

"Can I send a message to my...family? Let them know where I am?" She needed to let Ayla know she was okay.

"Well, it looks like we're stuck here for the night. Feel free to run home and talk to them. Just be back before dawn. This ship's launching at sunrise—and I don't care how many of Viven's guards we have to kill to get out of here."

Bryn stepped forward. She couldn't go to the brothel—it would be much too risky. But how would she get a message to Ayla? She couldn't simply disappear. Her Sister would worry her poor head off. But she had no idea how to get a message to her friend. Roses were not trained in the art of reading or writing. Whatever she sent to Ayla had to be enigmatic, yet obvious enough for Ayla to figure out Bryn was safe.

Xander fell into a chair unlike anything she'd ever seen before. It was ornately carved out of rare wood, with a tall back that seemed to be the image of...

"You like that?" Hawke went to stand beside Xander, and placed a hand on the man's shoulder.

"Um..." She did. The wood had been sculpted into the erotic image of several men in sexual positions. They had large erections, and limbs, mouths and cocks were arranged in what could only be described as an orgy.

Bryn had seen orgies. Often, Jahns wanted two, three or even four girls at a time. Bryn didn't mind those Jahns. It meant she got to spend her time enjoying the bodies of her Sisters instead of being used as a man's sole purpose of pleasure. And a cock could really only fit into one mouth at a time, so it also resulted in allowing Bryn to share that particular task she hated so.

But again with the men together. Why did she respond so strongly to the thought? Being with a woman was a special event for a man. If women were able to live freely, perhaps things would have been different. But because women were protected and had no control over their own destinies, they had become nothing more than an article of trade.

Never had Bryn chosen to lay with a man. They'd always chosen her.

Now...it was different. The way Hawke was massaging Xander's shoulder, the erotic image behind them, the way they were both looking at her...

Holy Priestess.

Hawke touched Xander—running his hand lightly over his shoulder, across his back, and her heart started to pound. He palmed the back of Xander's head and she sucked in a breath as Hawke fisted a handful of Xander's hair.

They watched her. Were they testing her? Xander leaned back in his chair, his knees falling open to reveal an erection that strained against his trousers. Bryn's gaze landed there, and she felt her own sex responding.

Why? She'd seen hundreds of hard cocks. And she'd rarely—if ever—been sexually aroused by the sight of one. So now why was lust pooling between her legs? Why were her nipples tingling? Why did she feel a hot flush creeping up her neck?

Hawke reached around Xander and began unbuttoning his shirt. As his long fingers made quick work of the clothing, Xander's gaze locked on to hers. They weren't even touching, and yet she felt connected somehow, as if his own arousal was seeping into her body just through his stare.

Her own gaze finally dropped as Hawke pulled off Xander's shirt, revealing a chest so smooth and lean Bryn licked her lips. She wanted to lick Xander's nipples. She wanted to feel his skin, taste his skin. She wanted to...

The Captain dropped his top to the ground. "Are you a virgin, young Brian?"

"W-what?" she sputtered. She was a prostitute, hardly a virgin. "Why would you ask that?"

Xander leaned forward, resting his elbows on his knees. "You seem young, but not that young."

Not that young? She sucked in a breath and was about to retort but caught herself. A man looking for work on a ship wouldn't argue about such a thing. So she relaxed her stance. *You should do something manly...* Should she grab her crotch?

Maybe not. "My family has such genes. I am tw-eighteen years, Captain."

"Tweighteen?"

"Eighteen. Sorry. I overcame a speech impediment when I was a young, er, younger g-boy." She bit her tongue. She really needed to shut her mouth.

Xander cocked a brow. She shifted in her chair. Would he really believe she was seven years younger than her actual age?

Silence stretched before he finally said, "It's just that you appear a bit...naïve. Something about you gives the impression of inexperience."

"You think I'm an inexperienced virgin?" she said and then slapped a hand over her mouth. But the idea was so ridiculous... She straightened her back. "I am not a virgin, sir. I have lain with men." She knew it would be unusual for a lowly deck hand to be able to afford the services of a woman, so it would be likely Brian had been with men.

Well, at least that part wasn't a lie.

And wasn't that an understatement? Most likely she had seen and tasted more cock than all of the members of this ship. Combined. A hundred times over.

She wouldn't mention that last part.

Xander's gaze was still nailed on her. "We just wanted to make sure because this crew tends to be very active. Sexually. I'd hate to make you uncomfortable. You'd be surprised how many men start complaining after a while."

Her stomach dropped. "Does that mean... Do you mean sexual relations are a requirement to be onboard?" As it was, she wasn't sure how she was going to get by as a man, but if sex was a requirement she knew she was going to be doomed from the start. She could bind her breasts and pretend she was twenty, but a vagina was a bit tricky to disguise as a penis.

Hawke crossed his arms over his chest and grinned wickedly. "Not a requirement. But it's a lot more fun than just swabbing decks, right?"

"Um. I suppose."

"Suppose what? Are you saying you don't like sex, young Brian?" He shook his head. "Because I have to say, I just don't understand such a thing." He placed a hand on Xander's shoulder and gave it a squeeze.

"We just wanted to make sure you understand this ship tends to be a bit...rowdier than other boats. We sail. We search. We get paid. And we fuck."

Her mouth opened but nothing came out. His words shocked her...and aroused her.

They were watching her, obviously waiting for a response. Finally, she said, "Um. Okay. Can I watch?"

Xander barked a laugh and glanced at Hawke. "You can watch all you want, right, H?"

"But of course." His blue eyes darkened. "Watching is always encouraged on this ship."

"Damn straight," Xander said. "In fact, you can start now. We'll give you a little peek of what to expect."

"That's right. I'm his boy. His servant. Right, Captain?" But despite his elegant demeanor, there was something about Hawke that could only be described as male. His jaw was firm and strong, body lean yet solid-looking. He reminded her of the warrior servants, trained in the Far East to be fighters known to kill with nothing more than their bare hands. Talkative Jahns had spoken of them, and something told her Hawke would triumph in battle with such a manner.

So it was bizarre—and bizzarrely erotic—to observe.

Xander reached up to bring Hawke's mouth to his. Bryn could barely breathe as she watched the men kiss, their tongues dipping inside each other's mouths, their lips pressing together. The sight was shocking, exhilarating. Bryn unclenched hands that had been fisted at her side.

Hawke finally released Xander from his grip and looked toward Bryn. "You don't have do anything, Bryn. Participation is entirely up to you."

She swallowed. "Okay." Everything was surreal, it seemed as if she'd stepped into another world. She supposed in a sense she had. She was out of the brothel, on a ship, apparently about to witness two men copulating. Something she'd only glimpsed through distorted glass.

On shaky legs she went to a chair and fell into it. "I want to watch." The words came from a dry mouth, and her heart was racing. Normally, she was the one who was watched. She was the one people paid for. Now, a powerful rush surged through her at the thought of being in a position of observer.

And it was incredibly hot.

"As you wish, Brian." Why did Xander's eyes sparkle when he said her name? Like he knew.

Impossible. He would have turned her in if that was the case. Instead they were giving her total freedom. Their boat, their journey. And now, sex.

And she didn't have to do anything but watch. If she wanted to. The thought made her head spin.

Hawke knelt between the Captain's legs. Xander touched the blond man's head lightly as he removed Xander's boots and placed them on the floor. Then Hawke untied his trousers and pulled them down his legs.

From across the room, Xander's eyes fixed on hers. She knew the look of desire, certainly. So why did the way his brown gaze bore into hers—dark, dilated and wanting—go straight through her. Her pulse beat like a drum in her ear, and her pussy throbbed.

She sat there. Watching. Free to watch. The combination of freedom and arousal exhilarated her, and her chest seemed to swell from the power of it.

Hawke took Xander's cock in his hand. The head of his cock was shiny, dripping with a sheen of his own arousal. Bryn licked her lips. She'd tasted plenty of come, but she'd never wanted to before.

Not like now. She watched Hawke's tongue dart out to lick the head of Xander's penis, her gaze fixated on the way he licked around the tip. Bryn was jealous. She wanted to taste Xander's skin. And then something else, a vision came to her, and she had to squeeze her legs together as the longing became so intense it nearly overwhelmed her.

What would Hawke's mouth feel like on her own sex? She wanted to know.

But that would never happen. Because she was pretending to be a boy. Right?

She'd enjoyed sex, but had only experienced pleasure with women. She'd thought about this, wanted it. But before, the only way she imagined it would happen to her was if she was being purchased. Never of her own free will.

She could walk away any time. But she didn't.

Instead, she watched Xander. Saw the way his hands tightly clenched the arms of the chair as Hawke took his cock deep into his mouth. Her entire body thrummed with desire and lust. Her pussy dripped with arousal. She couldn't take her eyes off the scene before her. She watched the back of Hawke's head move up and down, up and down, striking a rhythm as he sucked Xander, strong, deep. To her surprised, Bryn found herself experience a twinge of envy.

Envy at sucking cock? What was wrong with her?

It was the novelty. It was the site of two men doing what she'd only seen women do to men. It was more. The passion, the emotion between the two men was palpable and as Xander threw his head back, his eyes half-lidded and still watching Bryn, she had to shift in her chair as the longing between her legs intensified, making her thighs shake.

Power. She'd never seen anything so powerful as what she was witnessing. She'd never known there could be power in sex, but here it was. Right before her eyes.

And her body responded with such force it made her feel as if she were floating.

Xander cried out. She watched every muscle in his torso clench, and his hips thrust forward. Impressed, she watched as Hawke took him so deep Xander's entire cock nearly disappeared in the blond man's mouth. Xander released the arms of the chair and buried his hands in Hawke's hair, holding him still as he pumped what Bryn knew to be his essence into the other man's mouth, his throat.

Finally they stilled, and Xander's breathing began to slow. Eventually he released Hawke's head, and the man stood. They looked at her.

Her own breathing hadn't slowed one bit. In fact she was practically panting, needing a release of her own. She didn't know what she was doing, but she knew she had to do something. Without thought, she started pushing herself out of the chair.

Xander shook his head. "Stay."

His command was sharp, and left no room for argument. She was so out of her head, she doubted she could argue anyway. "If you like to watch. You can watch. 'Cause we're not done yet."

Oh God. She wanted to run. She wanted to touch herself. She couldn't do any of those things. She couldn't even think.

Hawke picked up two pieces of rope and approached her. "Don't worry, pet. You can watch all you want. We like it."

111

"Wait—"

But it was too late. Before she even knew what he was doing, he was tying one of her wrists to the arm of the chair.

"No—" Panic coursed through her. They were going to restrain her? Why?

Hawke pushed away a lock of hair and placed a gentle kiss on her forehead. It calmed her in a way only Ayla had been able to do. Strange, now that she thought about it, there was something about Hawke that reminded her of Ayla. He had a similar serenity about him. Something about him made her feel at ease.

He's tying me to a chair. No choice anymore. Instinctively, she began to struggle.

He put a hand on her shoulder, and she stopped. Looking up into his blue eyes, she was again reminded of Ayla. Hawke's eyes were almost identical to her chamber-mate's, the blue unique and bright. And caring.

She wasn't sure why, but his touch soothed her. He kissed her again, this time on the mouth. She could taste Xander on his tongue, and her eyes drifted shut as she sank into the chair. Thoughts drained as he continued to lick her lips, taste her tongue. She felt this kiss everywhere—her breasts, her belly, her pussy. The only one who'd ever kissed her like that before had been Ayla. And, like when Ayla kissed her, she melted.

He released her. Slightly stunned, she opened her eyes. Hawke's eyes twinkled as he gave her one last look—was that triumph she saw there?—and crossed the room, toward the bed. As he walked, he started removing articles of clothing. He untied the string at the neck of his tunic and pulled it over his head. A new wave of awareness washed over her as Xander's movement caught her eye. He was naked and he was...magnificent.

They both were. And she wanted them. Wanted this.

Whatever *this* was.

Chapter Four

How strange. As a Rose, she'd been forced to endure men touching her, more men than she could begin to count. She'd had to pretend every second, had to pretend as if she enjoyed taking a man in her mouth. As if she enjoyed spreading her legs to allow a stranger to kneel between her thighs and fuck her. Now, watching Xander stroke Hawke's smooth back, his fingers lingering on the thin man's hips, she felt privileged. She was tied, but the restraint only fueled the lust raging through her. Her pussy throbbed, wet and pulsing between her legs.

Something in the dynamics of the men had shifted. Before, when Hawke had been sucking Xander's cock, there had been tenderness between them. Now Xander yanked off Hawke's trousers, threw them aside and placed a wide palm between the man's elegant shoulder blades and none too gently shoved him facedown on the bed. As if earlier had only been a tease for what was to come.

Bryn's gaze roamed the two men's naked bodies, landing on Hawke's ass. Exposed. He was so exposed...as Bryn herself had been so many times. But unlike so many of her experiences, he was making the choice to be fucked.

Xander moved his hands down Hawke's back, keeping him flat on the bed. Next to the bed on a table was a jar of oil, and Xander dipped his fingers into the liquid. She hitched a breath as she watched him rub the oil in his hands, then he reached around Hawke to grab his very rigid cock. Hawke threw his head back, his mouth open. Xander took Hawke's penis and began to stroke, up and down, and she could see his grip was firm and steady. Xander's dick was hard and long as he pumped away at Hawke, pressing his own body against the blond man's back.

Hawke fisted the bedcovering. "Yes, Xander...fuck."

"What do you want, Hawke?"

"You know what I want."

Bryn's breath hitched. Their language filled her head, and she ached to touch herself. Her arms jerked against the restraints.

Xander took Hawke's long hair in his hand and pulled sharply. Startled at the violent act, Bryn stilled. But Hawke only groaned louder and pushed his ass against the Captain's erection.

Xander jerked his hair once more. "Tell me what you want, man."

Fascinated, Bryn watched as Xander picked up a wooden paddle. It looked ancient and used and the Captain raised it as if... No... Was he really going to use it?

"Stop!" She couldn't stand to watch Xander hurt Hawke.

But when Hawke looked over his shoulder, he was smiling, and his blue eyes were dark and glossy. She knew that look. Desire.

Facing her, Xander held the paddle in one hand and stroked it lightly with his other. "We found this on an island in the Southern Coast. However, this isn't exactly the time for a geography lesson." This time when he stroked Hawke's back, she could see his touch was gentle. What was going on here? "Just watch, Brian. We brought you here for a reason. To see if you really wanted to be a part of this crew."

She bit her lip. How could she just watch someone being beaten? But Hawke didn't seem to mind. In fact, the look on his face was nothing short of joyful.

"Trust us," the Captain said, as if it was an order.

After a second, she nodded. Despite her hesitation, her body hummed with lust and—gods help her—she wanted to watch. She *wanted* to see what would happen. She'd thought she'd experienced all there was to experience in the realms of sex. But she'd never seen anything like this.

So she watched.

Xander placed one hand on the back of Hawke's neck. Then he raised the paddle and brought it down on the fleshy part of Hawke's ass. Bryn gasped as the smack resonated through the room.

"You didn't tell me what you wanted, H," Xander said.

"Hit me."

"What?"

"Hit me again. *Please.*" Hawke's voice was dry and scratchy, but there was no denying the fact that he meant it. He wanted this.

Xander raised the paddle again. He struck Hawke once more, in the same place. He continued the paddling, and each time the piece of wood landed on flesh, Hawke's body did something fascinating. Instead of tensing, he seemed to become more relaxed. His upper body went limp, sinking into the mattress. His cries became softer, more erotic, and the sound of the paddle hitting his skin became louder, more intense.

It was as if they'd forgotten she was there. Xander seemed as taken away as Hawke was. It was the two of them, as if only they existed. The connection between them seemed to grow, and the muscles of Xander's upper body flexed and moved as he continued the motion of paddling his friend. She could nearly feel it, feel the control exchanging between them. Feel the union. Feel the power Xander held over his subject.

Bryn had never seen or experienced anything like it.

Before her eyes, Hawke's skin was turning rosy, his ass glowing from the onslaught. She wondered how he could stand it, why he wasn't screaming from the pain. Even his hands, which had been clenching the bedcoverings only moments before, were now relaxed, spread softly on the material. She could see his eyes were closed, and his facial expression was soft.

Eventually Xander slowed, easing the blows, lighter and lighter until he ultimately ceased altogether. She heard Xander's heavy breathing as he stroked Hawke's back. What struck her was how compassionately he touched the other man. The contrast between the beating and the gentle way he stroked Hawke touched something inside Bryn, something that made her heart swell with an emotion she couldn't quite name.

Longing? Perhaps. But longing for what?

When Xander turned to her, she knew what she wanted. Power radiated off him, a power she'd never known. His eyes shone, his breathing was deep and steady. He stood straight and confident. He looked ready to take on the world. And win.

She wanted to know that, wanted to experience what it was like to be in charge. In control. Powerful.

It must have shown in her eyes. Xander shook his head. "Not yet, Brian. You're not ready yet. However..."

"What?" she asked, and her voice was high and breathy.

Still naked, he approached her. She couldn't help it. Her gaze roamed over his sleek, smooth skin. When he had been dominating Hawke, he'd exuded power and control.

Her heart pounded with the need to experience such power. She raised her eyes and bit her lip, silently pleading.

He untied her, and she could smell his spicy scent. "Come with me." He took her hand, and led her across the room to place her directly behind Hawke.

Xander palmed the rosy stain of flesh on Hawke's ass. "Do you want to get fucked, H?"

"Please," Hawke said. His tone was soft. Faraway. Wanting. "Yes."

Xander picked up a phallic-shaped item from a nearby table. Of course, Bryn knew what it was—a device used for fucking. She'd seen them before. Some Jahns liked to use them on the girls. But was Xander really going to use it on Hawke?

He handed it to her. "Your turn."

The glass piece was heavy in her palm. This had never occurred to her—doing to a man what had always been done to her, to the other girls. But the idea rushed through her, nearly making her tremble with the idea. Power. She held it in her hand.

Xander picked up the jar and poured some oil around Hawke's ass. He dripped a generous amount near Hawke's anus, and Bryn's sex pounded as she watched him use his fingers to ready Hawke for what was about to happen.

What Bryn was about to do.

Xander put down the bottle and with his clean hand he took her palm and placed it on his crotch. She could feel the solid strength of his erection. She clenched her hand around him, and when he gasped, her own sex responded. Two cocks. A fake one in her hand, a real one in the other. She fisted both, loving the control as it rushed through her. She'd always known having a dick equaled power, and she was right. Two men, and she knew she could use both of them. And it would be her choice. A choice she was going to take.

Turning, she gazed at the beautiful man before her. Hawke, with the white-blond hair. First he'd helped save her from her worst nightmare, now he was giving himself to her to use. Her heart swelled with tenderness. Everything that had happened so far this night had been about her. Her safety, her pleasure. Her control.

Xander removed her hand from his crotch, and her fingers trembled as she ran her fingers over Hawke's smooth skin. She leaned down and placed a soft kiss on the redeemed flesh where he'd taken his beating. She felt his sigh. Then she took the glass piece, slid it over his slick skin and touched the edge to the rim of his anus. She steadied her trembling hands. Holding her breath, she slowly pushed the smooth glass into him. He gasped, a sound of pleasure. And the glass slid deeper.

She exhaled. This was how it felt. This was how it felt to be in charge, to fuck someone. She pulled the glass out and pushed in again. He cried out, and his pleasure fed her. Everything inside of her buzzed with desire. Power, control, dominance, lust—it all came together in a heady wave that made her feel as if she were high.

As she continued to drive the piece into Hawke's ass, he squirmed beneath her. Each time she entered him he cried out, louder and louder. She knew those noises, had become an expert in reading them. He was close, very close...

She felt a warm presence behind her. Xander. The heat from his naked body sank into her as he leaned against her body. She buried the glass piece deep into Hawke's ass and stilled. He moved back, using his own rhythm to fuck the phallic item planted deep inside of him. It was too much. Her pussy was so wet, dripping, and pounding. She couldn't think, she could barely breathe.

When Xander pressed his erection against her ass and reached around to palm her chest, she froze. He cupped her breast... He'd know.

Oh God...

"Ssssh," he whispered in her ear. "You have nothing to worry about."

Fear landed like a sinking ship in her stomach. "No—I can't—"

"I said sssh." He then squeezed her breasts and ran his thumbs over the stiff peaks of her nipples. "It's okay, love.

You're safe with us."

From the very beginning, she'd felt this. Safe. Why? What about these men made her feel safe? Pirates didn't exactly have a reputation for their humanity.

She felt the heat of Xander's breath on her neck, and a sharp nip to her earlobe. She bit her lip as the moist air sank into her, making her toes curl. Hawke moved his ass slightly, edging himself away from the glass, and then back down on it. She still held the piece in her hand.

Bryn melted. Xander's naked body behind her, Hawke's very pleasure at the mercy of her own hand. It was too much.

Xander began to undress her. She lifted her arms and allowed him to remove her tunic. She removed the cloth binding her breasts. Xander's eyes were dark with desire as she removed the rest of her clothing. Then she was naked. Totally exposed.

She raised her chin, straightened her back. She's spent so many hours naked, an object for men. But with these two pirates gazing over every curve of her body, she felt appreciated. Valued. Respected..

The glass piece still in her hand, she leaned over Hawke's back, supporting herself on one arm. His warm skin under her as she fucked him nearly sent her over the edge, but oh God...

He glanced over his shoulder and his irises were dark, a deep indigo that reflected his arousal. "It's okay, sweetheart. You're safe here.

Xander pressed himself against her back. "We have you, honey." Hot male skin covered her everywhere. She was burning. Slowly. Exquisitely.

She never knew it could be like this.

Xander stepped between her legs, spreading her. Preparing her. Her pussy ached with want. She wanted him to fill her so much it hurt. His fingers were strong and sure as they opened her wet pussy, and she gasped.

"Yes..." she said, her voice hoarse. "Captain, please..."

"Xander. Say, 'please, Xander'."

"Xander. *Please.*"

He slid his cock into her damp folds, teasing her, knowing she wanted him inside of her, but using his erection to turn her on that much more. Her hips moved back, encouraging him to give her what she wanted. She wanted him.

"Fuck me, Xander. Fuck me while I fuck Hawke."

"Is that what you want, Bryn? To fuck a man while I ravish you?"

"Yes." And the fact that he'd called her by her female name barely made it into her foggy brain. Because, at that moment, there was nothing else. Nothing mattered but desire. Fucking and being fucked by these two men. Two men who knew what she was. Two men, who, for some unknown reason, she trusted.

With a steady hand he guided himself into her. Filled her. The cry that escaped her lips was unlike anything she'd ever heard out of her mouth. With a firm grip he fisted her short hair and pulled her upright. "I'm going to fuck you, Bryn. And you're going to fuck Hawke."

"Yes," she managed. The word was slow and heavy. Sensation overwhelmed her as she focused on her hand, fucking Hawke. His cries began to mingle with her own as Xander pulled back and thrust into her. He reached around once more to cup her breasts, taking her nipples between his fingertips and pinching. It stung. It stung so much it landed right between her legs in electrifying pleasure.

"Don't stop, Bryn. You just keep fucking him, or I won't keep fucking you."

She realized, in her ecstasy, her hand had stilled, the glass piece buried deep inside Hawke's ass.

"Okay," she whispered. Because she couldn't think. She could only obey.

Mimicking Xander's movements behind her, she pulled out the piece of glass each time Xander retreated. And when he thrust, so did she. Hawke bucked against the bed. She threw her head back against Xander's chest. His hands held her steady as he continued to bead her nipples. She felt the sweat of his torso, sleek against the skin of her back.

Skin hitting skin, groans of erotic pleasure, the scent of arousal...they filled the room. There was no world beyond the ship, no brothel, no hiding. She couldn't keep her gaze off Hawke's ass and how it was *her* fucking him. It was like having a cock, and as Xander continued to fuck her from behind, she felt her climax building. Legs trembling, belly quivering, nipples throbbing.

"Come on, baby," Xander whispered in her ear. "Come for

us. Come for us right now."

"Fuck!" She screamed the word as the climax ripped through her, ripping her apart. She couldn't move. She surely would have fallen if Xander hadn't been holding her steady, if his solid weight hadn't been like a wall behind her.

Hawke thrust himself deep onto the glass piece, and she heard him groan as if it were being ripped from his mouth. She knew he was coming. Coming because she'd fucked him. Even in her hazed state of mind, the thought affected her. And as she felt Xander plunge one final time inside her, his hands squeezing her breasts as he pulsed his hot jets of come into her, another climax ruptured through her.

Time? The very idea of time passing was like an illusion. Everything seemed surreal, and her head was swimming. Was she actually conscious as Xander withdrew himself from her body? As he took her hand and released Hawke? Was she dreaming as Xander placed her naked body on the bed? She was on her side, with Hawke embracing her from behind, and the back of Xander's body pressed firmly against hers. So content. She thought she'd never felt so content in her life. And protected. Safe.

As if reading her thoughts, she felt Hawke's soft voice as he spoke against her ear. "Yes, sweet. You're safe."

She sighed. But as her eyes drifted shut she remembered Ayla, and how worried her friend would be. "My friend... I need to get her a message before we set sail."

"Sweetheart," Hawke said, and despite the short time she'd known him she knew he was grinning. "It's too late. We set sail about an hour ago."

Chapter Five

Leaning against the hull of the ship, Xander took a drag from his hemp arre'te and wondered where the fuck they were going.

The ship rolled on the gentle waters. The sky was its usual orangey hue, and he couldn't smell a storm coming. That was good. But they were on the run, and as such had to be careful where they landed. So, as usual, he was headed north, to the Lost Sea. It was rumored there were islands there in which native plants and animals had survived the Burning Time. And that's what Viven had sent him to find. Xander hadn't. But he had no plans on ceasing his search.

Their small crew was busy. Adiv was checking the supplies, and the rest of the men had their hands full since they'd taken on extra duties. At some point they'd have to go back to the ruins for more supplies, but Xander was in no hurry to do so. Instead, he continued to sail, his crew working as hard as ever to keep them going.

They'd been at sea five days. On the run from Viven, and with a refugee on the ship. A woman, a prostitute. How did he get himself into these messes?

But the girl, Bryn, didn't feel like a mess. She felt right. Her presence on the ship made everything lighter, better. After only five days, he couldn't imagine not having her onboard. Of course, the crew had been let on to the fact that Brian was actually a woman. The "crew" consisted of himself, Hawke and Adiv and a few deckhands who had remained. Adiv could be trusted. As his purser, he'd proven himself as honorable. He'd been in charge of the ship's supplies and trade for over five years.

Still, harboring a prostitute was a capital offense, and if they were caught by the Priestesses, the punishment would be a lot worse than a stab in the hand with a burning stick.

They wouldn't get caught.

He drew his gaze away from the endless turquoise sea. Hawke and Bryn lay side by side on the deck, laughing. She ran a finger down his arm, and he smiled at her. They seemed content.

The time spent in the sun had brought out the red in her hair, and her skin was turning a tawny shade of gold. She looked healthy and happy.

Watching them touched something in Xander. He'd made his own family at sea, and, deep inside, he realized he'd just added to his clan. It surprised him. He and Hawke had shared women and men previously. It was uncommon to meet a woman, but they'd sailed to places where women were free, carefully protected on secret islands. He'd been searching for the lost island so long, his travels had given him unique experiences. He'd never been jealous when Hawke had lain with another person. In fact, Xander enjoyed watching his lover's interactions because those encounters were fleeting, and no threat to their bond. What was strange...it seemed normal and natural. Xander enjoyed watching their pleasure in each other. The situation seemed complete, and anything but fleeting.

Which meant they were under his protection, and Xander would do anything to protect what was his. Even if it meant risking his life which was a real possibility if they were caught.

I own you. And everything that's yours.

After one last deep drag from the arrat'e, he flicked it into a barrel. Fuck. Now they were on the run from that fuckwad, and if he caught up with them, Xander didn't even want to think about the repercussion of having Viven discover Bryn.

"Captain. Look west."

Xander followed Adiv's gaze westward. He was staring at the sky.

In all the years they'd been sailing, Xander had seen every environmental phenomenon. The Roar, when particles from the sun swirled in a brilliant light toward earth, was the most common. They'd seen every color imaginable, and Xander often followed The Roar when it was blue, believing that would lead him to the northern edges of the earth.

But he'd never seen this.

In the distance were puffs in the sky that looked like storm clouds, but this was different. These were white, pure. Bryn joined him, as did Hawke.

"What is it?" Hawke asked, placing his hand on Xander's shoulder.

"I don't know." He walked to the main mast and twisted the lever, pointing the hull of the ship toward the fluffy white mass in the sky. "But we're going to find out."

The closer they got to the white clouds, the more Bryn could feel a shift. In everything. The air became less salty, cleaner. The sky gradated from its orange hue to something almost...blue. Xander, Hawke, Bryn and Adiv stood at the hull, mesmerized. She could feel the energy radiating off Xander's body—he was wound up like a coil.

And then...

"Holy fucking shit." He ran a hand through his hair.

She saw it too. Green. So much green all she could do was stare at the image before them. But it wasn't an image, or a mirage. It was real. And it rose out of the sea in lush abundance. Bryn put her hand over her mouth. "What is it?"

Hawke's hands were fisted on the edge of the hull. "We've found it. We've fucking found it."

Adiv barked a laugh. "Or did it find us?"

Turning away, Xander glanced over his shoulder. "Doesn't matter. Prepare for docking."

A month had passed since their arrival on the shore. During their time on the island the men had taught her how to swim in the gentle waves of the ocean. She'd learned how to carve a fish for dinner with nothing but a sharpened shell. She'd spent hours just staring at the lush plants that grew here. She'd stood under drops of warm, warm rain. Rain that came every evening and passed, leaving no havoc in its wake.

Bryn never wanted to leave. She had no clue how she'd gotten this lucky. It was barely imaginable that only a few weeks ago she'd been a captive in a brothel. That was the only life she'd known, and despite her fantasies of escape and freedom, never in a million years did she think that would actually happen. Her only concern was Ayla, and how worried she must be. That thought continued to nag at her, but she had no idea how to fix it.

And she was so wrapped up in the pleasure of it all... Now, as she lay on a hemp blanket in the sand, with Hawke's face buried between her legs and Xander's cock shoved deep in her throat, she moaned with total pleasure. She had everything she wanted, right here. Freedom. Power. Control.

And Hawke and Xander. How had she lived without them? They treated her like a princess. And she'd been exploring her sexuality in ways she'd never thought possible. Now, her eyes watered from Xander's cock as he shoved it deep in her throat. She bucked against Hawke's face. Looking up, she saw Xander's eyes were dark with desire as he withdrew and rubbed his cock around her mouth, her lips, her face. "Yes..." she said. "Please." She loved this. Loved feeling his erection on her face.

Because she loved him. She loved both of them.

"Someone fuck me," she said. "I want you both to fuck me." Her sex hurt from want. She needed to be filled. Filled with these two men.

"Fucking beautiful." Adiv was on his knees next to them, his brown skin even more tan since they'd been docked on the shore of this uninhabited paradise. Clothing was an unnecessary item, and they'd all reverted to spending most of their time in the nude. He never participated in their threesomes, but he would often watch, all the while stroking his long ebony cock. The other crew members were exploring the lush vegetation of the island, but the four of them remained on the sand, because it was simply too hard not to touch these men. And Adiv? He loved to watch, and Xander had once said he had no problem accommodating his trusted purser's voyeuristic tendencies.

Bryn's skin had also darkened under the effects of the sun. The sun. How different it was here. It shone brilliantly, brightly. Clearly. Unlike home, the air was pure and the sun's rays were like a warm blanket on her skin. She smiled. The Madam would be shocked if she saw the tanned hue of Bryn's skin.

The rush of freedom still affected her as it had that first night she'd held the phallic piece of glass in her hand. It was exhilarating, and made her heart pound. She looked up at Xander. "Get on your back so I can fuck you."

He grinned. "If you insist."

"I do. And I want Hawke from behind."

"Whatever you want, sweetheart."

She glanced at Adiv, who was pumping his cock in long, slow strokes. His gaze on her sent a jolt of arousal straight to her sex. She loved to be watched. If she could, she'd let the whole world see her having sex because she wanted to. Because she chose to. Because she had that power.

With her palm on Xander's chest, she pushed him backward. Then she climbed on top of him, and lowered her mouth to his. When he went to kiss her, she jerked away, smiling. Teasing. But then she touched her lips to his as she, finally, sank her wet pussy onto his erection, sliding up and down, using his cock to pleasure herself.

"Mmm, Xander. You're so hard. So hot."

"I do what I can."

She glanced over her shoulder, to where Hawke was kneeling, stroking his cock. The tip was just inches from her ass. "Fuck me," she said.

"All you had to do was ask."

She turned back to Xander,. Using the strength of her thighs, she rose up and plunged back down. He filled her. "Uhhh," she cried. Her legs began to tremble as she rode him. Then she felt Hawke's erection behind her, rubbing around her damp sex. She knew she was wet. They always made her wet...

He used that liquid to coat his dick. Then she felt him pushing at her other hole. She was tight and he was big, but somehow the sensation was lovely, and as he pushed in deeper her entire body froze as the bliss of having both men overwhelmed her.

"That's it, baby," Xander said. "Fuck us."

She managed to open her eyes. "No. You fuck me."

And they did. They moved in rhythm, plunging in, out. Every nerve in her body felt them. Pure desire that electrified her fingertips and made her toes curl. She braced herself on top of Xander, letting them fuck her. She felt Hawk's hair on her back, felt Xander's slick skin on her breasts. "Yes..."

And she knew Adiv was watching. Watching her be utterly filled by these two men. It fueled her, and she could feel her orgasm building deep inside of her. In her core.

"Oh God! Yes. Fuck, yes. Don't you fucking stop. Either of you, don't you fucking stop."

"No one's stopping, sweetheart. We got you," Xander said. He gripped her shoulders. Hawke held her hips. They pounded into her.

The climax shattered her, the intensity of it throwing her into utter bliss. She couldn't think, only feel. And several moments passed before the wonderful fog in her brain began to clear.

She felt Xander and Hawke ram into her and still. Then the sensation of both men filling her with their hot seed.

She collapsed on top of Xander, and felt Hawke's weight on top of her. A sigh of contentment escaped her mouth. She could stay like this forever.

Time passed. She wasn't sure how long they lay like that. Eventually, gently, Hawke removed himself from her. He then picked her up and carried her toward the sea. Xander followed.

They walked into the smooth, warm water. When the water reached his shoulders, Hawke released her, holding his hands under her back as the gentle waves lapped at her skin. They kissed her breasts, her neck, her wet stomach. The sun she had come to love so much caressed her with its rays. Unlike the hellish heat in the Wasteland, here soft clouds meandered through the sky and diffused the rays.

She never wanted to go back to Kroy Wren. Ever.

"We must return," Xander said.

Her eyes popped open. "W-what?"

Hawke nodded. "He's right. We're running low on supplies. We need to restock."

"But we have everything we need here," Bryn said, swimming away. "Fresh water, plenty of fish and vegetation to eat. Why do we need to return?"

Xander shook his head. "Trust me, I wish we didn't. But this place... We don't know the storm patterns. We don't know if there are seasons, if it will be cold. We need to be prepared, and I don't know if we are."

"I'm sure we are." Bryn waved to the shore, where a large tree was dotted with small orange globes. Fruit. There were many such trees, each one producing a different type of food. Things she'd never tasted before. "What else could we possibly need?"

Xander dove into the water and reemerged a few feet away. He tossed his wet hair away from his eyes. "That's the problem. I don't know."

"But..."

She could see the concern in his eyes when he spoke. "Trust me, going back to the ruins for supplies is the last thing I want to do. However, I'm still the Captain of this crew, and I need to make sure my people are taken care of."

"But we are."

"We don't know that," Hawke said. "This place...it seems like paradise, but the fact is, we don't know. We don't know anything. We've discovered something so unique, so rare...how do we know what the seasons will hold?"

The fear of the Burning Time was implanted deep inside anyone that was left on the planet. Bryn did know, deep down, that preparation was the key to survival.

"And there's something else."

Bryn turned to see Adiv had swum out to join them. "Who's to say no one else will discover this place? What if we are attacked? We don't have an infinite amount of weapons." He smirked. "In fact, we barely have any. If we do decide to stay here, we need to be ready. For anything."

Silence stretched between them. Finally Bryn nodded, knowing they were right. The only way to ensure they could stay here was to do as the men said. To be ready for everything and anything.

"When do we leave?" she asked.

Xander glanced back to the expanse of sea. "The sooner the better. Who's to say when and if the weather will change? If we can sail back to the ruins, restock and be back on the ship before anyone knows we're there, we could be back here within a fortnight."

She tensed. Because by now she knew Xander, knew what he was thinking. "When do we set sail?"

She wasn't at all surprised when he said, "Now."

Chapter Six

For the millionth time, Xander wondered if he was doing the right thing.

Leaning against the ship railing, he drank in the salty sea air as he smoked the last of his hemp arre'te.

Was he making the right decision? The severity of it was tearing him apart. He couldn't live forever on an island without being properly prepared. That would be irresponsible, and at the end of the day, it was Captain Xander that was responsible for his crew.

His family.

And yet his decision was bringing all of them right back to the eye of danger. And Bryn had the most to lose. If she were detected...

A rush of anger coursed through him. He stroked the handle of the dagger strapped to his right hip. He would not let anything happen to what was his. And this was all his—the ship, the people on it. He'd just keep sailing. They would never be found.

"Sighting, Captain."

Xander went to the huge metal telescope Adiv was peering through and pushed the man out of the way. Xander had been praying they'd make it as far as the outer city waters without coming into contact with another ship. Of course, luck never seemed to be on his side.

Peering through the tiny glass hole, his entire body clenched. "God dammit." A huge ship was a dot in the distance, but he could tell it was about to become a lot bigger. The bow was pointed right for them.

Hawke was already at his side. "Can you see their angle?"

"Schooner. Headed this way." Xander stomped across the deck and hoisted himself onto the main topmast. He climbed to the top and extracted a small scope from his tunic pocket. It was a powerful little piece. He'd given a trader named Ezra a gallon of fuel for the little invention. Perched on the peak of the topmast, Xander squinted through it to get a better look at the schooner. His blood ran cold.

"God fucking dammit!" He scrambled down the pole, jumping the last six feet to land with a thud on the main deck. "It looks like Viven's ship."

Hawk ran a hand over his head. "How?"

"No idea." Xander went to a trunk and began extracting weapons. He threw a hand-canon at Adiv, who caught it adeptly.

Adiv began loading the gun. "Did you get a count?"

"No," Xander said, heading toward the larger cannon. It was ancient—they'd found it within the ruins of an island in the N'eanarret Sea. It had only been fired once, and that was after a bottle of C'uerveh and the target had been a sharp island of volcanic rock.

"What's going on?" Bryn approached him, her big green eyes full of concern.

As he gazed at her, something inside Xander swelled. It was that protection thing. Annoying, but he couldn't help it. And with Viven's ship cruising straight for them, there was a distinct possibility of them finding her.

What they would do with her if they discovered who—and what—she was made everything inside him ice cold.

He nodded toward the hatch. "I want you down in the hull."

"You want me to hide?"

He wanted her nowhere near this ship, but that wasn't exactly an option. "Yes. I want you hidden. Go."

Crossing her arms over her chest, she said, "No. No way."

Xander grabbed both her shoulders. "This isn't up for debate. Go. *Now.*"

She shook her head. "I can fight."

"Yeah. We saw that when we found you in an alley."

"That was different."

"You're damn right that was different, Bryn. They were three punks in an alley. We're about to be attacked by a schooner full of wild pissed-off pirates. Do you have any idea what would happen if they discovered who you are?" Just the thought hurt.

She lifted her stubborn little chin. "I'm not hiding down there. What if something goes wrong?"

He turned away and stalked toward the cabin. "Oh, you can count on that, sweetheart. Something always goes wrong."

Bryn watched Xander walk away. How could he just expect her to do nothing if they were being attacked? She couldn't, and he couldn't make her. Did he really think it would be possible for her to hide like a coward when the people she'd come to love were being assaulted?

Inconceivable.

"Look, Captain. They're sending out a tender."

Bryn peered out at the water. Indeed, a small structure with a sail was heading their way. It consisted of two long metal pieces connected via three posts spaced throughout the center. She could see a figure steering the sails, and another figure, which was huddled in a corner.

"What do they want?" Bryn asked.

Xander and Hawke flanked her. "I don't know." Xander's hand was on the hilt of one of his daggers.

Adiv pointed the hand-cannon toward the small boat. "Holy shit."

"What?" Bryn had already figured out that Adiv's eyesight was more acute than any predator. "What do you see?"

"I would bet my life they have a woman on that boat." He glanced to Hawke. "A woman who looks incredibly like your sister."

"What?" Hawke reached into Xander's pocket and pulled out the eyeglass he always kept near his heart. Hawke peered through the glass and she saw every muscle in his body go tight. "Fuck, fuck, fuck."

"Why would they have your sister?" Bryn asked.

Xander pulled a dagger from his pocket. "Revenge." She'd never heard his voice so dark. He took a deep breath and put a hand on Hawke's back. "Is she...alive?"

"I think so...she's upright. I believe she's gagged."

Silently, they watched as the tender sailed closer to the

ship. It stopped about twenty yards away.

Bryn gasped. "Oh my God." She glanced at Hawke. "You're Ayla's pirate brother?"

He turned to Bryn. "How did you know that?"

"She was my chamber-mate. At the brothel." Her heart pounded in her throat. They had Ayla? And she was Hawke's sister?

Hawke continued to stare at his captive sister. "The High Priestess assigned Ayla to the brothel. I was taken by traders until I met Xander. I never lost track of her though. The Wasteland is dangerous. I knew she was safe inside the fortress of a brothel."

Bryn ignored Hawke's pleasant view of life as a Rose. Instead she moved on to realize why she'd immediately felt comfortable around him. His manners were familiar, his touch comforting. It all made sense.

And now they had Ayla. Imprisoned. Bryn's entire body pounded with anger. She was going to kill someone.

A fat man with a scarf tied around his head climbed to the front of the tender. Gripping the mast, he stood and faced them. "Captain Xander. You thought you would simply sail away without paying your debt?"

Xander clenched his jaw. "What do you want, Kaz?"

"Viven owns you, Captain. And owns what's yours." He nodded toward Ayla, who was bound and gagged at the back of the tender. "This girl belongs to us. And guess what? We don't want her. Women on a ship are nothing but bad luck and a hazard. We just thought we'd bring her out to show you ingrates a lesson."

It was then Bryn noticed there was a rope attached to Ayla's neck. Kaz jerked at the rope, yanking Ayla to her feet. Bryn saw her face was bruised. White-hot anger shot through Bryn like an earthquake.

Kaz gave Ayla another yank. "Viven just thought you might need a reminder of what happens when you attempt to disobey." He pulled on the rope, and Ayla stumbled forward. "We're going to dispose of this girl. Because he owns her, just as he owns you. And yours." He snarled. "Although it was fun for a while. Nice, sweet pussy. A shame I'm going to throw her overboard. But I'm sure her brother will find some satisfaction in watching her drown."

Hawke placed his hands on the hull, and Bryn knew he was about to haul himself overboard. But Xander stopped him.

Still holding Hawke back, Xander yelled, "You wouldn't dispose of such a commodity, Kaz. What do you really want?"

"You think I wouldn't?"

Ayla's eyes were wide, and she looked scared as Kaz pushed her toward the edge of the boat. "Oh, I think I would. After all, nothing else seems to get through your thick skull, Captain. Viven is quite certain you need to be taught a lesson. And put in your place." He spat into the sea. "Plus, a woman on a ship is bad luck. Isn't that so, Captain Xander?"

Xander yelled, "Come on, Kaz. You know damn well you can be bought off. What do you want?"

Kaz put a finger to his temple, as if considering his options. "What could you possibly have to offer me?"

"Fuck," Xander said under his breath. And then, louder. "Fuck."

"Tell you what," Kaz yelled. "I'll give you a few minutes to think about it. And then I throw the girl overboard."

"You do it," Hawke said, "and you'll be dead in minutes."

Kaz glanced back to the ship he'd sailed from. It was twice as large as The Sugar Skull and Bryn could see a full crew of men onboard. "And if you try anything, my crew will attack and you'll all be killed. So, yeah. You go and think about how to get out of this. I'll just be waiting right here with this sweet little Rose." He gave Ayla a lecherous glance and licked his lips. "I can find ways to amuse myself."

Bryn's entire body shook in violent tremors. She couldn't allow him to hurt Ayla. She *wouldn't* allow it.

She gently touched Xander's shoulder. Looking up, she said, "Do you think we'll have a battle?"

She watched his jaw clench. "Definitely. We have nothing to offer. We have no other choice but to fight." He took her arms in his hands with a firm grip. "Bryn. Please. I beg you. Wait in the hold."

She looked deep into his eyes and bit her lip. He wanted to keep her safe, and it was killing him. She saw it in the hard expression on his face.

Finally, she nodded. "Okay. But I don't like it."

He gave her a chaste kiss on the forehead. "Thank you,

Bryn." Then he softly shoved her toward the hold. The crew became busy, preparing for battle.

She climbed down toward the hull, but made her way to the Captain's quarters. Once inside, she unlaced her boots and shrugged off her trousers. She then went to the collection of razor-sharp shells they'd collected on the island. They'd used them for de-boning fish. Bryn smirked. Yeah, something was about to get de-boned in about ten minutes.

Even Xander and Hawke, no matter how well they'd treated her, still thought because she was a woman, she was helpless. Powerless. A liability.

But some twisted fuck had kidnapped Ayla. Bryn *did* have power, and she was about to use it.

Daily swimming lessons on the island meant Bryn was proficient in the current of the water. While the men were still preparing for what may lay ahead, she dove silently into the sea. She kept her head low as she made her way to the tender holding Ayla. Her legs kicked steadily through the water, and it took only moments before she was sneaking up on the boat.

Bryn dipped beneath the surface and emerged between the tracks. Kaz was sitting on the opposite end of the boat, smoking an arre'te that was so foul she could smell it over the scent of the sea. His eyes bugged out when his gaze discovered Bryn treading water between the metal decks of the boat.

She put her finger to her lips. "Sssh. Wouldn't want the boys to know I'm here."

Using her arms, she lifted herself up a bit. Knowing exactly how the white tunic clung to her naked skin, she watched Kaz's gaze rake over her wet body. She looked up through her lashes, giving him that look she'd perfected so well during her years as a whore.

"You stupid girl. Who are you and what do you want?" he said.

"I came to make a trade. Myself for her."

Ayla's eyes were big. The gag kept her from speaking. Good.

She lifted herself onto the boat, using her arms and legs to support her on either side of the decks. Legs and arms spread, she continued to stare at him. The tunic wetly hugged her thighs, giving him a peek of skin. But just a peek.

"Me for her. Take me."

"Why don't I take both of you?" Kaz spat. "In fact, I will. Before I kill you."

"You don't want both of us. I'll be all you need."

Kaz heaved himself to his feet and flicked the remainder of his arre'te into the sea. "Shut up. I'll fuck you while your friend watches. And then I'll shove you both overboard, and make your friends on The Sugar Skull watch."

Bryn's stomach turned as a drop of saliva dribbled from the side of his mouth. He came at her. Jerking her out of the water, he threw her to the floor of the boat.

"Please," Bryn said. "I just want you to release my friend. Take me instead."

"Fucking worthless whores, the both of you." He yanked her legs apart. "Stupid too. But who needs a brain in a whore? I just want your cunt."

"But you'll release my friend?" she asked, searching his eyes. Pleading.

He knelt between her thighs. "Fuck no." He laughed, and she felt his spit hit her face. She flinched. "I'm not releasing anyone. I'm going to see if your worthless Captain has anything of value. If so, I'll take it. Either way, my ship is still gonna blow apart The Sugar Skull and take the remains back to Viven. If there are any remains, that is."

"But..." Bryn said, squirming under his obtrusive belly. "Just take me and leave all the others alone."

The smack across her face had her seeing stars. Collecting herself, she tried to focus on him. "I'm begging you..." she said, her voice shaky.

"Not yet, bitch. But you will be." He went to move her tunic up her thighs.

"Please..." Bryn begged. "Just let Ayla and my friends go. Take me."

"Yeah. Right. That's gonna happen. Now shut the fuck up. You Roses talk too much. That's why I shoved a rag in your friend's mouth."

She felt his erection pushing against her. It all came back in a rush. The powerlessness, the vulnerability. The helplessness. It swarmed over her, entered every muscle of her body. Her heart pounded in her throat.

With his big chunk of a hand, he squeezed her breast until

she wanted to cry from the pain.

"Take it, you brainless slut."

"Please...no..." She shook her head from side to side. "Please..."

But his eyes were wide, crazy.

Good.

She slammed her legs together. He screamed. Jerking between her legs, he tried to get away. But the sharp shells she'd strapped to her thighs were buried deep in the sides of his legs. She felt his blood pouring out of his flesh, sticky on her skin.

He struggled. But the harder he fought, the deeper the shells cut into him. Looking straight in his face, she clamped tighter. "If you think I'm letting that fucking cock anywhere near me or my friend you're the only stupid cunt I can see on this piece-of-shit boat."

His eyes were dark as he stared down at her. Reaching down, he tried to open her legs in an attempt for release.

But the month of hiking and swimming in paradise had made her strong. And he was a fat, drooling slob. Also, he was probably in massive amounts of bloody pain. The battle only fueled her strength with a river of adrenaline. It seemed she was using no effort at all.

She moved her legs like scissors, using her thighs to slice his skin. More blood spilled—she was getting covered from it.

He screamed again. "Fucking whore!"

Reaching into the back of her tunic, she withdrew the dagger strapped to her back. Looking up, she smiled. "Not anymore."

She then plunged the dagger straight into his heart. Blood gushed from the wound. Grimacing, she turned away. "Gross."

He spasmed, and she watched as the man died. A big bloody mess, his eyes finally went dark, and he collapsed on top of her.

"Ew." She shoved him off. Then she climbed over to Ayla and released her gag. "Are you okay?"

"Bryn?" Ayla shook her head. "I've been so worried... What are you doing here?"

"I'll explain later." She cut the rope off of Ayla's neck. "Let's get back to the ship." She yanked her friend to her feet.

"Bryn. You know I can't swim." Ayla shook her head. "And neither could you ."

"I've learned a lot since you last saw me, Sister." She took Ayla's hands in hers. "It's okay. Trust me."

"Do I have a choice?"

Bryn grinned. "No. You don't."

They turned to the water. With a last glance at each other, they grabbed hands and jumped into the sea.

"What the fuck?"

Xander and Hawke rushed toward them. Hawke went straight to his sister and wrapped her in a fierce hug.

Xander, on the other hand, did not look happy. He grabbed Bryn's shoulders, stepped back and raked her over in one all-assessing swoop of his gaze. The sea had washed away all the blood from her body, but her tunic was still stained.

"Holy fuck. Are you okay?"

She nodded. "Yes. I'm fine."

"What did you do?" He gave her a shake. "*What did you do?*"

Releasing herself from Xander's grip, she unstrapped the shells from her legs. "I saved Ayla."

"By yourself?" Xander said incredulously.

She threw a belt of shells to the floor. "Um. Yeah?"

He just stared at her. She wondered if he might kill her.

But he yanked her into his arms and buried his nose in her hair. "You...*fuck*, Bryn."

She hugged him back. The adrenaline that had been coursing through her was ebbing, and she felt her body begin to shake. He held her tight.

Still clutching Ayla, Hawke turned to Bryn. "If you didn't just save my sister...I'd throttle you."

Bryn managed a smile. "But I did. So you can't."

"I'm impressed."

The words had come from Adiv, and they turned to look at him. He was gazing at Bryn with an expression of admiration. "I can't believe you had the balls."

She couldn't help but smile back at the big man. "Yeah. Well, turns out...you don't need a cock to be a fucking man."

Epilogue

Lounging on the deck, Bryn glanced at Ayla. They were wearing scarves around their hips and breasts. Hawke refused to let his sister run around the ship naked, so both women had been obliging enough to cover up their female parts.

Bryn took Ayla's hand. "He's looking at you again."

She saw the flush creep up Ayla's pale neck. "You think?"

Glancing at Adiv, who was checking stock in the infirmary trunk, Bryn grinned. "Um, yeah. I do."

"He is kind of..."

"Hot?"

Ayla's cheeks turned red. How strange to see a former prostitute blush. She turned toward Bryn and bit her lip. "He is, isn't he?"

"He's a voyeur, but something tells me he wants to be a bit more participatory when it comes to you."

Ayla looked to Adiv, who quickly whipped his gaze off the gorgeous redhead. He went back to sorting hand-cannons.

"Yeah," Bryn said. "He is so into you."

Xander walked over to the women. "It's bad luck to have women on a pirate ship."

Hawke came over and took his place next to the Captain. Their shadows cast out the orangey light of the sun. Bryn couldn't wait to get back to the clear sky of their haven.

"Bad luck to have women on a ship, you say?" Bryn said.

"Yeah." Hawke took a seat on a nearby stool. "But you rescued Ayla, killed the captain of Viven's ship. I'm beginning to wonder if that little idiom is true."

Bryn gave him a nonchalant look. "Don't forget. I bought off the rest of Viven's crew with my jeweled earbob."

"Right," Hawke said. "Can't forget that."

Bryn tilted her head and grinned. "So. You still think women on a ship are bad luck?"

Taking her hand in his, Xander squatted next to her. "I suppose we can make an exception." He kissed the back of her hand. "In fact, I can't imagine being on this ship without you. Or your new partner-in-crime."

Hawke looked at Bryn, and his eyes were dark and serious. "Bryn." He nodded toward her. "You have my ever-long devotion."

"That's not necessary. I was just saving my friend."

"And I am indebted."

Bryn lifted herself onto her elbows. "Is that so?"

He nodded. "Indeed."

"Then get us back to the ruins, get our supplies and get us the fuck back to paradise."

Xander squeezed Bryn's hand. "That's affirmative, woman. And after we leave the ruins, it's nothing but us, the open seas and..."

"What?" Bryn asked, searching his eyes.

"When we reach land, you girls are going to have to remain on the ship. It's too dangerous for you to be wandering around the ruins."

She touched Xander's arm. "What about Viven? He'll still be looking for you. He'll be more angry with you than ever because of what happened at sea. Will you—*we*—ever be free from his wrath?"

Xander's eyes went cold. She felt the muscles of his arm clench beneath her touch. He said, "Don't worry about Viven."

Hawke was staring at Ayla. "We're going to pay that man a visit. And he won't be bothering us again. We have things to protect now."

A chill raced up Bryn's back. She was afraid for the men's safety, but she could see the determination in their eyes. She knew if she was going to choose this life there would be risks, and scary moments. But Xander and Hawke weren't stupid. If they had a plan to take care of Viven, she would just have to trust them.

If she were to choose this life, she was going to have to

trust them.

She did.

Xander took her hand, reassuring her with gentle strokes from the pad of his thumb. "We'll return from the ruins. Safe and sound. And Viven won't be bothering us again." His eyes darkened, and he held her gaze. "And then you know what awaits us?

"Freedom. There can't be just one island... I believe there's an entire new world to be discovered. One with no rules, no castes, no trading yourself for a life of servitude."

Bryn's heart swelled. She knew what he meant. During the weeks they'd been sailing since the incident with Kaz, Xander had made it glaringly obvious the only man who was ever going to touch her again, other than himself, was Hawke. Thanks to these men, she'd never see the walls of a brothel again.

Bryn was fine with that.

Settling back onto the hemp blanket, she closed her eyes and felt. Felt the sea, felt the waves beneath the ship. Felt freedom. She smiled. "Let's do it," she said. "Let's just sail. The world is more than we ever imagined, and I want to discover everything that's out there." She squeezed Xander's hand. "With you."

"You got it, baby. After we get re-stocked at the ruins, we'll find our oasis."

Eyes still closed, Bryn grinned. "Oh. I think we already have."

About the Author

Lillian Feisty expected to write typical boy-meets-girl tales. But so often the characters wanted to be tied up by each other. Lilli had to oblige. Her love of writing spicy romance evolved, and the next thing she knew, she was published. Her first erotic novella was released in March 2007, and she's been consistently pursuing her passion ever since.

Lilli was born in the San Francisco Bay Area. She spent the majority of her twenties working just enough to pay for extended trips to Europe. Some of her fascinating employment titles included makeup artist, secretary and perpetual student. She owned an art gallery for several years, holds a degree in Creative Arts and was just a thesis short of her MA when she decided to drop out of school to write romance.

For more fascinating Feisty information go to www.lillianfeisty.com.

Look for these titles by
Lilli Feisty

Now Available:

Sting of Desire

The Breeder

Eden Bradley

Dedication

To my fellow Smutketeers: R.G. Alexander, Crystal Jordan and Lilli Feisty, for developing this world with me, for being their fabulously smutty selves, and for being my partners in crime, always.

Prologue

In 2012, the world came to a grinding halt as radiation hit from a massive solar storm. Crops died, animals perished, cities fell and humans became little more than beasts themselves. Under the threat of starvation, civility was reduced to mere memory. Only the strongest men survived, and physically weaker women and children wasted to nothingness.

More than a century later, humanity struggles in the desert Wasteland. The solar radiation rendered most women infertile, and the population dwindles more with each year that passes. Scattered up and down coasts, isolated cities eke out an existence from fishing, foraging and hunting for what little game is left. Outside the city walls, men face the threat of pirates and raiders.

Few women remain, divided into four classes—Whores, Breeders, Priestesses and Wanderers. They are as reviled as they are worshipped, a commodity any man must pay to touch. To touch a Whore, a man must sacrifice his riches. To touch a Breeder, a man must sacrifice his freedom. To touch a Priestess, a man must be chosen by the gods. And to touch a Wanderer may end up costing him his life.

There is only one rule in the Wasteland—survive.

Chapter One

The scent of burning sage hung heavy in the air, along with the tinkling of cymbals and a keen anticipation. The citizens of Kroy Wen filled the Temple of the Great Goddess—The Unnamed One. Hundreds of men gathered together in the vaulted caves that housed the Temple, pressing as close as the guards would allow.

Nitara watched, silent and filled with yearning, from behind the curtain which kept the novitiate Breeders hidden and separate from the men, for no Breeder was seen or touched by any man until the day of her Sacrifice. Today was such a day.

Seti, one of Nitara's sister Breeders, walked down the center aisle of the vast Temple, the floors and walls impossibly smooth, the ceiling arching high overhead. No one knew how this place had been made, but it was said the Goddess had carved the Temple from the mountain herself, and polished it to reflect her own perfection.

Seti's dark head was held high as she moved, her curved body clothed in the sleeveless red tunic of the Breeders, the cowl pulled over her head so that her face was shadowed, hidden from view. Her narrow waist was belted by a wide blue sash, signifying her transition into womanhood. The firelight of the torches gleamed in her hair, which fell to her waist in a soft curtain.

Cymbals clanged, the chanting of the Crone Priestess growing louder as Seti approached the altar, a high stone slab, which was draped in furs and linens. A eunuch stood guard at the head of the stone slab, his eyes on the citizens, most carefully not watching the young Breeder who moved slowly toward the altar, and the man who was bound there—naked, drugged, erect.

The Sacrifice.

Nitara's heart beat faster as Seti stopped, bowed before the altar and lowered the cowl, the draped fabric falling to bare her stomach and the rise of her lush, round breasts. A cheer went up from the onlookers at Seti's dark beauty, and Nitara saw a small smile light her friend's face before she walked up the stone stairs of the altar. Seti climbed onto the stone slab, standing over the Sacrifice, one bare foot on either side of his body. Nitara saw the strain of his muscles, his skin sheened in sweat. He was a man of the Wanderer clans, as the Sacrifices always were. The men of those bands which wandered the Wasteland were hardy, survivors, and kept the blood of the children the Breeders bore to the earth strong.

The Sacrifice moaned as Seti untied her sash and laid it over his stomach, then pulled her tunic over her head. The crowd cheered, tension rising at the sight of her female figure, something which was denied them unless they were lucky enough to be chosen to breed in the monthly lotteries, to indulge the pleasures of the priestesses, or could afford the brothels, which the young Breeder girls knew of only by whispered rumor.

Seti's body was ripe, her breasts and hips full, her skin a deep, lovely brown. Her nipples were hard, her sex shaved in preparation for the ritual. A dagger hung from a cord around her hips in its ceremonial sheath. The precious leather was inscribed with ancient images of the Great Goddess, the fertility symbols which had existed longer than anyone could remember, predating even the Burning Time, the punishment of the earth by the Angry Sun over a hundred years earlier.

Cymbals clanged, and the Crone's chanting grew louder, faster. The Breeders watching from their curtained alcove joined in the chanting. Nitara said the words, warm and familiar on her tongue, without thinking of their meaning. She was too entranced watching Seti as she began to sway, her hands running over her naked flesh. Nitara's sex ached, reminding her of her lessons with the High Priestess Xian, who had trained her in the sensual arts since Nitara was twelve, and which she would use very soon, in preparation for her own Sacrifice.

Soon...

Her pulse raced. It was not only the anticipation of doing

her duty to the Goddess which excited her, but the prospect of being touched by a man for the first time. The sensation of a cock filling her, finally. She had waited her whole life for that moment. Witnessing Seti sacrifice her virginity to the Goddess was an exquisite kind of torture, her body heating, the heat pooling between her thighs.

She watched as Seti cupped her breasts, her fingers brushing the hard tips, then smoothing down over her hips, between her rounded thighs. Nitara let out a small sigh, and another as her Sister lowered herself over the hard cock of the Sacrifice. He groaned aloud, and Seti began to pump, raising and lowering her body. The crowd hushed, the chanting stopped. Even from where she sat, Nitara could hear the collective panting of Seti, her Sacrifice, and the watching citizens, all of them joined together in a quickly rising sexual frenzy.

Seti's hand was working between her thighs, and the big hands of the Sacrifice, allowed just enough give within the binding ropes, went to her hips, his fingers digging into the soft brown flesh. Nitara couldn't tear her gaze from his face, beautiful in his lustful agony. His eyes were tightly shut, his lips parted. He was trying to thrust up into Seti, and she ground down onto him. Soon her panting turned to cries of ecstasy. She threw her head back, shuddering as she came. His body tensed, and something in that moment hit Nitara like a hard kick of lust deep in her belly. She went damp, wanting. And as Seti continued to arch her hips over him, milking him of his seed, Nitara could hardly stand it, to watch and not to have it for herself. She was shivering. Needing.

Soon...

Seti's motion slowed, and he groaned, his head falling to one side. She thrust once more, grinding onto him. Then, taking the dagger from its sheath, she raised it high over her head. The blade glinted in the torchlight, the flames reflecting red and orange on the polished metal as her lips moved in prayer, asking the Goddess for bounty, for a child. He looked up, his eyes fluttering open, his staring gaze on the curtain behind which Nitara stood with her Sisters. There was fear on his face, in his dark eyes, pure and frightening. Stark. And it was as though he could see her standing there, watching.

Nitara held her breath, her body filled with desire and a

vague sense of panic she had never felt before, no matter how many times she had watched this same ritual. As she watched, Seti took a breath, and brought the dagger down, plunging it into the chest of the Sacrifice.

The crowd cheered. The Sacrifice made no noise as the blood spouted, splashing Seti's naked body, pooling on the linens and the furs. His mouth widened in a grimace of pain, his eyes wide with grief. Seti pulled the knife from his quivering body, and still joined with him, used the point to trace the outline of the eight-pointed star tattooed in red just below her navel, leaving it marked in blood.

Nitara was shaking. She didn't understand the sensations warring in her body, her mind. Her heart. This was the most sacred of rituals—the Sacrifice of a Breeder's virginity to the Goddess, often resulting in a child, a gift to the scorched and barren earth. She should be joyous. But something in the face of the Wanderer...

She had seen his humanity.

How had she not recognized this before? Had she been so blinded by her duty to the Temple that she'd never realized the Wanderers, the men Sacrificed on the altar in the name of the Goddess, were more than animals who roamed the Wasteland, fierce and primitive and soulless?

It came to her that her own mother was likely a Wanderer now, if she still lived. Nitara hadn't seen her since she was six years old, but that connection remained in her heart. Once a priestess, she had been caught in the arms of her lover, a Sun Guard of the Temple, in the city, and had been banished for the sin of unconsecrated sex. Nitara, chosen as a cherished Breeder from birth, suffered no consequences for her mother's actions. But her twin brother, Nikkan, had been castrated, and had since served as a eunuch guard to the novitiate Breeders, the only men they had contact with until reaching the age of twenty, and the ritual of Sacrifice.

She brought her gaze once more to the altar, watched as Seti was helped down by the guards. The High Priestess Xian stepped forward and blessed Seti, praying over her and smearing the blood of the Sacrifice onto her forehead, her breasts, her belly. Nitara whispered the prayers with her priestess, but she did not feel the presence of the Goddess within her. She felt only a dull ache that had nothing to do with desire, but was instead a tight pain in her chest.

Her heart was a hammer, loud and fierce. Her very doubts frightened her. She barely took in the scene below as Seti was led, naked and covered in blood, back up the aisle in a small procession. Xian led with Seti behind her, followed by a pair of guards, then lastly the Crone, chanting in praise of the Goddess.

Nitara pressed one hand to her chest, trying to calm herself. She felt torn suddenly between sympathy for the Wanderer and the duty she owed to her Goddess. One she would surely pay, no matter her feelings.

She could not look at the dead man on the altar. She could not think of him any other way, suddenly. As an animal. A Wanderer. The Sacrifice.

She would have to calm down. To accept her fate and that of the man she would have to kill in little more than a month's time.

Nitara floated in some lovely place, light, airy, warm. Not her sleeping rooms, nor the vast caverns of the Temple. Not the dark and womblike subterranean Sanctuary she had seen only once, when she'd reached maturity, and where she would someday spend her Taming Moon.

No, just light and air and the warmth of a body next to hers.

She turned into the hands reaching for her. Fingers stroked her skin—her belly, the undersides of her breasts. Her nipples peaked hard, aching, but it was nothing compared to the ache between her thighs.

"Please," she breathed.

Palms smoothing over her thighs now, but the skin was rough. Not the hands of a priestess, but the rougher hands of a man.

Hands she had never felt.

She sighed, spread her thighs, pleading silently for what she desired. What she was born and bred for. Trained for. What she *needed*.

The fingers feathered over her sensitive flesh, down, down, over the insides of her thighs, so close to her sex, which was pulsing with desire.

"Please," she said again, her voice a lost echo in the misty light.

Why should she have to beg? Any man of the cities would pay to have her. Would die to have her.

One man would, very soon.

A finger slipping into her damp cleft, over the hard nub of her clitoris. And she came, shattering, her body clenching in a pure, dazzling pleasure that left her panting, blinded. Smiling.

"Wake up, Nitara." It was Leilin's soft voice.

Nitara sighed, stretched, opened her eyes. "I'm sleepy, Sister."

Leilin was her sister in truth, by birth, not only a sister Breeder of the Temple. She was much older than Nitara, retired now, having birthed twelve children. Now she helped care for the young novitiates, and for the Temple itself—cooking, making beautiful pottery from the clay brought in from the deserts, weaving fabric on the big looms in the rooms set high into the mountainside, where the light of the Sun shone most brightly.

"Lazy, Nitara," Leilin scolded gently. "It is the day of your initiation. You must not leave Xian waiting."

Nitara sat up, throwing back the sleeping furs and rose, naked, from her bed. Her heart was beating a hard rhythm again, as it had the day before during the Sacrifice, that strange combination of desire and doubt. "Of course not, Sister."

She washed quickly in the clay bowl of precious water, drying her face on a small woven towel. Leilin helped her slip the red Breeder tunic over her head, smoothing the cloth over her rounded hips, then tying the white sash signifying purity.

"Let me help with your hair, Nitara. It looks as if you've been standing in a high wind rather than sleeping." Leilin picked up the comb carved from precious shell and began the task of dragging it through her long hair. A Breeder never cut her hair, and Nitara's reached nearly to her knees, long, waving strands of fine, light brown.

"No one can comb my hair the way you can," Nitara sighed, enjoying the attention. Her body was buzzing from her lovely dream, but still held that edge of discomfort she didn't know how to identify. "Leilin, did you dream of men before your Sacrifice?"

"We all do. It is a sign from the Goddess that you are nearly ready. And after all, you will turn twenty in three day's time. Go

151

to Xian now, and may the Goddess bless you, Sister."

Nitara kissed Leilin's cheek, then turned and followed the corridors cut into the mountain, the flat sides polished smooth, the ancient green and white tiles blurring together at the edge of her vision in her haste. She was too excited to think as devoutly of the Goddess as she should on such an important day, a problem she had all too often. Excited and tense with anticipation, she picked up her bare feet, moving faster toward the Priestess Xian's rooms. She paused in the doorway to catch her breath, nervous suddenly.

Xian had her back to her, still involved with her morning bath. The Priestess was naked, her lush figure all lovely curves, her skin a smooth expanse of faint gold. Her black hair hung like a sheaf to her waist. When she turned at the sound of Nitara's entrance, she saw her unusual violet eyes, large and tilted at the corners, the irises edged in brilliant blue.

Nitara thought Xian the most beautiful of Priestesses. But of course, she was biased. Xian had been mother, sister, lover and friend to her.

"Nitara, there you are."

Xian slipped into the robes of her station, a long, high-necked drape of simple, dark blue cloth. The front panel was sheer, exposing the length of her body from neck to toes, in honor of the sacred sexuality of the Goddess, of which the priestesses were an incarnation on Earth.

Nitara stepped into the room. "Good morning, Xian." Moving closer, she took a necklace of twisted copper wires and bits of sun-glass from the Priestess's dressing table and handed it to her.

"Good morning, Nitara." Xian fastened the necklace around her throat. "We will go to the Crone this morning to receive your fertility mark."

Nitara nodded, smiling.

Xian reached out, stroked her cheek with a soft fingertip. "You look nervous. You do not remember receiving your Breeder's mark—you were too young. They will give you herbs to drink to dull the pain."

"It's not the pain that worries me, Xian."

"What is it, then?"

"I...I wish my mother was here to see..."

"I know. But be sure never to let anyone else hear you

speak of her, but Leilin or myself or your brother, Nikkan."

"I am always careful. But even though she's been gone all these years, I miss her. And I will never understand why she had to be banished. Or why my brother had to pay for her sins by being made a eunuch."

Xian's voice was soft. "These are the ways of the Temple. We must accept."

Nitara sighed. "Do you never question the rules, the rituals, the ways of the Great Goddess?"

Xian bit her lip, her gaze serious. "Nitara, this is not the time for you to doubt your devotion to the Goddess. You are to become a woman today. Tell me you are ready."

"I am ready. It's only that my mind wanders sometimes..."

"You must rid your mind of these distractions. You must show faith in the Goddess and in the rightness of what we do to see that mankind continues to flourish on the earth. This is your purpose."

"I'm sorry, Xian. I will not disappoint you. I will put my mind at ease, and trust in the Goddess."

Her mind was still turning.

"Good girl." Xian laid both hands on Nitara's shoulders. "Think only of the Goddess. Focus on your duty to Her, your love for Her. Your obligation to mankind. Let your mind empty of all but prayer, so that you are pure for the marking ritual."

Nitara nodded, and did as Xian asked. She took a long breath, training her mind on the image of the Goddess, all that was female and fertile. Sacred.

"We'll go now, to prepare you to be marked."

Xian held out a hand, and Nitara took it. Her touch was warm, familiar, helping her to push those traitorous ideas to the back of her mind. They would linger there, waiting, those questions which would never be answered to her satisfaction.

Today she must not think of these things. Today she would become a woman. And soon after, she would begin her Taming Moon, the month-long period with the man who would take her virginity, a sacrifice to the Goddess. The moment for which she had been trained most of her life.

Xian led her out of her chambers and along the corridor, then down a long flight of stairs, into the bowels of the Temple. Nitara remained quiet, searching out that meditative place within herself, calming her thready pulse.

Xian led her into a dim room she had never seen before, deep beneath the earth. A fire burned in a pit in the center of the room, and it was warm, stuffy, smelling of sage and burning coal.

Next to the pit sat Meidra, the Crone, the eldest Priestess of the Temple at Kroy Wen, on a small stool. Her face and hands were lined, her black eyes small and weary-looking. It was by her hand the Breeders and priestesses of the Temple were marked, and had been for as long as any could remember. With her were two younger priestesses, newly initiated and training to learn the art of the tattoo as Meidra neared the end of her lifespan.

They each bowed their heads as Xian entered, a sign of respect to the High Priestess.

"I bring you Nitara," Xian said.

Meidra gave a small nod of her head, and the two younger priestesses silently took Nitara by the arms and brought her to stand before the Crone.

"Drink this," Meidra told her, handing her a small ceramic cup. "The taste will be bitter, but your marking will be easier for it, and after you will sleep and dream."

Nitara took the cup and drank, and it was as bitter as Meidra said it would be. She glanced at Xian, who stood on the other side of the fire pit, her face somber. Then the two younger priestesses moved closer and quickly stripped her tunic from her. Nitara shivered, even through the heat of the room, waiting. She focused on the motions of the Crone as she mixed the dark red ink in a bowl made of polished bone, muttering a prayer as she worked.

Soon Nitara found herself floating, as she did in her dreams. And when the two young priestesses began to smooth their hands over her naked body, the sensation of lightness increased, their sensual touch helping to soothe her, to release her mind.

Their fingers were sweet and teasing at her nipples, the cleft between her thighs. She grew wet, her body softening with sensation. She didn't know how long it went on, the gentle stroking, the sensual shivers in her body.

After some time Meidra said, "We are ready to begin."

The priestesses held Nitara's arms firmly, and began to

chant quietly as Meidra dipped her needle, a long, hair-thin length of sharpened metal wire, into her bowl of ink, and brought it to Nitara's belly.

There was no pain at first. Just a scratching sensation as Meidra worked the ink into her skin, just below her navel. The scratching became harder, burning a little. She was aware of Meidra's bent head, inches from her body, but it was almost as if she watched from some far-away place.

It was over quickly. The two young priestesses took her to a bed piled high with furs and laid her down on it. Her naked skin was hot, fevered, and the eight-pointed star, the fertility symbol of the Goddess, engraved on her belly in red, burned as if branded there.

Xian stood over her, her beautiful face looking down at her. "You will sleep now, Nitara. And you will dream. Dream of the children you will give to the Goddess. To the earth."

A cool hand on her cheek for one moment, then Xian was gone, leaving Nitara to drift, her mind leaving her body, the heat and the burning pain behind.

He was dark—eyes and hair and demeanor. Beautiful. Angry.

A stranger. But somehow, she knew he was for *her*.

They were in a dark place, lit by torches set into the walls, by candles made from animal fat, making gray smoke. She could smell it, could feel it in her nostrils when she inhaled.

He was watching her. And as he watched, she ran her hands over her full breasts, down her sides, over her curving hips. His gaze on her was animal, sexual.

He was the one, her Sacrifice. He would desire her. He would take her virginity on the altar of the Goddess. And then, as had been ordained for more than a hundred years, she would take the sacred knife and plunge it into his heart.

There was chanting in the air, along with the smoke, the chanting of a hundred priestesses, like some dark music in her head. And she knew she was meant to sink into it, to feel the Goddess inhabit her body. This was the beginning of her purpose in life. Her duty to her Goddess. Why then, did it hurt her?

She held the knife over his chest. His breath was a ragged pant of need and fear and fury. But she could not do it.

She could not do it.

Tears ran down her face, tears she had not cried since she was a child.

The chanting grew louder.

Please stop.

It was a storm in her ears, a crashing thunder.

Stop...

But the words were only in her head, and the chanting continued, mocking her, demanding of her.

She raised the knife, which was wet with blood. His blood. But she hadn't done it yet, had she?

She looked down, found him still breathing, his dark eyes pleading with her.

She could not do it. *Would* not do it.

The chanting was inside her head now, drowning out all other thought. She struggled against it, against the drugs making her dizzy, making her feel as if she couldn't move, her body lying nearly paralyzed on the bed.

"Sacrifice."

No.

"Sacrifice."

No!

"Sacrifice."

"No!" she screamed.

All went black. And all she could hear were her own tortured sobs ringing in her ears.

Chapter Two

Nitara came awake. She was shaking. Glad to open her eyes and find Leilin sitting next to her.

"Ah, you're back, Little Sister."

Nitara blinked, trying to clear the images from her mind. But they lingered, dark and frightening.

"Leilin, I dreamed."

"You're supposed to dream."

"But it was not of the babies I would bring to birth."

"No." Leilin smoothed a cool, wet cloth over Nitara's face. "I watched you as you slept. I knew your dreams were not the birthing dreams. Tell me what you saw."

"I felt as much as I saw. It was the Sacrifice. *My* Sacrifice. But there was no joy in it. There was only a terrible sorrow and blood and...tears. What does it mean? Does the Goddess reject me?"

Her heart was a hammer in her chest, her fingers gripping the furs laid over her body.

"I was waiting for this," Leilin said, sighing.

"What do you mean?"

Leilin's voice was so low she could barely make out her words. "I hoped it wouldn't happen to you. It seems the women of our line are doomed to suffer for our service to the Goddess."

Nitara sat up too suddenly, and her head spun. "I don't understand. Doomed? Leilin, you frighten me."

"I had the dreams, too, at my marking. So did our mother."

"Our mother? How do you know this?"

"Shh. You must keep your voice down." Leilin glanced over her shoulder, at the doorway, then back again. "You must not speak of this, do you understand? Not to anyone."

"Leilin, I don't understand."

"It is better not to. Put it out of your mind. Here, look at your mark. You are a woman, now. A Breeder."

She pulled the furs back, and it was then Nitara realized she was in her own bed.

The star on her belly was drawn in red ink, a blaze against her pale skin. She reached down to touch it, but Leilin grabbed her hand.

"It will be healed by the next moon, the time of your Sacrifice. Your Taming Moon begins the day after tomorrow, the day of your twentieth birthday."

The dream was fading from Nitara's mind, along with her doubts, and she felt the long-awaited elation of what was to come: her entrance into womanhood, her service to the Goddess.

"You will spend these next two days preparing yourself with baths and herbs," Leilin told her, "purifying your body. Then you will go down to the Sanctuary to meet your Sacrifice."

A small shiver ran through Nitara, a flashing image of blood on her hands. Then it was gone. She couldn't seem to get her mind to focus.

"I'm so tired, Leilin."

"It is the drugs. Sleep now. Tomorrow you will begin."

Nitara lay back on her furs. Her body was humming with a sensual buzz, the response she had been trained to since puberty.

Her Sacrifice. The first man to touch her.

She shivered, a lovely wave of desire, like heat just beneath her skin, in her breasts, her sex.

She closed her eyes, heard Leilin's footsteps as she left the room. She was so sleepy. But her body was alive with need.

She spread her thighs, slipping a hand between them. Her cleft was damp, slick. She slid her fingers in between the folds, pleasure rising. The fog in her head threatened to overtake her, but she fought it off.

In her mind's eye, she saw a pair of hands, masculine, rough. Male. Her body burned for that touch.

Would he be gentle with her, the way Xian was? What would it be like, to feel him inside her, to feel him thrusting,

thrusting, coming into her?

She moved her fingertips over her clitoris, then lower, to tease at her entrance, being careful never to slip more than the barest tip inside. To preserve her virginity. She must remain untouched for another month.

She squeezed her eyes tight, her hands becoming the hands of a lover, the hands of a man, circling her swollen clitoris. She pressed harder, rubbing until it nearly hurt. And heard in her head a deep voice, saying her name...

Nitara.

Her body tensed, trembled on that lovely edge. She pressed down on her clit, her hips arching as she came. Her sex clenched, flooding with heat, and she gasped, trembling.

She was floating again, this time on the last waves of her climax. The waves shivered over her skin, gently, gently. Until finally, she slept once more.

Akaash opened his eyes, tried to sit up. But he couldn't move.

All was dark around him, but he remembered now...

They had come upon him at night. He'd been alone in a small cave in the mountains, sleeping after a long, successful hunt, and three days in the Wasteland. He'd thought it was road pirates, come to steal the meat he'd killed. They were on him so quickly, and in such numbers, that they had him bound and thrown onto the back of a horse before he understood they were the guards of the temple.

But he was no longer bound to a horse. He was lying on the earth, iron cuffs on his wrists attached to long lengths of precious iron chains. All was silent around him. And although the chains had some give to them, he could not move a muscle.

He'd heard of the drugs they used to keep their prey calm and still. To seduce the men of the Wanderer clans into serving their purposes with aphrodisiacs, using them as breeding stock to keep their bloodlines strong. He'd heard the girls used as breeders were beautiful, but of course, none of the Wanderers had ever seen them and lived to report back. Only those men of the cities chosen in the lottery to breed with them each month saw them. Except for those few Wanderers who were kidnapped, used. And killed.

He knew what his fate would be if he didn't escape. But he

could not move a muscle.

He wondered what Dhatri, his bonded lover, would think if he knew. Dhatri was the Chief Warrior, the best fighter of the Mutairi clan, fierce and brave. He would be ashamed, as Akaash was himself. Even if he escaped now, he could never overcome the disgrace of being taken. He had been a Warrior. And now, he was fallen prey.

He peered through the dark, trying to see...anything. And after a few moments, his eyes adjusted enough for him to see that he was in a cage of sorts, with bars made of the old iron, so precious since the Burning Time. He was in the dungeons of the temple, then. Impossible to escape, or so it was said.

He lay still for a long time, hours, perhaps, alone with his humiliation in the dark. He was thirsty, dizzy from the drugs. And his cock was hard, standing ready. He grew angrier by the moment, thinking of what they'd done to him, of this vile helplessness.

Finally, a shaft of light dazzled his eyes as someone came near with a torch. He blinked until his vision cleared. In front of him was a man, a guard of the temple, in a short, dark robe he recognized as the garb of the eunuchs who watched over the breeder girls. The man was young. His face was shaved smooth, his eyes a pale green, his features almost girlish in their prettiness. His body was lean, but his shoulders were broad. Had the situation been different, and had the boy been able, he was beautiful enough that Akaash would gladly take him to bed, part the smooth cheeks of his tender ass, and push into him...

He shook his head, reminding himself fiercely that this pretty piece of flesh was the enemy.

"You there," Akaash demanded, irritated at the unevenness in his voice. "Tell me where I am, and what is to happen to me."

The guard moved aside, and from behind him stepped a girl. She was petite, her head reaching to the guard's shoulder. Her long, waving brown hair was a soft veil around her curving form, touched with gold from the light of the torch. She wore the red garment of a Breeder, the cowl draped low in the front, revealing her full breasts, the fabric just covering her nipples. But it was her face Akaash found so arresting. Heart-shaped, innocent-looking, with high, rounded cheekbones, and the same pale green eyes as the guard. And her mouth...the pink lips full and generous, almost too lush in her otherwise-sweet face. Lips that could do wicked things to a man...

His cock filled even more, pulsing to life. He cursed its betrayal silently. This girl, too, was the enemy.

"You are in the Sanctuary of the Temple at Kroy Wen," she said, her voice soft and as sweet as her face. "You have been chosen by the Great Goddess, for the good of mankind and of the earth."

"Your goddess," Akaash said bitterly. "A goddess I don't believe in. This is why I am to lose my life? This is why I've been shamed?"

"Yes," she said simply, smiling.

His cock rose once more between his legs, and with it he felt a tingling in his fingertips. He still could not move, but the return of the sensation gave him the first glimmering hope of escape. He could not die here in this strange place, for a goddess he did not know.

"And why are you here?" he asked the girl. "What part are you to play in this?"

"I am Nitara, Breeder of the Temple. It is my duty to repopulate the Earth."

"And I'm to help you do it? I am to lie with you, to impregnate you? I will not do it."

But his hardening cock belied his words. His body wanted her, even as his mind rebelled. She was beautiful, this girl, lush and sensual. And he had not had a woman for a long time. Dhatri was a superb lover—he had no complaints. But the touch of a woman was different, rare...

"Tell me your name, Wanderer," the girl said, stepping closer.

"I am Akaash."

"You're more aware than I'm told the Sacrifice should be. More lucid. Do the herbs not affect you?"

"Apparently not."

Better that she not know he could barely move, how much effort it took simply to speak.

"Strange. I should tell the priestesses..."

He waited for her to turn away, but she stood there, watching him.

"What are you looking at?" he asked finally, gruffly.

"At you. You are more beautiful than I expected. And I have never seen a man other than our eunuch guards this close. You look different than they do. More...a man."

He didn't know what to say, so he remained silent.

"I should go," she murmured.

"Go then. Tell your priestess. Have me drugged senseless."

She turned, then, whispering to the guard, and they both disappeared, returning shortly with a small cup and three other guards. The eunuchs opened the gate and came into his cell. Two held his shoulders, another his face, and the beautiful boy with the green eyes held his mouth open with strong fingers and poured a bitter liquid in. Akaash sputtered, choking as it went down his throat, as he tried to struggle. But he was too weak.

Shame rolled over him in a heavy wave. How could he have let this happen? Only a man of weakness would end up like this—bound, a victim. He could never face his clan again. Never face Dhatri.

But soon the drugs began their work, and he couldn't think any more of his home in the Wasteland, the darkly beautiful face of his bonded lover, of all that he would never see again. The room seemed to shrink, his focus to narrow, until all he could see was the girl, Nitara. All he could feel was his cock swelling, aching, as she danced, her body swaying, sinuous as a snake. Her hands wove patterns in the air, over her breasts, down her body.

He wanted her.

She turned slowly, her long hair swinging, shimmering in the torchlight. She watched him over one shoulder, pulling her hair aside as she smoothed the fabric of her tunic down and down, until the pale flesh of her back was revealed. Lower still, and he could see a pair of dimples at the small of her back, then the high, rounded curve of her ass. There was no music, yet her body set a rhythm, one he felt in his blood, in his cock. And when she dropped the tunic to the ground and turned to face him, his cock pulsed with a need so powerful he felt dazed by it.

Her body was lush, ripe, her breasts full and round, the nipples two hard points. Between her thighs she was shaved clean, her pussy lips smooth and pink as her nipples. She ran her hands over her belly, her sides, her hips swaying. Then she cupped her breasts, kneaded the flesh, before her fingers brushed over the hard pink tips.

Akaash strained, trying to move, needing to touch her.

Had to.

But all he could do was watch. And want.

Her gaze was on his face, green eyes that glowed in the dim light like pale sun-glass. And her hand snaked down between her thighs, brushing her pink cleft.

He groaned. Desire was like a knife, cutting deep. He felt it everywhere—in his cock, his very blood.

Nitara...

He no longer cared that the drugs kept him as bound as any ropes might. All he knew was that he must have her. Touch her. Fuck her.

"Nitara."

She looked up at the sound of her name. Blinked, pausing in her sensual dance. He looked more closely and saw the rise and fall of her chest, signaling her panting breath. He knew if he put his hand between her legs he would find her wet. Ready.

"I will have you," he murmured.

She smiled, pulled her hand from between her thighs, stepped right up to the bars of the cage and knelt there. Her fingertips glistening with her juices, she reached through the bars and touched them to his lips.

He groaned.

"Yes, you will," she said.

Then she was gone.

Gods, he could smell her. And when he licked his lips, he could taste her. She was sweet, salty, full of smoke and need. Need as sharp as his own.

He knew it was the drugs that made him crave her as if he would die. That, and her sweet face, her ripe body. He didn't care. Didn't care that to have her he would *have* to die. At this moment, he would do so willingly.

I will die to have this woman.

The words echoed in his head, empty of any meaning. But full of images—him pushing between her round thighs, into her slick cunt. Thrusting into her over and over, pleasure soaring. Coming into her...

He was out of his head. But there was nothing he could do.

He was helpless against the iron bars of the cell that held him. Helpless against the drugs they'd fed him. Helpless against Nitara.

Nitara ran through the hallways and into her room. Tearing her tunic over her head, she dropped it on the floor. She knelt, naked, at the small altar next to her bed before the carved image of the Goddess, the small stone bowl holding bits of sunglass, bread and other offerings she'd put there before her morning prayers. She lit the candles, bowed her head and thrust her hand between her parted thighs, her fingers slipping in the moisture between the swollen folds of her sex.

"Great Goddess," she whispered urgently, "I offer You my desire, my willingness to serve Your needs."

She touched her fingers to the stone image, then moved her hand back between her legs, finding the hard nub of her clitoris.

She moaned, keeping her eyes on the image of the Goddess as pleasure filled her, shimmering over her skin. But in her mind's eye all she saw was the face of Akaash. Rugged. Dangerous. His dark eyes, glittering like coal in the torchlight. The white slash of his teeth between his lush lips. Lips she wanted to feel on her skin.

"Oh..."

She pressed onto her clitoris, harder and harder, and with her other hand she caressed her nipples, first one, then the other.

His hair was all long, dark waves punctuated by tiny braids, beads woven into them, and coils of metal wire. Beautiful. Strong. And his body...she had never seen that kind of muscle on a man. Long, lean muscles, covered in golden skin. The boldly patterned tattoo covering his left forearm, like heavy black thorns and swirling dots...there was something alien and masculine about it. What would that body, that skin, feel like beneath her hands?

Another surge of pleasure, sharp and hot, centering in her sex and spreading through her belly, her breasts, making her nipples so hard they ached, needing to be touched.

His name was Akaash.

"Akaash."

Even his name was like some sort of wild aphrodisiac on

her lips.

Desire was like the high tone of a bell, reverberating in her body, singing in her blood. She rubbed harder, circling her clitoris, closing her eyes.

Akaash...

She pinched one nipple hard between her fingers, pinched her clit just as hard. Her body tensed, and she came, shuddering. Pleasure stabbed into her, again and again, into her sex, her thighs, making her weak, dizzy.

Akaash...

She would have him. And during the month-long Taming Moon she would touch herself, come for him, over and over. Offer her pleasure to the Goddess. Do her duty.

She would not think about what would come after, on the altar on the day of her Sacrifice.

Akaash.

No, she would not think of it.

It was dark when Leilin came to Nitara's room and woke her, the hour late into the night.

"Nitara, it is time to go to the Sanctuary."

"Leilin. I've been dreaming," Nitara murmured, trying to drag her mind out of the fog of too little sleep.

The room was mostly dark, lit only by the candle her sister carried. Leilin's round face was pale, like a small moon, her green eyes dark in the shadows.

"Of what, Little Sister?"

"Of him. My Sacrifice."

"Good dreams? Fruitful dreams?"

Nitara sat up in her bed, pushing her hair from her face. "I dream he is touching me. That his body is hard against mine. I dream that I can feel the texture of his hair..."

"You want him."

"Yes. He's very beautiful."

"You're lucky."

"Was your Sacrifice beautiful?"

"He was average in looks. It didn't matter. I did my duty, anyway. But you are fortunate to desire him. It's a gift from the Goddess."

"Did you not feel desire at your Sacrifice, Leilin?"

"I felt the desire I was trained to. My body responded as it was taught."

"But your mind..."

"...was on my duty to the Great Unnamed One. That is often how it is for a Breeder."

"My mind will be on *him*. Too much, perhaps."

Leilin leaned in closer, clasped Nitara's hand in hers. "Be careful, Little Sister. You tread on dangerous ground. He is an instrument. He serves a purpose, as we all do."

"I will keep the intentions of the Goddess in mind, Leilin. But..."

"There must be nothing else, Nitara. Come now. Go to him, tantalize him, so that he'll be unable to resist you come the day of Sacrifice. This is the purpose of the Taming Moon. To tame him with his desire for you. This is the first step in fulfilling our purpose on the Earth."

"Yes, of course, Leilin. I'm being silly. I'll go."

Nitara rose from her bed, threw on the linen robe made for this purpose, closed it around her body. Leilin lit the candle on her bed stand and handed it to her, kissed her cheek and left.

The halls were cool in the evening air. Nitara's bare feet whispered on the smooth stone as she made her way down and down, into the deepest levels which held the Sanctuary. Her pulse was hot, fluttering. She was far too eager to see him.

Finally she reached the outer chamber, where a small altar stood. She bowed before it, touching her fingers to the rounded breasts and belly of the stone image of the Goddess before slipping through the doorway and into the small room opposite the cell which held her Sacrifice.

Akaash.

He was sleeping, his long body laid out on the bare floor, but came awake quickly. Too quickly—the herbs should have kept him sedated, as well as aroused. Still, she didn't think to run to the guards or the priestesses. She liked that he was alert, that he knew something of what was going on around him. That he could know *her*. She liked the way his long hair hung down his back, over the hard muscles of his wide shoulders, the contrast of black hair and sleek golden-brown skin.

He watched her with wary eyes.

"Is it morning?" he asked, his voice rough with sleep.

"You are to exist without sense of time or place. You are to exist only to feel a need which must be fed."

"Your drugs make me feel such need."

"Only the drugs?" she asked, letting the robe fall open, her belly and breasts bared to him. "Am I not enticing?"

Her body was going hot all over, seeing the hunger in his eyes.

"You know you are."

A small thrill went through her at his admission.

"Before the month of the Taming Moon is over, you will know it, as well, Akaash the Wanderer."

He only grunted, but he kept his gaze on her.

She slipped the robe from her shoulders, let it fall to the ground and stepped back, knelt on the pile of cushions placed on the floor for this purpose. She leaned forward, cupping her breasts with her hands.

"I like that you watch me. I like the need in your eyes." She feathered her fingertips over her nipples, and they grew full beneath her touch. "I wish these were your hands, Akaash."

Pleasure shafted through her as she said his name, teasing her nipples into two hard points.

"I want to feel your rough palms on my flesh, your mouth close over my nipple. To feel the heat and the wet. To feel you sucking."

Desire was like a storm raging over his face. She saw the rise of his hard cock beneath the loincloth he wore. He strained in his bonds, but said nothing. His silence was like a challenge to her. She would *make* him admit his need for her.

"Akaash," she said softly, simply because she enjoyed the sound of his name on her lips, "my skin would be sweet on your tongue." She lifted her breasts, offering them to him. "Tell me you want to taste it."

His eyes blazed. His jaw clenched.

She smiled and let her hands drop from her breasts, gliding them over her sides, the tops of her thighs. "I am even sweeter here," she said, slipping one hand into her cleft. "You had a small taste the last time I saw you."

A small groan from him, through his tense jaw.

"Ah, I knew it," she told him, smiling in triumph.

"Damn it, woman. What is this game?" His voice was rough, raw. "You're here to seduce me, that much is common knowledge. You're here to torture me with the sight of your body. Of course I want you. To touch you. To taste you. To fuck you."

She shivered, hearing the crude words from his mouth. That lush mouth. She remembered the softness of his lips on her fingertips. Unexpectedly soft...

She felt suddenly the power of her ability to do this to him. To make him suffer with desire. She understood that part of it was the drugs the guards fed to him. But she also knew the force of her own femininity. It was the first time in her life she had felt any sense of power, of control over anything. It confused her. Aroused her. Made her want more.

She spread her thighs apart, until she knew he could see the lips of her shaved sex. He watched her carefully as she massaged the swollen lips, and found the pleasure rising, sharp and swift. It felt different with him watching her do these things. Different than doing it to herself, alone. Different from Xian's touch when she taught her the ways of pleasure and seduction.

She slid her fingers between her folds. She was soaking wet. Aching. And when she slipped one fingertip inside, she saw every muscle in his body jump.

"Let me out of these bonds," he murmured.

"I cannot do that."

"Let me out and I will put my hand where yours is."

"Oh..."

She was shaking with need. Close to coming. Too close.

"Let me out," he said again, his voice a low growl, "and I will put my tongue there. I will taste you for myself."

She shook her head, spread her thighs wider and rubbed in a small circle over her clitoris. She moaned in pleasure, her body growing hotter, hotter.

"I'm told you breeders are trained in sex by your priestesses."

"Yes. We are taught to please a man using phalluses made of clay. And the priestesses train us to sexual response with their own touch, their hands and mouths."

It made her wetter to say these things to him aloud.

"So you know that ultimate pleasure of lips and tongue on your sweet cunt?"

"Yes..."

Every muscle in his body was tense as he leaned forward, as far as his restraints would allow. "I would bury my face between your lovely thighs, push my tongue inside you, lick your hard little clit."

His skin was gleaming with sweat, the iron cuffs biting into his strong wrists as he pulled against them. And the bulge of his cock beneath the fabric of the loincloth made her mouth water. To have his cock inside her...

Soon...

"Tell me again you want me, Akaash."

"I will tell you, but it will do me no good, will it? I will tell you, anyway. I want you. To fuck you. To grind my cock into your body until it hurts. Until you scream in pleasure. Until your cunt closes hard around me, clenching me as you come. Until I feel the wet heat of your come, until I can smell your pleasure. And then I will do it again, Nitara. And again, and again, until you cannot breathe, cannot move, cannot even beg for more."

"Oh...Goddess..."

Her body clenched in pleasure, her climax thundering through her. A dull white noise roared in her head, and she closed her eyes, her sex pulsing with heat, burning through her. She cried out, and heard his groans.

"Damn it, woman, you do this to me!"

She opened her eyes, looked at him. He was panting, covered in a fine sheen of sweat. His eyes were dark, the pupils enormous. He looked as if he might kill someone.

Dangerous.

Yes, but she loved the idea of that danger, contained as it was by the drugs and his bonds and his *need.*

Beautiful.

She got up on shaking legs, picked up her discarded robe.

"I will return to you soon."

With one last look at his beautiful, tortured face, she ran from the room.

She was beautiful. Beautiful and wicked and cruel.

His cock was so hard it hurt, and chained as he was, there was nothing he could do about it.

Their damn drugs weren't quite working, not as they were intended to. No, mostly it was the girl. That soft, white flesh, her rounded breasts, the nipples two perfect nubs of pink, full and luscious. He couldn't even think about her pussy.

He groaned, his cock pulsing. He was torturing himself, but he couldn't help it. Those pink lips peeking from between the smooth curve of her thighs. How tight she would be, the walls of her cunt clasping him as he slid inside...

He arched his hips, meeting nothing but the light cloth that covered him. It was agonizing. Almost enough to make him come. Almost.

He could not believe this was happening to him. Trapped like an animal, tortured with naked flesh he could not touch. Shame and desire warred in him in equal measures, and he didn't know which would win at any given moment.

He wished for the drugs. Wished they would work, make it all some sort of terrible dream. Except that it wasn't all terrible.

Nitara.

He couldn't stop thinking of her. He didn't want to. Didn't want to *want* her. It felt like some sort of betrayal. To his people. To his own God, El, and his consort, the Goddess, Ela. To his bonded lover, Dhatri.

But he could not think of Dhatri. It brought too much pain. Too much shame.

He focused on the shame, willing his erection down. And after some time, it worked.

His life would end in regret. Regret he would likely never have the chance to redeem. And here he was, yearning for some girl—one belonging to the city's temple—like a dog in heat.

Unbearable.

He was shaking, fury burning through him as fiercely as desire had earlier.

He must find some way to escape. To make his way home to the Mutairi. To earn once more his place in the clan.

Meanwhile, he would not talk to her again. There was something about that small bit of communication that made her seem all too human to him. Imminently desirable.

The Wanderers spoke of the breeder girls as just that—

broodmares for the temple. And he knew that was true. He hadn't expected one of them to have any individuality. But this girl, Nitara...she was, unexpectedly, a person. One he would not know.

Would not.

He could not prevent his physical desire for her. But he could avoid any other sort of attraction. Any other sort of thought, where she was concerned. He must remain as detached as possible, and focus only on his escape.

He lay on the hard-packed earthen floor for a long time, willing his mind to find some answer, some way out. But he came up with nothing.

Finally, too weary to think, he whispered a prayer to the Mighty El for strength and to the Goddess Ela for hope, and slept.

Chapter Three

Nitara's body was still humming with climax, her third one of the night. She'd come to Akaash's cell in the Sanctuary tonight, determined to make him speak to her, to torture him with her own pleasure until he could no longer help himself. But she had failed.

He had not said one word to her for fifteen days. She had visited him once each day, and once each night, as was the rule, sometimes spending several hours there, in the small space on the other side of the iron bars. She had brought herself to climax after climax in front of him, pleasuring her body in every way she knew how. His constant erection, his tense muscles, his glittering gaze and flushed face, had let her know he wanted her as much as he ever had. But other than the occasional grunt or groan, he remained mute.

He was a stubborn man. And a strong one. His strength—and his stubborn silence—made her desire him even more.

Her desire was like some rare fuel, feeding her and feeding her, yet leaving her always hungry. Even after coming three times, she craved his touch. And now, she craved even the sound of his voice—it had been too long denied her.

Her legs were shaking, her body weak, lamguid. His dark gaze was on her as she lay back on the pillows. She had come to know the bronze light within the brown depth of his gaze, especially when he was aroused or angry.

"You will not speak to me, Akaash?" She pushed her hair from her face, the long, silky strands sticking to her damp cheek. "I have given you my pleasure, over and over. That is all I have to give. Will you not indulge me?"

He stared at her, his jaw tightening. But he didn't look

away.

He never did. No matter how silent, he always watched her.

She sighed. "I understand your anger at being here. How this must injure your pride—"

"You think this is about pride?" he roared, startling her.

She sat upright. "Ah, you speak to me at last."

"This is not some battle you've won. Don't look so damn proud of yourself. I speak now because I choose to."

She couldn't help the smile on her face. "I am glad you choose to."

"Why?"

"What do you mean?"

"Why do you care if I speak to you or not? I'm your prisoner. Your victim. Why do you care one way or another what I do or say?"

"I don't know," she told him honestly. She leaned forward, toward the bars that separated them. His face was stormy with rage, but there was real curiosity in his eyes. "I only know that I do care."

His features softened the tiniest bit. "You shouldn't. There are rumors about what goes on in your temple. What happens to the men of the Wanderers who are captured and brought here. Who are never seen again. I can imagine it's not a good idea for a breeder girl to become attached to one of us."

"I am not attached."

"No?"

He looked at her, one dark brow raised. She felt...flustered, her cheeks heating. She picked up her robe and pulled it around her shoulders.

"I'm only curious about you," she said. It was partly true. The other part of the truth was that she wanted more than this build of sexual tension, his forbidden touch. But she didn't know what, exactly.

"What do you want to know?"

"Will you truly tell me, if I ask?"

"That depends on what you ask."

She nodded, thinking. "I know little of your people. We're kept separate from the rest of society, we Breeders. We hear things...from the priestesses, when they talk among themselves and think we aren't listening. Sometimes from the eunuch guards who watch over us. But I've never known what's true and what is only imagined. We're told that your people are wild. Primitives who live in the Wasteland like animals."

"Animals don't have speech."

"No. But I didn't expect you to speak this way."

"What way?"

"The way we of the Temple do."

"Did you expect us to be covered in fur and have tails?"

"Of course not!"

"I'm teasing you, girl."

She swore a grin tilted the corner of his lush mouth.

"I'm not a girl. I am a woman."

"Yes, I've seen that very clearly for myself."

"Why do you address me with such disdain, Wanderer?"

"Can you blame me?"

Her cheeks were going hot. "You should be overcome with desire for me."

"Ah, I am. You've seen my raging cock." He sat up on his heels, the muscles of his stomach flexing as he moved, golden skin over solid iron, his large hands gripping the chains that held him. "It thirsts for you, Nitara. Make no mistake. But maybe the reason you expect me to be some raving animal is because the men who are brought here are drugged beyond all reason." His tone was bitter again.

"But you are not."

"No. What are the drugs made of? Do you know the names?"

"Valerian and datura. Mandrake. Caltrop. Herbs, to quiet you, to stimulate you."

"Valerian I know. I've tried it to help me sleep when I was injured in the hunt. It's useless for me. Datura we use in our Manhood rituals. We have for generations. It's a strong hallucinogen, but works less and less well, in recent years. My people are becoming immune to its effects."

"Why are you telling me these things?"

His gaze went hard, his dark eyes seeming to look through her.

"Will you run and tell your priestesses, Nitara? Will you give them this information to use against the people of the clans?"

Her heart was a small hammer in her chest. She whispered, "No."

"I thank you for that."

He smiled then, a real smile, and her body seemed to light from within. His teeth were white, strong. His face was beautiful, all hard, fine planes, high cheekbones and that soft, lush mouth...

She *was* curious about him, that much was true. More now than ever. He was becoming more and more of a *person* to her. She knew it was dangerous. But she couldn't stop herself.

"I am told you have your own gods," she said. "That you worship some deity other than our Goddess."

"Yes. The God El and the Goddess Ela. God of fall and winter and Goddess of spring and summer. They're powerful. Fierce, as our people are. Wrathful and punishing."

"Even your Goddess?"

"Is your goddess not a punishing goddess?"

"She is called the Loving Moon. The female spirit is ever nurturing, and those of us who live within the Temple aspire to her loving nature. Our God is the Angry Sun. We live in fear of the Nameless God, who razed the Earth in the Burning Time. But we love the Goddess. You cannot worship what you do not love."

"Females cannot, in your view, be vengeful? Your goddess is not vengeful?"

"She is all love," Nitara said, then thought of her mother, her brother. "I...the Great Goddess does punish those who work against Her." She twisted a strand of her long hair between her fingers. "It is Her right. Her choice, made in Her divine wisdom. She has Her reasons, and we must not question. We're only human, Her servants."

"And yet you look sad."

Nitara shook her head, pulled her robe tighter around her.

"What does a breeder girl, who lives, pampered and protected, have to be sad about?"

There was a bitter edge to his voice once more. Resentment.

"What do you know of my existence?"

"I know it's far easier than my own. But one I would never trade for."

"Nor should you. I live in ease, it's true. I'm fed and

175

sheltered, protected from the dangers of the cities and the Wasteland. Yet I am not allowed outside the walls of the Temple, nor will I ever be. I know enough to understand that there is a world out there which I will never see. I'm caged as much as you are at this moment."

"I'm surprised to hear you say such things."

"So am I."

She felt her eyes blazing. With fury. With tears. Her mind was a whirl of confusion.

"I'm sorry, Nitara." His voice was soft. "The world is a terrible but beautiful place. It shouldn't be denied anyone."

She hung her head. "But it is being denied you now. Because the Temple holds you here for the purposes of our Goddess."

"Yes."

When she looked up he was watching her once more, but his expression was softer than she had ever seen it.

"Akaash. I'm sorry."

His dark brows raised. "You surprise me again, girl."

"I surprise myself. I did not expect..."

"What didn't you expect?"

"To...feel for you."

"Are your people so cold, then? Do they not love?"

"I love my sister, Leilin, and my brother, Nikkan. I love the High Priestess Xian, who has trained me in the ways of sensuality. I love my Sister Breeders. And I love the Great Goddess, of course."

"There's another kind of love," he said quietly.

She wasn't certain of what he meant, but his tone compelled her. She approached the cage, laying her palms flat against the bars. She had been this close to him only once. That first time, when she had touched her fingers to his lips. Now she took a few moments to really look at him, taking in the hard swell of muscle in his arms, his bare chest. The dark stubble that had grown into a short beard in the last weeks. His beautiful mouth. His dark eyes watching her, wary and filled with desire and something else she didn't understand.

"Tell me," she said. "Tell me about love."

He glanced away for several moments, and she saw his jaw clench. When he looked back to her, his eyes were shadowed.

"I have a bonded lover. His name is Dhatri. He's strong and brave. Beautiful. Wise beyond his years. He's our fiercest warrior, a trainer of our young in weapons and the hunt. His love is fierce, powerful. He joined our clan, the Mutairi, when we were both sixteen. We've been together ever since. He wears the mark of our clan on his arm, as I do. He is one of us. He is...part of me."

"It sounds wonderful."

"It is until you're parted from those you love."

She saw grief on his face, and her heart melted. She wanted to comfort him, to put her arms around him. And she wanted more. She didn't know what her need was, other than to be close to him. But any real sex was forbidden until the day of Sacrifice. Even this conversation would be forbidden. Knowing that left her feeling strangely bereft.

"I understand your pain."

"Do you?"

She nodded. "I have been parted from my mother since the age of six."

"Did she die?"

"She was caught lying with her Sun Guard. Unconsecrated sex is forbidden for a priestess. She was sent away, into the Wasteland. I don't even know if she survived."

"Then you have some idea of my loss."

"Yes."

She wrapped her fingers around the bars, the iron cool beneath her palms.

He lifted one hand as though to reach for her, but the chains allowed him only a few inches of movement. "I'm sorry for yours, Nitara."

She nodded, emotion a hard knot in her chest. What was happening to her?

"Akaash, I must go."

He shrugged, but she could see emotion on his face. Was she only imagining that some of it was for her?

She knew it shouldn't matter. He was an instrument, as Leilin had said, as everyone was an instrument of the Goddess. His purpose was to aid in the loss—the gift—of her virginity. To hopefully impregnate her. To aid in her sacred duty to carry on the human race. Her duty should be her only desire. But her desire had shifted, had become her own.

She was feeling something for this man.

Akaash.

She understood that to feel anything beyond sexual need was a sacrilege so profane, she could not imagine it had ever happened. She could not imagine what the Goddess's punishment might be.

Clear your mind. Purify your heart.

Yes. She must go to the altar in her room and pray to be cleansed of these impure thoughts.

He was watching her again, as if he could see the thoughts churning in her mind, his brows drawn together.

"Nitara—"

She took a step back. Tears stung her eyes. "I must go..."

She turned and ran out the door.

Akaash's chest ached as much as his swollen cock. What in El's name was he thinking?

This girl was part of this place, these people who justified kidnapping and using his people for their own ends. He was her victim as much as he was the temple's. And yet, he found himself feeling...sympathy for her.

Ridiculous.

He glanced down at his cock, straining against the loincloth.

That, too, was ridiculous. He would never feel the touch of this girl, would never sink into her lovely flesh, other than just before his death. Still, he craved that more than anything.

Maybe even more than his escape.

He thought of Dhatri, his dark, beautiful skin, the warmth of his flesh. His cock, large and full, thrusting into him...

He may never touch him again. Never struggle against the strength of his lover, their coming together a pure, animal fucking, full of lust and the rage of a warrior. Intense. Powerful. A battle they both won, in the end.

He would win nothing here.

He must escape. Forget Nitara. Forget her sad story, her lush body that tempted him beyond anything he had ever imagined.

If only his cock would let him forget. But it throbbed and

ached, even as he fell into exhausted sleep.

He dreamed he was lying beneath a canopy of stars, glimmering silver in the night sky. She was in his arms, her skin the softest thing he'd ever felt in his life.

She was naked. So was he. His cock was hard, pulsing with life and need. She turned to him, raised her face to his, and he took her mouth, hungry for it. Hungry for *her*. Ravenous.

He pressed his cock against the softness of her belly, and she reached down and took it in her small hand.

Oh, yes...

He wanted to fuck her. Needed to.

He turned her onto her back. She spread her thighs for him and he settled his body between them. The tip of his cock nestled at her opening, and she was wet, ready for him.

He pushed in, her cunt enclosing him like a fist, tight and hot.

Pleasure surged through him, as brilliant as the stars. His sight dimmed, went dark. He was going to come...

He groaned, coming awake instead.

Damn it!

Nitara.

He needed to have her. *Needed* to.

Damn this place. Damn this girl. Damn his own body.

Nitara.

His fondest wish. His worst nightmare.

It was morning. Nitara stood on the small terrace on the edge of the mountain, overlooking the City of Kroy Wen, the seemingly endless maze of adobe structures punctuating the flat, dusty earth. The terrace was, by custom, curtained, keeping the Breeders out of sight of the citizens. But the girls often peeked through, looking at the city, at the men who walked or rode the rare horses in and out of the tall gates.

Nitara had often been curious as to what the city looked like up close, what went on there. She'd heard talk of the simple matters of life, knew the men lived in the sprawling adobe buildings, that they slept there, had places where they went to eat, to trade: weapons, furs, meat and fish. But she couldn't begin to comprehend what else went on there, what their lives were like. All she had was this tiny glimpse of them walking, riding, fighting.

The fighting, which often ended in injury or death, was the most interesting. There was nothing like it within the Temple. Except for the blood shed during a Sacrifice, but that was a sacred ritual.

Was it really any different?

She felt momentarily stunned. Then immediately remorseful. She had spent far too much time questioning the ways of the Goddess recently.

Akaash had only made that worse, raising questions and doubts in her mind. Making her yearn for things she could never have.

He had talked to her of love. A kind of love that seemed alien to her, strange. Utterly desirable.

Especially when she thought of him.

Akaash.

She must stop thinking of him this way, in any way beyond physical desire.

She raised her gaze to the hot yellow sky. Clouds hung heavy in the air. There were rumors of rain, which was rare. But because something was rare didn't mean it could never happen.

She wanted to know more about love. She had no one but Akaash to ask.

It was time to go to him. She wanted to. But she was afraid. Afraid of what he made her think, made her feel. But she couldn't stay away.

She made her way down and down, into the bowels of the Temple, to the dark and womb-like Sanctuary. She paused outside the door of the chamber, her pulse a heavy thud in her temples, her sex.

She had to see him. Talk to him. But she must learn to steel herself against her own traitorous thoughts.

He was sitting on the bare floor, as usual, his strong arms held by the chains. His golden skin and dark hair were damp, letting her know the guards had been there this morning, bathing him. She could see tiny droplets of water beaded on the tips of the long, narrow braids in his dark hair, shimmering in the torchlight. She didn't know why this touched her. Perhaps because it made him seem human to her—the need to be bathed. Or perhaps it was simply the small sensual thrill at the sight of his wet skin.

She wanted to reach out and touch him, to rub the water into his flesh...

"Nitara. Good morning. Or good evening, I don't know which."

She sighed. "You are not supposed to."

"Yes, I know."

He sounded resigned today. Almost defeated. She stepped closer to the cage.

"You are not yourself today, Akaash."

"Ah, it's morning, then." He waited, his brows raised, but she could not answer. "Never mind. It's not important. I'm glad to see you."

"Are you?"

Her pulse sped, heated.

He nodded, his watchful gaze on her.

"I shouldn't be. I shouldn't care."

"Neither should I," she said, her voice a low whisper. She moved closer, laid her palms on the rough iron bars. "I should not be talking with you. I should not know you. I should only desire you, and make you desire me, so that on the day of my Sacrifice we are brought together in irresistible need. But I do know you, or at least part of you."

"And?"

Her chest went tight, as though a heavy weight rested there, pressing her down into the hard, cool earth. "And I don't know how I will do this. Sacrifice you to the Goddess."

He remained silent, but his chest rose and fell with ragged breath.

"Akaash..." Her eyes filled with tears. "I don't know how I will fulfill my duty to the Goddess. Yet not to do so would mean my death, as well as yours."

He said quietly, "I don't want you to die for me."

"How can you say that? How can you care for me at all, after what has been done to you by the Temple?"

"Because you understand this is wrong."

She nodded, the tears pouring down her cheeks.

"What will you do, Nitara?"

"What can I do but obey the laws of the Temple, handed

down by the Goddess herself, to ensure the continuation of the human race? My responsibilities are...enormous. But I don't want them." She wiped her tears with an angry hand. "I've always had doubts. Ever since my mother was taken from me there have been questions in my mind. And recently, it seems as if the Goddess herself is sending messages to me...but it is sacrilege to even think so."

"I'd comfort you if I could, Nitara."

His face was soft with sympathy.

"Akaash," she said, his name coming out on a sob. "I would not see you dead. Tell me what to do."

He leaned toward her, as much as his chains would allow. "Tell me, is there anyone within the temple you can trust utterly?"

"My sister, Leilin. And my twin brother, Nikkan."

"Twin?"

"He is the guard who brought me to you the first time."

"The guards have more freedom than the breeder girls, I would think."

"Yes, although he is a eunuch, so he remains always in the temple, unlike the Sun Guards, who accompany the priestesses into the city. Why?"

"Can he get a message to anyone outside of the temple?"

"I don't know. But I'll find out. Tell me what I will do if he can?"

"I must try to get a message to Dhatri. To the people of my clan. Even shamed as I am, they may help me to escape."

"None have ever escaped, that I know of."

"I must try. Will you help me, Nitara?"

"Yes."

She was damned in even considering this. She didn't know how the Goddess, or worse, the angry God of the Sun, might punish her. But she had to try.

"Akaash, if you cannot escape, you will die at my hand. There is no other way. Unless I refuse..."

"And then your people will kill you before they take my life."

She nodded. The tears were burning in her eyes once more.

"Nitara, if I must die, let it be at your hand. Let me touch you first."

His own eyes were bright with emotion. She reached

through the bars, her finger stroking his cheek, and he held perfectly still. Then he turned his head and laid a soft kiss on her fingertips.

A jolt of need, desire and emotion rocked her body, her mind. Her heart.

"I will try my best, Akaash."

He nodded.

"Do something for me now, Nitara."

"I will do whatever you ask."

"Give me your pleasure."

She smiled, light filling her heart. He wanted from her the one thing she was able to give.

She stripped her robe off and stood close to the iron bars. His gaze was hungry as she stroked her palms over her belly, her thighs, her breasts.

"Yes, draw out your nipples as I would with my tongue, could I reach you. Ah, beautiful. I've never seen anyone so beautiful, Nitara."

She shivered, holding the hardening flesh of her nipples between her fingers, stroking, pulling on them. Pleasure suffused her. Her clitoris grew hard, needy. The anticipation of awaiting his instruction was strange and thrilling.

"Tell me what you want, Akaash."

"Part your thighs for me so that I can see your lovely cunt. So pink...I can see how wet you are. I need to taste you again, Nitara."

She slipped her fingers into her slick juices. She was shaking with need as she held a trembling hand between the bars that separated them, held her damp fingers to his lips, as she had done before. He leaned forward, took her fingers between his lush lips, and sucked.

"Ah, Akaash..."

Pleasure was like the sun, burning into her skin, arcing through her body.

He let her fingers go, but she couldn't pull away. Instead, she explored the contours of his face, tracing over his mouth, his beard-stubbled chin, finding a long scar on his cheek. It only made him more beautiful, somehow, that he had survived hardship.

He turned his face and kissed her fingers as he had done

before, lingering kisses, his lips soft on her skin. She turned her hand over, and he pressed his mouth to her palm. Her heart fluttered in her chest.

She felt stunned by his touch. Immobilized.

"Nitara," he whispered, his breath warm on her palm. "Come for me."

It was only then, at his instruction, that she was able to pull away from him, but only far enough that he could watch her.

She spread her legs and slipped one hand between them, her fingers feathering over her hard clit. She was hot all over, sweat dampening her skin. His gaze on her was purely erotic, as was the cool air on her skin, her own long hair brushing her spine. She began to rub, circling her clitoris with her fingertips.

"Beautiful, Nitara. Show me what brings you pleasure. Show me exactly how to please you."

She raised her free hand to her breast and caressed the full flesh, pinching the nipple lightly.

"A little pain mixes well with pleasure. The contrast of hard and soft. I know it well." His voice was ragged with desire. He was up on his knees now, his hips arching into the air. His engorged cock was clearly outlined beneath the thin layer of fabric. "I would touch you the same way. And I would have you touch me. I would have you touch me now..."

"It is forbidden," she said, watching him, still stroking her swollen cleft.

"Yes..." His dark gaze was burning. "Do it, anyway."

She pressed against the bars, one hand still working between her thighs. And with the other she reached through and touched her fingertips to his loincloth.

"Ah, Nitara..."

His eyes closed momentarily. Then they were on her again, burning hotter than ever.

She traced the outline of his cock through the fabric, and he moaned. She wet her lips with her tongue as she moved it aside and looked at his solid shaft, the head swollen and purple, making her mouth water.

"I've never seen this before. I have seen drawings from the sacred texts, the clay phallus used to train me. But never did I imagine it to be so...beautiful."

He smiled. "I'm glad you find it so."

"I want to touch it..."

"Yes."

She wrapped her fingers around his cock, and it was hard as the iron bars that stood between them. But the flesh was soft, softer than her own. She began to stroke, pausing to cup his balls, then stroking again.

"Nitara..." His voice was a hard gasp. "I can't take this for long. Not after you've tortured me with your body all these days. But I want you to come with me."

"Yes, Akaash."

She worked her clit with her fingers, pressing, pinching, pleasure a strong, steady rhythm in her blood. One she kept time with in stroking his cock. He grew even harder, his hips pumping. Her own were thrusting in time, into her hand. Her legs grew weak, and she rested her weight against the bars, the cold iron a strange and lovely contrast against her aching breasts, the flesh of her belly.

They were moaning together, panting. She had never imagined the power of sex between a man and a woman, so different from her training with Xian. Akaash was more primal, more purely sexual—his body, his scent.

Finally it was too much for her. Her body clenched, pleasure pouring through her in a hot tide, heavy and thick. She shook with the force of her climax, her mind going blank of everything but her pleasure, and his, as he arched into her fisted hand.

"Ah, Nitara..."

He pumped hard, and she felt the heat and the wet of his come flow into her palm. She was still shivering with her own climax as he came. She felt as if they were oddly connected. One orgasm. One overpowering sensation.

"Akaash..."

She fell against the bars, her hand slipping from his softening cock.

She was weak all over. And afraid.

What had she done? Surely the Goddess would punish them both. But at this moment, it seemed worth any punishment.

"Nitara." He had settled back on his knees. His face was so

beautiful, she could barely stand to look at him. But she couldn't draw her gaze away. "Stay with me. How long can you stay?"

"Another hour or more. I don't want to go."

She reached for him again, taking his hand. He squeezed her fingers in his. His skin was rough. Warm.

"I cannot bear to leave you," she told him. "I cannot bear that you will die."

"We must find a way for me to escape. And you must come with me."

"What? Leave the Temple?"

Her heart thumped, fear rising, threatening to choke her. But just as frightening was the idea of never seeing him again.

"Will you do it? Come with me, if we can find a way? Will you stay with me, Nitara? Live with me in the Wasteland?"

His gaze was steady on hers, his hand gripping until it hurt.

She knew she could not let him go without her.

"Yes," she whispered, knowing she was damned either way. She would lose everything that was familiar to her. Or she would lose him. Perhaps both. And perhaps even her life in the process. But she would do it. "Yes," she said again, her voice stronger this time. "If we can find a way, I will come with you."

Chapter Four

Akaash watched the doorway for a long time after Nitara left. His body was still humming with pleasure, his mind whirling with possibilities.

Would escape truly be an option? He knew Nitara would do whatever she could. He felt in his gut that she would be true to her word. If he did manage to get out of this alive, she would go with him.

He couldn't think any further than that. He understood too much depended on her siblings' willingness to help. And that if either of them were more loyal to the temple than to their sister, it could mean death for both him and Nitara.

The idea of his own death didn't scare him. Death was part of the cycle of human existence, something a warrior and hunter faced every day. But he couldn't bear to think of anything happening to her.

His body yearned for her, his cock hard again already. But his heart yearned just as much.

This girl had touched him deeply. Her innocence. Her sweetness. Her sincerity. His feelings for her were different than what he felt for Dhatri, his partner of ten years. His love for Dhatri was deep and abiding, strong with history. What he felt for Nitara was a sort of tenderness he'd never felt with a man. More tenuous, being new. But powerful.

Maybe something in him responded to her femininity. The female Wanderers were different from the women of the temple. They were as fierce as the men, with none of Nitara's softness. She was like some ethereal creature. And her blatant sexuality combined with her innate sweetness was devastating.

His cock rose, hardened even more. He was certain that

even without the drugs he wouldn't be able to get enough of her.

Footsteps in the outer hall had him on the alert, and he sat up, but relaxed as he saw Nitara enter. A guard was with her, and he had one tense moment, wondering if they had been overheard earlier. But he saw immediately that it was her twin brother.

"Akaash, this is Nikkan."

He could see the resemblance in their pale green eyes, curving cheekbones and fair skin. Nikkan's hair was a shade darker, but they had the same mouth, the same solemn expression.

Nikkan's voice was soft, youthful. "My sister has told me of your plans. I want to help."

Akaash bowed his head in gratitude. "I know this puts you at great risk, Nikkan."

He shrugged, the casual motion at odds with his serious expression. "My life is nothing but service to the Temple, and will never be more. To give my sister the opportunity to have some choice in her path will be worth the risk. We'll also speak to our older sister, Leilin. She will be willing to help in any way she can. Tell me what I must do."

Akaash leaned forward, keeping his voice low. "Can you get a message into the city?"

Nikkan nodded. "One of the Sun Guards, Hel, is a loyal friend. He goes there regularly."

"A note must be delivered to a trader I know there. He'll get a message to my clan, and to my bonded partner, Dhatri. This is how you'll find him."

They spent the next hour making plans, then Nikkan left Akaash alone with Nitara. Her face was tense with strain, her hands wringing.

"Is this too much for you, Nitara? It's a lot to ask, I know."

"It's frightening. I understand what the cost may be, if we're unsuccessful. To us both, and to Nikkan and Leilin, if their involvement is discovered. I feel selfish, asking them to do this for me. Except that it is for you, regardless of what happens to me. I cannot accept your life being taken, even in service to the Goddess. It seems...cruel. Unnecessary."

"The citizens thirst for blood as much as they do for sex. The rituals of your temple give them these things. It helps to keep them under control."

"I'd never thought of it that way before."

"You've been taught to exist on blind faith."

"Yes. I've always thought there was something lacking in me that I questioned our ways. But do the people of the Wanderer clans live without questioning their god and goddess?"

"We're an independent people." He grinned. "And we love nothing more than a good argument."

She smiled, and some of the tension he'd been holding in his neck and shoulders eased.

"You're beautiful, Nitara."

She knelt before the iron bars, reaching for him and grasping his hand. "So are you."

That made him smile. "I've never thought of what I look like. Dhatri seems pleased enough with me. So have the other lovers we've taken, separately and together."

"I hadn't thought to ask...but Akaash, if we manage to leave this place, to go into the Wasteland, back to your lover, what will happen?"

"I can't say for certain. You'll be unusual to our people. Rare. Desirable. Dhatri will find you beautiful. Among the Wanderers, we take lovers as we choose. Dhatri and I are bonded, which means we live together, sleep together. But we take other lovers, male and female."

"You said separately and together..."

"It does nothing to change our bond."

"So..." Nitara bit her lip. "Does that mean that I would be with you, and with him?"

"That will be up to you. And to him."

Her green eyes were enormous, pleading. "But I will not be separated from you?"

His fingers tightened around hers. "Not unless you wish it. There may be another of my clan you find more attractive."

"Never!"

He laughed. "You haven't seen them yet."

"And I may never."

"That's true. How long do we have, Nitara? I have no sense of time in this place."

"You've been here for sixteen days. There are two weeks

remaining until my Taming Moon is over, and it is time for my Sacrifice."

"Why is it called the Taming Moon?" Akaash asked.

"Our Goddess is the Loving Moon, our God the Angry Sun. The female spirit can tame the wildness, the hunger and anger of the male, through seduction. It is only through Her love that the God's anger can be tamed, allowing human life to flourish on the earth once more. This month, the period of one moon, is to be used to tame the Sacrifice, so they will be calm and accepting for the ritual."

He stroked the back of her hand with his fingers. Her skin was warm. His cock was hard again. It had been since the moment she'd walked into the room, and nearly every moment she'd been absent. But it was pulsing with need now.

"Tame me once more, Nitara."

She smiled, let his hand go and stood to let her robe slip from her shoulders and flutter to the floor. She stood before him, all lush breasts and full hips, her skin flushed and glowing in the amber light of the torch.

"Akaash, I cannot wait to feel your hands on my body. On my breasts. On my thighs. And between them."

Her hand lowered, caressed her naked sex.

"Ah, you torture me, Nitara."

"Do you want me to stop?"

"No. Never."

She kept her gaze on his and rubbed the swollen nub of her clitoris. Soon her hips were arching, her breath coming in gasping pants. His cock was a hammering pulse, heavy with desire.

"Nitara...make yourself come. For me."

"Yes, for you, Akaash."

She rubbed her fingers over the lips of her sex, the moisture glistening in the dim light. He was dying to touch her, to taste her skin.

"I wish it were my hand there, Nitara. My mouth. My cock. I need you..."

She dropped to her knees, reached through the bars and took his cock in her small hand once more. Pleasure arrowed deep into his belly.

"I will come inside your beautiful body some day, Nitara,"

he murmured.

"Yes, Akaash."

Her hands were working her clit, his cock. They knelt almost hip to hip, on either side of the iron bars. If only the damn chains had a little more give, so that he could touch her, feel her body against his... But there was something about being bound in this way, the heavy weight of the chains holding him down, that was erotic to him. Knowing he couldn't move, that he was helpless against her touch...

She tightened her fist, and he could imagine it was the tight clench of her cunt.

"Ah, Nitara..."

"Akaash!"

Her hips arched, her hands pumping on his cock, between her thighs. He saw her body tense, small sobs escaping her lovely pink lips as she came. And his cock swelled, driving into her hand as he climaxed, groaning.

She kept her hand on him for a long time as they both caught their breath. Her eyes were half-lidded, the green a glimmer from beneath her long lashes.

"I should go," she whispered.

"I know."

She picked up her discarded robe, slipped it on. "I will be back in the night."

He nodded. "I'll look forward to it."

She smiled, then she was gone. He was alone in the half-dark once more, contemplating his future, his death, his feelings for Nitara. They were all entwined, somehow, and he had no idea what the end might be. But he had a chance. At life. A life with her. That would have to be enough to comfort him for now.

It had been twelve days since Nikkan had sent the message into the city. Nitara waited to hear the outcome. With hope. With fear. They could be discovered, betrayed, at any moment. The only thing that saved her from going mad was her time with Akaash.

They came together in the only way they could, and when they were worn from climax after climax, they talked. Akaash told her of the life of the Wanderers. It was a hard life, a challenging one. But they were free of the strictures of the Temple, of the city and the council. Free to live as they chose, to love as they chose.

She loved him.

Akaash.

She'd known for a while. Perhaps even since he had first spoken to her of love. He was her first thought when she woke. He was in her dreams each night. His scent, his voice, had become a part of her. She lived now between her visits to him only to be with him again.

Nitara sat on her bed, combing her hair, waiting for nightfall. Her body hummed with yearning, her heart, her mind, filled with nothing but him.

"Nitara."

It was Nikkan. He came quickly into the room.

"I have heard from Hel, Xian's Sun Guard. The message has been delivered."

Her heart was a hammer in her chest. "We have only a few days before my Sacrifice."

"It was delivered some days ago. I have just received confirmation."

"Then there is nothing more we can do."

"Little Sister, I'll help in any way I can. I'll be in the Temple that day to create a distraction as we discussed with Akaash."

"It will take more than one person, Nikkan. What can you do alone?"

"I have already asked Leilin to come here."

"We put her at risk."

"She'll take it willingly."

"I will, Sister." Leilin walked in, took Nitara in her arms.

Nitara's eyes pooled with tears. "It is much to ask of you both."

"There is nothing too great to ask of those you love. Are we not asked to give our bodies, our lives, to the Goddess because we love her? Should we not do as much for those people we love?"

"It feels right. But it seems counter to what we're taught. Our service to the Goddess is supposed to come first. And if you believe in those tenets, how can you be willing to help me now?"

Leilin pulled back to look at her. "Because ever since our

mother was taken from us, I've questioned the ways and the rituals. Little Sister, we are born under a curse," she whispered harshly. "We cannot serve the Goddess, faith strong in our hearts, allowing us to do what we must without pain. We're born doubting. Our mother prayed we'd be stronger than she was, that we wouldn't share her same fate. She cursed herself for having brought this on her children. For leaving us. For Nikkan's fate. I've spent my life fighting it. I bit back the tears at my Sacrifice, as I brought the knife down, into the chest of the man who lost his life in the name of the Goddess.

"I gave our people twelve children. I did it for the Goddess. But also because our mother asked that I watch over you. I would wish something more for you. This is your chance. If you can have a life, it will be worth whatever I have to give up in order for that to happen."

"And for me, as well," Nikkan said. "I have an idea... I'll need Leilin's help. If it works, it will get you and Akaash out of the temple."

"I will never see either of you again." The tears spilled, hot on her cheeks.

Leilin stroked her hair. "Live for us, Nitara. You're the only one of us with any hope of that."

She nodded, embraced Leilin. Nikkan's hand was on her shoulder, firm and reassuring.

If only she could be sure that this would work. She had nothing to rely on but the efforts of a handful of idealistic humans against the Goddess herself.

It was sacrilege. It left her with no familiar ritual, no Goddess to pray to. Her altar was nothing now but a statue made with human hands, an empty bowl. Her religion, her very perception of who and what she was, was shattered. If she made it out of the Temple alive, she would have nothing to hang on to but Akaash.

But she loved him. And he would be enough.

The morning of Nitara's Sacrifice began before dawn. Leilin came to wake her, accompanied by the Crone, Meidra, as well as several of her Breeder sisters—Seti, Tilan and Fareen. They took her, naked, from her bed, down into the bowels of the Temple.

Today is the day my fate is decided. And Akaash's, as well.

Her pulse was racing. It was all she could do to draw a breath, and even then it was shallow, uneven.

She had never gone so deep before, until the smoothly polished hallways ended and turned into close tunnels of rough-hewn rock. It was cold, the air smelling of molding stone and water.

They followed the tunnel until it let them out into a large cavern lit by torches. In the center was a small, still pool. The damp scent was stronger, and when Meidra lit a bundle of dried sage, the smoke mixed with it, making Nitara dizzy. Or maybe it was the feelings of dread and hope, battling within her heart.

Akaash.

Today could mean freedom for them both. Or their deaths. And she could not even pray.

Meidra came to stand before her, a bowl of dark mud in her hands.

"Today you become a woman," the Crone said, her voice rough with age. She dipped her fingers into the bowl and smeared the mud on Nitara's forehead. "Today you begin your true service to the Goddess." She dipped her fingers again, and pressed the cool mud to Nitara's breasts. "Today you open your body to mankind, so that you may give back to the earth what was lost."

Once more, Meidra smeared Nitara's skin with mud, just below her navel, over her red tattoo. Meidra nodded to the Breeders, and the four surrounded Nitara. They were naked now, as she was. With their hands on her arms, they drew her into the pool, breaking the serene surface.

The water was so cold it made Nitara gasp. She forgot for a moment the prayers she'd been taught. Leilin gave her hand a small pinch, and Nitara spoke softly.

"Great Goddess, I purify myself for You. I offer You this vessel, my body, to do Your work on the earth. I pray that You find me worthy of Your love, that I am fertile and willing and pure."

Four sets of hands came to rest on her head, pushing her beneath the surface. The cold was numbing, and she came up sputtering. Her sisters held her up while Meidra prayed over her. Her legs were cold, growing number by the moment, and in her head she prayed only that this day would be over. That she might know what her future held. If she would have one.

Finally she was led, naked and freezing in the early air, up and up, until they reached the highest point of the Temple. They went through a high, arched doorway and onto the flat terrace that was open to the dawning sun, so that the Angry God may look down upon their offering and be soothed. Her sisters laid her out on the smooth ground. It was cool on her bare back, but the sun was beginning to heat already, drying her skin.

The Breeders placed spiraled lengths of copper wire on her naked belly and breasts, at the vee between her thighs, along with bits of sun-glass and dried flowers, all things precious, while Meidra continued her murmured prayers. She watched the sun rise overhead, the sky turning from black to orange, and finally, a hazy golden yellow.

Her sisters stroked her skin with their soft hands, but she wasn't gentled by their touch as she should be. She was shivering, her muscles tense and aching, her mind whirling, unable to concentrate on the prayers being spoken above her. Unable to think of the Goddess she would betray today. She focused instead on Akaash, taken from his home, his people. She knew in her heart what she was doing was right. Her only option in light of her love for him, and in the stark clarity of the evil truth about what the Temple demanded.

Her sisters helped her to her feet, and took her down once more, into the chamber behind the Temple's altar. Her hair, still damp, swung behind her, making her shiver in the cooler air of the subterranean Temple.

She was led to the small holding chamber at the foot of the nave, the long center aisle that ran the length of the Temple. Meidra followed, praying constantly, her whispered words like some foreign language to Nitara. She knew she must concentrate on playing her part. She must make her body respond in the way it should, or it would surely be noticed.

It was easier as her sisters began her preparation. They surrounded her, their gentle hands stroking her skin once more: her shoulders, her breasts, making her nipples hard and ready. Her belly, her thighs, and then between them. She closed her eyes, imagined it was Akaash's hands on her.

Her body heated, her sex going damp.

Akaash.

Seti's fingers slipped over her damp cleft, joined by

Fareen's, pressing onto her clitoris. And she let her body respond as it had been trained to. Pleasure rose, spiraled, and she grew dizzy with it. The heat was a steady drumbeat between her thighs, and when she was on that keen edge, they pulled away.

"It is time," Meidra said, stepping forward and fastening around Nitara's hips a narrow cord that held the sacred dagger in its sheath. "Go to the Goddess, and make your Sacrifice."

Nitara nodded, her heart racing. She was dizzy with nerves and a sensual excitement she couldn't help. This was the purpose she had been bred for, and her body seemed to have a mind of its own. Desire poured through her, even as her mind argued with it, tried to suppress her yearning.

Do what you must.

Her sisters slipped her cowled tunic over her head, pulling the cowl over her hair, then tied the blue sash around her waist.

Leilin leaned in and whispered to her, "I will love you always, Little Sister. No matter what happens today."

Nitara didn't dare to look at her. She knew Leilin would understand. She moved through the curtained doorway and into the Temple.

The air was warm, stifling, and acrid with the scent of too many bodies. A low rumble vibrated in the air as the men muttered among themselves, the citizens of the city of Kroy Wen. All of them come to the Temple to witness this: sacred sex, sacred death.

Her stomach churned.

She caught sight of Nikkan waiting in the north transept, next to one of the iron cauldrons that held a bundle of burning sage. He nodded, acknowledging her.

Leilin was on her right, holding her arm. When they reached the high stone altar and Nitara caught sight of Akaash, his naked body held down by the hemp ropes that were traditional in the Sacrifice ritual, she gasped.

"Shh, Nitara," Leilin whispered. "Be brave. Be strong."

Nitara blinked back the tears stinging her eyes, and focused only on Akaash.

He was beautiful, his long, lean muscles straining against the ropes. His cock was as golden as the rest of him, hard and proud between his strong thighs. He was watching her, that dark familiar gaze. There was hunger in his eyes.

She would know his body, finally. Would feel his cock between her thighs, driving deep inside her.

Her body heated, her sex clenching hard.

Meidra raised her voice in prayer. She was joined by the stronger voices of the priestesses. Nitara looked to the platform behind the altar and saw her beloved Xian there. Would she ever understand what Nitara would do today?

But she must not think about that. She must think only of Akaash.

She was several feet from the altar itself, and could see now the rich darkness of his long hair, the smooth texture of his skin, his tattoo in stark, black relief against his gold skin. Closer, and her Breeder sisters left her side as she moved up the stairs, until she stood on the stone slab itself, covered in furs and linens.

Akaash watched her, his eyes gleaming with meaning. With hope. With love.

She melted, going weak all over.

Need him...

She straddled his body and removed her blue sash, laid it over his stomach. The crowd surged, and the Priestess's chanting grew louder. When she drew her tunic over her head, the crowd cheered. She cared nothing for their approval. All she knew was the desire in Akaash's eyes, in the arching of his body toward hers.

Akaash.

She formed his name silently with her lips, and he did the same in return, whispering, "Nitara," soundlessly.

She was wet, needy, desire pounding through her like a storm, fed by the importance of what lay ahead. Sharpened by the possible finality of this one act.

She held perfectly still, waiting, wanting this moment to last as long as possible, no matter her hunger for him. She smiled to Akaash, and it was as though he was drinking her in with his eyes. She could read so much emotion there, pouring out of him and into her heart.

The crowd was going wild. And still she did not move, but only stared into Akaash's eyes.

She loved him.

He tried to lift his hand, to reach for her, but the ropes allowed him only a few inches of movement. But it was enough, that effort. To see his need.

He wanted her. And she was going to have him, inside her body. *Now.*

Her sex went tight and wet. She went down on her knees, her sex open to him. The tip of his erect cock grazed her opening, and she sighed. Tilting her hips, she ground down, impaling her body on his.

Chapter Five

Nitara moaned as Akaash began to pump, his hips thrusting, his cock driving into her. There was pleasure, then pain. But it was gone in moments, dimmed by the other sensations—his skin against hers, his body, which was hard and strong. And his scent, stronger now and mixing with hers, now that he was a part of her.

She was only vaguely aware of the chanting of the priestesses, the dim roar of the crowd. All she knew was Akaash, the pleasure surging through her body as she rocked against him.

His gaze was on hers, glittering in the light of the torches and candles. She saw his pleasure, an exquisite agony on his face. His cock was solid muscle, driving deep. She bowed over him, taking him deeper, her sex holding him inside her. And his hands...he had only enough slack in the ropes to raise them to her thighs, to grip her there. They were rough, the skin hardened, but impossibly warm. She wanted them everywhere: on her face, her breasts, pulling on her swollen nipples. And in her soaking wet cleft, pushing inside her, pinching her hard clitoris...

If they lived through this, she would feel his hands on her, his arms around her.

He whispered through gritted teeth, "No matter what, this is worth it, Nitara."

She raised herself over him, came plunging down, trying to take him even deeper. Her climax was like a swarm of pleasure, waiting, waiting. And as his body tensed beneath her, his cock seemed to swell, to pulse inside her, sending her over that keen edge. She came, shattering, pleasure a brilliant, blinding light.

She moaned. He groaned, writhed. She felt his hot come shooting inside her. And when she opened her eyes, still trembling, his dark gaze was hard on hers, as always, as though he looked inside her very soul.

She pulled the dagger from its sheath, raised it over her head. The crowd roared for blood. And through that noise she whispered, desperation like a hot tide, threatening to drown her, "Akaash, know that I love you."

"As I love you," he said, his voice low. "Whether we live or die. Even if I must die by your hand."

She was shaking all over. She whispered to the Goddess, but not for a child, as was the custom. But for mercy.

She glanced up at Nikkan, who nodded, and she watched as he spilled the brazier of burning sage onto the trail of oil he'd spread throughout the Temple earlier. Flames shot into the air, bursting from every side, from between the feet of the watching citizens, even as far as the altar itself. A priestess screamed. And Nitara brought the dagger down in one hard stroke.

Akaash rolled to the side as the blade cut his ropes. He grabbed the dagger from Nitara, pulling her into his arms as he leapt to his feet. He saw Nikkan pushing his way through the frantic crowd, saw the High Priestess Xian being pulled to safety behind the altar by her Sun Guard, Hel. Then Nikkan was at their side, grabbing Nitara's arm and guiding them into the crowd of panicked men.

"Stay with me," Nikkan yelled.

Nitara was trembling in his arms, but her feet were steady as they moved through the sea of flames and bodies pressing toward the doors at the back of the temple. It seemed to take forever, but finally they reached the north transept, where Nikkan had been stationed earlier. The two men lifted Nitara over the burning brazier, the flames hot, the air full of smoke. Behind it was a small doorway. Nikkan pulled them both through.

Standing in the dim light of a torch was a man, dressed in leather pants and vest, his dark skin beautiful, lustrous, his hazel eyes gleaming. He wore the mark of the Mutairi on his left forearm.

"Dhatri. You came."

His lover pulled him into a brief embrace, and his heart

lifted.

"I came for you, Akaash. I would not abandon you. I started on my way here as soon as I realized you'd been taken. I was already in the city when your message came to the trader."

"Dhatri, there is much to explain... This is Nitara."

"Nikkan has told me everything. We'll talk more later."

"Yes." He turned to Nikkan. "What is this place? We will be trapped."

"The Temple is full of passageways and tunnels," Nikkan said. "This one branches into the eunuchs quarters to the right, and deep into the earth to the left. It will take you to the sea." Nikkan pulled a leather bag from a niche in the wall and shoved it into Akaash's hands. "Take this. It is clothing and food, a cask of water, a piece of flint. And take the torch from the wall where the passage splits. Hurry!"

"Come with us," Nitara pleaded.

"There is no life for me, Little Sister. I will stay and lead the guards in another direction, if I can."

"And die if they discover your part in this, Nikkan. Come with us."

"No, Nitara. For our mother's sake, go!"

Akaash gripped her shoulder. "We must go quickly." She looked up at him. He'd never realized how tiny she was before, never having had the chance to stand beside her. Her green eyes were enormous, filled with tears. "Will you come with me?"

She nodded. "Anywhere you go, I will go with you."

They ran.

They had been walking for hours. Nitara had been quiet, uncomplaining. Akaash knew she must be tired. She was unused to physical activity. But she never said a word. She just held onto his hand tightly.

The tunnel had been quiet behind them, but they hadn't stopped, other than for several brief moments to dress in the clothing Nikkan had given them—a white, hooded tunic for Nitara and a loincloth for Akaash. He wanted to be certain Nitara would be safe. The only sound had been their footsteps on the smooth floor, the occasional skittering of rats moving in the dark and their own harsh breathing.

Finally Nitara asked him, "Are we safe yet?"

He heard the fear trembling in her voice.

"We're away from the temple. I don't think they know where we went. We're safe from them, anyway."

"But there are other challenges ahead…"

Dhatri said, "Your brother made sure to supply us, and we're hunters, Akaash and I. We won't go hungry. And we have nothing to fear from the road raiders—they know to leave the clan's warriors alone. But once we reach the surface it'll be hot. You're not used to it, and the sun will burn your fair skin. We must find a way to cover you. It won't be an easy journey back to our clan, and will take several weeks on foot. But we'll take care of you, Nitara."

"You don't have to care for me," she said, her voice soft.

"You are Akaash's, and therefore you are mine, as well."

Akaash looked at Dhatri. Reached out to stroke one long, soft dreadlock. His mate smiled.

"I didn't think I'd find you alive," Dhatri told him, his voice rough.

Dhatri was not a man of many words, but he didn't have to say more. Akaash felt his love in the few he spoke, felt his acceptance, despite his own sense of shame. He nodded, smiled.

They walked on.

Nitara wasn't afraid of the darkness, only of the unknown. The only certainty she had at the moment was her love for Akaash, her trust in him. And his love for her. But Dhatri seemed kind and strong, and if Akaash trusted him so utterly, then she could too. She knew they would care for her. Still, there was so much about the world that would be new. Her mind was spinning with every step.

The tunnel narrowed as they progressed, until they had to walk close together, and when she stumbled Dhatri took her free hand and didn't let go. The last hour they walked side by side, the two men holding her up when she would have faltered, her bare feet torn by the rough surface, littered with rock and other debris.

Finally there was light ahead, just a small pinpoint. Akaash's grip tightened on hers.

"We're almost out of this dank place," Dhatri said, picking

up his pace.

Soon they were approaching a small opening, and Nitara could smell the sharp scent of salt. It was strange. Wonderful. When they got there Dhatri went first, having to bend almost in two to slip through. He held his hand out for Nitara, and she bent her head and went into the sunlight.

She blinked, dazed by the brilliance of the sun, something she had been exposed to only rarely. She could feel the warmth on her skin. There was a strange roaring, a heavy white sound, and fear was a rumble deep in her body, her heart fluttering.

Akaash stepped through, pulled her close to his side, and she felt for the first time the full impact of his embrace. It chased away her fears, her doubts. She pressed her face to his bare chest, inhaling the scent of his skin.

"Don't be afraid, Nitara. The ocean is vast, powerful. Beautiful. Open your eyes and see."

She did so slowly, keeping her head close to the safety of his beating heart.

The sight astonished her. Overwhelmed her.

She'd heard of the ocean, certainly, but had never hoped to see it. It seemed as endless as the night sky. Gray and blue and green, a moving, glorious entity. She felt its power, saw it in the waves that crashed on the shore.

"It's so...enormous."

Dhatri laughed. "Yes, it is. It's the home of the pirates and fishermen. Not for the people of the Wasteland. But we can use it as a guide to tell us where we are, by measuring the sun's position on the horizon."

Akaash nodded. "We head north. There's a rocky incline farther up the beach. We can find a place to make camp for the night. Our day has been long enough already." He bent and laid a kiss on the top of Nitara's head before pulling up the hood on her tunic. "Keep this on always during the day, Nitara."

"I will."

Akaash took her hand, and they moved over the sandy beach. She'd never felt anything like the fine graininess sifting between her toes. It was a wonderful sensation, sensual.

"Akaash..."

"Are you all right?"

"Yes. But...I want to touch it. The ocean."

He grinned, and Dhatri, coming to stand beside him, grinned, as well. She had a moment now to see how beautifully made Dhatri was. A few inches taller than Akaash, his skin was a gorgeous, smooth brown, as dark as the earth. His hair hung in long, flowing dreadlocks. It was woven through with metal wires, studded here and there with beads made of clay and bone, some of them intricately carved. His smile was lush and wide, a short goatee surrounding his mouth. And his eyes...they were a stunning hazel. Silver and gold and green all mixed together, framed by long, curling lashes. His smooth chest was crossed with long scars that ran down over his ribs, but did nothing to lessen his masculine beauty.

"You should touch the ocean," Akaash said to her. "You should experience everything you've been denied."

Dhatri tugged on her hand. "Come on, girl. Let's touch the ocean together."

The two men led her to the water's edge, and her pulse sped as they neared it. They stood at that point where the water reached its foaming fingers onto the sand, and it was surprisingly warm as it flowed over her toes, even as it stung the cuts on the soles of her feet. The next wave splashed her ankles, making her smile.

Dhatri reached out, stroked one finger across her cheek. "You're beautiful, girl. Too sweet for a pair of old warriors."

"Never too sweet," Akaash protested, smiling at her, his dark eyes gleaming in the yellow sunlight.

She felt safe with them. Cherished. Desired.

Heat seeped between her thighs, despite the long journey, the terror and excitement of the day.

She wanted them both.

"Akaash..."

He leaned in and kissed her, pressing his lips to hers. They were soft. Lovely. And when he opened her lips with his tongue, she went soaking wet all at once, her legs trembling.

He pulled away. "I want you even now."

"Yes," she murmured, tilting her chin to be kissed again.

"Dhatri wants you too," he murmured.

"Yes. I want him."

She felt another pair of hands settle on her waist, then slip around her. Turning in their arms, Dhatri pulled her close, his gaze on hers, those beautiful eyes watching her closely. "Only if you say yes, Nitara."

"Oh, yes. Please."

He smiled, then lowered his face to hers and kissed her.

His lips were fuller, more plush, his kiss a little rougher than Akaash's. Another rush of heat between her thighs. She was filled with the sound of the rushing waves. The scents of the two men. And an overwhelming desire.

Akaash's voice was a low growl behind her. "We must find a camp. *Now.*"

Dhatri laughed, stroked her hair. "Yes. Now."

They took her hands once more and pulled her up the beach, so fast she was breathless. In minutes they reached the rocky outcropping at the northern end of the beach.

"I'll scout ahead," Dhatri said, running ahead to climb over the rocks, disappearing behind them.

Nitara and Akaash waited, and he looped his arm around her waist, his hand wandering over the curve of her thigh.

"I can't wait to have you, Nitara. To really have you. And for Dhatri to be with us..."

Dhatri's face appeared at the crest of the rocks. "There's a small cave here. Come."

Akaash helped her climb. They found a narrow path up into the hill overlooking the sea. Dhatri waited at the opening to the cave. It was small, as he'd said, but would shade them from the harsh rays of the day's sun, and roomy enough for the three to stand in together. To lie in together. Nitara shivered.

Akaash took her immediately into his arms, his mouth coming down on hers. He kissed her hard, his tongue slipping into her mouth. His hands were on her shoulders, then moved down to her waist, her hips. She felt Dhatri come up behind her, his hands joining Akaash's, their fingers twining at her sides. Their bodies were burning, as hot as Akaash's tongue in her mouth. And she was melting with desire that rose higher and higher.

Akaash pulled back, smiling at her, then he leaned over her shoulder. She felt Dhatri moving in, turned her head and saw the two men kiss, their mouths coming together.

Her blood sang, her sex going damp all over again. She had never seen anything like it. Had never expected to respond this

205

way, with a torturous, sharp need that overpowered her. She wanted to see the two of them together, every bit as much as she wanted their touch herself.

"Ah..." she moaned, pressing her breasts against Akaash's chest, feeling the gentle scrape of her tunic against her nipples.

The men's joined hands moved lower, over the front of her thighs as they kissed. She could see the curl and clash of their tongues, flashes of their strong white teeth. And then their hands pressed between her thighs, over her aching mound.

"Oh, please..."

She heard Dhatri's low, husky laugh once more, then they both stepped back and one of them pulled her tunic over her head. Akaash fell to his knees before her, his mouth going to her belly, kissing the tender skin there. Dhatri's hands came around from behind and cupped her breasts. She thought she might come at that very moment.

Fingers teased her nipples into two hard points while Akaash moved his mouth over her skin, kissing her, nipping gently, his tongue darting out to lick. She was pure liquid, her body hot with need. Her beasts, her sex, ached so terribly she could hardly stand it.

Akaash grabbed her hands and brought them to his chest, and she explored his smooth skin, tracing the narrow path of hair that ran down the center of his chest and belly to his navel. Moving her hands back up, she found his flat nipples, and brushed her fingertips over them until they hardened.

"He likes to have them pinched," Dhatri said from behind her. "Watch how it makes his cock jump."

She pressed Akaash's nipples between her fingers, glanced down and saw the solid ridge of his erection press against the loincloth he wore.

"I want to see you," she told him.

He sat back on his knees, his dark gaze on hers, full of hunger. Dhatri stood behind her, his hands cupping her breasts, his thumbs teasing the hard nipples until she could barely hold still.

She watched as Akaash untied the leather cord at his waist, drew the loincloth off.

His cock was even more beautiful in the full light of the sun than it had been in the torchlight of the Temple. The skin was a deep gold, going darker at the swollen head. Her mouth watered.

"Dhatri," she said, breathless with need. "I want to see you too."

She felt Dhatri's hands slipping up, over her shoulders, then he was standing next to Akaash.

"And so you shall, girl," he said, smiling.

He stripped off his vest, then his pants, letting them fall over his thighs.

His cock was as hard as Akaash's, a rigid shaft of beautiful brown skin. She reached out, then paused.

"Do you want to touch me, Nitara?" Dhatri asked.

"Yes, please."

"Touch me, then." Dhatri reached out to her, took her hand and folded her fingers around his rigid shaft. She heard the gasping intake of his breath, and pleasure swarmed her.

"Stroke me," he whispered.

She moved her hand up, then slid it down.

"Ah, perfect," he said, his head falling back.

"I love watching you do this to him," Akaash told her. He slipped his hand between her thighs, over her wet slit, and she cried out. "Ah, beautiful. You're so wet for us, Nitara. Tell me, are you too sore?"

"No. I want you."

"Then spread wider for me. Yes, that's it."

She moved her legs apart, and Akaash leaned in, until his breath tickled the tender, shaved skin of her sex. He breathed out, warm and enticing. She looked at her hand, working on Dhatri's cock, then to Akaash's dark head moving closer and closer. His hands came up and grasped each of her thighs, and he planted his mouth on her cleft.

"Oh..."

His tongue darted out, licking first at the swollen lips, then burrowing between them to find the hard nub of her clitoris. His tongue was soft and rough at the same time, and when he sucked her clitoris into his hot, wet mouth, she nearly exploded.

"Akaash!"

"Hold back, Nitara. Try not to come yet."

"I...don't know if I can..."

"You can. Give me the pleasure of watching you like this.

Seeing your juices on your pink lips. Tasting them on mine."

He pressed a finger to her entrance, and she took a gasping breath.

"I'm going to fuck you with my hand, Nitara. I want you to hold back. And as I fuck you, I want you to stroke Dhatri harder. He likes it hard..."

Dhatri groaned.

She tightened her grasp on his cock, felt him pulse with pleasure.

"Ah, just like that...so damn good."

Dhatri's muscular thighs tensed, his hips arching into her fisted hand. A new wave of desire swept through her, simply seeing his pleasure.

Then Akaash was back between her thighs, his tongue darting out to flick at her clitoris as he pushed two fingers inside her.

"Oh!"

Her sex clenched, her body one long, undulating shimmer of pleasure.

"Akaash, please."

"Please what, little beauty?"

"Let me come."

"You must make Dhatri come first. I'll help you. Hold his shaft tightly. Yes, exactly like that."

Keeping his fingers buried in her sex, he turned his head and licked the tip of Dhatri's dark cock. Pleasure stabbed through her once more, simply watching him do it.

"Ah, you two torture me," Dhatri said, his voice rough as gravel.

His hands went into Akaash's hair. And Akaash went to work with his mouth, the lush lips closing over the head of Dhatri's cock, his mouth sucking him deep, until she could feel his lips on her hand. She squeezed Dhatri's cock harder, moving up and down the slightest bit, sliding over his rock-hard flesh. And all the time Akaash's fingers were deep inside her, thrusting, thrusting.

Dhatri pumped, into her fist, into Akaash's mouth, and crying out, he came. She felt the hot, liquid rush, over her hand. She kept pumping even as Akaash pulled away, reached up to lace a hand behind her neck, pulling her face to his. He kissed her, and she tasted the salt of Dhatri's come on his lips even before he opened her mouth with his tongue.

With Dhatri's come sweet in her mouth, Akaash drove his fingers into her, his thumb pressing on her clitoris. She came, pleasure like a thousand stars going off in her head, blinding her. She was shaking, her climax pounding into her like the waves of the ocean so loud in her ears.

"Akaash! Ah..."

In moments she was lying across Dhatri's lap on the ground, and he was spreading her thighs with gentle hands. Akaash knelt between them, held her chin in his hands.

"I will fuck you now, little beauty," Akaash whispered, his eyes glittering.

"Yes. Please."

He moved over her, used his fingers to spread the lips of her sex, the tip of his cock pressing against her.

"God, to see you come like that. To feel your hot little cunt. You will drive me crazy, Nitara. I need to be inside you. To come into your body."

"Yes, do it."

She opened her thighs wider, loving the way Dhatri's big hands closed over hers. It was purely erotic to her, the way he held her open for his lover. *Their* lover. Akaash thrust, his cock driving deep.

There was no pain this time. Only the most exquisite pleasure. As he plunged into her, over and over, Dhatri's hands caressing and pinching her nipples once more, the pleasure built, crested. Then she was coming again, shivering, crying out in their arms. And still Akaash went on, his breath warm in her hair, pushing pleasure ever deeper into her body.

Soon he tensed, his hips thrusting hard, bruising her. She didn't care. All she needed was to see his face, twisted in beautiful agony as he came. To hear her name on his lips as he called out, "Nitara!"

He collapsed onto her, and she went limp in Dhatri's lap.

They were both kissing her: Akaash's lips on her face, her neck, Dhatri lifting her hands to lay soft kisses on her palms. She was tingling all over, sated.

"I never knew...lovers could be like this. All of us together."

"Mmm, yes..." Akaash sighed into her neck.

"You've taken a third lover before..."

"Many times," Dhatri answered. "Most often a man. Never with a woman like you."

Nitara smiled, feeling the gentle power in being female, all the more so with these two warriors. *Her* warriors.

She felt that way. But what would it be like when they were back among their own people? Would Dhatri—or even Akaash—abandon her?

She felt fairly certain of Akaash, felt his emotions were more than gratitude for her taking part in his escape. But Dhatri she had just met. As wonderful as the sex was, would he feel any attachment to her in the long run? She already felt a connection with him, a sense of safety. But she had no Goddess to pray to, to ask for some illumination of the future. Her entire world was unsafe, uncertain, with only Akaash, and perhaps Dhatri, to anchor her to the earth.

She shivered, and Dhatri's arms tightened around her. "Are you cold, little beauty?"

"No. I'm fine. Wonderful."

And when Akaash kissed her she *was* wonderful, sinking into the soft sensation of his lips on hers.

She would have to accept her fate, whatever it might be. She herself had been instrumental in setting the wheels in motion. She would have to follow this journey through to the end, no matter how it might turn out. And with that realization came the understanding of her own strength, a strength she'd never recognized before. Had never had any reason to.

That was her last thought as she fell asleep in Akaash's arms.

They had been traveling for more than three weeks, walking each morning, resting in the heat of the day, walking again into the evening. They made camp wherever they could, the men always finding the most protected spot. The desert was a wonder to Nitara: sand and rock, cactus and sagebrush. The vast yellow sky was a constant mystery to her.

Twice they had stayed at the same camp for several days, the men taking turns hunting, bringing back small game. They took her into the caves, showed her how to find mushrooms and edible mosses, how to prepare the meat, to make a fire, to cook.

Each night they laid together, a tangle of arms and legs, warm hands and wet mouths. Each day they grew closer, and she was becoming as attached to Dhatri as she was to Akaash.

They were only another day's walk from the caves where the Mutairi lived. Nitara was growing more nervous about meeting their people, wondering if she would be accepted, how she would learn to live among them. She was intimidated by what they'd told her of their women, how they were warriors, hunters, just as the men were. Nitara was afraid their people would see her as being of no use. And that eventually, Akaash and Dhatri might, as well.

They stopped at a small clearing near the top of a hill, a flat area with a clear view of the Wasteland valley below, and a small curving overhang in the rock that would shield them from the sun and the wind.

Night fell, and Akaash built a fire. The stars came out, dazzling pinpoints of light against a black sky, the moon hanging like a disc of silver. Nitara laid across Akaash's lap, watching the moon rise while the men talked of people and places she didn't know. The moon watched over them, a silver eye in the night sky, and Nitara wished she could see her loving Goddess there. She raised her hand up, letting the moonlight turn it into a dark silhouette, wanting...something. Some sense of connection. That sense of knowing where she belonged she'd had her entire life, and that was now gone in the span of a few weeks.

"Nitara, what is it?" Akaash's voice was a warm breath in her hair.

"I'm coming to accept my place in the world. Or, my lack of place."

"You have a place. With us."

She turned to look at him, touched his cheek, rough now with his dark beard. "Will I, Akaash? How will I change things for you?"

"For the better." He caught her hand, brushed a kiss across her knuckles.

She turned to Dhatri. "And for you?"

"We get along well enough, don't you think?" He was smiling at her. He always seemed to be smiling.

"But do you feel...as if Akaash being with me takes him away from you?"

"Why should I? He's still here. I don't see it as anything being taken away. With you, we are multiplied. Love is multiplied. There are no limits to it." He laid a hand on her stomach. "And if we're lucky, maybe we truly will be multiplied."

She smiled then. "You've just given back to me my place in the world, Dhatri."

"It's true," Akaash said. "You can bring children to the earth no matter where you are. And if you can bear children, you'll be valued by the Mutairi above anything else. You'll be a gift to our clan. And maybe the only reason why I'll be welcomed back, after the dishonor of allowing myself to be captured."

"Then you must try again to impregnate me," she said with a grin. "As often as possible. And if you both try, it will be all the more likely."

Dhatri made a grab for her, pulling her out of Akaash's lap and into his own. "We can try right now."

She went willingly into his embrace.

Dhatri pressed his lips to hers, and she laughed as Akaash pulled her away, setting her on the ground before tackling his lover with a growl. She watched as the two men wrestled, muscles flexing, one on top, then the other as they rolled on the ground.

In moments there was more to it than humor. Dhatri grasped Akaash's face and kissed him hard. Akaash yanked the fastenings of Dhatri's leather pants open, yanked them down over his long legs. When she saw Dhatri's erect cock, her sex began a low pulse beat of desire. Dhatri turned Akaash over onto his back, straddling him and pulling his loincloth off. Akaash was as hard as his lover, and as Dhatri knelt over him, his hips arching, their rigid shafts came together, the swollen heads rubbing against each other.

They were wrestling, taking turns pinning each other down, thrusting their cocks at one another, their hipbones crashing, their hands rough. Akaash was on top, and he leaned down and bared his teeth, then sank them into Dhatri's throat. Dhatri groaned in pain and pleasure.

Akaash called to Nitara, "Come to me."

She crawled over to him, and he held one hand to her lips, holding Dhatri down with the weight of his body. "Take my fingers into your mouth, make them wet."

She sucked on his fingers, swirled her tongue over the tips. Then he withdrew.

"I'm going to fuck you now, Dhatri," Akaash said, eyes gleaming, cock rigid.

"Ah, yes..."

Akaash drew Dhatri's legs over his thighs, kneeling up, and his hand slipped down between Dhatri's muscular buttocks, and in between them. Another rush of desire poured through Nitara's body. She watched Dhatri's face as Akaash pushed one fingertip into his anus, then another. They were both hard as stone.

Akaash pulled his hand away, guided his cock between Dhatri's buttocks, and with one quick thrust he was in, his lover groaning beneath him. Dhatri's fingers dug into Akaash's thighs, and Akaash's hands held Dhatri's narrow hips, raising him up, giving him access.

Nitara had seen the two of them together, kissing, using hands and mouths on each other, but she had never seen this. Her legs were weak, she was shaking with desire, her breasts, her sex, aching, needy.

"Nitara..." Dhatri gasped.

She went to him and knelt over him, kissed him. His mouth was hungry, demanding. His tongue was soft and hot as it slipped between her lips. She was going soft all over, desire making her limbs heavy. She could feel the resonating thrusting motion of Akaash's hips as he ground into Dhatri's ass, and knowing he was fucking this strong warrior was impossibly erotic to her.

"Nitara," Akaash said, his voice a harsh panting breath. "Let him taste you. Let me watch."

She pulled her mouth away.

"Ah, yes..." Dhatri murmured as she stripped off her tunic, turned, and got on her hands and knees.

She knelt over Dhatri's face, and he pulled her down, his big hands on her hips, until her soaking sex was poised over his mouth. She felt the warmth of his breath, then his tongue, a lance of pure heat sliding over her cleft.

"Make her come," Akaash demanded, driving into Dhatri.

Dhatri's tongue pushed into her, pumping like a small, wet cock. She was shivering with pleasure, each thrust of his tongue pushing deeper into her body. Soon she was panting, barely able to breathe. When she felt Akaash's wet fingers pressing against her tight anus, she thought she would come.

"Wait," Akaash told her, as he so often did. He loved to make her hold her climax back, to let it build and build, so that when she came it was like a wall of sensation coming down on her.

She could feel the rhythm of his hips as he fucked Dhatri, Dhatri's hand stroking his own cock and Dhatri's tongue pushing into her soaking wet sex, in and out, then pausing to lick at her clitoris. She waited, forcing her body to relax, and Akaash pushed the tip of one finger into her ass.

Sensation layered on sensation, until she couldn't separate what she was feeling—Dhatri's tongue in her sex, Akaash's finger in her ass, moving deeper, deeper. She no longer knew where one of them began and the other ended. She was nothing but sensation, pure pleasure that spiraled into the night like a cloud.

She closed her eyes and began to move, her hips gently undulating in time with Dhatri's probing tongue, Akaash's gentle fingers, and his thrusting cock in Dhatri's body.

Akaash was the first to tense, to cry out. He thrust hard, harder, and Dhatri's hands gripped Nitara's thighs, hanging onto her as Akaash pumped into him. And before Akaash's groans had faded, Nitara came, pleasure surging, hot and sharp.

"Dhatri... Akaash..."

Then Akaash was lifting her, Dhatri helping with his strong hands, and together they lowered her onto Dhatri's pulsing cock.

"Oh..."

Pleasure crested once more, and she was coming almost as soon as he pumped up into her. Akaash knelt behind her, one arm around her waist, one hand teasing her hard and aching nipples, his mouth hot and wet on the back of her neck. And again she was assaulted by sensation, her climaxes coming one after another.

Dhatri thrust, impaling her over and over, his cock a solid shaft of flesh. There was no end to her orgasm, her sex clenching, her body writhing. Soon Dhatri was coming, his hips pistoning. They were a tumble of hard hands and panting breath, falling together onto the ground.

They lay in the lovely, breathless aftermath of sex, and all seemed well with Nitara's world. With her head pillowed on Dhatri's muscular chest, and Akaash's arm around her waist, holding her close, she slept.

It was twilight on their final day of travel, the lowering sun turning the sky a hazy orange. They crested the last hill, looking out over the valley where the Mutairi lived. The clan camped near the mouth of the cave at the bottom of the hillside. Their scouts would have seen them by now. They would know Dhatri and Akaash were their own, and that they brought another with them. But they would also respect them, allow them to make their own way home.

Akaash was relieved, glad to be alive, to be coming home to his people. And hoping to rid himself of the shame that washed over him anew at having to face them.

He had been taken in his sleep, when he should have been alert. He had grown too complacent, and had almost paid with his life. It seemed that Dhatri did not judge him. But he would judge himself, and find himself wanting.

He had failed the Mighty El, had been brought down as though he were the hunted and not the hunter. He had failed himself as a warrior, failed his people. Dhatri's love for him, and Nitara's, was his only redemption.

He looked at Nitara, standing by his side. She turned to him, her green gaze on his.

"Akaash," she said, reaching for his hand, then Dhatri's. "I have something to tell you both. I think...I am with child."

"You're pregnant?" Dhatri's smile was beautiful, radiant.

"I am fairly certain."

Akaash picked her up, held her tightly in his arms.

"Akaash," Dhatri scolded. "Put her down. You'll risk our child."

"Our child," Akaash repeated.

His or Dhatri's, it didn't matter. It would be *theirs.*

Perhaps that was what the God and Goddess had planned for him. That he would risk his life, the risk itself an offering to them, so that he might bring this woman back to his people, so they would flourish on the earth.

"You are my love, Nitara," Akaash told her.

"*Our* love," Dhatri said, his face close to theirs. "As you are mine, Akaash."

They would spend this final night together on the hill, Akaash decided, before sharing with the clan. The three of them, together.

Nitara held onto their hands, absorbing their warmth, their strength, the sense of solidity she felt between them, and that they gave to her, as well.

"My life is about to change," she murmured, her gaze on the darkening valley below. Fires burned, and she could see the silhouettes of the people of the Mutairi moving about.

"It has changed already, Nitara," Akaash said, his fingers tightening on hers. "We have taken you across the Wasteland, away from the temple."

"Yes, and safely. I'm grateful."

"Your life changed the moment you decided to help me escape. You went against everything you knew for me, even your goddess. I'm the one who's grateful."

"As am I," Dhatri said, "for bringing Akaash back from certain death. To me. To our people."

"I'm a little afraid," Nitara said. "Even if I bring a child to your clan, will I ever be one of them?"

"You're a part of us," Akaash told her, and she felt the truth of it in her heart, in her very bones. "We'll care for you. Teach you whatever you need to know. The clans are unlike the Temple. We're cast-offs, rebels, Wanderers on the earth."

"I suppose I'm a Wanderer now. I have no other home, but with you two."

Dhatri enfolded her small hand in his, took Akaash's with the other. "You're home now, Nitara. We all are."

Her warriors smiled at her and she felt her heart swell. With pride in her lovers. With love for them both. With the hope they gave her.

Tomorrow would begin a new day. A new day to survive the heat of the arid desert, the challenges they each faced to live on what was left of the earth. The love Akaash had told her about, that he and Dhatri now gave her, eased her fears.

The sun went down over the ravaged Wasteland, the clear black sky lighting up with stars, the moon casting silver over the earth. She laid her hand over her belly, feeling the life budding there. Hope for the Mutairi, and for her. Love meant they would build a new life together, the three of them. As one. Together, they would build a future for the Wasteland.

About the Author

The author of a number of novels, novellas and short stories, Eden Bradley writes dark, edgy erotic fiction for Samhain Publishing, Harlequin Spice, Berkley Heat (as both Eden Bradley and Eve Berlin) Bantam/Delta and Phaze Publishing. Her work has been called 'elegant, intelligent and sensual'. One erotic novel was profiled in *Cosmopolitan* magazine.

Eden appears regularly on Playboy Radio's Night Calls, Dissident Radio's Breaking Taboos, and the West Coast In the Flesh readings. When she's not writing, you can find her wandering museums, shopping for shoes and reading everything she can get her hands on. A California native, Eden currently lives in Los Angeles. You can visit her website: www.edenbradley.com.

Look for these titles by
Eden Bradley

Now Available:

Tempt Me Twice

Midnight Playground
The Seeking Kiss
Bloodsong
The Turning Kiss

Celestial Seductions
Winter Solstice
Spring Equinox
Summer Solstice

The Priestess

R.G. Alexander

Dedication

For Cookie—Love is the reason. To Beth, my Armageddon Encyclopedia. And to my fellow Smutketeers—Eden Bradley, Crystal Jordan and Lilli Feisty—I couldn't end the world with a finer bunch of deviants.

Chapter One

"Shall I kill them for you?"

Xian turned from the small altar on her private balcony and smiled softly. "You've asked each time I come back from a meeting with the council. What would you do should I ever say yes?"

Her Sun Guard quirked his lips. "Obey with haste and enthusiasm, High Priestess, as I always do."

She shook her head. "Much as I am tempted today, I'm still not sure the Goddess would approve."

But then, she wasn't sure She wouldn't. Not after hearing the men of the council spitting bile and demanding blood for the loss of the recent Sacrifice. That, combined with the previous disappearance of several Roses, prostitutes from the brothel, had them shouting recriminations and fear for the return of The Burning Time.

Chamberlain Vey kindly pointed out that though there had been incidents in the past, they had been rare until now. Until Xian. No Sacrifice, no Wanderer taken for seed and returned to the Goddess, had ever turned the tides and escaped, taking a Breeder with them.

During the meeting, he actually demanded that the Temple must increase the Sacrifice rituals. To kill two—even three Wanderers at a time to make up for what was lost. They cried faith, but it was greed and thwarted lust she saw in their eyes. They did not fear the reprisal of an angry god, nor did they respect the Goddess. They were children throwing tantrums at having their toys taken away.

Nitara.

Xian knew the Breeder was safe. Knew now that Nitara had

willingly chosen to save the Wanderer, the desert warrior, and run with him. She'd spoken privately with Nikkan and Leilin, Nitara's siblings and accomplices. She'd loved the young woman like her own flesh and blood. What hurt most was that Nitara hadn't trusted Xian enough to tell her that she'd had more than first-time nerves. To tell her that she'd spent her Taming Moon with a Wanderer whom their soothing draughts had not affected, and formed an attachment to him.

A bitter chuckle escaped her lips. Why would she? It was Xian who had placed her on her path. Even when, after years of study under the former High Priestess, Xian still didn't understand why the ritual was necessary herself. Oh, she knew what she'd been taught. In order to soothe the Sun's anger, in order to aid the Goddess, it must be a life for a life—sacrificial blood for a virgin's blood. But it felt wrong.

That feeling didn't stop her from forcing the murderous burden onto her charges...too many times to count. If her predecessor had not seen Xian's birth veil or markings as a sign that she would be a Temple leader, she too could have been a Breeder, could have been called upon to kill the father of her child moments after conception. As it was, she was born with blood on her hands, since her true mother had not survived the birthing process. That too, was considered a sign.

"My Priestess, if you do not stop looking so sad, I will have no choice but to believe they have offended you beyond repair and slay them all. What troubles you? Do they continue to blame you for the young Breeder's escape?"

Hel, her Sun Guard, was the only one involved that she hadn't spoken to yet. She didn't want to admit, even to herself, that he had kept it from her. He was her confidant, her protector. For six rotations of the starlit sky, since her predecessor had passed and she'd been given the mantle of High Priestess, he had never wavered in his commitment to her. Even during Akaash and Nitara's flight, he had wrapped Xian in his arms, protecting her from the fire and the angry mob with his own body.

But he hadn't told her why he'd been instrumental in helping them escape.

She turned to study him more fully. The sun through the sheer blue curtains that separated her from the harsh daylight cast his skin in shades of dark bronze. A testament to his tolerance for and life beneath the hot sun.

All Sun Guards were impressive compared to the ordinary citizens of Kroy Wen and the eunuchs. They spent their entire lives training, after all. But Hel was...more. Strong and broad-shouldered, he was taller than most of the others. Blue-black hair curled against his neck with the heat of the day, and eyes the color of the healing malachite stone glowed from his darkly tanned face.

He'd made many a Priestess flush with his mere presence. The eunuchs would often share the Temple gossip with Xian. They told her how the others wished Hel would enter the lottery just once, that one of the reasons they imagined he didn't, had to do with speculation about his relationship with their High Priestess.

There was none. No male touched the High Priestess. But Xian would be lying to herself if she denied her fantasies. How often had she completed a fertility ritual by the light of the moon, or taught a newly blooming Breeder the ways of self-pleasure, and found an image of Hel in her mind? Too often.

Her role in the Temple forbade such selfish urges. Her passion and energy was for Kroy Wen and all her charges, not for herself. As she was trained. As it was meant to be. She was chosen by the High Priestess Ani and the Goddess to be mother to all, and could never be mother, or lover, to one. Certainly not to a Sun Guard who was duty-bound to follow her every command.

You didn't command him to help Nikkan save Nitara.

Friendships between eunuchs and outer guards were rare indeed. As they should be. The eunuchs had been created to protect the Breeders in the inner sanctum of the Temple. Some were chosen at birth, some were the result of punishment when her predecessor had been forced to make an example.

The Sun Guards worked outside, also protecting those who dwelled inside these walls, but they did not befriend, or in many cases respect, the inner guards. It wasn't something Xian necessarily approved of, but she'd been taught that the separation was necessary for the safety of the Breeders. She supposed she'd just had that lesson reaffirmed.

Hel was not merely another Sun Guard, loyal only to her. He had secrets. A life separate from hers. It rattled her, thinking she might not know him as well as she thought.

225

She crossed her arms, determination steeling her spine. It was time. She couldn't back down now. "Hel, arm yourself and gather any supplies you believe we'll need. I must journey to The Vault." She hesitated. "I would prefer that you not share this information with your fellow Sun Guards."

His lashes flickered in surprise, but he didn't question her. Bowing low he backed into the room, toward his own small adjacent one to comply.

She knew what he wanted to say. They had already made the perilous journey once this year. It was only done when those Priestesses who had trained to understand the stars and their meaning deemed it safe. When the Crone foresaw a clear path. When other Sun Guards stood at the ready to make the journey with them.

This was not one of those times. Yet Xian felt compelled. She glanced down at the altar with the carved, lush figure placed in the center. Perhaps the Goddess was guiding her steps.

Perhaps.

"She knows, Hel."

Hel pressed Nikkan against the wall in the smooth, circular hallway. "And how would she unless you told her, eunuch? I did not believe you would be so free with your tongue, especially with so much at stake. For all of us."

A female voice broke the tense silence behind him. "I told her, Sun Guard."

He didn't take his eyes away from Nikkan, knowing that for an outer guard to look upon a Breeder would mean death. "Why?"

A soft feminine sigh echoed in the narrow walkway. "She was as much sister to Nitara as I was. And she is our High Priestess. I knew she would not rest easy until she knew the how and why of our actions. Nikkan's...mine...yours."

Nikkan adjusted his tunic when Hel released him, looking flustered. "I wanted to warn you so you did not lie when she asked you. Unless she has already?"

Hel ran a hand through his hair, his mind racing. Had she? The moon had filled only to empty again since that night, and once his charge had left her self-imposed isolation, she'd been different. Quieter. She used to tell him everything. He knew far more about the inner workings of the Temple than he should. But she'd barely spoken to him in days.

"She's said nothing. Asked me nothing."

Nikkan's sister spoke from behind him again. "This is good news, Sun Guard. By rights she could reassign you, banish you. Just as she could have had both Nikkan and myself punished. Instead she keeps her silence. Protects us all from the council and the judgment of the others in the Temple. Protects us from my mother's fate."

"No, you don't understand, Breeder. This is not good news. But I don't have time to explain. She has told me we set out for the old ruins tonight. Alone."

Nikkan paled. "Tonight? Without telling anyone? But there's been no preparation, no prayers. The rains have only just come. Why?"

Hel towered over the eunuch. "I do not know. But she is the High Priestess. She has kept your secret, so you will keep hers, or by the Goddess I will remove more body parts than you can stand to do without when we return."

"You are quite protective of Xian aren't you, Sun Guard? More loyal to her than to the Temple? I am glad. She deserves that kind of loyalty."

Hel dropped his chin in acknowledgement of the woman's words, stepping back to leave. Nikkan stopped him. "Hel, you have been a good friend to Leilin and I. Getting word to the trader for the Wanderer, not stopping Nitara and her lover from escaping when we all know you could have. If you should come across word...if anyone knows how she fares..."

"I will let you know. But I am no paragon. I did not do it for you." Hel turned his back on them both and strode down the hall toward the west entrance, and the Sun Guard barracks. He needed a few special supplies.

As he walked his mind returned to her. His High Priestess. She was in pain. He could see that. He just had no idea how to fix it. An enemy he could fight. He could tear apart the council chamberlain who looked down his nose at her while ogling her sex through the sheer panel of her skirts. But this quiet pain, this silence, it nearly unmanned him.

She was his reason.

For what he was, what he did, why he stayed. It had always been her. Xian. How much had he done to ensure a place at her side when she reached her majority and required her own personal guard? How far would he have gone, had he gone, to achieve his rank? All for her. The gods of the Wanderers and those who dwelt inside the city walls be damned. She was his altar, his religion and the answer to all his prayers. Or perhaps his punishment. Being so close for all these years without being able to touch her...

He closed his eyes and saw her, a vision of perfect curves and golden skin covered in the swirled markings of her rank. Her breasts were heavy and lush. Her hips swayed to a siren melody that had always drawn him in. Onyx hair hung straight and shimmering to her waist...and that face. It was exotic and otherworldly. Almond eyes an unusual violet and blue in hue, framed by thick coal-colored lashes. Her full lips always looked pink and freshly kissed behind her sheer veil. When she smiled it fell on him like gentle rain in the desert. Necessary.

Damn him back to The Burning Time. He spoke blasphemy. A Sun Guard's belief sustained him, kept him loyal to the Temple. But then, he hadn't always been amongst them.

A fact that his High Priestess could never know.

The warmth of the evening sun hit his face and a familiar voice greeted him. "Follow the Path of the Peaceful Sun, Hel. How are you this day?"

"May the Goddess guide you through the darkness, Fyral. I must speak with our Father." Hel smiled at his brother in arms, and the bald, dark-skinned man grabbed his arm in greeting, pulling him farther into the Sun Guard camps.

The Sun Guard of the High Priestess was the only outer guard allowed to dwell inside the Temple. The rest lived in barracks, mud-brick longhouses adjacent to the outer mountain wall of the limestone Temple, where they shared everything. Food, laughter, fighting and friendship. Raised to be guardians, warriors. Raised in strength.

They were the men who guarded the Breeders and Priestess class. The men who captured the Sacrifices meant for Kroy Wen. They kept all usurpers, pirates and overzealous traders at bay for the growers, herders, fishermen and artisans of the city. Hel felt a surprised jolt of pride as he watched the men training in hand-to-hand combat and weaponry on his way to the main longhouse. This had been his family for so long. Though they did not start out that way.

Fyral had trained with him beneath their Father, the man who had taken responsibility for their education, for years. Fyral pointed to the sparring guards. "We are all on high alert, since the loss of the last Sacrifice. You can tell our High Priestess it will not happen again. She need have no doubt that we will change loyalties either."

Hel stopped, tensing beside his friend. "Why would that be a concern?"

Fyral snorted. "That bastard from the council tried to talk to our honored Fathers, claiming that war with the Wanderers was the only way to appease the Angry Sun. That it was necessary to ensure the continuation of the civilized world. He said the Temple had twisted the old ways, grown soft. That the High Priestess was too compassionate for her own good, and had no doubt helped a valued Breeder escape. He attempted to convince them that a new hierarchy of councilmen and Sun Guards would be beneficial to all of Kroy Wen."

Rage burned, a living thing in Hel's chest. "Chamberlain Vey and I may have to have a private talk before too long. He goes too far."

"Be at ease, Brother. It is resolved. The Fathers made it clear that he would not be welcomed in the barracks again. No citizen will go against one Sun Guard, let alone all, and live to tell about it. Chamberlain or no. The Wanderers are warriors, yes. But they fight mostly amongst themselves. Admirable in their skill and survival instincts, but no threat to our way of life. We have no issue with them." Fyral patted Hel's back. "Father is inside. I must train the youngest of us, but I hope you'll come back when I'm through. I've missed sparring with you."

Hel smiled and nodded, heading for the longhouse. Fyral might underestimate the Wanderers. They had no desire to dwell in the cities, true, but they grew in number, stronger each year. They had more than just survived. They had advanced. And he knew that in the six years since he'd been assigned to the Temple, their clans had only increased. How much longer would they allow their warriors to be taken for their seed and killed for these citizen's entertainment?

He pushed back the curtain made of thick hide and saw his Father sitting by the hearth, sharpening his favorite long spear. His bushy beard and full mane of hair had gone white with age, but his body and movements were still those of a warrior. A Sun Guard. He spoke without looking up. "Hel. You honor an old man."

"Your instincts are sharper than ever, I see. Honor? This is your way of saying I never visit, yes?"

Father just smiled. "You have known your path from the start, as have I. I am revered above all Fathers to have one of my own as Sun Guard to the High Priestess. I know all that is required of you that takes you from us."

Hel knelt at the older man's feet. "I have never forgotten all you did for me. How much you risked."

"You must risk much to gain much. There is no need to speak of it again. Why have you come?"

Hel lowered his voice. There was no easy way to ask this. "I seek to borrow some things from your collection."

The tip of the spear was at Hel's throat before he could take a breath. The old man's eyelid twitched. "What collection?"

"Father, I do not test you. I seek only that which may protect the High Priestess."

"Why?"

"I cannot tell you. By her command."

The craggy face so familiar to Hel studied him, before nodding and standing abruptly. "If it be for the High Priestess, it is for the Goddess. And for the Goddess, I have sworn to do anything." He shook his head ruefully as he pulled a lose brick from the wall beside his bed. "I do not know why I thought you wouldn't remember these. You were there when I found most of them."

Hel remembered. He'd watched the powerful man digging through the rubble of shimmering stone and sharp-edged rocks to find his strange treasures. He'd been fascinated. By all of it. He'd even kept a few things of his own, things he would take with him now, in case he needed to trade to keep Xian safe.

He wouldn't have to if he spoke out now. Why wasn't he calling the ready guard for this journey? Why, instead, was he preparing in secret, when he knew how the Temple and the Sun Guard would react to the High Priestess leaving the city unscheduled, and with only one protector?

He could say it was because he was bound to follow her orders, but that was not the case. There were some laws even the High Priestess was bound to. Most meant for her safety, to ensure the continuation of their way of life. But that was not why.

The true answer came readily enough. He wanted her for himself. A few days with no one but Xian at his side. A few days where she wasn't called upon to train the Breeders, encourage the midwives, overlook the artisans or soothe the citizens of Kroy Wen with her sensual rituals.

The High Priestess was the most sought-after person in the city. Hel often wished she would rest, take some time to herself. But she never did. She gave of herself every day, and would until she died. As would he. It was their path.

The only thing she did not participate in was the lottery, a fact with which he could only feel relief. The thought of another man touching her made his blood boil. She was his. It was a primitive feeling, one she'd never encouraged or reciprocated, but it was strong. From the moment he'd seen her as a young boy he'd known it. A quiet voice inside him wondered if, without the demands of the Temple weighing on her shoulders, she would know it too.

His Father made a pleased sound, and pulled out several unusual objects. "Here. This is no doubt what you were thinking of. I was going to give them to you anyway. Consider them my gift to you."

Hel smiled. "You are too generous, thank you. Follow the path of the Peaceful Sun, my Father."

The old man nodded, reaching once more for his spear. "May the Goddess guide you through the darkness, boy."

Now he just had to get a few more things in order, and he would be ready to take his Priestess anywhere she wanted to go.

Chapter Two

Xian handed the sealed hemp scroll to the courier. "Timing is essential. High Priestess of the Temple of The S'Anilorac is to receive this at the Wild Moon. Not a moment before or after. Is that understood?"

"Yes, High Priestess." The swift-footed eunuch bowed his head, leaving the main prayer chamber with his head lowered in reverence. Xian had no worries for him. In the camouflaged, protective garb of a courier, running the coastlines, he should safely avoid all enemies...including the pirates that scoured the shores. There were several caves and overhangs along the route to protect him from the strongest light of day, and he could do most of his running at night. She prayed for him, and that her fellow High Priestess would understand the missive.

She noticed Hel appear in the hallway, his nod causing her heart to pound. All must be ready then. He hadn't told his brothers in arms, elsewise they would have been demanding an audience.

Was she truly going to do this?

Yes. She had to. If she was to serve the people in the name of the Goddess, there was no other way.

Xian tried not to let Hel's presence distract her as she took care of the rest of her Temple business. She wasn't sure how long she'd be gone, and she wanted everything to be settled before she left. Though she admitted she should have been done much earlier. She was hesitating.

This main prayer hall had always inspired her, given her strength. It had high curving walls, polished smooth and glistening with beautiful shades of red, brown and slate gray in the torch and candlelight. She used to sit in the corner, watching her mentor guide her fellow Priestesses, guide the spiritual life of the city, and marvel at her power. Hope to be like her one day. She was praying some of that power would rub off on her now, so she could do what she needed to do.

She heard a harsh snort echo off the chamber walls, and sighed, knowing she could no longer ignore the Crone. The older woman had come up from her seclusion several hours before, and was standing in the corner of the large room, beside the brazier smoking with white, purifying sage. Xian's throat tightened.

From the youngest of ages her High Priestess mentor had taught her the hierarchy of their order. Stargazers who charted the sky, in search of signs of the Sun's returning anger. Midwives who aided in bringing new life to the world and took care of the infants until they could be settled into their proper caste. Crafters who made strong netting for fishermen and pretty baubles out of sun-glass and other gems for trade, as well as pottery for food and precious water. Herbalists who specialized in healing tonics and aphrodisiacs. All of them, along with those Breeders who had already proven to be fertile and had participated in at least one Sacrifice, were eligible for the lottery, the annual choosing of citizens for a night of sexual revelry, a night that often led to multiple conceptions.

Only two types of Priestess were restrained from participating. The High Priestess and the Crones. The Crones were chosen at birth, just like she and all the others had been. They dwelt for a time in the Temple, but when they came of age they retreated deep into the sacred caverns, the Womb of the Goddess, and spent their days ingesting herbs and inhaling steam from the deep chasms below in order to aid them in their visions.

When Xian was younger, she'd often envied them. They were not expected to learn all that she was, to be responsible for an entire community, though it was clear *they* did not see it that way. They looked up, look within, returning to the Temple halls to create the mark for each Breeder and Priestess, and to share their future visions with the High Priestess in order to bring her clarity. They were special.

Did Meidra know about her plans? Would she share it with the others? She stood and gave the woman her attention. "Crone, Goddess blessings upon you."

Those dark far-seeing eyes looked into hers as she walked slowly forward. "Do you remember when I gave you your first mark, High Priestess?"

Xian notice Hel step closer outside the doorway, and she tried to ignore the nervous flutters in her chest. "Of course, Meidra. Your skills were beyond compare, even then."

The older woman reached out to trace the crescent-moon birthmark beneath Xian's breast, the dusky desert red of the tattoo curling around it. "Four symbols intertwine around the sign of the Goddess on your skin and these same ones were repeated on your back. To surround you with strength. Protection. Passion. And the fourth, and most important...Sacred Truth. Each High Priestess is given markings similar in style but unique to them. The Crones saw special things for you, Xian. From the beginning, you were different."

"What are you trying to say, Meidra?"

The Crone tilted her head, smiling the secret smile that had always sent a chill up Xian's spine. "Nitara followed her own path. It is not your fault. You must follow yours to its end. The Goddess demands no less from you."

She turned and walked away, stopping next to Hel in the doorway. He stood at attention, his eyes hovering somewhere over her right shoulder. Xian knew it was his training. The Sun Guards weren't permitted to make eye contact with their charges. Yet she'd often wished he would shed that rule with her. She'd stared up at those understanding malachite eyes as she'd told him of her worries about Kroy Wen, her concerns for the future of the Temple.

He'd been there the first time she'd had to decide where a babe was to be placed, when she'd been shocked to realize she wasn't completely sure she'd made the right decision. The Goddess had not whispered in her ear to assure her that the young boy child was to be a fisherman or a grower. He had known how unsettled that truth had made her. But she never knew if he really heard her. Really saw her.

The Crone chuckled beside Hel, drawing Xian's attention once more. "I've seen you as well, great Sun Guard. Don't think I haven't. If you'll take some advice from an old woman, I will offer it. Be willing to share more than your cache of fine goods for the safety of your High Priestess. Her safety and happiness mean salvation...more than you know."

Hel jerked his chin in acknowledgment, and the Crone was gone.

"All is ready, High Priestess."

Xian bowed to the larger statue of the Goddess, coming to walk beside her guard. "I need to gather a few more things, Hel."

She studied the honeycombed halls of her secure home closely, as if it were for the last time. "Wait here." She slid the stone door closed, looking around her private sleeping quarters. It was separated from the rest of the temple, the only room facing the ocean. Xian remembered the first time she'd been allowed into this room, the first time she'd seen the view from the balcony and the moment the hazy orange-yellow sky gave way to blue and green sea. The Temple had been built into the rock on the far edge of town between the ocean and the center of Kroy Wen. The best position for defense. The cliff beneath her was too steep for a pirate to scale, the mountain impenetrable. To her right, she could see the fishermen gathering, so small, so busy at their tasks. To her left, endless sky.

Xian sat on her bed and hugged her pillow to her chest. The Crone had said she must follow her own path. And Hel. Would he follow it with her to its end? She'd never been alone with him, and after his recent actions, she wasn't sure why she still trusted him. Yet, she did. Just thinking of him made her body heat, her nipples harden. Need, not trust. But it was enough.

She knelt on the floor and reached for her traveling pack from under the bed. She slid her hand beneath her stuffed mattress and smiled. The cool metal filled her palm before she quickly pulled it out and slid the chain over her neck. The small, strangely shaped keepsake slipped down to hide between her breasts. The key. She had everything she needed now.

It was time to go.

They went down into the tunnels that only a select few knew of, hidden deep beneath the Temple itself. One path led out to the sea, one to the Womb of the Goddess where the Crones dwelt, and it was down that path that it split off, heading into the Garden of the Moon.

It was a strange path, one that Xian had marveled at the first time she'd seen it for its perfect, cylindrical shape. Hel knew it well. He'd told her that part of the Sun Guards training was to walk this path, to clear out any of the creatures that sought to make it home, paving a safe path for the High Priestess and her annual journey to the Vault.

They traveled in swift silence until she noticed movement in the low light. "You've acquired a horse? But Hel, I did not ask you to—"

The welcome neigh silenced her for a moment. A mare was tethered to the entrance, a beautiful, pure white mare, and Xian couldn't hide her surprise. "The Garden is a walk of meditation and reflection. One is not supposed to be at ease, but to recall all those who walked through darkness without comfort after The Burning Time."

Hel chuckled. "One is not supposed to travel through the Garden of the Moon during the wet seasons. I will not take chances with your safety. I'm on strict orders from the Crone, you'll recall. I trust you and Luna will get along just fine."

Xian couldn't help the smile as the mare pressed her soft, flaring snout against her shoulder. How often had she wished to ride one of these rare, magnificent beasts? Her predecessor taught her that a High Priestess must walk amongst the people, not hold themselves above them, lest she lose perspective. But the child in her had longed to race with the wind through her hair as she'd seen the Sun Guards do on their way into the Wasteland. Longed to feel the kind of freedom Hel offered her.

He smiled down at her as though he could hear her thoughts. Before she could tell him to send the mare back to the city, that it was too fine a beast to waste on her journey, he gripped her waist with his large, callused hands and lifted her into the air.

She had a sudden flash of that night. The night Nitara stole away with her Wanderer. The explosion of the brazier, the crazed push of the mob...and then, Hel was there. He'd wrapped his muscular arms around her and swept her away, back to the safety of the inner Temple. Her mind had been in turmoil at what was happening around her, but her body had exploded with sensation.

The heat of his body, the warm, rich smell of his skin—it was intoxicating. Xian had performed the fertility ritual beneath the moonlight before the citizens of Kroy Wen, revealing her sex and reveling in the pleasure of the Goddess to ensure the growth of plants and herbs, gentle weather and new life. She taught young Breeders how to find relief with their own hands, how to seduce, arouse and satisfy their chosen Sacrifice's in order to ensure conception. But she'd never felt what she had in Hel's embrace.

Her face had been buried in his neck as he'd carried her, and when he'd set her down she'd seen the intensity in his eyes and known that passion dwelt inside him. He'd left too quickly for her to process her own reaction, let alone his. She'd spent the rest of the night going back and forth between worry for Nitara, and arousal for Hel. When she could stand it no longer, instead of praying at her personal altar for strength and guidance, she had closed her eyes and pictured him, using a tool made of polished sun-glass to fill the void inside her and find relief.

"High Priestess? Xian, answer me."

The horse was skittish beneath her, impatient, and Xian realized that her hands were clenched tight around Hel's shoulders. How long he'd been holding her, hovering above the blanketed mare she couldn't say.

Her cheeks filled with heat, and she released him, sifting her fingers through the satin mane in order to distract herself from the desire knotting her stomach. "Thank you, Hel. We should get moving."

He turned away from her to grab the braided reins of hemp, but she was sure she heard the smile in his voice. "As you say, Priestess."

They headed into the cavernous expanse, and Xian tried to tell herself that she wasn't glad to be alone with Hel these next few days.

She prayed that the Goddess would forgive her the lie.

Hel walked ahead of the mare, half his attention on the path ahead, the rest on the woman behind him. There was a lightness in his heart. It had appeared the moment he'd seen her reaction to the horse, and it had been growing with each step they took away from the Temple, and the people who took Xian's attention and energy.

She was his. For now.

"I don't believe I've ever noticed how beautiful the Garden is. How could I have missed all of this?"

Hel looked around at her words. The rains had come recently. Those hard rains that above meant danger, death, but down here meant life. The High Priestess was only allowed to make her journey during a time when there was no chance for flooding, so Hel was glad she could see this.

The Garden of the Moon was in bloom. The small central stream had swelled in size, framed by newly sprouted plants and strangely shaped and colorful fungi. Thick roots knotted the ceiling of the cavern and climbed down the walls. And up ahead... "High Priestess, look up."

He turned to watch her expression as they entered his favorite place. It was easy to believe in magic, in the stories of the chosen that survived The Burning Time, sheltered by the gently penetrating light of the Goddess, when you saw it. Green and blue glowing tendrils of incandescent light flowed from the water, up the ropy walls of the tunnel to cover the overhang above them like a star-filled sky. He could see his own awe mirrored in her expression. A joy he hadn't seen in too many moon risings to count.

"Hel, could we stop here for the night? I had no idea. I would have gladly braved the dangers of rising water if I'd known I could see this... It truly is a Garden of the Moon. It is beautiful."

She was beautiful. "It should be safe for the night. Let me set up your hammock, and then I will gather some fresh herbs for our meal."

The High Priestess slid off the horse as though she'd been born on one, shaking her veiled head adamantly. "You are only one Sun Guard. Gather what you must, I can make my own bed. I am the High Priestess, not an invalid."

He bowed his agreement before heading deeper into the darkness, just outside of sight. Hel felt like a child again. Watching from the shadows as she struggled with rope and vine. Her travel robes offered him no glimpse of her bare, pale gold sex, the copper nipples that had tormented him day after day. In a way, it was even more tantalizing, knowing what was beneath, knowing what she concealed for the journey.

She bent over and he bit back a groan, his usual restraint swept away by this place, this isolated place. None of his peers were looking on to judge him, none of the priestesses were stealing his charge away. No one and nothing could stop him from taking her into his arms, from touching her. Nothing but honor. Honor and the belief that she would hate him if he tried.

His cock was hard as stone. He needed relief and fast. Before he took the woman he loved by force and brought the wrath of her Goddess down upon him.

Chapter Three

"What is taking him so long, Luna?"

Xian slid her palm across the beautiful horse's flank to soothe the creature's nerves. Or her own. In the silence she'd been hearing strange rustling sounds, unnatural noises that had sent her imagination into overdrive. The stories of what survived beneath the surface along with what remained of humanity were tales told to terrorize young Priestesses into avoiding the tunnels. The Crones had survived well enough, but as High Priestess, Xian knew that part of their education included weapons training with the eunuchs. It was believed to help focus the mind, but Xian could see now how it might also protect them should the need arise.

"This is ludicrous." She took the small torch light he'd left her and started off in the same direction he had. There was flora enough beside their camp to serve them, and any other reasons for his absence should have been long taken care of.

A light ahead followed by a splashing noise slowed her steps. Was he bathing? Why hadn't he told her? Why had her Sun Guard left her unprotected for something like that? Oddly, Xian didn't feel offense or anger, just...intense curiosity. She slid her torch into a crevice in the wall and moved closer, swallowing the gasp that pushed against her lips at her first good look at him.

Great Goddess, he was stunning. Naked men were not unknown to her. She'd seen Wanderers prepared for Sacrifice, overseen the lottery to ensure the safety of her Priestesses and Breeders. But to her, all paled in comparison to Hel beneath a fall of water.

His body rippled with coiled power. His wet hair fell in

heavy curls to his shoulders, wide back flexing in time with the rhythmic movements of his hands as he washed. Her gaze followed the line of his body as it tapered sharply into his narrow waist. He had a strange curving scar climbing his back, disappearing beneath his hairline, and a symbol for the sun on his shoulder, the mark of the Sun Guard. She barely had time to study it before he turned slightly, and she lost all ability to reason.

He wasn't washing. He was pleasuring himself, his fist wrapped tight around a thick and impressive erection that made her thighs tingle. Flushed with blood and desire, and slick with water, his cock fascinated her. Her mouth dried, and she bit her lip, wondering if it would be hot to the touch, wondering how it would taste.

Though she had never seen a man pleasuring himself without another man or woman, the men of Kroy Wen did not believe in self-denial. There was no shame in passion. It was the way of the Goddess, how she soothed her savage consort. It was the way of women, and how they soothed the men. Xian wished to soothe Hel's passion, but it was not to be. Not for her. But even knowing that, she couldn't make herself leave.

His hips rocked in time to the slide of his grip on his cock. Xian trembled, and felt her own hand slide down her belly through her robes, toward her achingly empty sex. She glanced up at his face, at the look of agonized pleasure, the jaw clenched with need, and she pressed her palm between her legs.

What would it feel like, to have him inside her? Not cold, like the glass and clay phalluses in the temple. Nor soft like her own hands, or the hands of those she instructed. His cock would fill her with heat, burn her as surely as the sun. And she would revel in the flames as he wrapped his strength around her and took her against the cold tunnel wall.

Desire was a living thing within her. The motions of his body, his beautifully masculine face, making her blood pound, her body shudder as she came closer and closer to the edge. The cloth of her robes grew damp with her arousal as her fingers circled the sensitive nub faster, harder. Matching his rhythm.

She had never felt this kind of intensity. To her, pleasure had always been a warm glow, a sensual, clear stream that eased her. Healthy and good. Of the Goddess. This was madness. Dangerous. This was temptation.

His free hand curled around the rock beside his head and his strokes grew more powerful. The tip of his cock pearled with arousal, and his back arched as though he were in pain. The most addicting kind of pain.

"Xian. Oh, Xian."

He called her name, and her gaze flew back to his face. His eyes were closed tight as he came, with her name on his lips. Had she been in his fantasy the way he'd been in hers? The idea sent her flying into her own release, blood filling her mouth where she'd bitten her cheek to hold in her cries.

"I thought you were sent from the stars to save me, but now I see you're just as real as I am. Even better. I admit I wanted a good fuck before I died."

The deep, rasping voice was followed by large hands, one squeezing her breast, one covering her hand between her legs.

Xian screamed and tried to throw him off. She felt his hands relax, as if he was about to let her go willingly...and then he was flying. She whirled in time to see a naked Hel straddle the stranger's chest, sharp dagger raised above his arm.

"Hel, stop!" Her words froze him before he could bring the weapon down.

The man opened his brown eyes and wrinkled his brow. "Cock, huh? Well, it wasn't my first choice, but how many options does a dying man get?" His lashes fluttered, head dropping to the ground with a loud thud as he passed out.

He wasn't dressed like a citizen of Kroy Wen, but it was impossible to tell, since most of him was covered in blood. "We have to get him cleaned up, see where his injury originates."

"Xia—High Priestess, please." Hel spoke through clenched teeth. "This man molested you, would have done worse if he'd had the strength. That is an offense punishable by death. Do not stay my hand, let me be done with him."

Xian was shaking, her adrenaline high, but she was determined. "He will not die by my word. He was obviously out of his head with his wounds. Help me get him undressed and into the water."

Hel stood and looked down at her body. She followed his gaze, cringing when she saw the bloody handprint on the fabric that strained across her breast. "He touched you as though you were a Rose, a whore. As though he had the right."

Xian stared at Hel's nipples, entranced by the single bead of water that clung tenaciously to the hard tip. She licked her lips. "It was not his fault. To him I was just a woman, nothing more."

He was silent for so long that Xian lifted her lashes, only to gasp when her gaze clashed with intense, malachite eyes. She could see the anger there, the frustration...the desire. She was breathless with the power of his attention turned on her.

"High Priestess, no one who has ever met you has any doubt of your gender. Or your beauty. But no man, regardless of class or culture, should be allowed to touch a woman without permission."

He thought she was beautiful. And he was naked. "You should get him cleaned off. I'll find the necessary moss and herbs to see to his wounds."

He hefted the man over his shoulder. "Do not leave my line of sight. Anything you can't find around here we can gather on the way back to Luna and our camp. I'm not sure why you left in the first place, though I'm glad I was nearby when he showed up."

She turned before he could see the heat filling her cheeks. Would he put it together? Would he realize that she'd been watching him touch himself? That she'd heard him say her name?

Bending beside the stream, she listened to Hel struggle with the limp man who'd touched her. No man had ever touched her before. Not like that. It was disconcerting. Goddess forgive her, but all she could think about was how much she wished it was Hel who'd touched her.

What was wrong with her? This was not why she'd come on this journey. Clarity. Answers. A reason for the doubts that had been growing in her mind for years, that had finally overwhelmed her after the loss of Nitara. She needed understanding. What she didn't need was to throw away everything she'd been taught, everything she knew, in order to satisfy her selfish urges—urges that were admittedly getting harder to ignore with each moment spent alone with Hel.

Was the stranger a sign from the Goddess? Caring for an injured man would indeed be a barrier to further intimacy with her Sun Guard. For some reason, she found no comfort in that thought.

Hel was angry. At fate, at the interloper and at Xian. He sat, a stoic sentinel at the edge of the fire as he watched her tend to the unconscious man. She was wiping down his body, cooling the fever that had appeared as soon as they'd returned to camp. Touching him, this man who had arrived out of nowhere, in the Garden of the Moon, a path kept secret and sacred for years. He was obviously on the run. The wounds on his body were made by a jagged weapon, and the broken skin and bruising on his knuckles told Hel it wasn't a one-sided fight. Were his attackers nearby? What had he done to deserve this kind of punishment?

He'd checked out his body as he'd cleaned him. The man had no markings on the back of his neck, so he wasn't born to the Wanderers. In fact he had no particular markings to speak of. Nothing to identify him to city, job, or people. He was, in short, an anomaly. A dangerous thing, when Hel traveled alone with Xian.

But his worries weren't completely about protecting his High Priestess. Watching Xian touch another man's bare skin, even one who was apparently unconscious, was driving him mad.

She had tended to the wounded before, with those Priestesses schooled in the healing arts. But, standing guard outside and watching were two entirely different things.

He couldn't hold his tongue. "Your food grows cold. You won't be able to care for anyone if you do not take care of yourself."

She pushed her hair back with a tired sigh. "You are right, as usual. The Goddess can do more for him now than I can. That and rest."

Hel clenched his hands into fists on his thighs as she came to sit beside him, close enough to touch. The smell of her. Sage and another scent that was spicy, intoxicating. He had to do something to take his mind off how intoxicating. But there was no way he was going to leave her alone. Not with that man.

"High Priestess, may I ask you a personal question?" He watched her look up in surprise, their eyes locking again. He didn't look away, and she didn't tell him to. "Why have you not asked me about the escape of the Sacrifice?"

She swallowed the bite of food she'd just taken, choking a bit until he handed her some agave juice. He could see she hadn't been expecting that, but he had to know.

Instead of answering, she asked him a question in return. "Do you recall the incident when the Priestess was discovered with a Sun Guard in the city? The banishment that followed?"

Now it was Hel's turn to be surprised. "That was a long time ago. I had nothing to do—"

"No, no," she interrupted him. "I wasn't suggesting you did. You must have been twelve then. I was merely ten. The Priestess was Nitara's mother." She broke eye contact and leaned her head back against the cavern wall. The position gave him the freedom to study the perfection of her features in the firelight, and wonder what she would do should he remove her veil.

"My mentor, High Priestess Ani, turned it into a lesson to be taught to all Priestesses, all Breeders. The pressure on Nitara, on Nikkan and Leilin was extreme." Xian sighed. "It is no secret that I favored Nitara above the others. Her innocence. Her inquisitive mind. Much was expected, from the both of us, so we understood each other. She was more than a pupil. She was my friend. *Is* my friend. A friend I don't want turned into another tale of immorality."

Her voice grew raspy with emotion, and Hel let out a low curse. "I am sorry, my Priestess. I thought it was what you wanted."

She placed her hand on his arm. "You thought I wanted...?" She was silent for several long moments, just studying his features, as if she were seeing him for the first time. "May I ask *you* a personal question, Hel?"

"Of course."

"Why did you never enter the lottery?"

Hel swallowed. Damn. One question he didn't want to answer. Not now. "How do you know I haven't?"

"I know what goes on in my Temple, Hel. And I know that those in charge of gathering names often bemoan the fact that the most handsome and esteemed Sun Guard in Kroy Wen refuses to share his exceptional genes."

She blushed and his lips curved upward. "Exceptional?"

Her startling violet gaze narrowed on him. "Do not change the subject. Why?"

He shifted, uncomfortable and more aroused than he should be. What man could fault him? The woman he desired above all things was asking about his sexual activities. "I am the Sun Guard of the High Priestess. You are above reproach, and I must be as well. Which means those within the Temple are safe from my attentions."

"You know there is no judgment in passion, only joy. All men are encouraged to help replenish the population, regardless of station. You should not feel restrained by your office. By me." She hesitated, biting her lower lip. "Those within the Temple? But not out?"

He saw the look on her face, and chuckled. "When a Sun Guard is on leave he is allowed to visit The Dusty Rose. I do enjoy the curves of a woman, if that is your question."

She leaned closer, watching his lips move as he spoke, and his cock grew painfully hard. Did she know what she was doing, looking at him like that? What she was asking for? His earlier need for release was nothing compared to this compulsion, this craving. He had to kiss her, touch her, damn the consequences.

A male voice, groggy with sleep broke through the heated tension. "That is too bad, Sun Guard. I was hoping you might want to cuddle."

Chapter Four

His name was Siraj. He was the most unusual, outspoken man Xian had ever met. It had taken an extra day to arrive at the tunnel's end because of his injuries, and they'd stopped to have a meal until moonrise, safe from the heat of the day.

The stranger made the time pass quickly. His fever had broken early that morning, and he was healing rapidly, though obviously still in pain. He took it in stride though, and Goddess knew there was nothing wrong with his voice.

He'd spent the last day telling stories, impossible tales of adventure and feats of daring. The things he knew. He knew she was a Priestess, knew about Kroy Wen, but he insisted he wasn't from there, nor did he care to go. He spoke of traveling with the traders, raiding island ruins with pirates...even spoke of the Wanderers as though he knew them.

It was obvious Hel doubted the truth of his words. "The Wanderer clans would never allow an outsider into The Rites of Spring. It's sacred to them. Private."

Siraj flicked his long, mahogany braid over his shoulder, his brown eyes twinkling. "They would if one of the clan leaders personally invited him in return for saving the life of his first born." He shrugged. "However, merely observing a sexual feast left me rather...hungry... You would be as well if you'd seen that kabu temptress. I believe my host told me her name was Kadira. Beautiful dark hair, and that body..." He shivered, winking at Xian. "But, it was obvious she was already spoken for, and I decided to leave before I was gutted by a possessive warrior. I did get some fuel for my treader while I was there. Some of those Wanderers are very handy to have around. I'm sure you know what I'm talking about, right, Sun Guard?"

"Fuel? Treader?" Xian looked at Hel, confused. Her mind was full of the images he'd described. Wanderers, rituals, pirate islands. It sounded dangerous. Exciting.

Hel glared at Siraj before lowering his head to Xian. "The Sun Guards have often shared tales around the campfires of the increasingly elaborate metal contraptions made by some of the more inventive Wanderers. Fast as the swiftest horse, loud and terrible and billowing smoke. They can move higher into the mountains this way, through terrain that would be near impossible on foot and difficult on a steed. We have learned it's something to avoid, and the Fathers have forbidden traders from selling certain...items...in our city that would arouse fears. Those autos, like his treader, included. The citizens are already intimidated by the Wanderers' strength. It would only worsen if they knew of their intelligence."

Siraj grimaced. "Of course. Who needs progress? Not me."

Something, a memory flashed in Xian's mind, and without thinking, she stood and rummaged through her travel pack. She pulled out the large book and sifted through the pages until she found what she was looking for, trying to ignore the sharp inhalation and swearing filling the large cavern behind her.

There it was. In the very back, the page yellowed with age even inside the protective covering. Machines. A faded image with large black wheels, like the wheels of a cart, only thicker and not made of metal.

The handwritten notes from one of the former High Priestesses told of the machines that had been saved below ground with the foresight of the Goddess. Those that worked on heated water and pulled power from the sun.

They had been used to build the Temples and brothels carved into the sides of the mountain, by command of the Goddess, before they fell into disrepair. With no one knowing how to fix them, they were made into sculptures or used to create much-needed tools for the citizens. And the Wanderers had these? Had they found them, or found the blueprints to build them? And how had she not known?

"Why did no one inform me?"

Hel was standing beside her, his jaw grinding as he hid the book from Siraj with his body. "It has long been a silent agreement between the Fathers and the High Priestess. The less known about the origin of the Sacrifice, the better. To prevent panic in the city. Apprehension amongst the order." Hel lowered his voice. "What possessed you? No High Priestess has ever removed The Book of Knowledge from the Temple. It is too precious. Too valuable."

She took a step back, intimidated by the censure in his tone. "I do not answer to you, Sun Guard. I have my reasons."

Hel gripped her shoulders, and she gasped, burned by the heat of his touch. "You answer to me when it comes to your safety. I gave a blood oath to protect you with my life. An oath you seem to be doing everything in your power to make more difficult. It is a crime to remove this from the Temple. For anyone."

She was trembling. In part from fear that he was not as loyal as she'd first believed, in part from the need coiling in her belly at his touch. She was going insane, Goddess help her. Hel had to understand.

He must have seen something in her expression. He sighed and released her arms, sliding one hand down to the small of her back and guiding her away from Siraj with a terse, "Don't move," to the smirking man reclining on the ground.

Xian could barely hear above the pounding in her ears. Would he refuse to continue on this journey? Worse, would he expose her crime to the council and those within the Temple who looked to her for guidance?

She saw the rope ladder ahead. The ladder that led up to the surface. They were so close. The old ruins sat above them, the Vault mere hours away. So close. Would she never have her answers?

Xian turned to meet Hel's gaze. "Please, let me—"

Hel's blazing green eyes silenced her. He took the book from her hands and set it on a small ledge in the rock, safe from the damp ground. He gripped her hips and lifted her high against the ladder, throwing her off balance so that she instinctively gripped the rope above her with her hands.

He moved closer. "Please let you explain? Please let you get yourself killed? Break every law Kroy Wen has without letting me in on what you are planning to do?"

Her new position had her lips even with his, and they were so close, she could feel his breath caressing her cheeks. His voice grew thick and rough as he pressed against her. "You can trust me, my Priestess. You must know that by now."

Could she? He was a man. Men, she'd long been taught, were ruled by the Sun. Ruled by hot emotions—lust, anger, ego. He was also a Sun Guard, raised in loyalty and faith. More than that—he was Hel. And yes, she trusted him. Isn't that why she wanted him and no other beside her on her quest?

She studied his face. He was right. She had broken so many Temple laws already. Put the both of them, and now Siraj, in danger because of it. Did she dare, in this isolated darkness, break another?

Her grip tightened on the rope ladder, and she leaned forward. The small space between their lips disappeared. The prickly growth of hair on his face scraped her cheek as she angled her head to kiss him. It was strange, unfamiliar. She had never kissed a man before. It sent shivers of delight throughout her body.

Hel froze against her for an instant, long enough for her to doubt her impulse a thousand times, and then he shuddered. Hard. Groaning, he pulled her hips against him. His lips softened, gentled, opening to taste her.

Oh Goddess. She'd no idea his lips would be so soft, when the rest of him was solid as granite. Silk covered granite. She melted into his embrace, her own mouth opening instinctively as he traced her full lower lip with his tongue.

He tasted like dark cinnamon and agave liquor. Tasted of every dark desire she had in the night. Her tongue slid against his, inspired by the noises of encouragement erupting from his throat. The sensation soaked her sex in instant, overwhelming arousal. What would that tongue feel like against her skin? Her neck? Her breasts?

Hel pulled back. "Priestess. Xian. Wait..."

"No." She moaned in denial. She didn't want this moment to end. Not now. Not yet. But she soon realized he had no intention of ending it. He wanted more. He began to untie the side lacings of her traveling robe, unwrapping her slowly, like a treasured gift.

When the fabric was spread apart it revealed her High Priestess robe. Its sheer panel was unable to conceal her peaked nipples, and between her thighs, the damp fabric. He pushed the outer robes down her arms, as far as they could go, and he reached for the ties at her shoulders, the ties that would lower her dress to her waist.

Their harsh, expectant breath filled the silence. When she was finally bared to the waist, Hel took a step back, his jaw working and his face flushed with need.

"You cannot know how long... I have to... I must..."

Xian cried out in surprised pleasure when his head bent to take one aching nipple between his lips. His large hand cupped her heavy breast, lifting it higher as his mouth opened wide, filling his mouth to overflowing with her flesh.

Yes.

His other hand gripped the edge of her skirt and lifted, and as soon as she felt the cooler air on her thighs she wrapped her legs around his waist. His erection was burning her through the fabric of his pants, and her body was angry that the thin, rough cloth stood between them. That anything did. She needed him inside her.

She started to release her grip on the rope, to reach down and tear his laces off if she had to. She was crazed. Frenzied. Alive.

Hel sensed the movement and stopped her, lifting his head from her breast with a menacingly sexy growl. "No, Xian." He grabbed the dangling lacing from her robe and wrapped them around her wrists in swift, practiced movements. A thrill shot through her even though she desperately wanted to touch him, stroke him.

He pried her clinging thighs off his hips and dropped to his knees. He met her gaze and smiled tightly. "Not that. But I can give you this. I need to give you this."

Xian swallowed as he placed her legs over his shoulders, giving him a clear, unhindered view of her sex. "So perfect." His fingers spread the delicate lips apart, and his thumb pressed against her. "Delicate and perfect." He inhaled deep, his eyelids flickering as he took her scent in.

She watched, fascinated by the sight of this strong warrior at her feet, all his attention focused on her. Her eyes blurred from not blinking. How could she? Hel was burying his face between her legs, his tongue lapping at her arousal, drinking greedily from her swollen, sensitive lips. She'd never felt anything like it. It was as if he were consuming her. Ravenous for her taste.

The rope scraping her back through the robes, the laces restraining her, and Hel's tongue filling her sex were so forbidden, erotic. Was this what Nitara, what Nitara's own mother had felt? Why they were willing to risk their lives, everything they were, to have it? To have this feeling. This all-encompassing feeling of being claimed again and again.

And Hel was claiming her. His fingers had joined his tongue, thrusting deep, curling inside her, gathering all she was into him. Glutting himself on her juices.

She arched her neck and caught a glimmer of movement behind Hel.

Siraj.

He held one finger to his lips, smiling mischievously, as if they were two children sharing a secret. She gasped, and Hel groaned, his tongue pressing deeper, harder inside her.

She looked down at Siraj's body, still healing from his battle wounds. He'd opened the lacings of his pants, revealing a long, hard erection, his own fist wrapped around it as he watched them.

Hel didn't sense the intruder, too intent on bringing her pleasure. Siraj leaned against the cavern wall, stroking himself as Xian watched. Long, lazy strokes that riveted her gaze. She hadn't noticed before how attractive his lean, sinuous body was. How sensual.

What was wrong with her? It was Hel's body she'd fantasized about. Hel kissing her, bringing her to the brink. Yet...feeling Siraj's gaze on her body, watching him watch them...it only seemed to increase her desire.

Her heels dug into Hel's back, hips pushing against his mouth and his fingers and tongue picked up a faster rhythm, making her cry out in pleasure, so close to the stars.

Siraj's pace quickened as well, his face tightening with arousal, his white-knuckled grip on his cock holding Xian spellbound. He snared her gaze with his own, the brown eyes dark, bottomless. He wanted her to watch him. When his orgasm overtook him, Xian moaned, hiding his harsh breath with her own full-throated cries.

He lifted the hand, wet with his own come, and sucked his fingers into his mouth slowly. Wickedly. His eyes flashed as he studied the kneeling Hel once more. Then Siraj was gone, and Xian was consumed in the fires of her own climax. Taken over by it.

Lost.

A part of her mind knew Hel was standing, untying her arms and lowering her to the ground. That he was carefully redoing her robes, his lips, damp with her arousal, kissing her heated forehead with an aching gentleness. She knew, but she couldn't seem to pull herself together. Couldn't meet his gaze, or thank him for the pleasure he'd given.

Falling from such heights in a heartbeat, she berated herself for what she'd done. A few days away from the confines of her safe Temple walls and she'd thrown herself at her Sun Guard and allowed an outsider to observe her sin. Despite High Priestess Ani's lessons, despite a lifetime of following the destiny she was born to. She'd wanted more. If he hadn't held back, she would have given herself completely.

Why had he? He was a man. He seemed to want her. Why had he stopped her, kept her from touching him? Perhaps he was more loyal to the Temple than she thought.

Another blessing in disguise from the Goddess. She'd saved Xian from breaking the rules for someone who didn't want her. Not as much, she was beginning to realize, as she wanted him.

Chapter Five

She was here at last. Her body was still vibrating from her ride on what Siraj called a treader. Hel had been right. It was loud and billowed smoke. But it had taken hours off their journey and after Xian had overcome her fear, she found she'd truly enjoyed the ride. Did other cities have access to this kind of marvel? Why had she not been told? Her mentor was strict and upheld the ways of the Goddess without exception. Could that be the reason Kroy Wen was so isolated? So trapped in the past?

Xian knew Hel was angry. He'd demanded she ride with him on Luna, but she wasn't ready to be so close to him again. To wrap her arms around him and pretend she was no longer affected, that they could go back to before he touched her. Before she lost control.

He'd wanted the pretence. She could sense it. Once he'd guided her back to an innocently waiting Siraj, Hel had stayed away from her, playing the part of distant Sun Guard. It may have been for the other man's benefit, because he didn't know that Siraj had witnessed their passion, participated, but his actions hurt her nonetheless. They made it clear that she'd been right in her fears.

So she'd ridden with Siraj on his treader instead, with Hel keeping pace on Luna behind them. Xian was thankful that Siraj made no comments about all he'd seen. Not that she'd had an easier time touching him. Whatever had awoken within her from that first kiss with Hel seemed to be growing in strength. It hungered.

They had made it through the ruins without running into scavengers or incident. Jagged, oddly formed shards of metal pushed up from the ground, and sun-glass covered the ground, glinting under the moon's glow like an ocean of light.

The night sky pulsed with colorful clouds moving in a mystic, mournful dance. It was called The Roar. A near constant reminder in the night sky of the pain the Goddess suffered to protect humanity. What She'd lost. On those nights when the sky was clear, full of only stars, Kroy Wen celebrated it as a good omen. A sign of healing. She could have used such a sign tonight.

No matter. She had finally arrived. Safe within the familiar confines of The Vault, with the men waiting outside, giving her the privacy she needed for what came next.

Xian looked around, clasping The Book of Knowledge to her chest. It had come from here. All the wisdom of their ancestors, all they'd needed to remake their world. Ingredients for healing draughts, gardening in harsh environments, meditations on serenity and creating sustainable water and sewage systems...it was all inside this book. It had been bestowed upon the first of the Priestesses by the Goddess.

The room was large, but sharply angled and box-like. The walls, not layered with color and life from the stone, but unnaturally shaped tiles of a single hue. The floor beneath her was littered with a thick kind of ash.

According to the story, The Vault had once been a place of unlimited knowledge. Books had covered the walls from floor to ceiling. Xian could not fathom such a room. The book she held was one of only a handful she knew of, and all of them were the property of the few Temples scattered along the coast. They were sacred. Reading was meant for the Priestess order alone. A sacred law, to protect the rare tomes and the wisdom within them from being misused. To think there had once been so many, and all in one place. It was unbelievable.

And yet... She opened her book and noticed, not for the first time, that each protected page was a different size, each with unique lettering and relating to different topics. It was as though they had not been made at the same time, or by the same person. But hadn't the Goddess guided the first of their order to create it? Who was she to ask the how and why?

But she did. She questioned everything of late, it seemed. It was why she was here. It was why she'd brought the key. The reason she was about to break a sacred oath to her mentor, one that had been passed down faithfully since The Burning Time.

She set the book down and lifted the chain from around her neck to study the small key. "I vow never to bring this to The Vault without intent. Never to intend without reason. And to be prepared to face the repercussions of the Goddess."

The wording of the vow did not expressly forbid use of the key, though her predecessor was careful to add her own warning. This was the only key, and the responsibility was a heavy burden. It was one of the few times she'd seen fear in High Priestess Ani's expression, and it had been enough for Xian.

Until now.

When she'd taken the mantle, learned what it meant to be High Priestess of Kroy Wen, she'd thought she understood. All played their roles for a reason. The castes were there for a reason. Men and women kept separate for a reason. The will of the Goddess. The whim of The Angry Sun. But there had to be more.

She could not shake the feeling that this world was...wrong. That innocents like Nitara and her mother before her should not be considered criminals for feeling compassion. For feeling love.

Wasn't She the Goddess of love and empathy? How then could She have made these rules? The rules that forced Xian to take a babe away from its weeping mother and plot its course in life before it had the chance to open its eyes, let alone make a choice. The rules that took people away from their communities and drugged them in order to drain them of their life force, then soon after, their life.

And then there was the council. Created to keep balance, to keep peace, it had long since become a vehicle for angry men to proclaim themselves leaders while doing nothing. Nothing but decrying every institution put in place for their safety, protection and quality of life.

Six trips to The Vault since she'd taken her office, and she'd never wavered. Outwardly. Inside, her need for more answers, her need for clarity, continued to grow. Today she would use the key. She only prayed the answers were there, and that the Goddess would forgive her.

Xian knelt in the crumbling pile of dust, marveling anew at the strange circular tins, empty now, but once used to store food, lying upended on the floor. A white chair covered in cracks and dust sat in the corner, a hole in its seat that grew the only plant life for miles. Some strange contraption that reminded her a bit of a piece of Siraj's treader stood guard in the opposite corner of the room.

It had all been left untouched by the High Priestesses who made their pilgrimage here. Small and large odd trinkets, the meaning of which had been lost to time, peeked out from the disintegrating paper.

Light from her torch in the doorway caught on the black, rusted metal of the box. The box she was looking for. The hair stood up on her arms. It seemed so innocuous. It was hard to believe so many generations had been afraid of it. Yet, she could not deny that she too was trembling as she picked it up and placed it on her lap.

She studied the locking mechanism. The unusually shaped hole matched the key perfectly. She placed it inside, watching it slide into place and held her breath. No lightning struck. She was still here.

It wouldn't open. She tried to push the key in farther, wiggled it, and something clicked. Sending up a small prayer that she wasn't making a huge mistake, she lifted the lid.

"Oh my."

Xian knew her eyes had gone wide with wonder. Inside was a treasure beyond all her imaginings. Covered in the same clear protection as the pages in The Book of Knowledge were several folded pieces of paper. Beneath them, two small books.

Unfolding the one on the top she gasped. It was large and filled with images and strange symbols. Islands and continents and more oceans and streams, more bodies of water than Xian had ever imagined or seen.

"A map." The Priestesses had maps of trade and courier routes as well as the tunnel systems, and she knew the Sun Guards had created maps of the eastern half of the Wasteland, in order to plan their raids more efficiently. But this map was different. She wished she understood what it meant. Particularly the large landmass at the very bottom of the map. It had been circled in red with arrows pointing to it. The circle did not appear to be a part of the original map.

Xian folded it carefully, painstakingly, and returned it to the box. She lifted the other slippery page and opened it up. It was full of words and clear images that looked like some of those in The Book of Knowledge. Bold letters drew her eye.

The End is Near? Solar Flares and Earthquakes increase as the Mayan Calendar Enters Final Countdown.

What did that mean? Were they speaking of The Burning Time? Had it been prophesied? Xian narrowed her gaze to read the small print. So many of the words were unfamiliar. But the image of The Angry Sun breathing molten fire in a dark sky was clear enough. These Mayan people had known. They must have been similar to the Crones with their visions. And, at least according to this scribe, very few listened to their warnings. Those few who did were deemed insane by their fellow citizens.

She placed that back inside the box as well, a surge of excitement making her dizzy as she reached for the small books. Books no one had seen or touched in generations. They were in a clear sealed bag. One cover was simple brown, a single multi-petaled flower in the center. One soft with age, the tops of several pages folded down, as though to be remembered for later.

She studied the sealed section of the bag. There was no ribbon or lacing binding it together. No melted wax. She tugged lightly on the two ends and it opened with several small clicking sounds. How amazing.

With hesitant and gentle reverence, she lifted the brown book out of its container and felt the weight of it in her hands. She was afraid to open it. Afraid it would fall apart as the others in The Vault had long ago. But this book looked well intact. It had been protected from the elements for all this time. Protected from the warmth of the air. She had to open it.

It's been five months since it happened. I'd forgotten this journal was in my bag. It was supposed to be a birthday present for my daughter...

They were right. The lunatic survivalists that trapped us here beneath the library were right. This was not like the Y2K scare or any of the others. This was real. This was apocalyptic.

Mark is gone. He must be. He worked in an office on Wall Street. All our family and friends...gone. And the reports we've gotten from what's left of the military... Nothing remains. Any life that survived above has been destroyed by the radiation. A solar storm, they say. A fire that scorched large portions of the Earth. That melted glaciers and boiled oceans. Who could live through that?

The military apparently. Though they did leave one suit and some testing equipment behind for us to share so we could see the wreckage for ourselves, perhaps find more supplies.

How do I tell Tessa her father is dead? That it was a freak accident and not fate that brought us to the library in time, not to pick up a copy of her favorite story, but to be taken belowground by some foul-looking men with knives and a few crazy librarians? Yet they saved us.

They saved us. But is this really salvation?

Xian turned the page, tears streaming from her eyes as her hand opened to capture the image that slipped out at her action. So lifelike, it showed a blonde woman, her arms wrapped around a tall, dark-haired man who held a grinning child in his arms. They looked so happy, surrounded by lush green trees and colorful flowers.

And the sky...

"It was blue."

She wiped her cheeks, blinking through the tears as she soaked in the colors. They stood in the sun, uncovered and uncaring, beneath a sky that mirrored the ocean in its beauty. So much beauty. All gone.

She continued reading.

We've met others. People who happened to be in subways or mines when everything burned. People who lived beneath the city in places I never knew existed—some of them say there are animals being kept safe underground as well. Tessa was pleased at the news.

More military, though they seem to have their own survival plan now, separate from ours. Some of them have already lost touch with what it means to be civilized, showing allegiance only to each other—like a clan or tribe of warriors. But at least we are not the only ones left. And if there are more here, there must be survivors all over the country. The world.

We can be outside now, mostly at night. There was rain, though very little, and it was cleansing. They are saying we need to rebuild, that everything we need is in the books that were saved along with us. And those books have become valuable.

A couple of raiding parties have tried to take them, and a few of the women were raped and killed in the process. This is not the first time the men have attacked, several women are pregnant even now, but for my Tessa, I will try to make it the last. She is too young to understand, and I hope she never does.

The women held an emergency meeting. We are weaker, but we must gain the advantage. We have to protect ourselves. Our children. We will be smarter than they are. We hear the men talking at night, fearing another solar storm. Fearing God's wrath. Maybe we can use that to our advantage. Convince them that protecting us is a way to soothe that anger. And we must use the information we have here as a form of control as well. They must not be allowed to hurt our children. To hurt Tessa. One of the older librarians has been reading a book on Goddess worship and pagan mythology. She thinks she's stumbled upon something that might help. I wouldn't have chosen this path, but there is no man like Mark among the survivors. There are few men who can be trusted. The women must survive. It's the only way we can have a future. Tessa must survive this wasteland, she must be given a chance.

Hel wasn't sure what to do. What had happened? She'd been standoffish since he'd touched her, preferring to finish the journey with Siraj instead. But this. This was something different.

Xian had come out of The Vault with an expression on her face he'd never seen before. More than lost. More than broken. As though someone had told her the moon would never rise again. She'd asked to be taken to the cleansing cave—a nearby cavern that held a spring of clean, hot water where travelers could bathe or refresh themselves. He'd taken one look at her and agreed immediately, not arguing when Siraj wanted to join him to ensure her protection. All he could think about was Xian. What was wrong?

Siraj crossed his arms and leaned against the rocky opening, staring out at the emerging orange dawn. "If she were mine, she wouldn't be in there alone. Especially not when she looks so beaten up."

Hel stiffened. "She's not yours. She's not mine either. She

belongs to no man."

Siraj snorted. "That is a shame. If any woman in the Wasteland was ripe for pleasure, it's our curvy Priestess in there. If I'm not mistaken, you don't go burying your face between the thighs of any female unless she's a Rose...or she belongs to you."

Hel had Siraj's front pressed against the rock face, his body leaning heavily against him and a dagger pressing against his neck before the man could blink. "I should kill you now."

Siraj chuckled breathlessly. "Probably. Though I doubt Xian would think highly of you if you did. I'm still recovering from wounds *she* tended. So, my dear Sun Guard, I see you can be aggressive when you want to be." He pressed his ass against Hel, and Hel was shocked to feel his own reaction. "Much as I enjoy the rough stuff, I can tell your Priestess needs it more. She needs a passionate distraction, a lover who can take the reins. Take her mind off of her troubles."

He was tempted. Oh, so tempted. He relaxed his grip on Siraj. "I am a Sun Guard. To sleep with a Priestess outside of the lottery is to be banished. To sleep with her...would mean death. No doubt for us both."

Siraj rubbed his neck, turning to meet Hel's gaze. "There is nothing here but ghosts and regret. I won't tell if you won't. I'd be willing to bet you my treader that our lovely exotic flower will welcome your breach in protocol." He eyed Hel's knife warily. "She knew I was watching when you touched her. She enjoyed it. And I could tell she wanted more from you. She was yours for the asking."

Hel's grip tightened on his dagger, but it wasn't from the desire to use it. Just desire. Xian had known? He felt a flash of jealousy that Siraj had seen her, the woman he'd worshipped for so long. Worshipped but not known. Not the way he wanted to. He was beginning to realize that this might be his only chance. She had responded to him. Wanted him.

Siraj seemed to sense him weakening. "She needs you. I've got good instincts, I've had to, but I don't need them to know that."

Something stirred within him. Shifted. "You may be right." He thought about how long he'd fantasized about Xian, how many things he'd always wanted to do to her, things he'd barely admitted to himself. He'd spent so many years protecting her, he even did it in his mind. Perhaps it was time to stop.

He smiled wryly. "I don't suppose you'd want to wait out here?"

Delight transformed Siraj's handsome face. "I don't suppose I would."

Hel sighed and shook his head, trying to act nonchalant. Inside he could hardly contain the primal excitement burning in his veins. He felt a moment's worry, a moment's pity for Xian as he began to enter the cave.

Who would protect her from him?

Chapter Six

Xian knelt beside the pool of bubbling water, staring into the liquid, unblinking, as though it would give her all the answers. Answers that would make more sense to her than the ones she'd found in the box.

She piled her hair on top of her head, using a jeweled bone to hold it in place. Lowering her robes to her waist, she scooped a handful of the cleansing water and let it slide down her arm. She bathed herself slowly, studying the markings that covered her body. Marks of the Goddess. Sensual spirals twirled down her arms, her belly, even her sex. Her destiny had been written into her skin, her soul, for so long, she was not sure she could process what she'd found today.

The journal showed her what had been. The image of the man, woman and child, so happy together. The words of sadness, regret and resolve. Words that, in gifting Xian with a window into the past, had caused the small cracks in the foundation of her faith to split wide open.

She hadn't been able to finish the journal, nor examine the other book in the package, not with her stomach in knots, her eyes blurred with tears. What those women had done to survive was understandable and, in itself, incredible. But what did that mean for her? What was she now? Where did she belong?

"Xian."

She wasn't surprised to hear his voice. Her heart had been crying out for him since she'd arrived. She continued to wash without looking up. "Xian? Yes, I suppose that is appropriate, isn't it? I am no High Priestess. Not here. Not today."

He knelt behind her and she could feel the heat of his body against her bare back as he agreed. "No. Not today. Today you are Xian."

Her broken chuckle was tinged with bitterness...and hope. "And who is she? Do you know?"

Hel's blunt fingertips touched her chin, turning it until she had no choice but to look up into his eyes. "I have always known her. She has haunted my every dream, tempted me each day that I breathe air. She is all that is beautiful and strong." The determination in his malachite gaze made her shiver. "Xian is mine."

His kiss was not the gentle request it had been before. His lips were marking his territory. Taking everything. She loved it. When he lifted his head she was breathless, aroused, all thoughts of what she'd seen, what she'd learned, gone with the power of her need. She noticed Siraj over Hel's shoulder and startled in his arms.

She'd never seen that kind of smile on her Sun Guard before. It was confident. Sexual. "I know Siraj is here, Xian. This time, I know. I wish only for your pleasure. What would you do should I ask you to invite him to stay?"

He was studying her carefully. So carefully he must have seen the excitement sparkling in her eyes. Her voice was trembling when she answered. "Obey with haste and enthusiasm, Sun Guard, as I always do."

They shared a secret smile as both remembered the last time those words were spoken. Before their world had turned upside down.

A splash drew both their gazes to Siraj, who had already stripped bare and now stood in the heated pool, the water lapping low on his lean hips. "This is hotter than I'd imagined." His smirk told her he wasn't merely speaking of the water temperature. "What say you, sweet Xian? May I stay?"

She looked up at Hel once more, unsure where this was leading, but unable to deny her desire to find out. "Yes, Siraj. You may."

Siraj came closer, his warm brown eyes drawn to her full breasts. "I have the stars' own luck it seems. Though not in all things. Your Sun Guard is still woefully overdressed. As are you."

Hel shook his head at Siraj. "You're to follow my lead. That is our deal."

Siraj shrugged. "A deal I am more than happy with. I

believe I'll enjoy your brand of, um, leadership. I merely grow impatient for your first command."

She'd thought Hel disliked Siraj. They must have reached some kind of understanding. She shifted in Hel's embrace, her tight nipples scraping his bare arm.

His jaw clenched. "Xian. Stand up and remove your robes."

Xian found herself obeying instantly. The tone in his voice thrilled her. She stood and the loose robes that had rested at her waist fell to her feet. She had no desire to cover herself. She wanted to be seen. To enjoy the masculine admiration in their expressions as they traced the heavy globes of her breasts, the dip in her waist, her sex bare but for her markings of fertility.

"By the moon, she is stunning." Siraj had lowered his voice reverently. He came closer, and Xian could see his long erection skimming the top of the steamy water.

Hel stood beside her, setting his weapons and boots on the ground before slowly removing his clothes. "Yes, but she is so much more than that. There are no words to describe her. There never have been."

Her heart jumped at his words. She wasn't perfect. "Careful, Hel. I would not wish you to be disappointed. I've never—I don't—"

He placed his thumb against her lower lip, stopping her words with a touch. "You could only disappoint me if you sent me away."

She sighed. He stood there, naked, something so pure and beautiful in his gaze, and she was overcome with emotion. "Then you will never be disappointed."

Hel lifted her easily in his arms and stepped into the water beside Siraj. "That is what I wanted to hear, my Xian. Now. Let us pleasure you."

The two men shared a look, bending together to kiss her neck, her breasts. Hel lifted his head to join Xian in watching Siraj take one hard nipple between his teeth, biting with just enough pressure to make her gasp and arch in Hel's arms.

"You like that, Xian? I didn't think I would. Didn't think I would enjoy seeing another's mouth on your skin. Thought I would kill whoever tried." He slid one hand beneath the water, between her legs. His fingers pushed inside her sex, her arousal easing his way, and he growled. "You more than like it, don't you, my innocent Priestess? You love it. Love driving both of us wild, watching us go mad with wanting until all we can think about is fucking you. Claiming you."

Goddess, his words. She knew words had the power to arouse, but she'd had no idea she could be so effected. Siraj was leaving a trail of not-so-gentle bites over her torso while Hel continued to thrust inside her with his fingers, the sensations enhanced by his graphic words.

She did love it. Less than a week ago she had never been touched. Men barely met her gaze. Women called her leader. Now, pressed between these two strong men, so different, but both desirable—now she felt right. A woman. A goddess. She had lost her usual serenity, her usual control. But she wasn't afraid.

Hel would keep her safe. She trusted him, always had. Though she had never seen him like this. Controlling. Masterful. He was different. But so was she.

Siraj's hand brushed against Hel's where it touched the skin of her upper thigh, and she felt Hel flinch. She looked up at him, wondering at his reaction. It was known the men of Kroy Wen, even many of the Sun Guards, participated in same-sex relationships in between breeding times. It made sense when no lottery was scheduled, when they did not have enough to trade for a Rose, that they would seek satisfaction where they could find it. It was even promoted by the Temple to decrease frustration. Xian had the distinct feeling that Hel had never sought it out...and that Siraj had. The idea was evocative. Enticing.

She lost her train of thought as they moved closer, and she felt two hot cocks burning against her hips. Hel's fingers, Siraj's lips, they weren't enough. She needed more. Craved it as she'd never craved anything before. She'd dreamt of it since she'd overseen the lottery, witnessed the Breeders and Priestesses open their bodies for the men's primitive invasion. Flesh sliding against flesh, forcing two into one. Longed for it since Hel first took her in his arms.

Her body was aching. Empty. "Please."

"You cannot torture her, Sun Guard." Siraj was panting against her neck. "Not this time. She is too ready. If you do not take her soon, then I surely will."

Hel snarled. "She is mine. You'll put your cock nowhere without my permission." With that warning he dragged Xian higher up his chest, until her breasts were crushed against his body and her mouth being ravaged under his.

He pressed his forehead against hers. "Stop me now if you must, Xian. There is no going back after this."

"No. Don't stop. I beg you. I want you to. I want it to be you."

Xian wrapped her legs around his waist, clinging to him as she remembered how he'd pulled away before. His groan was pained. "Have no worries, my love. I know exactly what you need."

She felt his hands grip her hips, guiding her body until she could feel his shaft brushing against the lips of her sex. "Yes."

"I offer myself to you, my Priestess. Soothe my anger. Sate my passion. Know me."

The ritual words uttered at the start of the lottery. She could see he was trying to show her honor and reverence. To pay tribute to the courtship of the Goddess and The Angry Sun. They were words she never thought to hear anyone say to her.

She responded in kind. "I accept your offering. Come inside and I will sate you with my body. Know me."

Hel skimmed his lips across hers, sharing his breath as he lowered her onto his erection. Her mouth opened on a soundless cry, and he took full advantage, filling her mouth as he filled her body.

Too big...too much. She'd pleasured herself, used tools made of clay and sun-glass to simulate, to train others, but she wasn't prepared for how different this felt. This true intimacy. This connection.

His heartbeat pulsed through his skin inside her. When she thought she couldn't take any more of him, he angled her hips and lowered her another inch. She felt stretched to the point of pain, but it was a good pain. A beautiful pain.

He tore his mouth from hers and pressed his forehead against her shoulder and a fine tremor passed from his body to hers. Xian wrapped her arms around his neck, her hands in his hair. She felt connected to him, beyond the physical. She knew he was still holding back, still protecting her from the strength of his passion.

She began to rock against him, circling her hips slowly, sensually. Her breath caught and a sudden image flashed in her mind. Xian was kneeling in the Temple, surrounded by

Priestesses before the last lottery. Several had expressed nervousness at that years' chosen. They were too rough. They did not know how to bring pleasure. She had invited them to her personal chambers, reminded them that they had the true power in the sensual struggle. They could please themselves. As they cried out in ecstasy around her, from their hands, their clay phalluses, she recalled seeing something out of the corner of her eye.

"Did you see us that day, Hel? Was I right? Or was it just wishful thinking?"

Brilliant green eyes flashed with knowledge and desire. He knew what she spoke of. He'd seen her.

She bit her lip and smiled. "You can tell me. I watched you too. In the Garden before Siraj appeared. I wanted you then. I do now. All of you."

Hel gave up the battle. His training, everything he was demanded he take care not to hurt her, not to overwhelm her with his passions. Sun Guards ate, slept and breathed restraint. Do not look. Do not touch. You are more than a man. You are all that stands between the future and chaos. It was hammered into him again and again until it was a part of him. But inside his feelings were far more primitive. Volatile. And her words, the knowledge that she wanted him, set the beast within him free.

Need erupted from his throat with a roar. He stood straight and flipped Xian onto her back at the edge of the hot spring. With one of his hands he gripped her wrists and held them over her head, gaze riveted to her breasts heaving with each panting breath.

He barely recognized his guttural voice. "You want all of me, Xian? Your wish is my command."

His free hand gripped her knee, lifting it high as he began to fill her with long powerful strokes. Years of pent-up desires filled each hard thrust. Hel knew he was being too rough. Knew it was her first time, but her Goddess forgive him, he could no longer hold back.

"Take it." He punctuated each word with a sling of his hips, watching her body arch off the ground with the force of his penetration. "Every. Last. Inch. All of me."

The sleek heat of her body burned his cock, her hungry sex

squeezing him tighter, as though her body recognized his, didn't want him to leave. She cried out, calling his name the way she had in his dreams. But this was real. Her body was real beneath his. He couldn't get enough.

She came. Came again. Tears of climax slid down her cheeks. Her body writhed, and her hands curled into claws in his grip and still he couldn't stop. He never wanted this to end.

He was bent over her, half in, half out of the splashing water, when he felt the strong male hand on his back. Hel was about to shrug him off, focused on claiming Xian, but the gruff voice stopped him.

"You said I could put my cock nowhere without your permission, Sun Guard. You said nothing about my hands. Or my tongue."

Xian's body jerked beneath his at Siraj's words and drew his gaze. Her eyes were wide and her pupils dilated from surprise and...interest? Hel's mind was spinning with unsated hunger, his muscles rope-taut. When one hand joined another and lowered to his ass, he was too aroused to resist.

Hel continued to pump his hips against Xian's, watching her beautiful face contort in ecstasy. He was focused on her, but he was also waiting, holding his breath in anticipation as he sensed Siraj kneel behind him in the water.

Xian's tongue slid out to wet her lower lip as she felt Siraj's kiss. He kissed her calf where it met Hel's heated side. Her ankle where it clung to Hel's tailbone. Siraj continued to kiss her as his hands spread Hel's cheeks, his wet thumb slipping down the seam of Hel's ass.

He slowed his thrusts, unsure what he should do. What he should feel. When Siraj pressed his thumb inside the ring of muscles, easing its way with the firm stroke of his tongue, Hel's shout echoed through the small cave.

The feelings. He wanted to rip Siraj away, to push against his mouth and demand more. Each flick of his tongue sent a charge like heat lightning up his spine.

Xian bucked her hips against his, her voice breathless. "Show me, Hel. Show me how he touches you."

Hel groaned. "You will undo me, love." He took her mouth without another word, thrusting and swirling his tongue, mimicking Siraj's mouth. He let her hands go and she lifted them to his shoulders, nails digging into his skin as she moaned against him.

His cock grew harder inside her, and blood burned in his veins. Too much sensation. The feel of Xian's sex clinging to his cock, Siraj's thumb pressing deeper inside his ass, along with his talented tongue, sent Hel over the edge.

His vision blurred as instinct took over. He ate at Xian's mouth, taking her hard and fast, loving her screams vibrating against his lips. His climax rocked him to his soul. Everything he had, all that he was, poured into her. Xian. He felt the power of it as he had with no other.

He lifted his head and looked into indigo eyes gone soft with satisfaction. Siraj had moved away from them, and Hel sunk into the water, dragging Xian's limp body down with him.

She buried her head into his shoulder, laying a kiss on his neck. Hel's gaze clashed with Siraj's, dark with unresolved passion. Nothing had gone the way he'd imagined, but he hadn't lied to her.

Now that he'd had her, there would be no going back.

Chapter Seven

Hel was hot and angry. He'd gone to gather their packs and bring Luna into the shade of the cave's overhang. Alone. He was mad at himself for not thinking of it earlier, not taking care of their supplies and the rare animal that was, even now, looking at him with disappointment. He was mad at Siraj for playing up his injuries this morning, relying on Xian's compassionate nature to save him from the task.

Those injuries hadn't been on anyone's mind last night. But Xian had smiled up at him, and he knew he could not deny her.

Last night. After the first time, he'd been insatiable. Xian had been more than willing, as had Siraj. They hadn't spoken of what he'd done to Hel, and there'd been no repeat of the intimacy. Hel was thankful. He wasn't ready to think about how much he'd enjoyed the other man's touch. The two of them had silently agreed to work together to bring their sensual Priestess as much pleasure as humanly possible. And they had.

The memories of what they'd done stirred his arousal yet again. Xian's mouth filled with Siraj's cock as Hel took her from behind. Hel's head buried between her thighs while Siraj fucked her voluptuous breasts.

Siraj had been true to his word in letting Hel set the pace. He wasn't sure if he'd ever be able to truly share Xian. In his mind, in his heart, she had always been his alone. But he had to admit, he loved enhancing her pleasure with Siraj's help. As long as he was the one in control.

When he walked back into the limestone enclosure, taking his shirt off to wipe down his sweat-soaked body, it took a moment for his mind to register what he was seeing. Xian and

Siraj were lying on her robe beside the pool, naked bodies entwined in an erotic embrace. Siraj's reddish brown braid was draped over her thigh, his eyes closed as he feasted on Xian's arousal. Her hips rocked against his mouth as her own full lips wrapped around as much of his long cock as she could take.

The blood rushed to Hel's cock so fast his head spun, and a new wave of anger washed over him at their moans. He had been dutifully seeing to their safety and supplies while Siraj had taken full advantage. Injuries his ass.

He stood, still as stone, watching the two of them find their pleasure. When Siraj lifted his mouth to cry out in climax, Hel moved swiftly, yanking him away from Xian's mouth as he came.

Siraj's neck arched at Hel's grip on his hair, his seed dripping down his cock. "Shit, Sun Guard. Oh, fuck that was good. Why did you stop us before she came?"

Hel glanced over at Xian. She'd come up onto her knees, her arms covering her breasts as she stared at him in surprise. Her wide eyes and flushed skin told him she was still in the grip of passion, still unsatisfied.

Good.

"You didn't follow the rules, Siraj."

The idiot smiled serenely. "Not true. I was merely showing her what I did for you last night. It was she who decided to pay me back in kind. I did not break my vow, for I put my cock nowhere. She took it."

Hel didn't crack a smile. "You aren't a Sun Guard or a Wanderer, and you definitely aren't an ordinary citizen from the cities—so you don't know. There are punishments for those who don't follow the rules."

Siraj narrowed his eyes dangerously. "Are there now?" Hel watched his gaze drop to his pants, his erection straining against the fabric. "What kind of punishment did you have in mind?"

Hel swore. He couldn't deny what he wanted. Couldn't deny the knowledge in Siraj's eyes. But he could show them both who was in charge of their pleasure.

They'd drive him insane.

He unlaced his pants. "Xian. I want you to stay right there, spread your legs and keep your hands on your knees where I can see them." He looked over at her long enough to ensure she obeyed, then turned his stare on Siraj. "You can show her how you use that talented tongue of yours from here. Or do your injuries hinder you?"

Siraj licked his lips, still wet with Xian's juices. "I can take whatever you can, Sun Guard."

Xian held her breath, her body shaking in reaction. She wasn't sure what had happened with Siraj. She'd been curious about what he'd done with Hel, and he'd known. One moment he was telling her of the time he'd sailed with a group of highly sexed pirates, of what he'd given in payment for safe passage down the coast, and the next he'd lowered his head between her legs. It had felt so good, and his erection had looked so painful, that she'd had to respond in kind.

When Hel returned she'd been frustrated, aroused...and guilty. It seemed wrong to experience that kind of pleasure without him. It was him she'd wanted. Hel had awoken this need inside her, not Siraj. But still, there was something about Siraj. He wasn't constrained by the rules that held the rest of them back. His view of the world, the way he spoke to her— without hesitation, without reverence—was attractive. She was drawn to him. Not like Hel, but still tantalized.

She watched Hel wrap Siraj's braid around his fist, watched Siraj reach inside the open flap of Hel's pants and grip his thick, blood-flushed shaft with firm fingers. Her nails dug into her thighs.

Great Goddess, but they were beautiful together. Siraj kneeling at Hel's feet took nothing away from his masculinity. There was no submission, only power as he took Hel's cock into his mouth. Only strength as Hel pumped his hips, growling as Siraj took everything he gave and more.

Her body was shaking with the need to come. She dragged her hand up her thigh, needing relief, needing to join them in their passion. Before she could touch her sex Hel's malachite gaze pierced her flesh.

He shook his head, skin tight over his face. "Do. Not. Fucking. Dare. You watch. Don't touch what is mine."

Siraj lifted his head and grinned. "She likes watching us, don't you, sweet little Xian? She loves it. I bet she'd love to see more."

Hel snarled. "I don't believe I said you could stop."

Siraj chuckled, but instantly wrapped his lips around Hel's erection once more.

Hel spoke to Xian through clenched teeth. "Is he right? Do you like watching him swallow my cock? He's good. I've never had anybody able to take this much."

Xian whimpered, but he wasn't finished. "Do you want to see me fuck him? Are you that curious?" Siraj moaned against his flesh, and Hel bared his teeth. "I can see he likes that idea. Or would you rather I just bent you over and took your ass, High Priestess? Let us feel firsthand what it is we've been missing."

She was surprised by the sudden rush of fear and curiosity. High Priestess. What was she doing here? Breaking every rule put into place to protect her, to protect the future. She stood, grabbing her robe to wrap around her as she ran outside, ignoring the male shouts of denial.

The harsh rays of the sun hit her like a physical blast. She was vulnerable. Out in the world with no protection, in more ways than one. For a moment she wished for the ignorance of yesterday. Before she'd read any of the journal. Before she'd known a man. Before she understood what it meant. What love meant. "What have I done?"

"Changed everything." Hel spoke into her ear before pulling the fabric of her robes over her head protectively, shielding the rest of her from the strong light of day with his body. "And damned if I'll let you out of my sight long enough for you to change it back."

He picked her up and carried her back inside. She watched him share a look with Siraj for a long, tension-filled moment.

Siraj sighed and reached for his pants and boots. "I should go tinker with my treader, bring it closer so Luna'll have something to commiserate with." He reached for his belt and untied one of the small pouches, setting it on the ground. "You'll need this. Trust me."

Xian and Hel were alone. He sat, still holding her in his arms, and rocked her as though she were a child. As though she were precious. She didn't feel like a child. Not after what she'd seen and experienced. Not with the hard ridge of his erection pressing against her bare bottom. But he had something else on his mind.

He spoke in a hushed faraway voice that had Xian straining

to hear. "I was nine when Father found me in these ruins. I don't remember much before that. I was the child of a warrior. A Wanderer. I'd wanted to prove myself. I was too young to go with the raiding party, but that didn't stop me. Unfortunately they were overtaken. Everyone died, but I escaped. I ran away."

She felt his chest lift with a shaky breath. "I think I was scared. Ashamed. So I came to live in the ruins. It wasn't long before I saw Father. He was a part of the Sun Guard, scouting ahead prior to the High Priestess Ani's arrival. I'd injured myself, I was sick with fever, and I followed him." He chuckled. "Father almost killed me, but when he saw how young I was, how ill, he took care of me. Hid me out of sight and smuggled me back to his longhouse."

Xian lifted her head from his shoulder in surprise. He wasn't born in Kroy Wen? Wasn't chosen by the High Priestess from birth to be a Sun Guard? She looked at the scar on the back of his neck.

He noticed the direction of her glance. "I did that myself. Not very well, I admit, and Father never let me forget it. I wanted to blend in. But not at first. Father told the others I was one of the lost. A young Sun Guard lost in the Garden of the Moon during training. It's not an unusual occurrence, so it was easy enough. Still, he risked everything for me. But I didn't understand that then. I almost ran away, back to the Wanderers...my family. Despite my shame, everything I'd learned about the heretics of the city, the cruel foreign Goddess of the Temple told me I would surely be killed if I stayed."

"Why didn't you?" It was suddenly important for her to know the answer. Why would he have stayed? Become a Sun Guard no less?

Hel met her gaze, unblinking. "I saw a young Priestess being chased by her tutor. She couldn't have been more than seven or eight, but she was sneaking out of the Temple to watch the horses go by. Fearless."

Xian felt her eyes widen. Her? Was he talking about her?

He smiled. "When they'd passed, she allowed the older Priestess to drag her away. She looked up at me as she went by, her eyes a color I'd never seen the rival of...and she smiled. I heard her tutor scolding her, saying she needed a keeper." Hel shrugged. "As quickly as that, I found my destiny. I knew that I wanted to be the one to protect you. I wanted to be the one you smiled at again. So I embraced my new life and never looked back."

Xian's heart was pounding so loudly she was sure he could hear it. "Why are you telling me this?" The knowledge of what the elder Sun Guard had done, in the wrong hands, could have Hel and his Father killed. Especially since Hel had become the personal Sun Guard of the High Priestess.

"I'm trusting you with everything that I am. All my secrets. I'm trying to tell you that I—"

She covered his mouth with her hand. She wasn't ready to hear more. Not now. She replaced her hand with her mouth. Showing him without words how she felt.

Hel soon took control of the kiss. Lowering her to the ground, he pressed his body between her thighs. The loose laces of his pants dug roughly into her flesh, the sensation only exciting her more. He pushed down his pants and she moaned into his mouth, loving the feel of his bare skin on hers.

He lifted his head, his cheeks flushed. "You're right. No more talking. Let's see what Siraj left for us." He reached out to grab the pouch and a small vial slipped out.

Xian recognized the liquid. The Priestesses who worked with the herbs that drugged and aroused the Sacrificed, also created this. An oil that heated the body and eased the way for men and women alike. It was a popular item, always in high demand with the traders.

Hel's rough chuckle told her he recognized it too. "Good man. Now what were we talking about earlier? Trying something new?"

She shivered beneath him. He meant taking her as a man takes another man. The idea was as intimidating as it was thrilling. "What if I can't—"

"Take me?" His smile reached his brilliant green eyes. "You can, Xian. Trust me."

Adrenaline made her giddy. "I do, Hel. I trust you with my life. And my body."

His smile wavered slightly. "Two out of three. Good enough, Priestess. For now." He kissed her again and she lost herself to it, until she felt him lift his hips and apply the oil to his erection.

She jumped at the first brush of his thumb along her sex, and lower, along the seam of her ass. A warm tingle penetrated her skin instantly, her arousal building swift and strong. Oh, Goddess. "Hel."

His voice was rough. "I feel it too. The heat. Fuck, Xian, I need you."

"Then take me."

Hel turned her over, spreading her legs wide and entering her sex in one movement. Xian shouted in surprised pleasure, her body beyond ready for him. She pressed her forehead into the ground, her breath coming out in joyful sobs as he claimed her.

When he pushed his thumb inside the tight ring of muscles hidden by the full curves of her ass, she arched her back, opening for him, loving the stretch, the sting. The oil set her nerves ablaze, and there was no room for anxiety or tension—only desire.

"You're ready for me, aren't you? Damn, you don't know how long I've been dreaming of holding those sweet curves in my hands. Being inside you."

She nodded against the ground, every part of her screaming in agreement. Begging for more. For him. She groaned in denial when he left her body, her brow furrowing as he turned her on her back.

"I want to see you, Xian. I need to see those eyes." He lifted her legs high over one shoulder, his thumb thrusting inside her ass, coating her already-tingling flesh with more oil.

She didn't need any more help. She needed him. She reached out, her hand grazing his hip, his cock, and wrapped her fingers around him. A rumbling, primal sound emerged from Hel's throat as he thrust instinctively against her. He pushed her hand away and she gasped, feeling the head of his erection pushing through the snug barrier.

"Fuck. Xian, open your eyes. Look at the man who takes you."

Xian couldn't help but respond to the command in Hel's tone. She lifted heavy lids and looked into the face more familiar to her than her own. He snared her gaze, refusing to let it go as he slowly slung his hips forward.

She couldn't breathe, couldn't think. This was beyond anything she'd experienced before. Ecstasy and pain, panic and exhilaration. It was as though every inch of her body, inside and out, was focused on where they were joined, sensitive to each thrust and drag of his cock.

It was the most intimate experience of her life. Her soul felt as though it was floating, leaving her body to merge with his. For long, wondrous moments, there was nothing but the sound of their breath, the beat of their hearts.

They came together, still staring into each other's eyes as the inferno blazed around them. Hel looked the same way she felt. Staggered. Bewildered. Overwhelmed.

Dear Goddess it was true. She loved him. More than her calling. More than her people. More than anything.

He smiled tenderly and separated from her body. Lifting her in his arms, he carried her into the steaming pool beside them and bathed her with gentle hands. She still felt dazed, still felt like she was floating. As he held her she found herself telling him about everything. Her doubts. Nitara. What she'd read of the journal, and the reason she'd stopped.

Hel was silent for long moments. "This woman sounds very wise."

Xian pushed back to study his expression for signs of mockery. There was none. "Wise? If what she wrote is true, then the world we built wasn't the design of the Goddess. Our world would be a lie based on—"

"Xian," Hel interrupted her. "I know men. I have fought with them, lived and bled with them. I know the evils they are capable of. Without the Sun Guards to protect the Temple, the chamberlain and the other men of the council would have taken over. Perhaps never attempted to recreate any type of civilization at all after The Burning Time. And the Sun Guards were created because of faith in the Goddess. Without that..." He shrugged.

"You're taking this very well."

Hel kissed her brow. "My faith was never for the Goddess. It was always for you. Meidra believed in you too. She said you were important. That you would bring salvation by finding your own path."

Xian shook her head, certain he was wrong. "I am no one's salvation. I have no answers. After the last few days all I have are more questions."

Hel lifted her out of the pool and began to dry her off with her outer robes. "You need to finish reading the journal. After Siraj returns we can go for the box. Together."

"Siraj has returned. I hope we have enough food for company. I've brought some old friends."

Xian turned to the cave entrance, puzzled by the strange tenor of Siraj's comment. Hel stiffened beside her at the same time she saw them. Three men in desert gear surrounded Siraj. The largest one held a knife to his throat.

Chapter Eight

Hel laced his pants, standing in front of Xian as she frantically pulled her robe up over her body. He used the time to try assessing the situation. His weapons and ruin artifacts were in the corner of the cave. They were outnumbered, and they blocked the only exit.

He cursed himself for not being more aware of their surroundings. He'd been so lost in Xian, in his own selfish desires, that he hadn't protected her properly. Now they were all in danger.

Hel knew from their ragged dress and hostile manner that they were criminals and renegades. Desert pirates. They followed no law. They were less trustworthy than the ocean pirates. More volatile than the warriors.

He attempted to distract them from Xian. "So, Siraj, I see you have made another strong impression. Do you know these men?"

Siraj's jaw locked. "Only too well. We had a slight misunderstanding recently. They believed they could ransom a clan elder's heir for fuel and supplies. I, humbly, disagreed."

The larger man snorted. "You more than disagreed, Siraj. You stole him from us. Do you know how hard it was to get him? How much danger you put us in? We should have killed you the last time."

Xian shocked Hel by stepping out from behind him, hands on her hips. His Priestess. The warrior. "So you are responsible for his injuries when we found him?"

"Xian, be silent." Hel swore silently when the three men's gazes focused on her.

One particularly grungy man with a thick scar from his

forehead to his chin sneered. "Siraj, you do well for yourself. A Kroy Wen Sun Guard and a Priestess? Perhaps there is hope for you to live another day. Shall we make a trade? Your life for these two. We'll also be taking that fine-looking mare outside."

"Oman, if you think the Wanderers were difficult adversaries, than you must know the Sun Guards would be just as deadly should you take a Priestess. Soon you'll have to move to the southern desert, just to get away from everyone who wants you dead."

Oman pressed close to Siraj's side, his large, crescent-shaped blade caressing his hip. "I gave you shelter. Took you in and shared scarce supplies because I thought... But you don't have what it takes to survive in the Wasteland. Other than your quick tongue and ready cock, you are useless to me. No wonder you have no family, no group of your own. You betray everyone." He walked forward, studying Xian. "You, however, are something different. I know a particular clan in the Wasteland who would readily agree to trade with us for the chance to get their hands on you and your protector. They've lost many healthy young males to your bloody sacrifices, pretty one. A chance for payback may be worth food and fuel for us."

Hel was enraged at the threat that put fear on Xian's face. If there were time, he would kill him slowly, painfully for that. But he could see that the three men were on the edge with nothing to lose, and that made them dangerous. He had to get to his weapons.

He didn't count on Xian having a plan of her own.

"What if we can give you something even more valuable to trade? The treasure of the Temple is hidden in these ruins. Would you let us go if we show you where it is?"

Hel watched Siraj make a pained face, closing his eyes at Xian's words. Mistake. He couldn't agree more. What was she thinking? These men would take her bait...and she would be in even more danger.

Oman was true to form. "Treasure? I knew it. We've seen the Sun Guards march into the ruins, year after year, going who knows where. We knew there must be a reason. You have a deal, Priestess. You will take me to this treasure. If it is as valuable as you say, we may let Siraj and your Sun Guard live."

Xian took a step forward and Hel gripped her arm. "Don't do this."

She lifted her chin, every inch the regal Priestess. "I do not believe I gave you permission to speak."

Oman chuckled harshly. "He can fuck you, but he can't talk, eh? You're my kind of Priestess, my lady. Lash, Moyle, stay here and keep your eyes on these two. Careful with Siraj—he's slippery."

Hel growled, stepping toward Oman. He wrapped his fingers around his throat and lifted him off his feet. "You take her nowhere."

He heard an unusual crackling sound, like the rumble of a gathering storm. Felt a pinpoint zap that quickly spread throughout his body in waves of pain.

The last thing he saw were those eyes. Beautiful violet and blue, and so worried. For him.

Why had she opened her mouth? She'd seen the men with their weapons on Siraj, seen their expressions, and knew there was no way it was going to end well. All she could think of was getting them away from Hel and Siraj, getting them out in the open to give her Sun Guard a chance to attack.

She'd failed.

One of the renegades had slipped behind Hel as he'd held Oman in his crushing grip and touched him with an unusual weapon. Blue sparks had flashed from it into Hel's skin, and he'd fallen to the ground in an instant. His heart still beat, but she wasn't sure how much damage had been done. *She* had done that to him with her talk of treasure. She'd never forgive herself.

"Keep walking, Priestess." Oman laughed. "Never seen one o' those, have ya? That is what you get when you trade with the Wanderers and their inventors. Man said it picks up the static charge in the air, then slams bolts like lightning into the body. Would have killed you for sure, but your big Sun Guard'll just have a nasty headache. That is, unless we hit him with it again."

It wasn't that far to the Vault. Xian had to find a way to escape him. A way to circle back and save her men. Her man. Hel. If they got out of this she promised to tell him she loved him. Promised to never give him reason to doubt it again.

She stumbled, accidentally on purpose, and fell to her knees on the rocky ground. "I'm sorry. I'm not used to being out in the elements. Especially not during the day."

Oman sniffed without bothering to help her up. "Aren't you the lucky one? We can't escape the elements, as you call them. I call it a bloody evil sun and a soul-sucking desert. It's no way for a man to live. But at least it doesn't rob you of your manhood the way the cities do. The way your high and mighty High Priestess does."

"She does no such thing. What are you talking about?" Xian couldn't help but be insulted. The men had everything they wanted. They had freedoms the women could never dream of. It was the women who had to be hidden. The women who had to play roles.

"Oh sure, pretend you don't know." Oman shook his head, pushing her forward as soon as she got to her feet. "I know about your eunuchs. Well, you may as well have cut the dick off every man in that city. As it is you have them shackled by it. Don't do this or you won't get a Rose, don't do that or no lottery for you. Men aren't dogs, you know. You can't keep them in line forever with the promise of a sweet cunt. We need to be men. To fight and hunt and stalk our prey. Sooner or later your tame pups will turn and bite you. I know that much."

He had a point. The fact that she found herself agreeing at all with a filthy criminal who would probably kill her when he realized she'd been lying to him was disconcerting. But if it was true for the men, it was also true for the women. Nitara had proven that. The Roses who'd disappeared had proven that. Fear and faith kept people in line for a time, but sooner or later they would want to be free. To make their own mistakes. To fight their own battles.

Just as she had to fight hers. She stopped in her tracks, bending down to reach for a large rock. "Oman, you may be right. Women want strong men. Men who take what they want." She hid the rock in the folds of her robe and smiled sensually at him when he turned to study her suspiciously.

She arched her back slightly, showing her breasts to their full advantage, grateful for the sun's heat and the lover's flush it gave her body.

Oman whistled. "You are a lusty one for a Priestess. No wonder Siraj took a liking to you. He knows about the delights of the flesh."

Xian quirked her lips. "I bet you taught him everything he

knows."

"A few things." He nodded. "A few. I bet I could teach you something right now. I'm sure you'll still be a good trade even if you're a little used up."

Her heart thundered as she watched him slip his pack off his shoulders and plant his knife in the ground beside it. One hand began to unlace his pants, the other reached out awkwardly toward her breast.

Xian lifted the stone and hit Oman on the side of his head. He screamed and fell to his knees, gripping the injury. "Godless bitch! You'll pay for that."

She ran. She had no idea where she was going, farther into the ruins where she'd never been before. But she didn't care. She had to get away.

"You can't get away, bitch. I know these ruins better than you. If I don't get you the wild things that roam this place will. You're safer if you just give up and take what's coming to you."

She shook her head. She'd rather die. She crawled up a jagged mound of rubble, her hands and knees already scraped and raw, desperate to escape. Some loose stones shifted, and she was falling, unable to stop, tumbling down the other side.

She cried out when the sharp protrusion of metal pierced her side, trapping her, near blinding her with pain. In moments a shadow blocked the sun. Oman. His smile was not pleasant.

This was not the way she'd wanted it to end. Raped and killed in the Wasteland. As he scrambled down the hill after her, she had a moment of clarity. This was what the woman who wrote the journal experienced after The Burning Time. This powerlessness, helplessness. This was why they'd done what they'd done. Because of men like Oman. Men like Chamberlain Vey. Violent men who lusted after power and control, but were too weak to win out over other men, so they abused women instead.

"I'm going to enjoy this. I really am. I'll just have to get your Sun Guard to tell me about the treasure. As for Siraj, well, it will take years for Siraj to make up for what he's done to me." Oman pulled down his pants, spreading her legs. He ignored her shout of pain as the movement pushed the metal farther into her side. The pain was excruciating.

Xian closed her eyes, clinging to the image of Hel smiling above her, love in his eyes. His was the last face she wanted to see. That was the last memory. Not this. This was only a nightmare.

"What the fuck?" Oman squealed and his heavy weight flew off of her. Xian opened her eyes in time to see Hel fling him to the ground, one hand at his throat, the other clutching his dagger.

"You will die for touching her, you bastard. But not as quickly as your friends. I'll stake you in the sun with your insides dangling out for the wild dogs." Hel set down his dagger where Oman could see it, and began to use his fists to break the bones of the renegade's face.

"Oh, Xian. Sweet, you're wounded." Siraj's voice sounded far away. Xian couldn't take her eyes from Hel. So much rage. So much anger. Like the Sun. For her.

He wasn't going to stop.

"Hel. Don't make him suffer. Siraj, don't let him..."

Hel looked at her over his shoulder, hearing her words. Siraj leapt over the rock to lay a hand on his back. "Hel, she's hurt. We need to get her out of this heat, clean her wound. End it. Now."

"Traitor." Oman spit blood out of his mouth, his voice garbled with pain as he spoke to Siraj.

Siraj leaned over his bruised body. "I owe you nothing. You fed me. I fucked you. I never signed on for kidnapping. Or rape. You deserve everything you get."

Xian watched as Siraj took Oman's head in his hands and twisted sharply, breaking his neck. Hel snarled up at him, but Siraj sent him a bitter smile. "She is watching, Hel. Better me than you."

She slipped in and out of consciousness, getting bits and pieces of images. Hel carrying her, tending to her wound. Siraj wiping her down with a damp cloth, singing softly under his breath as though to soothe her.

When she woke, the cooler air told her it was night. She heard Luna's neighing and relief washed over her. She was glad the mare was safe.

"Xian? Don't get up too quickly, my love. Wait for me." Hel came over and sat beside her, helping her to a sitting position. They were back in the cave, the small fire pit lighting every corner. There was no sign that the men had ever been there. No sign of what had happened to them.

Hel noticed her expression. "They are gone. Dead. They won't bother you again."

"Are you all right?" Xian accepted the agave juice he handed her, the soothing liquid making her sigh in relief.

Hel shrugged. "I didn't enjoy that weapon. But it's ours now. You are alive. That is all that matters." He reached behind him and handed her the black metal box. "I brought this from the Vault. So you could finish reading the journal while you recover."

"Hel, I need to tell you—"

"Anything you need to tell me can wait until you read. Siraj has made us something to eat. You need food."

Siraj came inside, a metal plate topped with food in hand. "Talking about me? I'm just glad your Sun Guard hasn't killed me yet for putting the two of you in danger." He knelt down beside them, sincere concern in his eyes. "I had no idea they'd found me, Priestess. I swear to you."

Xian cupped his cheek with her hand. "I know. This, none of it, is your fault. Hel knows that."

"Hel knows that. He also knows that the next time dangerous men with weapons surround us, his woman will not decide to take it upon herself to save the day." Hel's growl drew her gaze back to his piercing green eyes. He didn't hide the emotion in his expression. The fear. "I couldn't take it again, Xian."

His woman. Not High Priestess. Not his charge. His woman. That was what she was. Her true destiny. "I know, Hel. I just wanted you safe."

He kissed her forehead and pointed to the box. "Eat. Read. Before I forget you're wounded and bend you over my knee for the spanking you so richly deserve."

A small thrill of arousal shot through her, but she nodded dutifully, knowing he needed that from her right now.

She ate the small bits of meat and herbs on her plate and opened the box, removing the journal with a sad sigh. She didn't want to finish this. Didn't want to read about any more pain or hardship. But Hel was right. She had to find out what happened. The whole truth, not bits and pieces.

She forced herself to read each and every entry. People had died. Of radiation. Murder. Women had died in childbirth. And babies had been born. Wounds had healed. And the rough outline of a society began to develop.

The last entry sent tears pouring down her cheeks and onto the old, strangely lined paper.

Tessa,

I give this gift to you along with the book we'd gone to the library to get that day. A gift so you will always know where you came from. Know that there was once a world where men and women worked together, laughed together and loved each other and their children. Your father loved you so much, Tessa. He loved both of us. He was a good man.

This wasn't what I wanted for your future. This is what had to be done. If I had been stronger I would have fled with a few of the others to those military wanderers. It is a rough life, but at least there is equality. There is a chance for families to live together.

When you are older, you may understand. I'll lock up this journal for safekeeping and give you the key on my grandmother's chain. Keep it hidden. When you are ready for the truth, you can return to this place and find me between the pages.

I also left you a map. One of the scientists that passed this way spoke of Antarctica. Of the possibility that life could thrive there now. That the solar storm melted the glaciers, but the land was not scorched beyond repair. Maybe someday you can go there with your family. Start again. Live the way you want to live. Not behind locked doors and hidden in caves. But free, as you were born to be.

I wish I could go with you.

I love you, baby. I always will. Remember me.

Xian thought of the mother she'd never known. The children she never thought she'd have. It was obvious this woman had done everything for love of her baby. A love that was shared by the man who had given of his essence to create it. It was so alien to Xian. And yet... She could easily imagine feeling that kind of love for Hel's child. As strong as the love she had for him. As the love she had always felt for the Goddess.

Meidra had said she would find her own path, and Xian could not help but think that this was destined. That this had all happened for a reason. After nearly two hundred star rotations in the Wasteland, surviving in a barren desert, they were being given a gift of renewal. Yet another chance to get it right. Everything she'd known had been proven wrong. She couldn't help but still believe a higher power had a hand in all this. That She had brought Siraj to them. That She had made sure Hel had found his way to Kroy Wen all those years ago. To her.

She looked up to find Hel and Siraj watching her with concern as they sat by the fire. She set down the book and they jumped into action, both coming to sit on either side of her.

Her smile was wet with tears. "I have made up my mind. I will not be returning to Kroy Wen."

Hel tensed. "They will come after us. They'll think something happened to you."

She shook her head. "I sent a missive to the High Priestess of S'Alinorac before I left. The Wild Moon is in two days. She will receive word that she must send her apprentice to Kroy Wen's Temple." She shrugged. "I wasn't sure where this journey would take me, and I couldn't leave my charges with nothing. The apprentice will become the new High Priestess when it is discovered that I am gone for good. And if they look for me they won't find me." She reached for Hel's hand. "You can go back. You still have high standing. A life. No one knows your secrets. You could protect the new High Priestess."

He flinched at her words. "Is that what you want, Xian? You want me to leave you?"

Her heart began to race. "No, Hel. I—I love you. I just don't want to take you from your destiny."

Siraj chuckled. "Are you blind, Priestess? I have known from the moment we met that you were the Sun Guard's destiny. His path is yours. And a beautiful path it is. One I intend to stay on for as long as possible."

A chuckle escaped from between Xian's lips, joy filling her soul as she saw Hel's smile of agreement, the look in his eyes. He wanted to stay with her. He loved her as she loved him.

Hel lifted her hand and kissed her fingertips. "Where do we go, my love? A High Priestess who is no longer a High Priestess. A Wanderer-born Sun Guard with no family but you. And, well, Siraj." He shrugged at Siraj's cackle. "Where do we go?"

That was when she showed them the map and told them the story. They listened with the rapt wonder of children. Siraj as understanding as Hel had been about what the women of The Burning Time had done.

He was also fascinated by the large map. "So much world," he marveled. "The pirates tell stories...but I had no idea. This map alone could be the most priceless thing in existence to them."

They spoke deep into the night, making plans.

Siraj told her of a pirate by the name of Captain Xander. He owed Siraj a favor, and he was always a savvy trader. Siraj was confident Xander's ship would be able to make the long journey, for the right price.

Hel showed her what he'd brought to trade with, things his Father had given him. They were bizarre contraptions that should fetch enough to take them where they were trying to go.

A pirate ship. Xian never imagined in her life that she would run away to a strange land on a pirate ship. With two men nonetheless. Yet, nothing sounded sweeter. This was right. A fresh start.

But how could she leave everyone behind? Leilin, Meidra, Nikkan and the others who depended on her. How could she abandon them to the whim of the council? Chamberlain Vey?

Hel was holding the old image of the man, woman and child. "The sky is so blue. Do you think this place, this Ant-Ark-Tika, will look like that?"

"I don't know. I suppose we'll find out. But first, we need to break a few more laws. I think the Goddess will approve."

Epilogue

She was dreaming. Her back cushioned by lush green grass, her feet in a cool stream of clear water. She'd dreamed that Leilin and Meidra had taken her words to heart. That they'd listened when she'd come back through The Garden of the Moon to tell them what she'd learned and where she was going.

From the news she'd gotten, the myth was spreading. Sun Guards training in the tunnels had seen the carving Siraj had so perfectly rendered of their map and been curious. Some even inspired.

Leilin and Nikkan had left Kroy Wen in search of Nitara and her family, to tell them of a place that The Burning Time did not touch. A paradise where life flourished. A place for new beginnings. Akaash had sent a message to Captain Xander. They were coming. Nitara, her lovers and family...and her child. Xian was overjoyed with the news. She knew they would decide to stay as some of the pirates had. Decide to start again. As she had.

She'd begun her own journal, finding the plants she needed to create her own ink. In it she'd spoken of the journey, both spiritual and physical, that had led her here. She spoke of her ocean voyage, which had been one surprise after the other. The two Roses who had disappeared from Kroy Wen had been aboard. Bryn and Ayla. Though there had been some tension because of what Xian was, the three soon became friends.

Bryn was a strong, sexual woman. And the stories she'd told Xian about what she did to Xander and his man Hawke on a regular basis...it made her blush just thinking about it. Bryn promised they would be back often. Already they'd brought back some small livestock and supplies, and several wonders created by an inventive trader known as Ezra. They'd even built a home here, though they weren't finished with their ocean adventures and exploration. It was a good sign of things to come.

"My love, I woke up and you were gone."

"Hel." She turned and took him into her arms. His hand slid over the curve of her belly, tight now with child, and down between her legs. She would never get enough of him. Never touch him enough, love him enough to make up for all the time they'd lost.

He caressed her features with his gaze. "You seemed lost in thought. Any regrets?"

Xian smiled. "Not a one. This place. You." She took his hand and placed it on her stomach. "Our child will be able to decide its own fate. And I will read Tessa's favorite story. A story about a young girl's brave adventure to a strange new world. How can I regret that? And you? Do you regret?"

A shadow crossed over his features. "Only that Father refused to come with us. And because of that decision, Fyral did the same." He pulled her closer. "But they were convinced they had to stay to ensure that another chamberlain did not grow mad with power after Vey met his...untimely end."

"Give them time. At least they understood. And they keep our secret. They love you."

Hel smiled, the shadow passing. "As long as I have your love, I am blessed."

"It is yours. Forever."

He kissed her, his lips and fingers arousing her swiftly, her body knowing well the pleasure that awaited her.

"Don't start without me."

She smiled against Hel's lips as she felt Siraj lay down behind her, his long erection pressing insistently between the cheeks of her ass. She wrapped her fingers around Hel's thick cock, loving his moans, loving how she affected him, even now.

Siraj entwined his fingers with hers, so they were both touching Hel, both stroking as he grew ever harder beneath their touch. Hel's malachite eyes narrowed dangerously on Siraj and he growled, but he didn't push him away, bending his head instead to take one of Xian's lush breasts into his mouth.

Siraj kissed her neck, and she could feel his smile. Xian

was smiling too. He had insinuated himself into their lives, into their hearts...and whenever possible, into their bed. He still allowed Hel total control, but there was no doubt that Siraj knew how to get exactly what he wanted from both of them. She could no longer see a future without him. Without the both of them.

Her last thought before she lost herself to sensation was that she had finally found her answers. Finally found her destiny. Where she belonged...who she belonged to.

Xian had followed her own path. And it had led her home.

About the Author

R.G. Alexander writes erotic romance for Berkley Heat and Samhain Publishing. She has lived all over the United States, studied archaeology and mythology, been a nurse and a vocalist, and now, a writer. She is happily married to a talented chef who is her best friend, her research assistant, and the love of her life. To learn more about R. G. Alexander please visit www.rgalexander.com. Send an email to R. G. Alexander at r.g.alexander@hotmail.com.

Look for these titles by
R.G. Alexander

Now Available:

Children of the Goddess Series
Regina in the Sun
Lux in Shadow
Twilight Guardian
Midnight Falls

Not in Kansas
Surrender Dorothy
Truly Scrumptious
Three for Me?

Wicked³ Series
Wicked Sexy
Wicked Bad

Shifting Reality Series
My Shifter Showmance
My Demon Saint

Can a god of fire melt the heart of an ice queen?

Melting the Ice Queen

© *2008 Savannah Jordan*

When a mysterious package shows up on the doorstep of self-proclaimed frigid bitch Cassandra Moore, she's more curious about who could have sent it to her than about the statue of the Egyptian god inside.

That night, the human spirit of her statue appears in her dream, giving her hottest sex she's ever had in her life. Emin is every girl's dream lover. He's mysterious, sexy as hell, and eager to satisfy every erotic whim Cassie entertains.

Yet Emin has secrets as deep as the myths of Egypt—he has sacrificed his magick and his life in the spirit world to be with Cassie.

The fires of passion blaze hotter with each encounter. But if Emin cannot melt Cassie's heart and convince her to love a fantasy, he is doomed to the hell between the realms.

Warning, this title contains the following: explicit melt-your-panties sex, graphic language, ménage a trios, and a demigod that will make you gasp and swoon.

Available now in ebook from Samhain Publishing.